PHL6

D1195163

UNWRITTEN

Center Point
Large Print

Also by Charles Martin and available from
Center Point Large Print:

Thunder and Rain

**This Large Print Book carries the
Seal of Approval of N.A.V.H.**

UNWRITTEN

CHARLES MARTIN

CENTER POINT LARGE PRINT
THORNDIKE, MAINE

ISBN: 978-1-61173-752-3

Library of Congress Cataloging-in-Publication Data

Martin, Charles, 1969–
Unwritten / Charles Martin.
pages ; cm.
ISBN 978-1-61173-752-3 (library binding : alk. paper)
1. Actresses—Fiction. 2. Priests—Fiction.
  3. Missing persons—Fiction. 4. Large type books. I. Title.
PS3613.A7778U59 2013b
813'.6—dc23

2012051786

For John Dyson

PART ONE

... never forget that you have promised me to use this silver to become an honest man ... Jean Valjean, my brother: you belong no longer to evil, but to good. It is your soul that I am buying for you. I withdraw it from dark thoughts and from the spirit of perdition, and I give it to God!

—Victor Hugo, *Les Misérables*

Death is the destiny of every man; the living should take this to heart.

—Ecclesiastes 7:2

Prologue

Christmas Day

She knelt. Genuflected. He sat alongside the kneeler. Hands in his lap. She pushed the curtain open, to smell the Vitalis and Old Spice. She liked being this close to a man who did not feel compelled to touch her. To conquer her. She looked past him. Beyond the present. "Forgive me, Father, for I have sinned."

"When was your last confession?"

She glanced at him out of the corner of her eye. "You should know. You were sitting right here." He held his watch to the light, allowing his eyes to adjust to the date. It was Friday. She'd been here Wednesday. She knew that he knew that. She also knew that his mind wasn't as old as his trembling hands or the spittle in the corner of his mouth suggested and reading his watch was little more than a deflection.

His thumb circled the bezel of his watch. It was government issue and still kept pretty good time but that wasn't why he wore it. "This is unusual."

She spoke without looking. "You of all people should know—" Another glance. "I am anything but usual."

She loved diamonds. Had a drawer full. Custom

9

made. Tennis bracelets. Pendants. Solitaires. Several of each. But for the last couple of months there'd been no glitter. No glisten. The only decoration she wore was the barcoded wristband from her last admission as a patient. He glanced at her wrist. "You planning on going back?"

She shook her head once. "Just making it easier to identify the body."

Normally, she enjoyed their back-and-forth. But today, she wasn't trying to be funny. Her cheeks were thinner. Drawn. She knew he noticed it. He dipped his thumb in the oil. Painted her forehead. "Bless you, my child."

They'd met when she was sixteen. And while they had both grown older in those twenty years, only he had aged. He was more wrinkled. Skin thinner. More dark spots on his hands. Voice weaker. Cracking at times. Mucousy at others. Maybe the effect of his pipe. He could never quite clear it. He was eighty-three now. Or, was it four? She couldn't remember. White hair combed straight back.

She had spent a lot of money to not change. To remain timeless. And, in everyone's eyes but her own, it'd worked.

Despite more awards than she has shelf space, her own star on Hollywood Boulevard, thirty-some-odd movies, an eight-figure price tag, several "most beautiful people" labels, a schedule booked years in advance, and worldwide name and face recognition, she had become fragile. Not so confident. Not so certain. Simply, a girl. More afraid than not. She tried to hide it but hiding from him was not as easy.

She always found him dapper. She once told him in a weak moment that he'd not be a priest now if she'd met him in his twenties. He had nodded. A pleasant smile. "I'd like to think you're right."

She turned, surprised. "You'd have left God for me?"

He weighed his head side to side. "I'd have asked His permission and prayed He gave it."

She studied the church. "You think He'd let you out?"

He eyed the walls. "He doesn't keep me here."

Sometimes she came here just to breathe.

She got to the point. "No drugs. No alcohol. No sex. And only three cusswords but no F-bombs." She shook her head and smiled. "In the last three weeks—thanks to you—I've had no fun at all."

He smiled. "When was the last time you had fun?"

She turned away. The stained-glass window rose some thirty feet above them. The light filtered through the crown of thorns and painted her skin red and purple. A sycamore tree outside fluttered in the breeze, flashing a disco ball effect on the marble floor. She shook her head. He leaned in to hear her. Was her voice that weak?

While petite, she could tower on the stage and owned Broadway. In her shows, there was no such thing as a cheap seat and that had nothing to do with the price. She managed, "Can't remember."

He raised an eyebrow. "Can't . . . or won't?"

She shrugged. "Take your pick."

He waited. "And your thoughts?"

She didn't answer.

He moved on. "How about your schedule? Last we spoke, you were going to spend less time pretending to be someone else. More time being you."

"We did." He handed her a tissue. She wiped her nose. "I told them."

"And?"

"I have a few days."

"And then?"

"They are considering three more projects." Her voice mocked her agent's. She rolled her eyes. " 'Roles of a lifetime.' "

"Are they worth it?"

She shrugged. "Eight figures."

"That's not what I asked."

"But you like it when I write checks for this place."

"What you do with your money is between you and God."

"You sound ungrateful."

He let out a breath, stared at her. He sought to make eye contact. She looked away. "What you are giving up is worth more than what you are getting."

She smiled. Another tear. She whispered, "Thank you." It's one of the reasons she loved him. He gave, wanting nothing. She stared through the glass.

He asked, "And your sleeping?"

She shrugged. "Here and there."

"Dreams?"

"None that are any good." A minute passed in silence. She picked at a nail, then looked out the window. The ocean shimmered. Two dozen pelicans in V-formation skirted the rooftops, heading north up the coastline. She was probing. "You ever had anyone tell you they were going to hurt themselves?"

"Yes."

"What'd you do?"

"I did what I could and left the rest to God."

"You have an answer for everything."

He waited. He had time for her. She loved him for that, too. She'd miss him. Not much else.

She turned. He knew she was deliberate. Purposeful. Finished what she started. Not given to exaggeration—which was odd given her profession.

"Yes?"

She spoke softly. "Do you think God forgives sins in the future?"

"He's outside of time."

She shook him off. "I don't really understand that."

He nodded, a shrug, a smile. "Me, either."

Another glance out the window. "Least you're honest about it."

"Why lie?" He finished his thought: "I think God sees and hears our past, present, and future all in present tense."

"That doesn't bode well for me."

"Or—" He smiled. "Maybe it does."

He waited. She turned her tissue in her hands, shook her head, pulled an envelope from her pocket. "Given the events of the last few months, I've had some time to think. Put a few things in order. I've named you executor. In the event that, you know—I'd like it if you oversaw everything. Just in case. And—" A quick glance. "Speak at my funeral."

He accepted the envelope. "I was thinking you might speak at mine."

She looked around, staring through the glass and the trees beyond, trying not to sound too terminal. She handed him a ring holding two keys. "My penthouse at Sky Seven and a safe-deposit box at the bank. Everything you need is in there. My attorney's name is Swisher. He drew up the papers."

"Shouldn't your agent or loved ones be handling this?"

A tear trickled. She whispered, "Loved ones,"

and managed half a giggle. She turned away. "Ex number three will be pissed, but you get it all. Do with it as you wish."

His eyes narrowed. "Should I be worried about you?"

She held his hand between both of hers. "I'm in no hurry. I'm better. Really." A contrived smile. "I'm just . . . planning. In the event, you know. That's all. In the daytime things aren't so bad." She dropped her head. "But when the sun goes down and . . . my balcony gets so dark . . ." She trailed off.

She checked the watch on his wrist, then the sun outside. "I'm late." She genuflected. "Oh, my God, I am heartily sorry—"

He slid forward on his chair, dipped his thumb again in the oil, traced a cross on her forehead, and laid his hand atop her head. His words echoed. The oil felt warm. *"Ego te absolvo a peccatis tuis in nomine Patris et filii et spiritus sancti."*

She stood, kissed him on the cheek with trembling lips, then a second time, smearing his cheek with her tears. Fighting the confession on the tip of her tongue, she buried it, sealed her lips, stepped down, and walked away. At the foot of the altar, she stopped—the distrust creeping in. A whisper. "And Father?"

He stood. His robes white. Leaning on a cane he did not need. "Yes?"

"This is between you and me, right?"

A nod. "Just the three of us." His voice was stronger now. The cross towered above him. He said nothing. A final genuflection, and she closed her eyes. She'd be talking with him soon enough.

He straightened. "My child—"

She waited.

He took a step.

She spoke softly. "Father, all movies end. All curtains fall."

He raised a finger. Eyes narrowed. Started to speak.

Avoiding the center aisle, she retreated beneath the side arches. Alone. At the rear side entrance, she pulled on the door. The salt air cut into her. She wrapped her scarf around her head, slid on her sunglasses, and walked out beneath a blue sky dotted with clouds. "Good-bye, Father."

Chapter One

Christmas Eve, eighteen hours earlier

I rubbed my eyes, blew the steam off my Waffle House coffee, and steered with my knees. I was neither passing nor being passed. Just fitting in. Drawing no attention. Something I was good at. My speedometer was hovering around seventy-seven miles an hour as was the rest of the northbound herd of nighttime travelers. Hypnotized by the dotted line, I counted back through the days. Nine years? Or, was it ten? At first, they moved slowly. Each minute a day. Each day a year. But, sitting here, the days lined up like dominoes outside the windshield. Time had been both a blink and a long sleep.

In a little over seven hours, I had crossed from the southwestern-most tip of Florida to the northeast corner. I changed lanes, wound through the spaghetti junction where I-10 intersects I-95 on the north bank of the St. Johns River, drove south across the Fuller Warren Bridge, and exited beneath the shadow of River City Hospital—a collection of a half-dozen or so buildings that rose up and sprawled along the Southbank. Jacksonville may not be as well known as Chicago or Dallas or New York but its nighttime skyline is one of the more beautiful I've seen, and the hospital features in that sight.

I spiraled up the parking deck to the sixth floor just prior to the nine p.m. shift change. Twice the people moving to and fro made it easier to blend in. I checked my watch. I had plenty of time.

In the cab of my truck, shrouded in the darkness of the parking deck, I changed into my dark blue maintenance uniform and slid on one of several pairs of thick-framed prescriptionless glasses. I twisted my sun-bleached hair into a tight ponytail and tucked it up under a matching ball cap. I pulled a white breathing mask over my mouth, dug my hands into elbow-deep yellow rubber gloves, and clipped Edmund's credentials over the flap of my chest pocket. At first glance, the credentials looked professional but anybody with a computer could determine rather quickly that Edmund Dantes was not and never had been employed with River City Hospital. 'Course, my plan was to not be around when whoever that was figured out that Edmund Dantes was really the Count of Monte Cristo and not a man working the trash detail. I fed earplugs up under my shirt and let them dangle over my collar while the unplugged end snaked around inside my shirt. With increased security concerns over the last decade, the hospital had been outfitted with dozens of live-feed, twenty-four-hour HD cameras and a host of rent-a-cops. The trick was knowing where they were, when to turn your back, lower your hat, or hug an exterior wall. Truth is, none of that explains my disguise but it had worked for years and would continue to do so as long as I did not draw attention to myself or stand out from the hospital's more than one thousand employees. The trick was simple: Be vanilla, not Neapolitan.

For the most part, people are not observant. Experts have conducted studies on bank robberies from actual eyewitnesses. Seldom can two or more agree on who actually robbed the bank, what they were wearing, what they took, and whether it was man or woman. Point being, being invisible isn't all that tough. In the last ten years, I've learned a good bit about being visible yet unseen. It's possible. Just takes a little work.

On the ground floor, I grabbed a yellow trash cart stowed outside the loading dock. About the size of a Mini Cooper, it looked like the bed of a V-shaped dump truck on wheels. I leaned into it and followed it onto the service elevator, where I turned my back to the first camera. The cart served several functions: It gave me a reason— most folks don't argue with a man who will take out the trash; it gave me a place to stow my duffel until I needed it; and it gave me something to hide behind. It also gave me something to shove between me and anyone after me, but I'd never needed it for that.

The children's wing was located on the fourth floor. The bell chimed with each floor as the camera above me filmed the top of my hat. The doors opened and the smells flooded me. I filled up, welcomed the memories, emptied myself, and filled up again.

River City Children's Hospital is considered one of the finest in the country—as are those who work here. What they *do* isn't easily measured as kids aren't easy patients. Most walk through the front door with two ailments—the one you can diagnose, and the one you can't. Knowing this, the doctors attack the first, then slowly work their way deeper. To the real wound. Doing so gives the kids reason to smile when reasons are tough to come by. It's slow work. Painstaking. And the endings aren't always happy. Despite their pedigrees, technology, and best of intentions, there are some hurts that medicine simply can't fix.

That's where I come in.

I'd wrapped each gift in brown paper, tied it with a red ribbon, and attached a simple card—a squared, preprinted white sheet of paper. Each read, "Merry Christmas. Found this on my ship and thought you'd enjoy. Get well soon. I'm always in need of new mates. You're welcome on my ship any time. Pirate Pete." I added a gift card to the TCBY yogurt store on the first floor of the hospital. Fifty dollars would buy them yogurt for months on end and since most of the kids could stand to gain a few pounds, it was a good fit. The guy that ran the yogurt place, Tommy, was a big, Santa-looking softy with two chins, hands the size of grizzly paws, a smile that could light up most any room, and the wingspan of a zeppelin. And since he was a hugger, he hugged everybody that stepped foot through his door. Figured if the kids didn't like his yogurt, they could at least get a hug. Most got both—along with a double scoop of gummy bears or crushed Oreos.

I exited the service elevator, routed around

the nurses' station, hugged an exterior wall, and emptied the first of several trashcans. I took my time—hunched, slow, a slight limp—looking at no one and inviting no one to look at or speak to me. Circling the fourth floor gave me eight cans to empty and a constant view of the nurses' station. After the third can, the nurses vacated their desk, and I turned ninety degrees toward the library.

Around here, hats are a big deal. It's not required but the walls are lined with hat hooks and most everybody wears one that can change daily. Literally, there are hundreds. All shapes, sizes, personalities, and attitudes. From umpteen styles of cowboy hats to ball caps to feathered things to visors to painter's hats to stockings to berets to watchman's beanies, to you name it, this place is spilling with hats. It began years back, when one of the patients—a young girl—started wearing a large, flamboyant purple hat with an even larger peacock feather spiraling out the top. Didn't take long for the trend to catch on. Whenever she was asked why she wore it—which was often and usually on television—she'd flip the feather and say with a mile-wide smile, "Because what I can imagine is bigger than what I see."

There were fourteen new kids plus the twelve who had been there long enough to hang artwork on the wall. That's twenty-six. Including staff and nurses, I had counted on forty-seven. Some, like the staff, had been there a long time so I knew their names. Others, like the new kids, I still knew very little about. It'd taken me months and several trips up here just to get them all straight.

When I walked in, Grant, Randy, and Scott were gathered around a game console playing a *Kung Fu Panda* game. Reading the body language, I could tell Randy was winning. Raymond and Grace Ann were lying on the floor—reading. Lewis and Michelle were sitting at a table playing checkers. Andrew sat staring out the window overlooking the river, talking to himself. Others sprawled on beanbags, recliners, and sofas around the room. Most wore hats and their choices were as different as they were.

I scanned the room, noting each face, and double-checked my mental list.

Grant was eight, often wore camouflage pajamas, liked macaroni and cheese with chicken nuggets from McDonald's, and wanted to live in a house on stilts with a swing in each room. I got him a couple of Paulsen books. *Hatchet* and *Brian's Hunt*.

Teresa was twelve, liked fried okra and fried chicken, wanted to live in Italy, did not like needles, had a lot of artwork hanging in her room, and especially liked to draw castles. Each with a prince in shining armor. *The Once and Future King* and *Princess Academy* for her.

Randy was turning ten, liked cheeseburgers, Nike shoes, the music of Justin Bieber, and had a stuffed lion on his bed. A box set of The Chronicles of Narnia.

Raymond was soon to be fourteen, wanted to live in a submarine or on a farm with dirt bikes, and would like to be able to talk one day and work as a news anchor. He has a rather vivid imagination. Voracious reader. *The Lord of the Rings* for him. Another box set and I threw in an older copy of both *The Hobbit* and *The Silmarillion*.

Grace Ann was thirteen. She wanted contacts and then Lasik, followed by plastic surgery to shorten her nose because she wanted to be an actress. She loved Oprah, and more than anything, wanted out of her wheelchair. I got her *The Color Purple* and *Jewel*.

I'm not sure how old Steve was. Thirteen, maybe, based on the zits on his cheek. He was studious, wore glasses, carried a briefcase—though I'm not sure it contained anything—and he talked of going to law school like his father, who I suspect was a figment of his imagination. I got him a couple of Grisham's thrillers, including *A Time to Kill* and *The Pelican Brief*.

Scott had to be close to ten and wore a two-holster belt every day to chemotherapy so I got him eight Louis L'Amour books, starting with *The Sacketts*.

Isabella was just five, so I got her two pop-up picture books: *Beauty and the Beast* and *Finding Nemo*.

Knowing these details isn't all that tough. Each wrote their hopes, dreams, likes, and wants in an essay that one of the staff had taped next to the photo on their door.

I pushed the cart between the Christmas tree and the camera on the wall and made a fair showing of emptying the adjacent can. Having replaced the dirty can liner with a clean one, and using the cart to hide my movements, I placed the gifts at the foot of the tree, turned my back, and began my slow retreat. My rule was simple and I'd never broken it—get in, do what I came to do, and get out. Never dally. Frankenstein was safe behind the woodpile as long as he did not venture out. But staying behind the trash cart was all the more difficult on Christmas Eve.

I pushed, one wheel squeaking. The noise drew Andrew's attention. He turned, looked at me, half smiled, and said, "Merry Christmas." His knees tucked up into his chest. He'd gained a few pounds. Looked better. His hair was growing out. I could see the bulge of the PICC line beneath his shirt just below his left collarbone. I nodded and said nothing.

I took my time, glancing at each out of the corner of my eye. Noting changes. Progress. Set-backs. Growth. Weight loss. These were the long-timers. The might-not-make-its. The poster children. The I-wish-I-was-anywhere-but-heres.

One last can. I pushed the cart into the library, hovered above it, letting my eyes scan the shelves. My old friends whispered to me. Most people enter a library and don't hear a thing. Eerie silence. I stand between the shelves and hear ten thousand conversations occurring all at once. Each ushering an invitation. The noise is raucous.

Blue slippers appeared at my feet. It was Sandy. She was nine. Red haired, freckled, and allergic to most everything on planet Earth. Anaphylactic shock had twice put her in a coma in the ICU. For her I'd left a set of The Enchanted Forest Chronicles and *Anne of Green Gables*. She, too, wore a white mask over her mouth. She tugged on my pants leg and pointed. "Mister, please." *The Wizard of Oz* rested above my head. I reached up and pulled it down. The worn cover and familiar feel. I remember when I'd bought it. Where I was.

I handed it to her and winked. She giggled and disappeared back into the game room. I placed a new liner in the can, wondering how the Wizard would have responded had the Tin Man said he was allergic to the Emerald City.

I backed out, and about the time I reached the door, Michelle beat Lewis in checkers and walked to the tree. The ribbons caught her attention. She knelt, digging. She slid the pile out onto the floor before her. "Hey! Look!"

The kids rallied. Michelle played Santa, passing out gifts. I lingered, untying and retying a trash bag. Making a poor show of making myself look useful.

Life has not always been so distant. So set apart. There were times when I lived in the middle of it. When I knew great emotion. Drank straight from the fire hose. Sucked the marrow. Stuck my finger in the socket. This was not one of those. This was a cheap counterfeit but it was as close as I could get.

I wanted to peel off my hat and mask and the name that wasn't mine, and sit in the middle while the misfits fell and piled up like pick-up sticks around me. Then we'd crack open a worn cover and I'd read, and the words would do what medicine can't, won't, and never will.

Of the six million species on the planet, only man makes language. Words. What's more—in evidence of the Divine—we string these symbols together and then write them down, where they take on a life of their own and breathe outside of us. Story is the bandage of the broken. Sutures of the shattered. The tapestry upon which we write our lives. Upon which we lay the bodies of the dying and the about-to-come-to-life. And if it's honest, true, hiding nothing, revealing all, then it is a raging river and those who ride it find they have something to give—that they are not yet empty.

Critics cry foul, claiming the tongue is a bloody butcher that blasphemes, slices, slanders, and damns—leaving scars, carnage, the broken and the beaten. Admittedly, story is a double-edged scimitar, but the fault lies not in the word but in the hand that wields the pen. Not all stories spew, cower, and retreat. Some storm the castle. Rush in. Stand between. Wrap their arms around. Spill secrets. Share their shame. Return. Stories birth our dreams and feed the one thing that never dies.

This is true for all of us—even those who hide behind masks, carts, and names that do not belong to us.

Andrew spoke first. His voice rising. "Hey! Pete was here!" Around here, Pete is an iconic hero but his identity is a mystery. Some think he's a local tight-lipped charity. Others think a wealthy heiress in her late eighties who was never able to have kids. A well-respected business, or maybe a collection of businesses. A group of professional football players giving back. Over the years, several posers have stepped forward and claimed responsibility hoping to cash in on the notoriety, but nobody really knows. All anyone knows is that he shows up a couple times a year —specifically around birthdays and Christmas —unannounced and leaving no trace.

Raymond held his package and smiled. Speaking almost to himself. "He came back. He came back."

The cart grew heavier. My feet dragged. Sweat beaded. I turned. Torn wrapping paper, and spent ribbons, piled at their feet. They turned the pages and smiles spread from ear to ear.

My window was closing.

But I was not finished. One gift remained. Liza wasn't in the library so I exited, turned right, and made my way toward the far end of the hall. Room 424. The door was cracked. Lights dim. I rested my hand on the frame. I knew this room. Spent many a night in here. Long ago, it'd been Jody's and had belonged to many children since.

I grabbed the present and pushed on the door. She was asleep. Her face pale. Hair stuck to a sweaty forehead. IV dripping. Her cheeks were pudgier—which was good in a ten-year-old survivor. Liza had been here longer than anyone. A house favorite. She could light up a room from down the hall. The artwork on her walls had been framed, evidence of her tenure. So had several pictures showing her with famous people who'd seen her on TV. A half-eaten, triple-layer birthday cake on the table next to her bed. Icing crusted in the corner of her mouth. Up here, you have two birthdays. The day you are born. And the day you are free. She'd been a Christmas Eve baby.

I stepped in, my worn boots squeaking on polished floors. I stood in the shadows and set the present on her nightstand, resisting the urge to place a cold, wet towel on her forehead. I hovered, watching her breathe. I did not know Liza, and she did not know me, but I'd known many like her and I'd watched her grow up in here. Watched her hair come and go and come again. Maybe it was her smile, the way the right side of her mouth turned up more than the left, but, of all of them, she reminded me that I was once alive. I stepped out of the shadow, slid my hand from the glove, reached across the chasm, and gently placed the back of my hand against her cheek. The fever had broken. When I turned to retreat, she spoke. Her voice cracked. "Thank you." I turned and her eyes shifted from me to the present on the bedside and back to me.

I nodded.

She sat up and her eyes were drawn to the red ribbon. I retreated slowly to the shadows. She said, "May I?"

Another nod.

She untied the ribbon, untaped the wrapper, and unfolded the paper, careful not to tear it. She read the title and clutched the book close to her chest. *Pirate Pete and The Misfits: The World Is Flat.* The smile grew. "It's my favorite."

I knew that. I whispered and motioned with my fingers. "Open it."

She did. Turning to the title page. It was signed. Not to her, because what are the chances of finding a signed copy for a girl named Liza when the author had been dead for a, well . . . a long time, but Elizabeth was another story, a more common name. She ran her fingers across the signature. Helen Keller at the Alabama pump house. "Elizabeth is my real name." I knew that, too.

I drank from the fire hose.

She looked up. "Where'd this come from? Did my doctors find it?" Her head tilted. A quiet moment. "Did *you* find this?" The emphasis was pointed at me—as was her finger.

Lost in another moment, I forgot myself and was in the process of answering, "I . . . ," when heavy footsteps squeaked outside the door. I turned quickly, grabbed the trash bag from the bathroom trashcan, and almost bumped into a nurse walking into the room. I tucked my chin to my chest, threw the bag in the cart, cussed myself for being such a fool, and made for the elevator.

I'd made it halfway down the hall when I heard the same high-tempo squeaky footsteps. Her voice was elevated. "Excuse me, sir."

I turned the corner and picked up a jog. The cart squeaking louder. I was almost running.

The sound followed me around the corner. The effort caused her to breathe heavier and speak unnaturally loud. "Sir!"

To my left, the stairwell. I could ditch the cart and run but my cover would be blown. I pushed the elevator button, and fed the earbuds into my ears. I stood in front of the cart, which blocked me from her, and tapped my foot. The doors opened and I debated. If I stepped in, she had me cornered. Unless I wanted to hurt her—and I did not. If I ran, I could make it down and out the stairs and disappear to the Riverwalk around the fountain, but that would only ensure my escape. Not my return. And the latter was more important than the former.

I stepped in, pulling the cart behind me. Sweat beaded on my forehead.

The doors were closing when she appeared and shoved her massive arm between the doors. The elevator jolted. An out-of-breath nurse stood holding a half-eaten, triple-layer birthday cake smothered in icing. I pulled the noiseless earbuds from my ears. She smiled, caught her breath, leaned on the cart, and offered. "If this thing stays up here, we'll graze on it for days, and I'm already knocking lamps off night tables as it is, so do a girl a favor and remove the temptation." I wanted to tell her that her smile was beautiful. That she lit a dark room. That the world needed it, and her.

I did not.

I accepted the cake with a grunt and a nod, and she stepped out of the elevator. When the doors closed, I stood—conscious of the camera above me. I exited at the loading deck, made a serpentine path through the parking garage, up six flights of camera'd stairs to my truck, and didn't peel off my mask, glasses, or hat until I climbed back up on I-95 and headed south.

I merged, tapped the steering wheel, and took my first bite of cake. The icing stuck to my lips. When I glanced in the rearview, the city skyline was brilliant and the hospital a white blur shrouded in halo.

Tears do that.

At five a.m., I found myself next to a parked tractor trailer at a rest area south of Melbourne. After the sugar rush, I pulled over, crashed, and slept—dreaming of laughter; tender, magnificent voices; of small victories and large defeats; of my place in the world; and days long, long gone. The idling diesel woke me—bringing me back. I stepped out, brushed the cake crumbs off my lap, and stretched—my neck stiff from sleeping against the window. I scratched my head and studied the highway. Jacksonville to the north. Miami to the south. I glanced at my watch and the date reminded me.

Today is Christmas. Time to see the old man.

Chapter Two

Miami is known for its vice squad, year-round tropical weather, professional sports teams, wealth, fashion, art-deco design, and bikini beaches. Maybe none more famous than Miami Beach. Just south of Miami Beach, across a little stretch of water and past the Miami Seaquarium—the original home of Flipper—is a barrier island called Key Biscayne.

Key Biscayne is seven miles long by two miles wide. It is bookended by state parks, which means that the real estate in the middle is rather pricey. The Ritz-Carlton is here, as is an exclusive condominium called Sky Seven. Since the area is threaded with canals, many of the homes are waterfront and most owners have several boats. Just across Biscayne Bay on the Florida mainland sits Coconut Grove, Coral Gables, the University of Miami, and an old church shepherded by an even older man.

St. John the Divine always struck me as simple, which is odd given that Catholics are not known for understatement. I'm not knocking them; my best friend is Catholic. Actually, he's my only friend but that's irrelevant. The point is that his church has not been dipped in gold like a vanilla cone from Dairy Queen. It's grand

33

without grandeur. That's not to say they've put no effort in it. The grounds are manicured. Lush. Succulent. Blooms everywhere. Hummingbirds gorging. Roses climb every arch and breezeway. Not a weed to be found. The thing on display here is not man's handiwork. That strikes me because it gives me no reason to leave—and I've been looking.

I reached Miami by morning but given that it was Christmas, and given that they ran four services back to back, I made myself scarce until late afternoon, letting the crowd thin. A single black Range Rover was parked in the lot when I arrived. Looking more like me and less like the Count of Monte Cristo, I stepped inside, took a breath, and leaned against the heavy mahogany. I liked this place. Incense burned in the far corner. Candles flickered. They say confession is good for the soul.

Maybe that depends on what is confessed.

He sat at the far end. Hands clasped on his knees. The confessant knelt opposite. Between the scarf and the sunglasses and the bowed head, I couldn't make out much but the curves suggested a woman in her late twenties. Maybe midthirties. She finished speaking, stood, and he handed her a tissue with which she wiped her nose, the skin below her eyes. A true confession. She took a step, then turned, leaned across the space between them, placed her hand on his cheek, and kissed him. Tenderly. Then a second time. Gathering herself, she stepped off the platform, crossed her arms and began her hurried exit. Steps from the altar, she stopped and whispered. He stood and responded. I could make out none of it. Satisfied, she crossed to the outside aisle and began her solo walk toward the side entrance—and me.

Her running shoes squeaked on the polished marble while my flip-flops smacked my heels. I moved aside. Removed my hat. Sun-bleached hair down to my shoulders. She passed. A careful distance. Careful not to look. A satellite in orbit. I'd seen her before. She came here often. Scarf, sunglasses, faded jeans. Nothing showing. Could have been anybody. Nobody. That she was hiding was obvious. She brushed by me, tears falling below the rims of the glasses. A tissue dabbing the end of her nose. A plastic hospital bracelet hung on her left wrist. I glanced at the confessional. He had that effect on a lot of people.

I walked beneath the arches. Approached the chair. A thin curtain separated us. I sat. Facing him. My spiritual umbilical cord. I pulled back the curtain. He was distant, staring at the door through which she'd disappeared. Her smell hovered over both of us. "What'd you say?"

He looked at me. Head tilted. Voice low. Father Steady Capris had been a priest for longer than I'd been alive. And, if he was anything, he was—

steady. Little rocked his boat. At eighty-four, he had few responsibilities at the church other than to care for the other priests and hear confessions when he could. He came and went as he wished, though he seldom left the grounds. For the most part, he wandered the halls, encouraging others, rubbing his beads, and whispering to himself. They fed him, gave him a room, took care of his needs, and put him on a platform from which he continually tried to climb down.

He glanced at me out of the corner of his eye. "Do I keep your secrets?"

I laughed and looked around me at the absence of people. "Evidently."

"Then don't ask me for others'."

"You're in a good mood." He stared at me but he wasn't looking at me. He was distracted—focused on the girl beyond the door. My eyes roamed the expanse of the cathedral. "You still like it here?"

"It's home."

"What would you do if it burned to the ground?"

He turned slowly. Unaffected. "God doesn't inhabit buildings."

"That's not what I asked."

He crossed one leg over the other. "Fire is not the enemy."

"No? What then?"

His pupils slid to the corners of his eyes. "The match."

"What do we do about the finger that strikes it?"

He waved his hand across the expanse. "We build cathedrals with them."

With Steady there was no pretense. Everything was what it was. And God knows I loved him for it.

He stood, wrapped his sweater about him, and pointed outside to the circular platform tucked beneath the trees, the blue water just beyond, where he heard other priests' confessions. He waved. "Walk with me."

"Merry Christmas to you, too." He smiled, nodded, and buttoned his Mister Rogers sweater. "It's nearly eighty degrees outside and you're wearing a sweater."

"My body is old. My spirit is not." He motioned again. "Walk."

"I'm not going out there."

He pointed.

"I'm not a priest."

"You'd have made a good one."

"I'm not even Catholic."

He turned. "Come."

I gave him my arm. He didn't need my help. He knew this. I knew this. And he knew that I knew this. He took it anyway. Our footsteps echoed, followed by the sound of his cane tapping the marble. I spoke. "I saw this once in a *Godfather* movie. Didn't really go all that well for the guy making the confession. He ended up in diabetic shock." He kept walking. We neared the platform. I stopped him, shook my head. "Steady, I love you, give you the shirt off my back but not today."

His nose wrinkled. "I don't want the shirt off your back."

He walked behind a fig tree, facing the other way. The branches separated us. The leaves were bigger than my hand. Masking him. He fingered his cross, rubbing his thumb along the wood. Oil from his fingers had darkened it over the decades. He proffered, "Try, 'Forgive me, Father, for I have sinned.' "

I pulled down on the limb. Poked my head between the branches. "Are you forgiving me or God?"

A knowing nod. "Told you you'd have made a good Catholic."

"You don't mind me questioning you?"

He smiled, shook his head. Leaves rustled beneath him. "I'd mind if you didn't." He pointed behind him. "But remember, you sat in my chair." He studied me. "You have bags under your eyes. You drive all night?"

Old, yes, but that didn't make him blind. He didn't miss much. "The fish were biting."

He reached out, took my hand, and smelled it. His eyes narrowed. "Are you really going to lie to me on Christmas?"

I shoved my hands in my pockets.

He nodded. Pleased with himself and, I think, me. "And how is my friend Edmund?"

What amazed me about Steady was not what he didn't know, but what he did. "He's fine."

"Working hard?"

"Something like that."

He let it go. "How long have we known each other?"

"Seems like all my life."

He nodded. A slight laugh. "True." He turned to me. "You realize, of course, I probably have fewer days left than you."

"You're still pushing for the confession, aren't you?"

"Yes."

I shrugged. "Let me make this simple. You know the ten commandments, right?"

He chuckled. "Seems I've heard of them."

"Well, I've never killed anybody."

He raised an eyebrow. "You sure?"

"That doesn't count."

"Killing yourself is still murder."

"Are you serious?"

"Don't kill the messenger." He shifted his weight. "That's an admission. Not a confession. Start with what hurts the most."

"It all hurts."

He took a deep breath. "I've got time." Then he shrugged. "Well, maybe not as much as I once had."

"Father, I—"

He waited, shuffling around in circles—like a one-legged duck.

I thought back, shook my head.

He was quiet a moment. "Do you have a favorite word?"

I thought a minute. " 'Epilogue.' "

He tilted his head to one side. "Good word. Interesting choice, but good." He nodded slowly. "Got another?"

I shrugged.

"Mine is 'do-over.' "

He often talked in circles. Or spirals. More like strands of DNA. Nothing was wasted. Everything connected. He waved me around the tree, hooked his arm inside mine, and led me away from the platform. The ocean lapped on our left. A southwest wind had flattened it. I took a deep breath. Salt filled my lungs. He nodded as we walked. "Yours is a painful story. It hurts to hear it."

"But I didn't tell it to you."

"Your face tells me every time I see you."

Bait fish schooled beyond the swells. "Ought to try living it."

He shook his head, staring south, back several decades. Bald head. His face a road map. Wrinkle leading into wrinkle. "Mine is enough."

He was quiet awhile, mumbling to himself. He always looked like he had one ear in this world, one ear in the next. He turned, studying my mouth. He nodded. "Your speech has really improved."

"It's amazing what you can do online these days."

"Wish it had happened sooner?"

"I wouldn't trade it."

"I've been told that most stutters stem from a father wound."

"Yeah, I've heard that."

He raised an eyebrow and did not respond. A few moments passed. He leaned on me, heavier. The air was thick. He was going to say something but changed his mind.

I loved this old man.

The path led to an old coquina building. Spanish residue, which due to four-foot walls survived hurricanes Wilma, Andrew, and others. The walls kept it cool in summer and winter. The priests used it as their chapel. Slate roof, arched ceiling, no glass in the windows meant it was open to the elements. It looked more medieval or European than South Florida.

We walked through the doorway. I shook my head.

He said, "What?"

"Seems like you ought to have a door there."

He trudged forward. "Not trying to keep people out."

"Forget people. Try mosquitoes."

We walked down the narrow aisle, mahogany

pews on either side, and sat down at the end. A padded bench staring out over an expansive eastern view. The stone floor amplified his shuffling.

"Sit with me and soothe the soul of a dying man."

"You talking about you or me?"

He nodded. "You don't miss much." He chewed on the inside of his lip and spit a piece of dead skin. "If you could paint one single picture that would explain you, what would the picture, or scene, look like?"

I thought a moment. "When I was a kid, I was working down on the docks. Odd jobs. Whatever I could do to make a few bucks. One of the fishing guides ran out of gas. Gave me two dollars and asked me to get him a cupful of gas to prime his engine. I stuffed his money in my pocket, ran to a trashcan and pulled out the biggest cup I could. One of those Big Gulp things. Sixty-four ounces or something like that. Ran across the street to the gas station. Paid the attendant. Set the cup on the ground and began pumping in two dollars. And then watched in dismay as that two dollars' worth of gas ate through the Styrofoam and spilled across the parking lot. I'm the cup. Life is the gas."

Moments passed. I had come to look forward to the stories he told me here. Finally, he spoke. Tit for tat. "We were bottled up. Hemmed in on all sides." I had not heard this one before. "Couldn't get the wounded out. Couldn't get medicine in. Gangrene became a problem. The smell was always with us." He ran his finger across his top lip. "We wore Mentholatum to combat the smell. Our triage tent looked like something out of the Civil War. We were reduced to working with a handsaw and a hot iron. We told the men that amputation was voluntary and that we had no morphine. Their call. They'd hold out a few days, hoping. Praying for air support. But the bullets were still flying, bombs still dropping, and their limbs were swelling, and the smell was getting worse. One by one they lined up. By night's end, the doctors were so tired they couldn't hold the saw. Passed it to me. By morning, I passed it back." He fell quiet. "I used to wake up nights, sweating, hearing those men scream, my hand cramped."

I leaned against the wall. He sat, staring a long way off. "Then came Christmas 1944. I was freezing my butt off at the Battle of the Bulge." His thumb unconsciously traced the bezel of his watch. "My platoon's sixth engagement. In a month, we lost more than nineteen thousand and treated forty-something-thousand wounded." He shook his head and spat. "Blood filled the tank tracks, froze, and stained our leggings. We'd stack bodies two high on one stretcher. I had to tie my hands to the stretcher because I could not physically carry another man. That night, I was leaning against a tank. Letting the exhaust warm me. Dead on my feet. Staring back out across the battlefield. My captain saw me and threatened to take away my stripes if I did not return to the battlefield. I waved my hand across the mangled trees, dead men's legs poking up through the snow like jacks and broken barricades. 'Sir, it's not fear. I'm not afraid, not anymore, but where? Where do I start?' He understood. He leaned against the tank. A good man. He lit his pipe and said, 'Steady, we can't help the dead. So leave them to God.' He drew on his pipe and blew the smoke from deep in his lungs. Then he waved his hands across the tree line. 'But . . . rescue the wounded.' The next day I carried him off the field. Before they buried him, I took the pipe from his shirt pocket."

Steady pulled the pipe from inside his robe, packed and lit it. He drew hard, his cheeks touching his yellowed teeth, and then blew smoke rings out across the pews. He shook his head. "I'm a priest with a blade. And my robes are stained." He turned his arthritic hands. Gnarled like old stumps. Dotted with age. "This may be my last walk across the battlefield." He was quiet awhile. A bony finger poked me in the chest. "It will be painful as hell, but I'm offering to cut out your gangrene."

"You or God?"

He smiled, his lips spreading. His eyes wet. "You are a good Catholic."

He wiped his face with a white handkerchief. Moments passed.

"Steady . . ." I searched his eyes. Shook my head.

He poked me in the chest with a crooked, arthritic finger. "In all your running, what have you gained?"

"Freedom."

He shook his head. "People in hell have more freedom than you." He drew deeply, his cheeks drawing tight against his teeth. He nodded once.

We sat an hour. Neither talking. Him breathing out. Me breathing in. Steady didn't need to speak to counsel me. The concert of his life spoke so loudly that I couldn't hear him even if he did open his mouth. A shrimp boat in the distance.

He paused, pressed his finger to his lips, and then straightened as the blood drained out of his face. He looked as if a steel rod had been shoved up his spine. Whatever had been bothering him since I'd arrived bubbled to the surface. He'd connected the pieces. Something clicked. He stood. Whispering aloud. "But, when the sun goes down and—" Urgency in his voice. "I need you to do me a favor."

"Name it."

He glanced back at the space in the trees, raising both eyebrows.

"Name anything but that."

"I'll explain while you drive." The sun had fallen. Dusk had set. "We may be too late."

I was in the process of objecting when he raised a finger and cut me off. His voice stern. "You owe me."

I chewed on my lip. "So . . . after this we're even?"

He shook his head. Sweat breaking out atop his forehead. "Not even close." His pace quickened. "We might not have much time." We turned a corner.

"Where're we going?"

"Sky Seven."

I stopped. "You mean the place behind the big walls that's monitored and guarded by ex–Navy SEALs?"

He nodded, walking faster.

"Just how do you plan to get in? They're rather protective of the famous gazillionaires who live there."

He dangled two keys.

"Where'd you get those?"

No response.

I crossed my arms. "And the gate code?"

He tapped his temple with his index finger.

"You know, the guards carry guns and probably don't need much of a reason to use them."

He pushed open a door. "I've been shot at before."

"Yeah, but I haven't."

He waved me on. "You'll get used to it. Besides—" He glanced over his shoulder. A slight smirk. "What do you care? You're already dead."

I nodded and spoke to myself. "Somebody should tell my heart."

Chapter Three

Steady began speaking before we'd pulled out of the church parking lot. "What I'm about to tell you is not a break in confidentiality. I'm not telling you anything you can't read in a gossip rag, popular magazine, or"—a shake of the head—"a counterfeit biography. Reams have been written and very little of it is true."

I knew him well enough to know that if he was prefacing his story with why he was telling me, then it was important to him—which meant it was important to me.

The rhythm of the turn signal interrupted the silence. He paused and squinted, staring beyond the end of the road, suggesting that this story would last the duration of our trip. Finally, he sat back and crossed his legs. How he started was evidence that he'd given it some thought. "She's the one. The one in a million. The standard by which others were, and are, measured. From Annie to Dorothy to Juliet to the queen, she's played them all. On the stage, she has performed before monarchs, heads of state, and on the screen, before the tens of millions. All have sat at her feet, marveling and moved—ranging from pin-drop quiet to raucous applause. I have seen women weep. Grown men cry. Children laugh. I have seen her make believers out of the cynical. And, when she's finished, reeled them in, I have watched as they all jump to their feet. Demanding role after role after role." He nodded. "And, to her detriment, she has obliged.

"Her sales are unprecedented. She owns the silver screen. The first twenty-five-million-dollar woman. Studios are lined up to pay it. And while films pay the most, Broadway is her love. Front-row tickets routinely sell for five hundred dollars. Box seats a thousand to fifteen hundred. Back-stage twenty-five hundred. Internet scalpers can get twice that now that she's won a third Tony. Sold-out shows are the norm and have been for a decade. Even the critics are kind. Using words like 'otherworldly' and 'angelic,' and phrases like 'Not humanly possible.' "

He paused. Reflecting. "Fame has brought homes, jets, glitter, a perennial residence in the top five, a staff of attendants, a personal trainer, world-class chef, crooning cosmetic companies, a twenty-four-hour spotlight, the loss of anonymity, a pedestal made for one, and her own private priest." Steady raised both eyebrows and slightly bowed. "The world has rolled out the red carpet and given her all it has to offer . . . including loneliness on a silver platter.

"Several men have tried to keep pace. Strong chins. Six-pack abs. Three-day stubble." He touched his ear. "A single diamond stud. Maybe a hat tilted sideways. Fresh tattoo to match their attitude. A hedge fund, record company, or clothing line and a designer fragrance in the works.

"With each, she gave unselfishly. Invested fully. Herself, her money, and her resources. They'd stand stoically. Resolute. Inching ever so slightly forward. Taking in while giving little. Truth was, they had little to give.

"Each a house of cards.

"Each had the same need. To be seen, known as the one who'd summitted and conquered her. She was a trophy. They'd bask in the glow but what they thought was their own private spotlight was little more than the residue of her reflection."

He shook his head. "They couldn't hold a candle."

"They'd stay awhile. Sleep in her bed. Brag about the sex. Attend the parties. Smile for the magazines. Take her money, drive her fancy cars, fly first class, demand better service and more champagne. As if everyone cared about them."

A final shake. "No one really did."

He glanced at me out of the corner of his eye. "Ever noticed how a spotlight is a focused beam? Not a flood? They were and would always be little more than footnotes and gossip fodder—never stepping out of her shadow. Didn't take them long to clue in. They couldn't cope so they stiffened. Became cold. Aloof.

"So, one by one, they packed up. Disappeared. Leaving her to deal with most of their baggage. Their parting words were fiery darts. Especially the ones they spewed through the papers and talk shows. She thought her tough exterior would shield her, maybe deflect them. Their words were silver bullets. Shrapnel.

"It didn't happen all at once. In her twenties, she found herself with a different last name and tied to no one. She was old-fashioned so this surprised her. Always believed in ' 'til death do us part.' Death had nothing to do with their parting. Unless death looks like a six-foot-two silicon blonde working the strip in Vegas. A few more years, a second last name later, she again found herself alone and shaking her head. Not to mention the two miscarriages that got lost in the shuffle. The doctors blamed a hectic schedule. Said she needed some time off. Slow down. Breathe some mountain air.

"She wasn't so sure. Neither was I.

"The view from the top of the world is endless. Stretches forever. 'Course, the reverse is true, too. Those below you—which is everyone else —can see your every move. Life under the microscope. Loved by all, yet known by none?

"Then, about a decade ago, for reasons I do not understand, things changed—for the worse. She's never revealed to me the reason, or reasons, but whatever it was, it is still painful to her. Maybe even the source of.

"She's pretty tough so she held off for a while, but then her weight dropped, she retreated to the pills, and occasionally, me. Sold-out shows were canceled. Her team of publicists stepped in: 'She needs rest. A performance schedule that was a little too aggressive.'

"She checked herself in. A desert oasis. The name on the gate said 'Spa' but those inside knew better. Her people kept it a secret. Weeks later, she was back on the stage, rejuvenated, clean, her voice, her presence, her command—stronger than ever.

"A smoke screen. It didn't last.

"Several months ago, a few days into the filming of her next great movie, one of the producers found her confused, her speech slurred, in the back of her million-dollar bus. Her team moved in. Citing 'mislabeled medication.' A quick relapse. Another stint in therapy. This one longer, more expensive. More difficult to hide. As was the scar on her wrist. The producer empathized, even apologized, but found another star. An up-and-comer. Her people filed a lawsuit against the maker of the drug. Another press release: 'She is unfortunately the victim of someone's neglect. Her team of lawyers will handle that. Now, she is spending time recuperating. Reading scripts. Focusing on what's important.' A plastic surgeon was employed to mask the 'accident' on her arm."

It didn't take a genius to understand that Steady was telling a story he had lived. Had invested in. His tone told me he relished in the memory of some of the moments, but winced in the recollection of others. A retelling that was both satisfying and painful. He continued, "Home again. A much needed vacation. I helped her find an oceanfront villa in Miami—" Another point out the passenger's side window. "With acreage, a twelve-foot-spiked coquina fence, and more security cameras than she could count. Months passed in freedom. Glimpses of normality. No spotlight. Few headlines. Moments of anonymity. She'd wrap a scarf around her face, don sunglasses, and come see me several times a week.

"Clean once again, her people stepped in. Her 'handlers' felt it was time. Play offense. Tell her side. 'Control the news rather than suffer it.' They figured the way to do that was to publish her authorized biography. I disagreed, felt they were pushing her too soon, that she was still too fragile, but word was leaked to publishers. New York came frothing. An auction was held. A seven-figure advance. Writers were interviewed.

She was introduced to a writer. Told she could trust him. I told her she could not but she is not the best judge of men. Anyway, he listened thoughtfully, convinced her he was different, compassionately poured more wine. So she agreed, and started at the beginning, telling him 'her story.' When he had enough, he transcribed his record-ings, penned his tale, and skipped town. Took her story with him. An insider's view. Sold it to the highest bidder. Millions. He made the rounds. All the late-night shows. The networks. His book is called *The Ice Queen* and is currently climbing the *New York Times* list.

"Because she is headstrong, fiercely deter-mined, and—I think—because she is not about to be outdone by a liar with a pen, she accepted a role for the stage, saying, 'The role I was born to play.' Publicists worked the frenzy around the clock. The much-awaited triumphant return." Steady shook his head in retrospect. "She can fool the faceless masses who throw flowers and praise and promise love untold, and she can pacify her handlers, but not me. That book did more damage than she let on. A crack in her dam. I told them so but they like the money she makes them and the power she gives them.

"With the audience seated, the orchestra tuned, the curtain string taut, the spotlight searching, she walked out on stage, a standing ovation. A triumphant return. But it was not enough. When they quieted, the music grew, rising, the audience on the edge of their seats." His voice softened. "I know. I was there.

"She looked around, measured her life, and found herself wanting. She did not open her mouth. No sound. No lines.

"A knee buckled. Unsteadiness in her eyes. She glanced at me, then gathered herself, turned, and silently walked out of the spotlight. Moments later, a stranger appeared. 'Ladies and gentlemen, we're terribly sorry. Our star has taken ill.'

"She was sick, all right.

"I found her in the bathroom of her suite with an empty pill bottle. I dialed 911 and held her while her breathing grew shallow. I had just started CPR when the paramedics arrived. They rolled her out the hotel lobby. Naked beneath the sheet. An oxygen mask, IV, a medic charging the defibrillator. White paddles held in the air." Steady's face grew tense. No longer retelling, he was reliving. His voice cracked. "Between the double doors leading to the street and a throng of people, the paramedic shouted, 'Clear!' and her body jumped."

Steady shook his head and oncoming headlights exposed the tears in his eyes. "No plastic surgeon would hide this.

"I sat with her that night. When I walked the hall for coffee around three a.m., stretched my legs, the paparazzi paid off one of the nurses. I don't know how many pictures he took, but based on what I've seen, it was a lot.

"The next morning—I saw it in her eyes. She was empty. Sucked dry. Played out." He recrossed his legs. "I walked downstairs for some antacids and one of the headlines at the checkout read THE LAST GASPS OF A BROKEN, AND REBROKEN, HEART." A false chuckle. "For once, they'd gotten it right." He waited while his words sank in. Then with a deliberateness I seldom saw, he said, "That was three weeks ago today."

I waited, allowing the hurt to ease. "How do you know all this?"

"I met her when she was just a kid. Still undiscovered. I knew the owner of a theater on the mile so I got her an audition. That was some twenty years ago."

I knew the answer but I asked anyway. "You feel responsible?"

A long pause. He whispered, "Yes, although—" A glance at me. "I am realistic about my ability to control another's actions."

"Does 'she' have a name?"

Steady waited, then said the name both with admiration and discomfort. "Katie Quinn."

Steady fell silent. Sky Seven towered before us.

Chapter Four

Miami is something of a New York City of the South mixed with a Cuba of the North. That makes for an interesting blend of cultures. Along with some really good food. For the young, nightlife is hopping and there are enough clubs to frequent a new one every night of the month. For the wealthy, oceanfront parties in fifteen-thousand-square-foot villas are the norm. Yachts average seventy-five feet, and can stretch to a hundred and twenty plus. Once in, keeping up with the Joneses is a full-time occupation. For some, an occupational hazard.

In South Florida, much of life revolves around the water. Most everybody owns a boat or two and a couple of Jet Skis. Empty trailers are common yard art, and in many cases, a person's boat costs more than their car. Weekends are not a question of what you're doing, but where (on the water) you're going.

Sky Seven is a waterfront high-rise where villas start in the "you can't afford it" range extending into the "don't even think about it" stratosphere. High-fenced, and gated, the property is patrolled by a team of ex-military wearing suits and ear-pieces who've found their retirement gig baby-sitting the über-wealthy.

A block away, Steady took the wheel and told me to slide down between the rear seats. Out of view. I didn't argue. We pulled up to the gate and a chiseled man with a flattop approached the driver's side door. Through the trees, Key Biscayne shimmered. Down the street to our left, a crowd of paparazzi stood in a narrow stretch of public parking access. Tripod-mounted cameras pointed at the top floor. One reporter stood illuminated, talking into the camera, Sky Seven serving as the background. The thought that Katie Quinn might actually be in the building had them in a feeding frenzy.

The guard shined his light and nodded. "Merry Christmas, Father." He punched a button on the wall, the gate lifted, and he waved us through in a reverse salute of sorts.

Steady extended his hand, touching the four imaginary corners of the cross, blessing the instantly penitent man, and returned to the wheel. We idled through and the lights of the gatehouse passed. I whispered, "They know you?"

He shrugged. "I make house calls sometimes."

"You mean you come all the way out here to hear her confession?"

After we drove through the gate, he turned. Stern face. "I carry the stretcher to the wounded."

"What about me?"

"You're not crippled."

"What am I?"

He glanced in the rearview, eyeing the restless crowd across the street. "Stubborn."

A marina was stuffed full of oversize boats and empty of the people who owned them. Many of the sailboats had converted their masts into fifty-foot, twinkling trees. Single man-size stars clung to the satellite dishes of most of the yachts. Several had continual music playing and one gargantuan boat had twelve life-size reindeer pulling Santa and his sleigh atop the helicopter deck. I scratched my head. Strange to be so lit up and yet so devoid of people.

Steady pointed and said she owned a boat. "One of those fast, cigarette things." He snapped his fingers. "The name is something catchy."

We drove into the garage and parked near the elevator. We found her black, tinted-window Range Rover parked in her spot. Unlocked and un-womanned. Steady touched the hood. "The engine's still warm."

We boarded the elevator and the doors shut. I asked, "Which floor?"

Steady inserted his key, turned it, and nodded. "The top."

The directory listed five villas on the top floor. "Which one?"

"All of them."

"She owns the whole floor?"

He nodded and watched the digital numbers climb on the wall display.

We rode to the top in silence. When the doors opened again, one enormous, dark wooden door stood opposite us. Think castle gate. The thing must have been twelve feet tall and the handle probably weighed twenty pounds.

We let ourselves in. Steady first, then me. A cross breeze sucked through the door as we entered, suggesting another door was open elsewhere. He stood listening, then muttered under his breath. "That's bad."

"What's bad?"

"She likes to be . . ." He waved his hand in the air looking for the right word. ". . . Attended to. Normally, this place is crawling with people—waiting on her hand and foot. Cell phones growing out of their ears."

The expanse was dark. Pin-drop quiet.

A light shone in the kitchen. On the table we found a "To Whoever Finds this Letter" letter. Steady picked it up, slid on his reading glasses, and read it. When finished, he set it down, folded his glasses, and stood thinking. Listening.

The interior space was huge. Ten thousand square feet or more. The floor was hard and slick. Maybe marble or tile. I could make out furniture across the room and a piano set against the far wall, which was made entirely of glass, giving an unobstructed view of the western side of Miami and the unlit Everglades beyond. I'd never seen anything like it.

The sliding glass stood open. While the east side of Sky Seven shimmered white and brilliant due to paparazzi and media crew searchlights, the west side stood dark. Silent. Whatever happened on the east side would be instantly public and, thanks to the Internet, worldwide in seconds. But whatever happened on the west side would not be known until daylight. Or later.

A sheer curtain waved gently across an opened sliding-glass door leading out to a porch with a western view, now encased in shadow and blackness. Steady looked at me, then back at the door.

We weaved our way through the three rooms between us and the door, stepping around the furniture. We approached slowly. Someone was muttering on the other side. Her voice shook.

A naked woman stood on the railing. Teetering. A rope around her neck. It trailed down her neck and spine, wrapped around her left hand, and ended at a coil below her. A strand of beads in the fingers of her right hand. I had almost cleared the door, when the woman stopped muttering. Her hands stopped moving. The distance was too great. I couldn't reach her in time. Without a word, without so much as a hiccup, she stepped forward. Then she was gone.

Feathers make more noise when they fall.

I seized the rope. It wrapped around me like an anaconda, tightened on my arm, and launched me into the railing, threatening to pull my arm out of its socket. In the same instant, Steady grabbed the end with both hands, giving me just enough slack to unwrap my hands. When he let go, the rope slid another ten feet, peeling most of the skin off the insides of my hands.

I lay flat on the slick floor and pushed up with my legs, bracing myself against the underside of the railing. Had I not, she'd have pulled me over. I could see a flash of movement, her fingers grasping the rope. The blood in my hands made the rope slippery. Steady reached in, grabbed the rope, and we worked hand over hand to lift her back up.

The closer she got, the more I could feel her kicking and twitching. I felt like we could lift her to the railing, but I wasn't sure how we'd get her over it. One of us would have to hold the rope while the other lifted her, or her body. I wasn't sure Steady could do that.

I was wrong.

We got her within reach. I braced myself, nodded, and Steady stood. Between the columns, I could see her hands—both of which were gripping the rope above her, taking just enough of the weight of her body off her throat. Her expression was one of panic—of life slipping away. Or being taken. And her eyes were about to pop out of her head. She didn't make a sound.

Steady leaned, grabbed her with his gnarled, arthritic hands, and pulled, drawing from a reservoir of strength I did not know he possessed. The rope fell slack, and she landed in a muted thud across his legs. He held her while I dug my fingers under the knot, and loosened the rope. I've never been married, never had children, and never witnessed one being born, but I am told that their first breath is an audible and unmistakable experience. The sound of her sucking in told me she was alive again.

Covered in coils of rope, my blood and sweat and maybe her urine, it struck me that this was not a publicity stunt. She'd not done this to attract attention. At least not while it was happening. I won't speak to her motivation but this was intended as a private death, permanent and absolute, no do-over, and the world would deal with it long after she was gone.

For several minutes, the three of us lay exhausted on the balcony. I studied my stinging hands. In a sense, she was lucky the rope slid through them. Had I been able to grip the rope like a vise, the rope plus her weight would have snapped her neck. As it happened, it tightened gradually—allowing us time to pull her up.

Soon, the sobs came. Steady sat up, cradled her head, and wrapped her body in his robes. I uncoiled myself and lay staring at the stars above us. I tried to stand, but my legs were shaking so badly I decided against it.

I wanted to get out of there before someone

found us. Accused us. Steady sat unfazed. Unmoving. She curled into a fetal position in his lap while he whispered in the air above her.

The circular burn around her neck was not going away any time soon. A tattoo sans ink. As were the burns on my hands. I made my way to the kitchen sink, ran cold water over the raw meat in my palms, and then handed a wet towel to Steady. He dabbed her neck. Soothing the skin.

She lay there, sobbing. Shaking uncontrollably. What I saw was not the woman who lit the silver screen, walked the red carpet, graced the cover of *Vogue*, *People*, or name your tabloid, but a broken human being at the bottom. I slid down the wall, and sat quietly, deciding something I'd long since suspected but never known for sure. Man, or woman, is not made to be worshipped. We are not physically cut out for it. Life in the spotlight, on the pedestal, at the top of the world was a lonely, singular, desolate, soul-killing place.

I whispered, "Shouldn't we call somebody?"

He looked down at the scar on her wrist and the oozing burn on her neck. He shook his head. He stared out the window, and down at the lights of the dock. "We need to get her out of here without being seen by the sharks below. Get her some-place where she can have a few days anonymity. Peace." He nodded. Like he'd made up his mind before we ever came up here. "Your place."

"My place? Why my place? Take her to your

place. Take her to a hotel. I'm getting out of here before somebody blames me—"

" 'Cause nobody'll find her with you and she needs that right now. And 'cause—"

Steady rarely, if ever, asked anything of me. " 'Cause what?"

" 'Cause you don't care who she is and don't care to profit off this."

I wasn't getting out of this. I leaned my head against the wall. "Maybe we should ask her."

He brushed the hair out of her face, whispered over her, and she pulled his hand across her heart and nodded.

He pointed at the kitchen. "The keys are hanging on a panel in the pantry. Only one with a floating key chain. The service elevator will spit you out the back of the building. Lower level parking deck. There's an exit in the far corner. You can wind your way through the dark and avoid the crowd. We'll be along in a few minutes. And"—a wrinkle appeared between his eyes— "don't let anyone see you."

I wanted to ask him how he knew all this but figured now wasn't the time. As it turned out I was right because with little notice, she turned, lifted her head, and vomited all over the balcony. He waved me off, so as to protect her from any more embarrassment.

I studied the sleek paneled elevator as I stood inside, descending. No security emerged. People here valued their privacy. Downstairs, I crept out of the loading garage and around to the docks, which sat at the end of a long cul-de-sac and out of earshot. The crowd of news media and cameramen had started on eggnog and grown animated. Pointing at the top floor and talking loudly about the injustices of the rich, they were oblivious to what had been attempted and almost happened in the shadow of the western side. I had no desire to tell them so I wound my way to the back. A forty-something-foot, go-fast boat, probably worth well over a quarter of a million dollars, sat dry on a lift a few feet above the surface of the water. Even out of the water she looked fast. The name on the back read *The Ice Queen*.

This meant we were taking the long way home and it also meant no one would ever know. Hopping in that boat at this time of night and killing the running lights was like dropping off the face of the earth. Which, given what I'd just witnessed, wasn't a bad idea. But none of that was my problem—or so I thought.

I dropped the lift, turned on the batteries, and ran the blowers while I made sense of the instrument panel—which looked more like a fighter jet than an expensive pleasure boat.

I punched the start button and all three engines roared to life then returned to a low hum and rumble characteristic of over fifteen hundred horsepower. Minutes later, Steady emerged on the dock leading a slow-walking, unstable, cloaked person clinging to his arm. She wore jeans and a dark, long-sleeved T-shirt. He and she stepped into the boat. She descended into the cabin, closing the door behind her. He whispered, "Cut the lights and you two ease out of here."

My head jerked. "What do you mean, 'you two'?"

"Security saw me enter. They need to see me leave. Otherwise, I may have to answer questions I can't answer."

"But—?"

He waved me off. "Pick me up at the Spear."

"The what?"

He frowned. Like I should know. He raised both eyebrows. "Piet Hein's Spear."

Yeah, I did know the spot.

I eased us out of the slip, through the marina, and into the open water and total darkness of Biscayne Bay—my navigational screen and GPS serving as my guide. I had no idea what I would say if she emerged from her cabin but luckily I didn't have to figure that out. At least not yet.

We crossed Biscayne Bay, west of the Seaquarium, then turned south where the dark shadow of Biscayne National Park appeared on our port side followed by the lights of the Old Dixie Highway and the Card Sound Bridge. Her cabin door never opened and she made no sound—least not that I could hear over the hum of the engines. The Card Sound Bridge is a toll bridge that hovers sixty-five feet above the water, connecting Florida City to North Key Largo. I have some experience with the bridge and the view from this perspective—from the water up—was strange. It looked taller than I remembered.

The granite obelisk of the memorial, or Piet Hein's Spear, rose up above the trees on my left. Just past it sat the dock that allowed boat access to the memorial. I nosed the bow of the boat up to the platform, where a white-clothed figure stood smoking a pipe. With surprising agility, Steady stepped in and then hung his arm inside mine.

Wasting no time, I reversed and began easing out into open water. I realized running without lights was in violation of most every law that governs nighttime watercraft use but I doubted if anyone could catch us and if they did I had no intention of still being aboard. I throttled up and planed out. No wind, and glassy water, meant that sixty miles an hour had never felt so smooth. Comfortable inside the pocket of air created by the windshield in front of me, I probed Steady. "How'd you know so much about this boat?"

"She donated a ride in a fund-raiser for the new parish hall. Part of the silent auction." He made quotation marks with his fingers. " 'Buy a hundred-and-twenty-mile-an-hour boat ride with a celebrity.' It brought a lot of money. Helped us finish the building. She let me tag along."

I glanced back in the direction of the parking lot. "What about the van?"

"I'll send someone to pick it up."

To the north, Sky Seven still sat lit up like the Taj Mahal. "And the letter?"

"Left it alone."

I looked at him. My surprise showing.

He said, "Throwing away that letter doesn't change what it says or the person that wrote it. She's going to have to deal with it sooner or later."

"What if somebody else finds it first? Like the vultures parked out front."

"You really think that matters?"

I rarely questioned Steady. "You sure you're not playing God?"

He paused. Shrugged. Shook his head once. "I hope not." He looked down at the cabin door. "But sometimes, God wears skin."

We cut across the channel south of the lighthouse at Bill Baggs Cape Florida State Park and, given a rising tide, right through the seven remaining renegade structures of Stiltsville—a community of houses that, as its name suggests, are built on stilts and sit some ten feet off the ocean's surface. At one time there were more than twenty-five weekend homes in a cluster on the flat just south of Key Biscayne but every hurricane to pass through has skimmed a few off the surface. I've always admired Stiltsville and the people who built it. Maybe that says a lot about me.

I took us to open water where a southwest wind had flattened the Atlantic. Two- to three-foot swells welcomed us with a rhythmic roll. I turned south-southwest and soon knew when Key Largo was on my starboard side.

We passed Islamorada and Lignumvitae Basin, which led into the Florida Bay. I turned northwest at Long Key, crossed under U.S. 1 at the viaduct and across the southern tip of Florida Bay toward the deeper water and grass flats of the gulf. Without the navigational system, I'd have never made it. Maybe Totch Brown, but not me. The waters of Florida Bay are shallow—averaging zero to three feet—and rife with Buick-size chunks of limestone sitting inches below the surface. Depth charts are essential. I swung wide, taking us around most of it, keeping to deeper water. We serpentined through the deeper channels of Little Rabbit and Carl Ross Key, and into the open water just outside Northwest Cape. At the Shark River, the water deepened, and I pressed the throttle forward and started skimming across the surface at over seventy miles an hour. I looked behind me. A frothy wake spread in the shape of a long Y. I smiled. I'd just done something I'd never done—cut across the southern tip of Florida in about thirty minutes. North of us flowed Marjory Stoneman Douglas's "river of grass" and the first of the Ten Thousand Islands. If conditions stayed calm, we were ninety miles and less than two hours from home. The drive would not be a straight one as shallow water would force us through more channels only wide enough for one boat. Navigating the flats of the Keys is dicey. On the surface it all looks the same, wide open and inviting. Underneath, it's anything but. Much like those who live here.

I'd fished this area a lot, and Steady knew it as well if not better than I, but more than one newcomer had sunk his boat because he got overconfident. Local charts are all printed with fine print that says "Local knowledge is essential to successful navigation." I kept my eyes on the screen and depth gauge.

Given the wind, the water was a sheet of black. Deeper water opened up beneath us and I pushed the throttle forward and trimmed the tabs. Our speed climbed from seventy-two to seventy-seven to eighty-six and finally eighty-nine. We were flying. Yet in a boat that big and heavy it felt like thirty. I wouldn't want to fish out of it but it danced across the surface of the gulf.

I turned my baseball cap backward and drove in silence—tucked in the vacuum. Steady sat to my left, staring well out beyond the bow. His robes waving in the wind. His lips tight. A wrinkle between his eyes. I don't know if what Steady was doing—what we were doing—was right or wrong, and I don't pretend to know what's best for that poor creature of a woman, but, I will offer this—if God wore skin, I think it'd look a lot like Steady's.

Chapter Five

Once in the gulf beyond Shark River, we passed several river mouths, including Lostmans and Chatham. The mouth of the Chatham meant home wasn't far. Tide was up so we motored across the grass flats at Chatham Bend, beyond Duck Rock, and around to the leeward side of Pavilion Key. Years back, somebody had built a house on stilts that backed up to the mangroves and looked out over the gulf. A great view and great proximity to the fishing, but given that its location sat in the direct path of most every hurricane to pass through, it proved unlivable. Later, it served as a fish camp or trading post for guys like me. As only the twelve barnacled posts remain, the camp did not fare well against the hurricanes, but it did allow safe anchorage for my home on the water, the *Gone Fiction*.

At three a.m., I came in out of the wind, cut the engine, and tied off the go-fast boat to the stern of mine. The woman was hard asleep so I lifted her off her bed in the cabin and carried her onto my boat and into my cabin where I set her quietly on the bed and pulled the door behind me. She never stirred. Whether she was acting, or truly asleep, I knew not.

Steady waited for me in the galley, only shrugging when I walked out. Having experienced more personal contact than I had in years, I climbed up on deck, and hung my hammock. Nighttime here is magical. I've stood on my roof and watched the shuttle spiral into space, followed satellites in their arc across the sky, and watched Mars creep across the black marble floor of heaven.

The Florida Everglades start as a river flowing south out of Lake Okeechobee, sixty miles wide and a hundred miles long. It flows across a limestone shelf to Florida Bay at the southern end of the state into two parks: Everglades National Park and Big Cypress National Preserve. Together they total 2.22 million acres—the largest roadless area in the U.S. While their map lines are set, their boundaries are somewhat fluid as they're shaped by water, fire, and man. They flood in the wet season: May to November, where they average five feet of rain a year, followed by drought in the dry months of December to April. The Glades' most famous spokesperson, Marjory Stoneman Douglas, coined the phrase "river of grass." The Seminoles called it *Pa-hay-okee*, or, "grassy water." And the Spanish called it the "Lake of the Holy Spirit." The terrain shifts between cypress swamps, mangrove forests, hardwood hammocks, and pine rock land. Some have said it is quite possibly the most primitive wilderness remaining in the lower forty-eight. Maybe. I wouldn't know how to measure that other than to say that it's certainly not civil.

I live on the outskirts in the Everglades—beyond the southern tip of Florida—in that magical soup of mangrove keys called the Ten Thousand Islands—a band or swath of trees and roots that grow up off the shallow shelf between the grass and the deep water of the gulf. A place with no beginning and no end. Where the roots of the mangroves weave through the water like interlocking fingers looking for safe purchase, anchoring themselves against the next hurricane.

Both the islands and the Glades are too low to live on except for about forty small oyster-shell island mounds probably built by the Calusa and Tequesta Indians. They range in size from two to twenty feet above sea level and from fifty feet across to a hundred and fifty acres. I'm never far from one of these. The last to live here were the Seminoles—the only Indian nation never to surrender to the U.S. The closest town is Chokoloskee, pronounced "chuck-a-luskee," which sits eighty miles west of Miami just off Tamiami Trail (U.S. 41). Note: I didn't say I lived "close." It's simply the closest place on the map.

Out here sugarcane grows wild. Along with

guavas, sugar apples, oranges, limes, grapefruit, papaya, avocado pears, and hearts of palm—called "swamp cabbage." Trees are buttonwood, poinciana, and coconut palm. Oysters grow rampant on the roots of mangroves. There's bear, deer, fox, raccoon, alligator, Burmese pythons, and more birds than most have ever seen. Whip-poor-wills, mourning doves, owls, turkeys, osprey, and eagle are common and plentiful.

Given so much water, I live on two boats. One is home. The other is play. There is a third, but we'll get to that. Home is a forty-eight-foot trawler built in the 1930s that drafts about three feet. Twin diesels, holds five hundred gallons of gas, four hundred gallons of water, two hundred of propane. If I'm frugal, I can stay gone for months at a time. About nine years ago, I was driving north on U.S. 1 and saw her lying on her side, weathered and rotting in a cow pasture miles from the water or the smell of salt. She had beautiful lines, peeling paint, and a yellowed waterline that spoke of gentle moments spread across the cut-water. Foreign shores. Tropical destinations. I paid the farmer five hundred dollars, hauled it to a warehouse, and spent a year, five thousand hours, and five hundred gallons of sweat turning it back into a faint reflection of her former self. When I got into the hull, I found a picture album and captain's log wrapped in oilcloth.

In her heyday, the *Blue See* cut her teeth

running from Key West to Cuba chasing marlin and tarpon as a charter boat. The log and accompanying charts gave a detailed history of the men and women who fished her and when, where, and how many and what kind of fish they caught and on what bait. In 1943, the boat was voluntarily taken out of charter service and used by the Navy to spot submarines off the Florida coast. Following her service in the war, she returned to charter service, though this time on the high end. Three of the most notable passengers were Eisenhower, Hemingway, and Zane Grey.

I don't know what happened to the captain or how his boat ended up in a cow pasture providing shade for Florida cows and rattlesnakes but the last entry read: "November 3, 1969. Starboard engine dead. Port fading fast. Sunset behind me. Been a helluva run. If I had any guts, I'd bury us both at sea where we belong. Seems a shame—the stories this girl could tell." The farmer said the boat had been in his pasture since he bought it in '71 and he didn't know how it got there or anything about the owner. In honor of the captain, and given the boat's penchant for stories, I renamed her *Gone Fiction*. Thought maybe he'd like that.

My second boat is where I spend most of my days. A twenty-four-foot Pathfinder called *Jody*—for reasons that matter to me. If you don't like to fish, chances are you won't like this boat—it's designed by fishermen, for fishermen. By now, she's well seasoned. I've fished her from south Texas, to Louisiana, Key West, the Bahamas, Matanzas Inlet on up to Sea Island and Charleston. But most of the time we find ourselves in the waters of the keys and the Ten Thousand Islands and as a result I'm rarely more than a two- or three-hour boat ride from Miami. The caveat to this is the migration. If the hundred-plus-pound tarpon are schooling in the Matanzas or the waters off Sea Island, well then so are we.

Chasing the fish like this means that I seldom stay in one place for more than a week. There are always more fish to catch and always a better place to do it. Over the years, I've caught tens of thousands of fish and learned that if the fish aren't biting, I'm either not throwing at them what they want to eat or not throwing it in the right spot. Truth is, the fish are always biting. It's the fisherman who's wrong, not the fish.

I suppose some may find it strange but I like living in a boat. I have no grass to mow, no property taxes, and no last-known address because it changes every few days. Between selling what I don't eat, my crab traps, odd jobs for Steady at the church, and boat repair work for cash in Chokoloskee, I manage.

Sunrise found me awake. One leg dangling. Swaying slightly. A book on my chest. My boat is packed with books. Thousands. Stacked up like cordwood. I never met a used bookstore I could live without. On the other hand, I don't own a TV, read the paper, subscribe to magazines, or listen to the radio, and I've only had meaningful conversation with one other person in the last decade. But don't think me friendless—I have hundreds. All tucked within the pages of these stories.

A breeze washed across me. Not really cool, but not hot either. I climbed out of my hammock and stretched, staring out over the flats into the first glimpse of daylight while one of the ten trillion swamp angels in the Everglades buzzed my ear. I used to swat them. Now they land, suck, gorge, and fly away.

I slid on my flip-flops, and hung my Costa Del Mars around my neck. Sight-casting is awful tough when you can't see "into" the water. Costas do that. Thinking Steady might be hungry, I grabbed the cast net, and checked it for holes. It took me six months to make the thing so I'm a little particular about mending it. I found two snags and knotted them closed. I hopped in *Jody* and eased toward faster-moving current in the leeward side of Bonefish Island. The wind in my face, I turned my hat around. Wheel in one hand, throttle in the other, glass all around—it was one of my favorite places—before you . . . all possibility. All future. Behind you . . . a deep cut that heals. A quickly forgotten past.

I cut the engine, walked to the bow, studied the surface, and slung the net. The surface popped with bait fish—I caught breakfast in one cast. Four trout feeding on the surface bait. I threw two back.

From the serenity of the water, I returned to the sound of slamming pans and shattering plates. Along with the screaming of a very angry woman. I tied off *Jody*, hopped downstairs into *Gone Fiction*, and found my houseguest making a mess of almost everything I owned. Steady was trying to talk her out of her rage and, judging by the pile of broken plates and glasses that surrounded her, not having much effect. She held a frying pan in one hand, interrupted in mid-rant about how she got here, and pointed it at me when I walked in. "And, who is that!"

Steady spoke softly. "He's the guy that saved your life and drove us here." He pointed at his feet. "This is his boat."

This registered in her mind, only serving to douse her anger with more gas so she reared back and launched the pan at me. "Why?" she demanded. It glanced off my shoulder, flew out the cabin door, and splashed behind me. Her face was red and a vein had popped out on her right temple. Her top lip was twitching. She was sweating. "What are you looking at? What do you want?"

She was maybe five and a half feet tall. Distinct features. Large, round, expressive eyes. Her body screamed aerobics, yoga, and Pilates. Julie Andrews meets Audrey Hepburn with a little Sophia Loren and Grace Kelly thrown in for spice and that lady from *Terminator*, Linda Hamilton, mixed in for spunk and attitude.

I looked at Steady as a plastic plate Frisbee'd past my head followed by a full water bottle. Over the last decade, I'd spent considerable time lining available wall space with shelves and then filling the shelves with books. An old habit. Given the abundance of stories shelved about her, she turned her attention to them. She pulled hardcover editions of *The Old Man and the Sea* and *The Count of Monte Cristo*. I didn't care if she threw every pot, pan, and dish I owned in the water, but those books were another story. She reached back and heaved both at once. I did my best to deflect them. Knocked them to the floor, picked them up, and tucked them safely under my arm. Then I held up my hands in stop-sign fashion. She was reaching for *Les Misérables*. The sight of raw, blistered, and torn skin on my palms gave her pause. She raised an eyebrow. "What's wrong with your hands?"

Steady answered. "He got to the rope first."

Her resolve weakened ever so slightly. "Does that hurt?"

I nodded.

She hardened again. "I didn't ask you to stop me from falling."

Steady spoke up. "Fall or jump?"

She shot a glance at him. "Whatever. Same thing."

She pointed her finger at both of us. "I want off this boat. Now."

I reached in my pocket and handed her the keys to her boat. She snatched them out of my hand and the tension in her face eased. "You're not keeping me here?"

I shook my head.

"Then what do you want and why am I here?"

Steady continued. "We thought it'd give you some space to think things out. Maybe take a deep breath."

She pointed at the door. "So I can leave any time I want?"

Stepping out of the walkway, I held open the door.

She jumped out the door, hopped in her boat, cranked the engine, and placed it in gear. The boat tugged on its mooring, satisfying her that we weren't lying and she could actually leave when she wanted. She stood stoically. One hand on the throttle, thinking. Threatening. She eased the throttle forward, stretching the stress limit of the line. Satisfied she was not a prisoner, she throttled down, cut the ignition, and stepped back into my cabin. Steady patted the cushion next to him. "Katie, please."

She wiped her hands across her face then

abruptly pointed her finger in my face. "I don't like you and I don't trust you. And I don't care what you did, just because I'm on your boat doesn't mean I owe you a thing."

I didn't say a word. I was in bad need of some coffee. I stepped into the galley, ground some beans, filled the coffeemaker, and clicked it on. I observed her out of the corner of my eye. She sat listening to Steady explain himself and his thinking but her attention was centered on the galley and me and specifically the coffeemaker. It finished, I poured myself a cup and sat sipping, hovering over the aroma. By now she was ignoring Steady, staring at me and my cup. She raised an eyebrow. She was calm, measured. Arms folded, legs crossed. One foot tapping the floor. "Black. No cream. No sugar. And warm the cup before you pour the coffee in it."

I never took my eyes off my coffee. I simply stepped aside and continued sipping from my mug. If she wanted coffee, she was more than welcome to it, but I wasn't serving her. She stood, slammed open a cupboard, grabbed a mug, washed it in the sink then let it sit under the hot water for five minutes while my precious fresh water ran through her mug and down the drain. Satisfied her cup was of the right temperature, she poured some coffee, sipped not disapprovingly, and then resumed her pissed-off posture on the couch. From the sweat on her top lip, to the narrowed stretch between her eyes, to the tension in her shoulders, everything about her said, "Leave me alone. I don't want you. Don't need you. Don't want to know of your existence."

I obliged.

I stepped outside and noticed the current along the back side of Pavilion Key. The water from the gulf pushes in through a small slough, or break in the key, creating a swift current that often fills up with trout. I grabbed one of my poles, a Sustain 3000 on a seven-foot St. Croix, and threw a popping cork with a soft plastic into the current. I fish twenty-pound Sufix braid with a thirty-pound fluorocarbon leader. In English, that means I can pitch in around shells and other barnacled structures. It also allows me to cast really far.

Ten minutes later, I'd caught three inside the slot—two trout measuring at least fifteen inches and a flounder slightly smaller. I filleted them along with the trout I'd caught earlier in the cast net, and while Steady reasoned with psycho woman, I dropped the fillets in two skillets with some clarified butter and salt and pepper and started cooking breakfast for me and Steady.

Again, her attention turned toward me. She paraded to the coffeepot, filled her empty mug, and stood observing me. When I didn't notice her, she returned to her throne on the couch.

The more I was near this woman, the more I wanted her off my boat. Just standing near her made the hair stand up on the back of my neck. I'd never met someone who was so cold, shut off, shut down, and just downright rude. The B-word came to mind but I kept it to myself. So did the words "high" and "maintenance." A stark contrast from my first glimpse of her kissing Steady's cheek at the confessional. I served two plates—a number that did not escape her. Steady was in midsentence when she pointed at me. "Who the hell is he!"

"His name is Sunday. He's a hermit, of sorts."

"A what?"

"Hermit. The church once called them 'desert dwellers' though he's"—Steady waved his hand out across the water—"thrown that definition on its head. It's a voluntary, solitary lifestyle meant to bring about a change of heart." She glanced at me. He continued. "A condition in which the participant withdraws. Given to penance and prayer." She recrossed her legs while her thumb traced the rim of her mug. Her eyes never left me. Steady continued, "In the Canon Law 1983, the church recognized the eremitic or anchoritic life by which the Christian faithful devoted their life to the praise of God and salvation of the world through a stricter separation from the world, through the silence of solitude, assiduous prayer, and penance." He motioned to me. "A hermit is recognized in the law as one dedicated to God in a consecrated life if he or she professes the three evangelical counsels of chastity, poverty, and obedience. And, in his case, a fourth."

I had no idea what he was talking about but I didn't interrupt him. He'd piqued my interest and I wanted to know where this was going. Technically, everything he said was true, but it had never been an official thing. She did not look impressed. "Fourth?"

He nodded. "Yes. Silence."

Steady had turned chatty. Taking the focus off her and placing it on me. "His profession is confirmed by a vow or other sacred bond in the hands of the diocesan bishop"—Steady smiled—"and observes his or her own plan of life under his direction."

She cut to the chase. "So, he lives alone and talks to no one?"

"Solitude is not the purpose, only a conducive environment for striving after a particular spiritual aim."

She slowly turned her head toward me. "I can think of few things that sound worse."

"He is a man who has renounced worldly concerns and pleasures to come closer to God. His life is filled with meditation, contemplation, and prayer without distractions of contact with human society, sex, or the need to maintain socially acceptable standards." She raised an eyebrow and measured me. "He maintains a simple diet with very few distractions."

"So"—she pointed at me—"he doesn't want sex?"

Steady laughed. "I didn't say he didn't want it. I said he'd taken a vow to abstain from it."

She shook her head. "Pitiful. What kind of a loser would vow that?"

Steady shrugged. "I did."

"Yeah, but you don't count. You're a priest. You're supposed to. He's nothing but a guy who's"—she painted her hands across my boat—"checked out and attached some religious mumbo jumbo to it to give him a sense of purpose. Living out here in the middle of nowhere with no purpose and no reason for anything."

I didn't even know her and yet she'd undressed me in a single sentence. She knew me better than I liked. I didn't respond. While what she said was true, she was also trying to turn my screws and get a rise out of me.

She thumbed at me. "Can he talk? What language does he speak?"

I turned to her. "I speak English."

One hand on her hip. "It is alive." She eyed me. "I thought you'd taken a vow of silence."

Steady explained. "He can talk. He has no intent to be rude. He simply chooses not to engage or initiate conversation, and avoids environments in which he might."

She looked at me, but spoke to Steady. "What's his name again?"

"Sunday."

"Sort of a sucky name." She bit her bottom lip.

"He didn't choose it."

"Still sucky."

She looked at me. "You're strange."

Another bait. I didn't bite.

She spoke slowly. As if doing so would allow her to produce the intended reaction or control the outcome. "Do you know who I am?"

Most in the civilized world knew her. "Yes."

"So, I know Steady. Steady knows me. Steady knows you. You know me. I don't know you. Who are you, besides a hermit?"

It was a good question. The answer was simple. "I am not the man I'd hoped to be."

My response was a speed bump. She rolled over it. "Which way would I go if I wanted to get myself out of here?"

I pointed through the glass toward the mangroves. "Head twelve miles that way. You'd lose a few pints of blood to the mosquitoes, but there's no need. I'll take you anywhere you want to go."

"Just like that?"

"Just like that."

She eyed me for a moment, assessing. Then she stood, walked to the galley, and grabbed both plates. She handed one to Steady then stood holding my breakfast on the other. She picked at the white, flaky fish, finally tasting it. She pushed it around her mouth, unable to hide her surprise. When the plate was empty, she set it down, and walked out on the deck with her mug. She climbed up on the foredeck and stood staring at the Ten Thousand Islands. Her arms crossed. A breeze tugged at her clothes, revealing the rope burn on her neck. Steady followed her and handed her a small tube of Neosporin. "Katie, if you'll tell me what you need, what you want, how to help, I—we—will."

She glanced over her shoulder and down at the galley where she had last seen me. "I don't like the way I treat people. I am . . . People deserve better."

She was a roller coaster. High highs, and low lows. Steady put his arm around her. "You can rest here. Take some time—"

She looked cold. Her eyes fell to the water's surface. Lost in a gaze. He lifted her chin. "Let's don't talk anymore today. Let's just take it easy. You're safe. No one knows you're here except us." She glanced at me. Steady looked at her neck. "This will heal."

She shook her head, staring out across the gulf. Tears were dripping off her face. She tried to speak and couldn't. She was waging a battle against the rising tide of her emotions and the tide was turning. She was losing. Finally, the words exited in a whisper. "If regret is an ocean, then I'm drowning."

Steady led her to my cabin, where she spent the day sleeping. He, on the other hand, walked the perimeter of the boat, his beads in his hands, eyes on the horizon. I cleaned, spooled, and oiled some reels, replaced one of the live well pumps on the Pathfinder, and watched my cabin door out of the corner of my eye for the next eruption. Late in the afternoon, we fished a little—live shrimp on an eighth-of-an-ounce jig head. Toward dark, I swam the fifty yards to the beach, gathered driftwood, and built a bonfire. Steady followed in the dinghy and, at dark, we grilled a few trout and two reds, quietly watching the boat for any sign of life.

None emerged.

Steady had something on his mind. Kept watching me out of the corner of his eye. He usually chewed on whatever he wanted to say for a long time before he spoke it. I'd learned to give him time. I fed the fire and watched the boat. With the moon high, the fire hot, and coals glowing white, Steady walked to the water's edge, filled a bucket, and carried it to the fire. Without speaking, he poured five gallons of water across my bonfire.

"What'd you do that for?"

He shook out the last few drops as darkness enveloped him and steam rose around him. His eyes were trained on the boat. "It does seem a shame to purposefully douse something so beautiful."

I nodded. "She is beautiful."

Steady tossed the bucket at me and climbed back in the dinghy. "I wasn't talking about her, dummy."

Gone Fiction has two cabins. One starboard, one port. Her royal highness was asleep in my cabin so Steady stretched out in the guest cabin, or since he was the only one to ever use it—his cabin. At midnight, I stretched my hammock across the posts of the aft deck. It's a Hennessy and I'd prefer it to most any bed but, admittedly, I'm used to sleeping alone. It also has a built-in mosquito fly, which can come in handy just before daylight.

I slept with one eye open, which meant I didn't.

Chapter Six

At two a.m., a door cracked. Then a zipper. A snap. Boards creaked. I'd been expecting this. The cabin door opened and closed slowly. I stared through the screen of my hammock. Moonlight lit upon her shoulders. She crept barefooted across the lower deck and untied her boat. Steady appeared just below me in the galley. We watched her push off into the current. He whispered, "This feels bad."

I nodded.

"You'd better go with her."

I grabbed my hat and the keys to *Jody*. In the distance, I heard the rumble of her engine. She was idling out—into the gulf. I turned the corner and watched as the blue LED lights from her instruments lit her silhouette. The water was a black sheet of glass. Not a ripple. That was good for her and bad for me—it meant I'd never catch her. I stepped into the Pathfinder, untied the bow, cut the running lights, and cranked the engine. Following her would be easy—all that power created quite a churn in the water. 'Course, it was nearly three times as fast as my boat, too. Neither one of us could throttle up, or gun it, until we reached deeper water. She needed four feet. Given my jack plate, I needed at least two and a half. More like three. She was nearly a half mile away when I heard her engine rumble, saw the bow rise up, and she started putting distance between herself and the island.

She had become a far-off speck when I pushed the stick forward. One advantage I had—and possibly the only one I had—was that her exhaust was running straight out the back. When she was on plane, I could see flames. Like following a candle across the water. Seconds later I was skimming the surface at sixty-two miles an hour. I wasn't catching her, but I wasn't losing sight of her as quickly, either. The trick would be following her while not being detected. If she cut her engine—or snuffed out the candle—and mine was still screaming behind her, she'd simply crank the engine, slam the throttle to the dash, and leave me in her dust.

I had one shot at this.

I adjusted my trim tabs and reached sixty-seven miles an hour. Too fast for my boat. A rogue wave or odd ripple and I'd flip, probably snap my neck, and Steady would have to swim home. Not to mention what would happen to the woman.

But my mind was not thinking about what might happen at that moment. It was thinking about the moments tomorrow. Next week. Next month. Playing the what-if and if-then game. Chances were good that if we, or I, convinced this girl not to end her life, that she'd stick around awhile. Where else would she go? She'd have to hide and I had a good hunch she'd not thought that through. Although, I'd bet my boat that Steady had. Which was why he said to bring her here. In fact, I'd bet he had thought that through the moment I appeared in his church after her confession.

In front of me, nearly a mile in the distance, she turned hard to port ninety degrees left—and continued her scream across the gulf. At this rate, she'd be in Cuban waters in about forty-five minutes. Maybe thirty. I cut the angle and soon came in behind her, a quarter mile back. She slowed, then turned hard to starboard and gunned it. We were now fifteen miles out into the gulf, where the depth was rolling between nine and fifteen feet. Another half mile and she turned hard again, followed by another. This erratic serpentine course continued for a mile. Then another. I couldn't figure out what she was doing until my eyes landed on the depth finder.

She was looking for deeper water. One of the reasons the gulf makes for such great fishing is the grass flats—a shelf of water that extends miles offshore that never grows deeper than about fifteen feet. The caveat to this is the occasional "hole."

I throttled back, idled, and watched her frantically searching for a watery grave. Didn't take her long to find it.

The candle disappeared.

I killed the engine and watched her disappear into her cabin only to reappear moments later. She was hunched over, moving slowly. Like she was carrying something heavy. While she fiddled with something below her, I coasted within a hundred feet, lowered the anchor, and slipped into the water—breaststroking to her stern.

I could hear her dragging something heavy across the floor of her boat. Then she lifted it onto the platform at the rear, balancing it next to the edge. I swam faster.

I reached her boat and hung silently from the stern while she stood on the ledge above me and muttered to herself. She busied her hands with something small. The heavy thing she'd brought up from the cabin was a white bucket, which now sat next to her. She had undressed again and stood naked save the rope that ran from her neck to the bucket. Obviously, she intended to finish what she'd started. Her boat was equipped with a sun pad—a padded platform directly above the engines.

Her hands were cupped in front of her, nervously moving. The mumbling continued. It sounded like she was saying the same thing over and over again. Or parts of the same thing. She stepped up on the edge of the boat, her toes dangling over the water. I listened, catching the last of a sentence. Her voice was breaking. I caught bits and pieces. ". . . mourning and weeping in this valley of tears." Then the moonlight lit the strand of beads in her hands.

The rosary.

Her prayer was growing louder. I knew that if she was hell-bent on killing herself, sooner or later she'd succeed and no power on earth, and certainly not me, would ever be able to stop her. She needed a choice, but she also needed to know what was at stake. Her legs tensed, knees bent. She sucked in a deep breath. Then let it out. All of it.

I said the only thing I could think of. "That won't stop the pain."

The sound of my voice was not what she expected. Nor was any sound. She screamed at the top of her lungs and fell backward into the boat—which was better than falling forward. She landed with a thud on the padded seats and began frantically crab-crawling backward into the cabin. Tethered to the bucket, she looked like a dog pulling against its own chain. Covered in darkness and her screaming, I pulled myself out of the water looking like the creature from the black lagoon.

I touched a button on the dash, turning on the interior lights, so she could see me through eyes that were now the size of Oreo cookies. She'd pulled her knees into her chest and sat saying nothing. I pulled out my pocket knife, opened the blade, and was about to cut the rope that led to the bucket, but then thought better of it so I left it alone.

Neither of us said a word for several minutes. Finally, I waved my hand across the bucket and asked the question that was bugging me. "Why this way? Why hanging and drowning? I mean, pick one or the other but not both."

She didn't respond.

I shook my head. "This is a horrible way to go. Nobody should go this way." I shrugged. "And why are you doing this?"

Silence. Another moment passed. Finally, she whispered, "I deserve it."

"Which part? The death part or the painful death part?"

"Both."

"Well"—I nudged the rope and eyed the bucket—"you're signed up to get both." I sat down. "Look, I don't know you, don't pretend to know what you're going through or anything about your life, but I do know this—I'm finished chasing you around and I'm getting off this boat. If you want to die, then die. Take a swan dive. Peter Pan yourself off the side of this boat and let the fish nibble on your body."

"You won't stop me?"

"No. I won't. I'm not signing up to be your protector. You want to go meet God, then go meet Him." I turned toward the bucket. "There's your ticket."

I stood but her voice followed me. "And if I don't?"

"Take that rope off your neck, put your clothes on, and stop taking yourself so seriously. It would do you some good to realize that you are not the center of everyone's universe."

She was quiet. Frozen.

I pointed at the Pathfinder. "Let me spell it out for you. Through door number one is life. That means you come back with me. Steady is pretty good at helping people douse the fires they start themselves." I touched the bucket with my toe. "Door number two is a cold, lonely, painful death that won't fix anything." I folded my arms. "Either way, it's a choice." The boat rocked gently in a slow moving wave. I leaned against the seat, deliberating my next question. Finally, I got around to it. "Can I ask you something?"

She stared at me.

"Do you really want to die or do you just not want to be you anymore?"

"What's the difference?"

"Well, you can do one without the other."

"How?"

I scratched my head. "That's door number three."

"Tell me about it."

"You really want to know?"

A nod.

"Door number three is one-way and you can only walk through it once. There's no reentry. No do-over. Ever. And you get to take nothing with you. You lose everything you've ever known. Name. Identity. Homes. Cars. Money—unless you have a bunch of cash stashed someplace. Every single tie you ever had goes up in smoke."

"What do you get out of this?"

"Nothing."

"And let me guess, you don't want anything, either."

"Nope."

She turned away. "Right. And I believe that."

"You can believe what you want, but that's the risk you take."

"What guarantees me that you won't sell my

little secret someday down the road or blackmail me with it?"

"You're assuming I'd do that."

"I know men. I've believed in and married three of them. Steady is the only man I've ever trusted who hasn't used me, taken from me, and left me with less than I started. Why should you be any different?"

"Miss Quinn, your distrust of me has nothing to do with me and everything to do with you. Think about it—I've saved your life twice and I don't even know you."

She shook her head. "That doesn't mean anything. I've been 'rescued' before. But in the end, every knight I've ever known has stormed the castle so he can name and claim his reward. So what will yours be?"

"Think what you want but know this: I don't want your money, don't want to know your secrets, and don't want to profit by whatever pain has got you in this boat and tied to that bucket. Miss Quinn, to be gut-level honest, I don't want anything to do with you."

She leaned her head back and stared up. Moonlight lit her tear-streaked face. "That'd make you different."

"Yeah, well, I've never met anybody like me, either."

She wiped her nose with her forearm, stood up, and dressed. She lifted the rope from around her neck and sat twirling it around her fingers. Moments passed. "I know one thing for certain—" She rested her foot on the rim of the bucket. "A pedestal is the loneliest place in the world." She shoved with her foot, toppling the bucket and sending it to the ocean floor without her. "And, I don't want to be me anymore."

I shrugged. "Then don't. Be somebody else."

"You really think it's that simple?"

"Never said it was simple. I said it was possible."

She crossed her arms, stared out across the water. She spoke, but I don't think she was talking to me. It was like she was finishing a conversation she'd started with herself sometime in the past. "I've been acting since I was five. I've played more roles than I can count. Somewhere along the way, the girl in the dressing room became the girl on stage. No difference. And now, I don't even know who I'm *not* being." She shook her head. "I'm tired of pretending."

I didn't respond. She turned to me. "How would you do it? I mean, door number three."

I glanced around us and chose my words carefully. "Well, I'd do it in such a way that left no doubt. That got everybody's attention and settled it once and for all."

"What would that be?"

"I'd set this thing on fire." A long minute passed as her eyes walked up and down the lines of the boat. The pieces fell in place in her mind. She crossed her arms, and was about to say something when I interrupted her. "Remember—it's a one-way ticket. No return trip."

She was quiet awhile. Finally, she turned. Arms crossed. Holding herself. "I'd like to go back now. To your boat. Please."

She followed me. The return trip took a while longer since I was traveling half as fast. Steady was waiting on us. We tied off, and stood on the back deck. I told her, "Your boat draws some attention. Sticks out. If it's okay with you, I'd like to hide it in some mangroves."

She nodded.

I made sure she understood. "It won't be easily accessible. And you'll need me to get to it, but I'll take you anytime you—"

"I understand."

Steady spoke up. "Katie—" He pulled an iPhone from inside his robe and turned it on. "You left this in your kitchen the other night. Figured you might want it at some point." He handed it to her. "If you're going to make an informed decision, then you should know that there are people in this world who desperately don't want you to leave it." She nodded as the flood of emails and texts began downloading. For the next thirty seconds it dinged, and clanged and beeped—her own private orchestra of communication. She clutched the phone to her chest, disappeared into my cabin, and shut the door behind her.

I waited on high tide and hid her boat. I pulled it up a small creek where I had to pull back the branches to make room. There was a deep alligator hole in the middle that would float her boat even in low tide. That meant the creek wouldn't be navigable but the boat would be okay. Given the bright colors, it could be seen from the sky but there was little I could do about that.

Two long days passed in which I watched her, or for her, out of my peripheral vision. Trying to look without looking.

She was thoughtful, deliberate. Whatever decision she made, it would not be rash. Most of the time she looked lost in conversation with herself. I paddled her to Pavilion Key and she spent the day walking across the few short beaches, arms crossed, barefooted, kicking at the sand. She stayed away from the gulf side and out of view of the occasional fishing boat. Her phone was never out of her hand. Her tether to the outside world. Every few seconds it would beep, she'd read whatever message had just come through, and then press it back against her chest having made no response.

Back on the island, Steady took her a blanket, and talked to her by the fire. I fixed some fish tacos but she just pushed them around her plate.

Steady took her a cup of mint tea around midnight, which he returned empty an hour later. They spent a lot of time talking. Mostly in hushed tones. Evidence that cutting free is painful.

The next morning, I woke before everyone, left a note, and took *Jody* up Chatham River to a hole where I thought the reds might be bottled up. They were, but they were all too small. No keepers. Still too early in the season. I returned around noon and found her asleep in my cabin— or at least in there with the door shut—and Steady napping in my hammock.

Late in the afternoon, I did something I never do. I turned on the radio. I'd been thinking about that note she left in her condo and whether her staff had found it.

They had.

It was all over the news. And, from what I could tell, most of the civilized world was in an uproar in a last-ditch effort to "find Katie." I told Steady about it and he nodded. He already knew. We kept it to ourselves. She had her phone. Chances were good she already knew if she'd spent any time browsing the web. If she wanted to talk, we would, but we thought it'd be best that she make up her own mind based on what she thought, not what she thought others were thinking.

I left again in the Pathfinder but didn't go too far. Duck Key. Well within radio distance. In the event that Steady needed me. I dropped the power pole, stepped out of the boat and waded, throwing a plastic up under the trees. I found myself thinking about the woman. Katie Quinn. My brief encounter with the radio had been an education. Around the red carpet, they called her "The Queen." Behind her back, "The Ice Queen." If I'd ever seen one of her movies, I don't remember but that's not unusual in that I haven't seen a movie in more than a decade. Between Steady's story, and what I'd heard on the radio, it was obvious that she was in a league all her own. A former costar on the radio had said, "She doesn't 'play' her character. She becomes her character. Makes you believe."

Most people would be impressed by all that and I guess on one level I was, but success isn't all it's cracked up to be and she was right when she talked about a pedestal being a lonely place. It is. But you can't really know that until you've stood on one.

When I cranked the boat, and dialed in the radio frequency, the anchor started his broadcast by saying, "Good evening. Tonight's one-hour special . . . Katie Quinn. 'All Hail the Queen.' " I turned it off.

The boat was dark. I skipped dinner and lay swinging in my hammock a long time.

She woke me at two. I rubbed my eyes. She handed me a cup of coffee and whispered, "Can I talk with you?"

Chapter Seven

She'd been crying. Arms folded. She didn't waste time. "I was wondering if you'd walk me through door number three." She had chosen her words carefully and the choice of "walk me through" did not escape me. Far different than "I'm walking through." The latter is an individual pursuit. The former is a shared experience. I didn't take it as a crutch. I had the feeling she could do most anything she set her mind to. It almost had the ring, or tone, of an apology.

"You sure?"

She nodded but didn't look at me.

We towed my boat out across the grass flats. A slow drive. Steady waited on the *Gone Fiction*.

Fifteen miles out, I found some shallow water, set it in neutral, and anchored the Pathfinder. A clear night. The explosion would be seen in Flamingo, Everglades City, maybe even Naples. Once lit, there'd be no going back. The shallow water meant that it'd be easier for search and rescue to find what was left of the boat.

I was readying to scuttle the boat when she tapped me on the shoulder. "Do you mind if we do one thing first?"

I shrugged. "Sure."

"This thing cost me almost half a million

dollars. I'd like to see how fast it will go before we blow it up."

"Okay."

We lit out across a sheet of black, moonlit glass. I throttled up, pushing the lever farther forward. Pressed against my seat, we ate up the ocean. I'd never been so fast in my life. We passed a hundred miles an hour in a matter of seconds and climbed from there. The boat was heavy, around twelve thousand pounds, but when I got her to a hundred and fifty, I doubted anything but the propeller was in the water. I inched it forward, feeling the knots in my stomach. We passed 160, 170, 180. With throttle yet to go, I got scared at 193 miles per hour. My palms were sweating and my heart was racing. But not Katie. Eyes closed, she was calm. Breathing normally. Hands folded in her lap. Another millimeter on the throttle and we hit 203.

I spoke, looking straight ahead. "Any faster and we'll need wings."

She nodded and then cut her hand through the air as if to say, "Enough."

I circled the ten miles back and the boat came to a rolling stop next to *Jody*. I ran my hand across the dash. "Seems a shame to sink something so—"

She opened her eyes. Pursed her lips. "It's a shell. That's all."

I got her settled in the Pathfinder, made some

adjustments to the gas line on her boat, and was about to crank the engine when I said, "You want to say anything? If Steady were here, he would."

She stared out across the water, beyond where the blackness ended. She slid her iPhone out of her pocket and threw it into her boat. It landed on the floor beneath the driver's seat. A whisper followed it. "Set it on fire."

We were about two miles away when almost three hundred gallons of gas ignited at once, sending her half-million-dollar boat in a million different directions. We saw the flash and heard the boom a second or two later. Flame spread across the water and burned orange and then blue while the gulf swallowed the back end of the boat. The hull came to rest on the shallow bottom while the bow pointed upward, nosing out of the water. Wouldn't be tough to spot. Word would spread quickly.

She spoke without looking. "How do you know so much about door number three?"

The flames rose, shining on the water. "Steady." The enormity of that struck me—how a name can say so much. The flames flickered. Soon, only the smoke would remain. And in an hour or so, it, too, would be gone. Like nothing ever happened. A watery grave.

We returned from the edge of the gulf, through

the gates of the grass flats, and started weaving among the mangroves. The white hull of the *Gone Fiction* reflected in the distance. I smelled coffee. She looked at me, tilting her head. "How long have you been out here?"

I counted backward. "A decade—give or take."

"How do you do it? How do you stay out here all alone?"

"My books."

"Why here? Why not some farm in the woods? A mountain cabin. Someplace on dry land. Any place but here."

About then, it hit me. Life as I'd known it the last decade was over. I glanced back in the direction of the smoke cloud rising above the mangroves and realized that more than just her life was going down with it. Without really thinking it through, I'd just signed up to help her figure out how to disappear. How to drop off the face of planet Earth. And when you're her, you can't just do that overnight. It takes time. And it takes help. And unless I was cruel, hard-hearted, and downright mean, I was that help.

My very private, very self-centered, very just-the-way-I-like-it life was about to get adjusted. Truth was, I knew what she needed. And, while Steady did, too, he needed me to pull it off.

I pulled the stick into neutral, turned, and watched our wake settle behind us. The churn and bubbles spread in a V through the outstretched arms of the mangroves. The water settled. Rolling glass. A mirrored picture of the heavens. I waved my hand across our path and shook my head. "Miss Quinn . . . no matter how wide or deep you cut it . . . it has no memory. No . . . scar." I pointed toward the bow. "Out here, it's all future, no past."

She nodded and turned. Placing her back between her and what lay behind us.

"I'd like it if you called me 'Katie.' "

"Katie is back there in the water."

She looked up at me. "So is Miss Quinn."

We heard a helicopter off to the southwest, flying fast. "I suppose you could change your mind and make up some story but . . . starting about now, the world is beginning to believe that Katie Quinn just died."

She reached slowly for my hand. She uncurled my fingers, spreading my palm. She traced the edges, her fingers confirming what her eyes told her. "I'm sorry about your hands . . . I'm very sorry."

We rode the last half mile in silence. I set the stick in neutral, gliding. Then cut the engine. She stood, her face two feet from mine. I felt like she needed comfort, or maybe I felt like I wanted to comfort her. I'm not sure. Whatever it was, one half of me wanted to offer it while the other doubted I was the one to give it or that she would find it comforting. I whispered, "You made one assumption tonight that may or may not be correct."

"Which is?"

Steady stood above us on the upper deck, looking down. His face calm. Rosary beads draped between the thumb and index finger of his right hand. Robes flowing. Pipe glowing. Smoke trailing from the corner of his mouth. White hair flittering in the breeze. Her face was close. Sweat on her temples. Emerald green eyes. Big and round and telling. I swallowed. "That your secret is more valuable to me . . . than mine."

⌣ **Chapter Eight**

We didn't say much that night. She didn't ask and we didn't offer. The circles beneath her eyes were deep and dark. She looked drained. Depleted. Bone weary. Having made her decision, she walked into my cabin, shut the door, and fell into bed.

She stayed there five days.

Every few hours I walked alongside the deck and glanced through the cabin window, where I found her curled up in bed, knees tucked up in her chest, arms wrapped around herself, seldom moving, pillow wet with drool. I think she'd been running on auxiliary, borrowing from reserves, for a long time. Like maybe longer than anybody suspected. When she did wake, she didn't eat, didn't talk. She quietly got up, went to the bathroom, sipped some water, and fell back in bed.

Steady called in and told them he was taking a few days off. They understood. They knew he was her priest and that her death would hit him hard. After he told them that he had been to Sky Seven the night before and that he was, more than likely, the last person to see her alive, they said, "Take all the time you need."

They found the boat that first night. Search teams scoured the water. Pictures of divers holding jagged pieces of boat covered the front pages of the *Miami Herald*. One diver held her burned and mangled iPhone. The fallout was immediate and total. Her death consumed every channel, every outlet, every network, for a week. The second night, I made my way into Chokoloskee, pulled my baseball cap down over my eyes, and drank a beer at the historic Rod and Gun Club bar.

The bar was full of media and mourning fans. On the TV, all the Hollywood A-listers were making the late-night rounds talking about the tragedy. About their friend Katie. One report told how her flame-scarred iPhone had sold for six figures in an auction on eBay.

I finished my beer, got in my boat, and slipped back out into the trees. Out in the gulf, a makeshift shrine developed. Somebody put a huge cross constructed out of white PVC pipe next to the hull of her boat. Covered it in a wreath. Others tied or taped notes to it. Some tossed bricks wrapped with plastic bags holding tearful letters. Others dropped messages in bottles that floated wherever the current took them. A continual procession of boats I'd never seen made their way from Chokoloskee to "the graveside." Some came from as far away as Miami. Within days, more crosses appeared. Some wooden, some metal, most were made from PVC or plastic tubing because it would last longer and weather the storms. Four nights after her "death," more than seventy-five boats had anchored in what was being called a "water memorial." A solemn affair. People talking in hushed tones. The smell of pot, stale beer, rum, and coconut oil. Some forty crosses now rose up in ordered rows out of the water. The networks had hired several barges, anchored close to the burned-out hull, showered it in a twenty-four-hour spotlight and transmitted around the clock as the ceremony continued and the number of boats grew—as if she might, at any moment, rise from the water.

But Katie Quinn was no phoenix.

One guy in a hundred-and-ten-foot yacht positioned two huge flat-screen televisions—maybe seventy inches—on the deck, wired them through speakers equally as large, and played her movies around the clock. The parties lasted all night. I drove the perimeter, outside of the light, amazed at the number of boats and people and their devotion to someone they did not know and had never met. I cut my running lights and returned under the cover of darkness. I knew it wouldn't be long before someone with a camera and microphone stumbled upon us and started asking questions. "Did you see the explosion?"

That night, Steady and I moved both the *Gone Fiction* and *Jody* deeper into the islands where only the ghost of Osceola could find us. Which was good because the water was crawling with boats. Katie Quinn had been a spectacle in life and her fans were making sure her death was one as well. On the sixth morning, tucked well back in the trees, she woke. It was daylight. Steady and I were sipping coffee, twiddling our thumbs. She shuffled in; her eyes were slits. She sat at the table, pulled her sweatshirt sleeves over her hands and held them under her chin. The circles beneath her eyes were still there, just not as dark, and maybe not as deep.

Steady poured her a cup of coffee and the three of us sat in silence. After a few minutes, she nodded out the back of the galley. "The view's changed."

Steady nodded. "A lot of people are looking for you."

She sipped. "What day is it?"

He spoke softly. "Saturday."

She sipped again. Calculating the days. "Which one?"

He smiled. "You've been asleep for the better part of six days." Steady held her hand in both of his. "Katie, I need to head back for a few days." He glanced at me. "Leave you here with Sunday." He smiled. "If you're good, maybe you can convince him to take you to his cabin in the Glades."

I spoke the only Spanish I knew. "*Mi casa es su casa.*"

He smiled. "I'll be gone a few days. So long as you stick with him, no one will find you here. If you need anything, all you have to do is ask."

She nodded. "Steady?"

"Yes."

Her fingers mindlessly turned her mug. "How can you declare me 'ashes to ashes'? I mean . . . that's where you're going. To my funeral. Right?"

He nodded, stared out across the water. "It is an ethical and moral dilemma but"—he glanced at me—"one I'm not unfamiliar with."

She shook her head. "I can't ask you to do that."

He laughed. "Too late."

"But . . ." Her voice cracked. "How can you do that when you know you're lying?"

He sat back, crossed his legs. "I once heard the confession of a German who hid Jews in his basement for two years during Hitler. Said the

SS routinely knocked and searched his house. He denied it every time. The family in the basement lived. Their children's children bear his name." He looked at me. "I think God looks at this the way He looked at that."

She said, "How's that?"

Steady patted the sweat on his forehead with his sleeve. "With a smile on His face."

There really wasn't much response when Steady started telling stories. We were silent a minute. I asked, "Why was he confessing that to you?"

"He wasn't."

"What then?"

"Towards the end of the war, he'd shot an SS officer in the face and wanted to know if I thought it was murder."

"What'd you tell him?"

Steady stood. His complexion changing. His cross dangling from his neck. "I told him it was not."

Chapter Nine

I drove Steady to Chokoloskee, where one of his priests picked him up. He had asked Katie for a list of things she needed, which she'd scribbled on a yellow sticky note. I made the rounds, picking up everything from toothpaste to feminine products to women's deodorant.

The story was everywhere and on everyone's lips. The general tone was remorse. Or loss. As in, "What a shame. What a waste." And most folks were left shaking their heads. Given its proximity to the explosion site, the networks had filled every parking lot with antennae-topped trucks and out-of-place reporters all saying the same thing: "Katie is gone. And nobody really knows why. Long live the Queen." Their attempts to make sense of it were getting nowhere. Probably good she wasn't there to hear it.

My last stop on the way out of town was Delilah's—a thrift store with shelves of second-hand and vintage castoffs. I guessed Katie's size as a four but bought everything from a two to a six. I bought a few bathing suits, couple pairs of jeans, several T-shirts, a sweater, more sweat-shirts, a windbreaker with a hood, some cut-off shorts, flip-flops, a wide-brimmed purplish hat fit for a lady, some big bug-eyed sunglasses that would hide half her face, a new pack of women's Jockey underwear, and three bandannas: blue, lime green, and red.

I stepped into *Jody*—Costas on my face—cranked the engine, and let her sit idling while I stowed my purchases. A voice sounded over my shoulder. "I'll give you five thousand dollars to rent you and that boat for three days."

I turned. A tall, skinny man, with dyed black hair in a ponytail, a voice recorder, and a point-

and-shoot hung around his neck stood at the water's edge. His eyes were piercing aqua blue; fingernails painted black, he looked to be wearing black eyeliner, and dragon-footed tattoos climbed up his neck and behind each ear. My first thought was Queequeg from *Moby-Dick*. A second portly man wearing a dumpy hat and carrying a large and expensive-looking video camera stood behind him. He reminded me of Smee in *Peter Pan*. Queequeg was my height, a little over six feet. Smee was shorter, stockier, had meatier hands. Both looked to be following the story and assured of their own importance.

I shook my head. "I'm not from around here. Wouldn't be much help to you."

The tall man shook his head and stepped down into my boat. The cameraman followed. "I doubt it. I'm a pretty good judge of people and based upon your weathered skin, the tan on your face from the sunglasses, the way you handled this boat coming in here, and the proficiency with which you navigated the stores around town while the rest of us are tripping over ourselves, not to mention the well-used look of this meticulously manicured boat, and the darkened cork handles on your fishing rods, I'd say you know these waters about as well as anyone." He held up a wad of cash. "Seven thousand."

It was about here that I started wondering if he'd witnessed my purchases at Delilah's.

"Thanks, but"—I patted the console and deflected it—"she's not for hire." I kept my eye on his cameraman because the moment he clicked that thing on and started pointing it in my face, he and his camera were going in the water.

He smiled. "What about you? Everything can be bought." I hadn't been around this guy more than fifteen seconds but I already wanted to take a shower. I untied the bowline and was returning to the console when he stepped between me and the wheel close enough for me to determine that the black lines beneath his eyes were in fact tattoos. Permanent guyliner. His voice was smug, giving insight into his elevated opinion of himself. "I'm Katie Quinn's authorized biographer. And the only one to"—he raised both eyebrows—"authorize her, if you know what I mean." He glanced away, then back at me while the success of his prowess resonated across the water. "I'm also the author of the current number ten on the *New York Times* best-seller list. Based on the feeding frenzy"—he tossed his head back—"I should be topping the list by tonight." He pointed toward the gulf and tried to sound casual. He thought I'd be impressed. I wasn't. He continued, "Based on recent events, we're releasing a new edition with a few new chapters. *The* authoritative work." He pointed at Smee. "CNN is producing a documentary on my research. Airs late next week and several more times this month."

I revved the engine. "Well, good luck on your work."

He put one hand on my shoulder while snapping behind him with his other. "Do I know you?"

I looked at his hand. "Doubtful."

"I rarely forget a face." Smee shouldered his camera, pointed it at my face. The red light on the front told me he was recording. I didn't hesitate. I bumped it into reverse and slammed the throttle down. Evidently, neither were boat people. The jolt threw Smee and his camera in the water. Queequeg landed on his butt in the bow. I knelt over him, my face inches from his. "You want to walk off this boat, or exit like your wet friend there?"

He stood, eye to eye with me, and said nothing. He was slick. Undeterred.

Frothing at the water's surface, Smee treaded water while cussing me and my entire lineage because his forty-something-thousand-dollar HD video camera was sitting in fourteen feet of water amid a bed of oysters. I'm pretty sure salt water isn't too good for digital recordings.

Queequeg stepped off. His wad of cash lay on the bow wrapped in a rubber band. I fingered it, then tossed it at him. He caught it and his eyebrows creeped together. A small crowd had gathered at the dock. Time to disappear. I pulled my hat down, turned *Jody* into the wind, and took the long way home.

What should have taken an hour took me almost four, which was more than enough time to convince me that with all the increased shark activity my boat was the last place Katie Quinn needed to be. She might as well be sitting on a bench in Central Park.

The sun was setting when I hopped up on the back of the *Gone Fiction* and found her sitting on the bow, back to me, knees tucked into her chest, staring out across the mangrove tops. I knelt and she sniffled, then wiped her face with her sleeve. She shook her head. "You'd think I'd be empty by now."

I didn't respond.

She looked up at me. "Do you think I'm wrong for doing this? For putting Steady in the position he's now in?"

I shrugged. "I'd say you are in uncharted waters. I'm not sure anyone like you has ever done what you're doing. If they have, they did it really well 'cause we don't know about it. This one's not black or white, but maybe several shades of gray." She tried to smile. "If it's okay with you, let's just deal with right now, right now. I think it best if we left here for a few days. I have a cabin . . ." I pointed northeast. "Up in the Glades. It'll be quiet. Steady knows where it is. He'll find us when he's finished"—I smiled and shook my head—"telling everyone how dead you are." I stood.

She stopped me. Suspicious. "Something happen in town?"

I thought about lying but decided I'd sidestep it. "The town and every square inch of water between here and there is crawling with people looking for any scrap of you. They're pretty pushy, too."

She tilted her head, her voice changing tone. "You didn't answer my question."

She was smarter than I gave her credit. "I bumped into a black-haired, ponytailed guy with tattoos running up his neck who said he was your—"

She stood and made quotation marks with her fingers. " 'Biographer.' " She shook her head. "He couldn't write his way out of a wet paper bag."

"He seemed to think a lot of himself."

"His name is Richard Thomas. Goes by 'Dicky.' Should be 'Tricky Dick.' "

"What's up with all the black?"

"It's the color of his heart pouring out his skin." She crossed her arms and began climbing below. She spoke over her shoulder. "Your place in the Glades, is it safe?"

I smiled. "Depends on how you define 'safe.' If you mean safe from snakes and alligators. The answer is no. If you mean safe from people, then yes. It's like going to Mars. Listen . . ." I glanced in the direction of Chokoloskee, trying to lighten the tension. "I just bought deodorant for myself for the first time in eight years. My social graces are not really up to date. If I offend you, well, it's not intentional. I've been alone a long time."

She stood on the aft deck, looking up at me. The breeze was warm but she looked cold. "You said you value your secret more than mine." She waited. It was a question. Not a statement. I didn't answer. She tried again. "Did you . . . murder somebody? I mean, is that why you're out here?"

I considered how to answer. I did so indirectly. "Have you ever murdered anyone?"

"Just myself."

I smiled. "Well then, you're in good company."

She stopped me. "Do you always answer questions with other questions?"

I answered without looking. "Only when I know that the answer will hurt me." I handed her the two plastic grocery store bags. "The things you asked for. Along with some clothes. I guessed at your size."

She half smiled. "Thank you."

A helicopter buzzed the treetops en route to the site of the explosion. "We'd better get moving."

Chapter Ten

We closed up *Gone Fiction*, left her anchored in a dense section of mangroves, and I cranked *Jody*. Katie stepped down holding a plastic grocery bag stuffed with her clothes. She shook her head. "It's been a long time since everything I owned could fit in one bag." She stowed it. "I once paid over five thousand dollars for a piece of luggage to hold my shoes, but I'm not sure it was as useful as that bag."

When I turned away from the gulf, she set her hand on my arm. The first time she'd touched me in some way other than anger. "Would you mind driving me by the—or *my* memorial?"

I would not say that I had grown comfortable with Katie Quinn. Nor her with me. Our movement around each other was more like oil and water—sharing a necessary border but not necessarily mixing. "Sure."

In driving her back to her watery grave, the idea occurred to me that dogs often return to their vomit, but I didn't share that with her. From a distance, we circled the growing circus. A small charter boat carrying a captain and one passenger floated near the site of the explosion. Death tours. Somebody was already making money off this. Katie stared at the singular frame in the back of the charter boat. She squinted, then shook her head once. "Silvia. My housekeeper." The woman knelt in the back of the boat, prayed, threw something in the water, then stood and motioned the charter pilot to return her to port. Katie shook her head. Her bottom lip trembled slightly. "No one will ever work for me again."

Despite her attempts to suppress them, Katie's emotions bubbled near the surface and her stoic ability to control them was fading. Cracks in the dam. Words dangled on the tip of her tongue.

I studied the boats—the muted party. It struck me as strange. So off-key. All these fans—the "show" of mourning—and yet the only two broken hearts belonged to Silvia and Katie. Most everyone else seemed saddened at the loss of a silver-screen someone they did not know and had never met but who had given them what they wanted. Who had filled their need. These rum-drunk, coconut-oiled people were saddened at what she had given them and what they could no longer get—not at Katie's tragic end.

Katie caught it in the look on my face. "Something bothering you?"

I waved my hand across the charade. "This might have more to do with their loss—than yours."

She nodded, then whispered in measured sarcasm, "You ever looked up the definition of the word 'idol'?"

I shook my head.

She turned her back to the circus. "I did."

We circled wide of the other boats and disappeared into the mangroves. Katie looked cold and yet it wasn't. I was learning that her minute facial expressions often said what her mouth did not. Right now, it was asking where we were going. I supposed that trait came with always being in control. I unrolled a map. "Here. I call it 'the Hammock.' It's a cabin . . . of sorts."

"You mean you have an actual house with walls and a floor?"

A shrug. "Depends on how you define 'house.' "

A slightly raised eyebrow mixed with an even slighter tilt of the head.

"Several years ago, I was fishing on a full moon. Snook everywhere. Heard a plane sputtering above me. Saw it go down. Trailing flames. The next morning, I found it several miles away on an island deep in the Glades. Both wings broken off. Nose stuck in the ground. No pilot. Just a lot of white powder in clear plastic bags. I didn't care much about the plane or the drugs but the island was another matter. Just two or three acres in size, it was nothing but a huge piece of limestone sticking up through the muck of the wiregrass. Surrounded by trees, hidden both from the sides and the air. I found several old Indian mounds, old pottery shards, a few broken arrowheads. I found a clear spring bubbling up in a little pool and some high ground. So, I began hauling in wood and other things as they drifted up onshore around the *Gone Fiction* or as I bought them in town. Over the years, it's become my winter getaway."

"Why winter?"

" 'Cause," I laughed, "I have a limited supply of blood."

"What do you mean?"

"Mosquitoes."

A few hours later, the water grew shallow. I raised the jack plate, lifting the engine completely out of the water, stepped out, grabbed the bow-line, picked my way through the tree branches, and pulled *Jody* up a small creek that only flowed during high tide. I walked maybe an eighth of a mile as the limbs closed behind us.

She said, "So, is there a story to how you found this?"

"I stumbled upon it while looking for a place to stash the airboat."

"You have another boat?"

I pointed at the airboat sitting to her right.

My airboat is ten feet long and six and a half feet wide powered by a two-hundred-and-forty-horsepower Lycoming four-cylinder airplane engine with a seventy-inch propeller. I call it *Evinrude* after that character in the Disney movie *The Rescuers*. It'll do sixty miles per hour but it gets pretty squirrelly after that, as you lose the ability to steer at high speed. Maybe life is the same way. An airboat is little more than a fancy johnboat with a four-foot lip angling up off the front that hovers over the grass. The bottom, or hull, is covered in a half-inch sheet of stainless steel, which is tough, glides over most anything —including asphalt—and comes in handy in the dry season.

I stowed *Jody*, and sparked *Evinrude* to life. Minutes later, we emerged out of the trees and began skimming across the tips of the grass at forty and fifty miles an hour. Airboats don't turn as much as they slide. Or glide. She sat in front of me. Her hands were white-knuckled around the base of her seat. I slowed, tapped her fingers, and mouthed the words, "Let go." She did, although uncomfortably. As the miles passed and her comfort grew, her arms relaxed. Eventually, she sat up straight, and let the wind pull at her hair. For a second, she closed her eyes. Deep in the mangroves, she spoke over her shoulder. I slowed, cut the engine. Her eyes were wide. "The roots—they tangle with each other. It's as if they make their own floor. Each holding each." She looked around. "They need each other."

From the Ten Thousand Islands we moved into the wiregrass of the Glades. At the sight of the first alligator she pulled her feet up beneath her, tucking her heels beneath her bottom, but after the hundredth, she let them back down. Seeing her enjoy the ride, I took the long way. Winding in and out, around. I sat behind her, watching layers disappear, peeled off by the wind. I would not describe her as happy, but it was the furthest I'd seen her from unhappy since we'd met.

Toward sunset, I slowed. Cut the engine. A crimson sun setting on the treetops. Seagulls filling the air and the background with noise. A few sandhill cranes perched in treetops. A single osprey floating high in the distance. I whispered, "Steady says riding in this boat is like walking on water."

The sun dropped. She nodded, whispered to herself, "He would know."

We reached the Hammock late in the afternoon. I tied off the airboat and she stepped onto the dock. Her eyes followed the walkway. Cabin. Screened porch. Wood-burning stove. Half a plane. Red hand pump indicating a freshwater well. Her eyes scanned the trees around her. "Where'd all the fruit trees come from?"

Around us stood a dozen or more orange, grapefruit, tangerine, and kumquat trees. I shrugged. "Indians, I think."

She peeled a tangerine. Juice dripped off her chin. "Sweet."

I grabbed a bar of soap and an unused razor. "Come on." I led her through the woods. She followed closely yet didn't cling.

Beneath a sprawling live oak, she tapped my shoulder and pointed at a single orchid hanging at eye level. Her own private discovery. I asked, "You like?"

She nodded.

I pointed up.

Scattered high up in the tree were fifty or sixty orchids.

She inhaled, smiling. Eyes wide. "I've never seen anything like it."

"I planted them."

It was one of the first things I'd said that got her attention. "Really?"

"They like this environment, so whenever I'm in Miami, I stop at one of those roadside vendors, buy a couple and then plant them up there. Most of them make it. Some don't but I think that has more to do with the vendor."

"You're pulling my leg."

"No. If you climb up there, you'll see the tags are still tied around the base to remind me what kind they are."

Moments later, we were twenty feet up in the tree reading the tags. One lay flat across her hand. "You weren't kidding."

I shrugged.

"You get more interesting the more time I spend with you."

I pushed away a branch, peeling back the canopy. "This is one of my favorite views." We could see for thirty or forty miles. All the way to the gulf.

She didn't say a word. Which said a lot. I pointed across her field of view. "Your boat blew up out that way."

She half smiled. "You mean you blew it up out that way."

"Yes, I did that."

After a few moments, she whispered, "How far from here to the nearest road?"

"Dirt or asphalt?"

"Whatever."

I pointed. "There's a dirt road about twenty miles that way."

"Talk about being in the middle of nowhere."

"I suppose we show up on some military satellite but they'd have to be looking." I smiled. She smirked and appreciated the image. "And if you want to find a dead person, you look in a cemetery."

We climbed down and I led her to the spring, where I stepped into the God-carved limestone bathtub big enough for ten people. A few leaves floated on top of the water. It was clear, about four feet deep, and a shelf rose on one side serving as a seat. She stepped in and we soaked in the lukewarm water for over an hour as I told her about the island, how I'd built the cabin and how I dumped all the cocaine in the water.

She tried not to smile. "Tell the truth—you

didn't sample just a little for yourself? Maybe stash some for a rainy day? It was probably the best of the best, straight from Colombia."

"No. Never did."

She waved her hand through the water. "Ever done any drugs?"

"No, although I still enjoy a good gin and tonic."

"Hmmm . . ." She smiled knowingly. "Liquid courage."

Once my fingers and toes were pruney, I stood, left the soap and razor and pointed toward the cabin. "I'm going to fix some dinner. Take your time. Nobody's watching." I turned, then turned back, waving my hand across the backdrop of trees. "Biologists estimate there are over a hundred and fifty thousand Burmese pythons in the Glades, slithering this way and that. Most are the offspring of escapees from aquariums after hurricanes flooded the pet shops. Some were released when they grew too big for the family aquarium. Just, FYI."

"What do I do if I see one?"

"Run real fast."

When I left, she had backed away from the edge and was slowly scanning the rim of the spring.

She returned a while later, smelling of Irish Spring, her legs shiny. Proud that she didn't get eaten by a snake. She set the soap down on the side of the sink, then nudged it closer. Watching me out of the corner of her eye.

I looked up from the pasta sauce I was turning. "That bad, huh?"

She nodded. " 'Ripe' would be a better word."

"Sorry."

After dinner, I returned from bathing and found her standing alongside the twin bed she was to sleep in, rubbing the sheet along the side of her face. I poked my head in. "Everything okay?"

She held the sheet in both hands and nodded.

Her face did not convince me. "You sure?"

She said nothing.

"I have other sheets if you like." I started digging through the closet. Some were mildewed. A few had been nibbled on by moths. Mice droppings covered those on top. "Maybe a different color."

"No, really, these are fine."

"Then why are you looking at them like they have cooties?"

She almost smiled. "When I traveled, on location, shooting a movie . . . my contract stipulated that I would not sleep in a bed with less than seven-hundred-count Egyptian cotton. That the mattress was a king-size Tempur-Pedic Rhapsody complete with seven pillows, each of a certain make and size, and that my room temperature would be held constant at sixty-eight degrees. Not sixty-seven. Not sixty-nine. Bottled water from Italy. Champagne from France. Bagels from New York. Salmon flown in fresh. Lobster.

Caviar." She shook her head. "Do you know how heavy that mattress is? I once had it flown into the deserts of North Africa and then the top of the Alps just so I could get some sleep."

"Did you?"

A quick shake. "No."

"I realize this is getting toward personal, but how much did you make for your last movie?"

"Twenty-five million."

I'm no expert on actors but somewhere I read that screen actors must relearn how to make facial movements because the camera picks up every little thing. The good ones learn how to say volumes with barely a twitch. In contrast, stage actors must make dramatic movements—almost overacting—so as to be seen by folks in the cheap seats. Katie gave away only what she wanted. Every movement, every breath, every thought, was thought out before it was acted upon or carried out. Acting was in her DNA. She'd have made a good poker player. "Lot of money."

"It's out of order."

"How so?"

"I have a—" She tilted her head to one side. "I *had* a townhouse in New York. Upper West Side. Central Park out the window. I used to stand on the back balcony and watch the street below. Waiting on the guys picking up the trash. They could empty every can on the street in less than eight minutes. Lot of trash, too. I used to wonder

131

what would happen if they didn't come around. Then one day, they didn't. Went on strike. Piles spilled out into the street. Flies. Maggots. The smell. I, or rather somebody that worked for me, checked into what they made. Their salary." She paused. "Thirty-six thousand. Thirty-six thousand lousy dollars a year to pick up filth unknown." She stared out her cabin window. "I made that in less than one minute on my last film. Just for standing there and looking pretty. But if he doesn't pick up the trash, stuff stacks up. Stinks. Disease. Not a pretty picture. If I don't come to your movie theater, what's lost? Nothing. Seems out of whack. Out of order."

I didn't say anything.

"I watched that street for almost a year. Same guy. Every Tuesday. Clockwork. He liked to sing while he worked. No teeth but great voice. I walked out one morning. Sunglasses. Scarf. So he wouldn't know me. Handed him an envelope with forty thousand cash." She teared up. Looked away. "When I got back to the balcony he was dancing in the street, singing at the top of his lungs." She shook her head. "Twenty million didn't make me as happy as forty thousand did that man."

I shrugged, pointed. "Those sheets you're holding, started at about fifty-count polyester but with seven or eight years of wear and tear, they're probably down to twenty-five threads per inch.

Which is a bonus when it gets warm 'cause you get better ventilation."

She made her bed and said little else.

An hour or so later, I was reading on the porch when she appeared around the corner. She asked, "Do you have any scissors? Like, for cutting hair." I reached in a drawer and offered them to her. "Thank you." Two hours later she reappeared.

With short hair.

As in not a hair on her head was longer than a few inches. It looked perfect. The only problem with it was that it highlighted the burn around her neck.

"You did that?"

She leaned against the door frame. "When I was first starting out, I knew exactly how I wanted my hair to look—"

"How?"

"*The Sound of Music* meets *Breakfast at Tiffany's*." A pause. "So . . . I worked at it. Once I figured out how to use two mirrors, it got easier."

I hadn't had a formal haircut since I started living on the water. When it needs cutting, as in grown down past my shoulders, I simply cut the end. All of it. At once. And I shave every few weeks, whether I need it or not.

I looked at myself in the mirror. Sun-bleached hair past my shoulders. Split ends. Several days' stubble. Unrecognizable. Perfect.

She swept up her hair and walked out, carrying

it in a makeshift dustpan made from a piece of paper. She held it aloft. Chest high. "A busboy in Germany once stole my underwear and sold them online for nine thousand dollars. If you bagged this up you could sell it on eBay. Probably buy another boat."

"Thanks. Three is plenty."

She turned, spoke over her shoulder. "In my experience, men with hair long enough to be in a ponytail aren't all that trustworthy."

I nodded. "Good policy."

Chapter Eleven

Around midnight, she blew out her gas lamp and shut her door. Saying not a word. I sat up, a notebook on my lap, listening to the alligators bellow us to sleep.

The next morning, she woke to find me sitting where she'd left me. She saw my mug. I pointed. "It's on the stove. A little old, but old and strong is better than none at all."

She rubbed her eyes and lifted a mug hanging on a nail. She milled around me as the caffeine hit her veins. Always a safe distance. Moments passed. I noticed she was standing on her toes. More fidgety than usual. After a few sips, she set down her mug. "Okay, I don't think I can hold it any longer." She proffered with one hand.

"Oh, sorry. Follow me."

I walked out back, fifty yards through the trees to the outhouse. I opened the door and showed her the roll of toilet paper hanging on a nail. She eyed it, weighed going versus holding it indefinitely, then slowly stepped inside and shut the door.

I got about ten steps away when the door cracked and she said, "Sunday?"

It was the first time she'd called me by that name. "Yes?"

She stepped outside, spoke through terse lips, and pointed. "A roach."

I nodded. "Yes." I opened the door. Wider. Showering the walls in light. Fifteen roaches crawled up the back wall. A few scurried along the wooden floor. One poked its head up over the toilet seat. She gritted her teeth. "Is there any other option?"

"Sure. Anywhere on the island, but if you want a seat . . ." I pointed.

She eyed the white seat, glanced at the crawling wall and the two tentacles fluttering like windshield wipers along the rim, pulled the paper roll from the nail, and disappeared down the trail toward the back of the island.

When she returned, she sat at the far end of the porch, finished her coffee then returned from her bunk with my shears in one hand and a towel over her shoulder. She stood behind her chair, turning the chair slightly toward me. She cleared her throat. I set down my pen. She said, "It's not often that I offer to do anything for anyone else. I'm used to being served. Not serving. It's not in my nature." She patted the chair.

I shook my head. "I'm good. Really."

She shaded her eyes against a growing sun. "You open for another opinion?"

I tapped the pen on my journal. "Thanks, but—"

She set down the shears. "What are you doing when you write in that book?"

"Record the tides. What we caught. Water temp. What's biting. Bait choice. Wind direction. Barometric pressure. I look back on it year to year."

"But we didn't fish yesterday."

"I record that, too."

"Can I see?"

I offered the journal. "You don't trust me?"

She glanced at the first page. "Your hand-writing is the fanciest and neatest I've ever seen in a man and better than most women I know. Like John Adams or Thomas Jefferson."

"I've practiced some."

"I'll say." She returned the journal without reading it. I was learning that she liked to lob atomic-bomb questions to catch me off guard. To judge my immediate reaction. Her next question was one of those. "Can I trust you?"

"You can trust that what I tell you is truthful."

"What about what you don't tell me?"

"You picked up on that distinction, huh?"

She turned, crossed her arms, and spoke, looking away. "When I was first getting started, I signed a few contracts without really reading the fine print. I was just happy to get in front of the camera and, as it turns out, so were the producers, just with less clothes than when I walked in." She shrugged. "Now, or rather up until a few days ago, I'd learned to say, 'define minor nudity.' Doing so kept me out of more than one tight spot. I know how that must sound. You've probably seen my movies and you're thinking, 'But I've seen you take your clothes off and walk across the screen in your birthday suit—' "

I held up a stop-sign hand. "I haven't been to a movie in over ten years and I can't say for sure if I've ever seen one of yours."

A pause while it sank in. "Really?"

"It's nothing personal. I don't own a TV, so—"

She pursed her lips, her bottom sticking out farther than her top. One eyebrow rose above the other. Her mind calculating. "So, back to the trust thing—"

"It's your call."

"So, I shouldn't trust you past the point where we are now?"

"At what 'point' are we?"

"No longer uncomfortable."

I scratched my beard. "Probably a good call."

She shook her head. "So, what you're saying is that you're not good and I can't believe in you." Her head tilted ever so slightly sideways. She was baiting me. "Is that really what you want me to think?"

"In my experience, trust is built over time and we haven't had much of that. So, let's—"

She shook her head once. "I once spent two years of my life living with a man who I thought would be the father of my children only to discover one night when I flew home early from a set that he was trying to be the father of my manager's children." The other eyebrow climbed to meet the first. She pointed at my journal. "You ask me if I trust you? You're writing in a journal, quietly, while I walk and talk around you. Several months ago, the firm that handled my publicity, in their infinite wisdom, hired this"— she made quotation marks in the air with her fingers—"'writer.' So, I could tell him my story and he could write it and the world could love me more and we could charge more and so they could make more money. Anyway, they told me they'd done their due diligence, that he'd written lots of stories and that I could trust him. He was handsome. They were in a rush to get it published, and he was willing to start right away. Said not to worry about the writer's contract, that lawyers took forever and he trusted me that it would all work out fine. Said I could trust him. Gave me his"—more quotation marks—" 'word.' So, I did. Some of my secrets." She shrugged. "Not all. Hardly any, to be honest. Anyway"—she made quotation marks in the air again—"my 'biographer'—"

I cut her off. "You're talking about the guy I met in town with the tattoos climbing up his neck and the black fingernails?"

A short nod. "Tricky Dick."

"You liked that guy?"

No response. She continued. "He spent weeks interviewing me, showing me drafts. He asked a lot of questions. Asked about my childhood, which I've always been notoriously private about. I didn't talk about that, at least. But thanks to the paparazzi, there was still plenty of material for him to work with. My management team felt this would be my chance to set the record straight.

"I told him how I'd been in a downward slide, had managed to hide it for years. But then my weight started to drop. The papers spread questions that led to rumors. A doctor prescribed something to take the edge off. Combat the circles beneath my eyes.

"A pill here. A little sleep there. Another doctor's order almost anywhere. I cycled much like regular folks and then the pain would pile up, I'd give in, pop the top off the bottle. Pretty soon I was eating them like Skittles. Sold-out shows were canceled.

"I checked myself into this treatment center for the burned out and soon to be burned up. My people kept it a secret. A hundred and sixty thousand later I was back on the stage, clean, and judging by my outward appearance, stronger than ever. Somewhere, some group gave me another award. Another spotlight. Another movie. Another number one. And then there was this biography that was supposed to tell how I'd gotten through it all.

"Anyway, my"—she held both hands in the air for more quotation marks—" 'biographer' fills up this recorder and goes off to write it. Next thing I know, instead of sending me the draft to review, he's selling my precious story to the highest bidder. Because he never signed a contract, there was little we could do to stop him. Where I hadn't answered his questions, he filled in the blanks on his own, altering the context and many of the facts. By the time he was through, I looked like a very different person than when I look in the mirror. And he didn't even know the worst parts." Her finger unconsciously traced the scar on her wrist and then her hand traced the outline of the angered collar on her neck. She made eye contact with me. "In my experience, 'time' doesn't prove one trustworthy and has very little to do with trust."

"Then, if I were you, I wouldn't trust me."

"But I want to."

"Then do."

"But you just said, 'don't.' "

"Okay, don't."

A long pause. "Don't you want people to trust you?"

"Did you learn to do that in acting?"

"What?"

"Pause like that. It was 'pregnant.' "

"The camera does strange things to time. My timing is hardwired."

I shook my head. "No. That's why I live out here and why you and Steady are the only two people who know I exist."

"Do you have family?"

"None that I know of."

"Well, what do you know?"

"I know how to fish."

She didn't hesitate. "Will you teach me?"

"You want to learn?"

"I want to learn to do a lot of things I've never done."

"You've never been fishing?"

She shook her head.

"Really. As in, never?"

"Not once."

I tried to process this and spoke out loud. "That's like saying, 'I've never taken a breath before.' "

"So—" She slid her hand inside mine.

"I tend to spend a lot of long hours on the boat. Often daylight to dark, and the only bathroom is the one off the back. As in, out in the open. Sound travels. Not much privacy."

"I don't mind."

"Is this important to you?"

"Yes."

"Okay."

She held on to my hand for a bit longer. "Before we go, tell me one thing about yourself."

"Why must you know?"

"What's the harm? Just one thing. I mean—" She waved her hand across the cabin, *Evinrude.* "How can you afford all this? We both know you're no hermit. No man devoted to penance and prayer. And I'm pretty sure your name isn't Sunday."

She was good. A quick study. "I was in manufacturing. I owned a company. Took it public. Sold it at the height. Made some residuals off recurring sales. Now I fish."

She had yet to let go of my hand. "And hide."

I nodded. "Yes, I do that, too."

"And your name?"

"I'd rather not."

"At least you're honest."

"I told you I wouldn't lie to you."

"Yeah, it's getting you to talk that's the tough part." She tapped her front teeth with her fingernail. "Guess you're stuck with 'Gilligan.' "

She eyed me. As in, walked up and down me with her eyes. She said, "Is it difficult for you to be around me? I mean—" She ran her fingertips along the curves of her figure.

I shook my head. "No. Not really."

"So, if I sunbathe without my bathing suit, you're okay with that."

I bit my bottom lip. "I'd probably go fishing while you did that."

She shrugged me off. "You don't think I'm pretty?"

"I've tried not to think about it."

"Why?"

" 'Cause Steady asked me to care for you. Not—"

She nodded, half smiling. "You don't need to be so flattering. It took a lot of money for me to look this way."

"Really?"

She pointed to her chin. Then her nose. Above her eyes. And finally, her breasts.

"Well—"

She chuckled. "Your face is turning red."

"Look, I don't have a whole lot of experience with women."

"You gay?"

"No, I just mean I don't date much."

"When was the last time you went on a date?"

"About eleven years ago."

"You ever been married?"

I shook my head.

She raised an eyebrow. She was a quick study. "You ever been with a girl?"

"Define 'been.' "

"You know . . . 'been.' "

I shook my head.

"How old are you?"

"Fortyish."

Her disbelief was difficult to hide. "You're over the hump and you've never slept with a woman?"

I didn't respond.

She put both hands on her hips. "Come on. Are you telling me the truth? I thought everybody had slept with somebody, or lots of somebodies, by the time they were your age."

"Never found the right—"

"The last romantic. Somebody should make a movie about you." She looked away, her mind spinning. "If I were still alive, I'd direct it and with your Coppertone face and island-man hair the tickets would sell like hotcakes."

"You're making fun of me, aren't you?"

"No. I'm being serious. I mean you're . . . you're not normal. I don't think I've ever met a man who hasn't been with a woman, and didn't want to be with me." I kept my mouth shut. She sat. "I guess maybe you would have a tough time with me sunbathing in my birthday suit." She curled up one side of her lip. Sucked through her teeth. "You sure you're not gay? I mean, it's okay if you—"

I nodded. "Pretty sure."

"How do you know?"

I turned away, smiling. "I just know."

She laughed. "Your face is really red." One hand on her hip. "Just how much did you see on my balcony and the back end of my boat?"

"I had other things on my mind."

"Yeah, but you still 'saw' me. You're human, right?"

"Yep."

"So, how much?"

"Enough."

She threw a pencil at me. "There I was the whole time thinking you were some guy like Steady."

I stared east through the mangroves toward Miami. A pause. "I'm nothing like Steady."

She stepped closer. This was the most talkative she'd been. And she'd just stepped into and violated the unspoken and yet consciously observed bubble of my personal space. "What do you mean?"

"Not a day goes by that I don't wish I was."

"How so?"

I paused. Tried to put it into words. "He sees clearly." I opened the screen door. "For what it's worth, I've talked more with you in the few days I've known you than any person other than

Steady for the last decade." She took another step. "Combined."

Her eyes narrowed. "Why?" It was a sincere question.

"Haven't wanted to."

She nodded, once. A long, purposeful blink. "Then—thank you for the gift of that."

So while the world searched, mourned, and tried to make sense of Katie's death, Steady returned to Miami, and I taught a Hollywood icon with her own star on the Boulevard how to bait her own hook, how to throw a spinning reel, how to read the surface of the water, how to tie a double surgeon's knot, how to connect leader to braid, and how to rub lime juice on her hands to get rid of the fishy smell.

All was not Edenic. Hurdles appeared. Not insurmountable. Just unexpected. The first morning, sunlight just breaking the treetops, I offered her a pole and a live shrimp. Still kicking. Her top lip curled. "Do I have to put that nasty, smelly thing on that hook?"

I considered this. "No." I offered the pole again. "But if you want to catch a fish, it helps."

She gritted her teeth, baited her hook, and we fished in silence. Easy with one another. Not talking. Not filling the air with nervous chatter. She didn't feel the need to give me her résumé detailing the worlds she'd conquered and I didn't pepper her with questions about what it was like to be her. We sat in the quiet, on the edge of the world where the Glades melted into the islands, casting across the current and letting arms of the mangroves envelop us in shade and easiness.

We watched each other out of the corners of our eyes. Comfortable but not demanding comfort. When she did talk, she did so in passing. Not in an effort to justify, but understand. Make sense of.

I listened. Something I've always been good at. Steady says the ocean is the bosom of God—if it is, then cradled there in that faraway place, we nursed.

And with every quiet moment that passed, every hook baited, every fish landed, every word unspoken, my wall—my very fortified, very carefully constructed, very calculated, protected, unscalable, and impenetrable wall—began cracking.

Chapter Twelve

Four days later, the call came in from Steady. I picked him up in the airboat and returned him to the island, where we found Katie comfortable on the porch. Hands in her lap. A thought on her mind, but not yet on her tongue.

We went inside.

He emptied his satchel and set the newspapers

147

on the table. "They buried you." She picked up the papers, studying the pictures. The color in her face had slowly returned—mixed now with hours in the sun. And yes, I'd long since had the thought that she was in fact the most beautiful human being I'd ever been this close to. She asked, "What'd they bury?"

"Memorabilia. Ticket stubs. Show programs. Posters. A scarf you sold for charity. Some jeans they said were your favorite." He waved his hand across an imaginary area of the table. "You've got your own section of the cemetery. It's a mausoleum, complete with all-night lighting and twenty-four-hour security paid for by your estate that, thanks to you, I'm now overseeing. Although . . ." A slight chuckle. "I'm soon to be embroiled in a nasty lawsuit with ex number three."

She waved him off. "All bark. No bite." She sat, reading the articles. Clicking her teeth on a single fingernail. She turned the article sideways, studying it. She nodded. "Yeah, I did like those jeans."

Steady had some questions, but he let her finish. When she laid down the papers, he opened his mouth but she beat him to the punch. Her words were cleanly articulated and echoed around the inside of the cabin. "I need to go to France." She said this with the same tone of voice with which she might order a Diet Coke.

148

Both our heads turned. I suppose our open jaws prompted her to explain. She drew a picture of the country of France in the air. "France. You know, west of Italy. North of Spain." She nodded. "You've seen pictures."

Steady sat back, realizing she'd made up her mind. He knew her pretty well. "I suppose you're going whether I like it or not."

"Oh, you'll like it 'cause you're going with me."

Steady looked caught off guard. "What?"

"It's your fault. You got me into this mess. I'm dead because of you."

I admit, I liked the thought of getting her off my boat and returning to my uncomplicated life. "I think that's a great idea."

He tapped his chest. "Sorry. Bum ticker. Can't fly. Doctor's orders."

She crossed her arms, chewed on her lip, and turned to look at me.

I didn't like what I saw.

She considered me for some time. Finally, she nodded. "You'll have to take his place. As long as you don't get in my way."

Being around her was like riding Space Mountain at Disney World. I looked at both of them. "Me? Why me?"

Steady smiled. "She obviously can't go alone." He placed his hand across his heart. "I can't go and you're the only other person who knows she's still alive." A shrug.

I spoke to both of them, shaking my head. "That does not mean I have to go."

She protested loudly. Reminded me of Veruca Salt in the chocolate factory. When I didn't react, she took a breath and said, "This is serious."

"I'm being serious."

"No, you're not. You're not even listening to me."

"Yeah, I did. You said you wanted me to go to France and I said no."

Steady interrupted. "She needs you."

His support of her was not what I had in mind. "She doesn't need me. She needs a priest and probably a good shrink."

She turned her thumbs in her lap, whispering below her breath. "It's important."

My voice rose. "What could possibly be important in France? I just helped you blow yourself to bits in the Gulf of Mexico!"

She crossed her arms.

Steady was still trying to get her point across. He patted me on the shoulder. "You should definitely go."

I looked at him like he had lost his mind and wondered how he'd gotten out of this so easily. He, of all people, should know that I couldn't go to France. I said, "You haven't answered my question."

She looked at me and spoke without emotion. *"Le coeur a ses raisons que la raison ne connaît point."*

I knew it was French, but I had no idea what it meant. My deer-in-the-headlights stare convinced her of this. She said, " 'The heart has its reasons that reason ignores completely.' "

"You make that up?"

A single shake. "Pascal."

She had me there but I tried not to let on. "Quoting dead philosophers sounds great but it's not getting me to France."

She looked at me out of the corner of her eye and spoke with conviction. "Writers die, not their words." Had me there, too.

"So, what's so important?"

"I'll tell you when we get there."

"Not good enough."

She responded quickly and without measure. A true emotional response. Uninhibited. She was yelling. " 'Cause it hurts. 'Cause I don't want to talk about it. 'Cause I can't. Haven't ever . . ." She hid her scarred wrist under the other.

Steady touched my arm. "A minute please?" I followed him outside. He slid the cabin door closed behind me. She sat arms crossed, glaring through the glass, shut out. Liking the idea that we were talking about her behind her back about as much as the fact that she had to beg us to get her way. The smell of salt washed over us. He spoke softly. "Go with her." He waited. Hands in his lap. Silence was response enough.

"Why?" I finally asked.

He pulled out a fingernail clipper and began trimming his nails. Trimmed three before speaking. "Because you need this."

"Me? This is about her." I waved a finger in the air. "This has got nothing to do with—"

He closed his eyes. "It has everything to do with you."

"What could this possibly have to do with me?"

He clipped a nail, which fell on the deck. His nails were always trimmed short. "That's for you to figure out."

"Steady, you of all people should know that I cannot do this."

Another finger. Another clip. "And you of all people should know that you can."

I shook my head. "Being around this woman is like walking across a dormant volcano. You're never quite sure when the mantle is going to blow. My primary thought every time I get within five feet of her is that I want her off my boat."

He switched hands. "If you go to France with her, she will be off your boat."

"That solves the second problem. Not the first."

He shrugged. "She's an onion."

"Meaning?"

"Multilayered."

"Oh, I thought you were going to say she leaves a bad taste in your mouth and brings tears to your eyes." He didn't bite. I said, "If she's an onion, what am I?"

He spoke matter-of-factly. "A coconut."

I tried to deflect. I countered. "Why, 'cause I'm hardheaded?"

"No, because a steady diet of coconut juice will give you the runs."

I was not winning this. "That's not funny."

He slid the trimmers back into his pocket, which meant this conversation was coming to a close and he'd made up his mind.

I turned and walked back through the door, intent on proving that she'd not thought this through. I stood across from her. "Let's assume for one minute that I agreed. That I said I'd go." She let out a deep breath. "You've got other really big problems."

"Such as?"

"Crossing the ocean. You don't have a passport and you can't get one without some black market help."

She looked away. Her voice softened. "I already have one."

"I'm sure Katie Quinn has one. I'm not so sure that"—I pointed at her—"you do."

She nodded. "I have a passport."

"How?"

"I've had it since I was fifteen."

"But—"

"Katie Quinn is not my real name."

Even Steady looked surprised. He asked, "It's not?"

" 'Katie Quinn' is the name I created when I needed it."

"It'll never work."

"It worked for Jason Bourne."

"He's fictional."

She raised an eyebrow. "I've been traveling back and forth to France for years without anyone knowing it."

"How?"

"It's simple, I make myself look like someone else."

I didn't respond. Steady smiled at me and whispered, "See, you two have more in common than you thought." I brushed him off.

"I'll pay you. I can pay you more than you make in a year. Or five years."

"You don't know how much I make."

"I've seen how you live. It can't be much."

"I don't want your money." I leaned forward. "And even if I did, you couldn't afford me."

" 'Course I could. I could buy everything you own ten thousand times."

"What's my trust worth?"

"Please don't make me beg any more than I already have."

Steady sat back. Almost smiling. He knew she was winning and he almost seemed to enjoy the banter.

"We have to go to the bank." She pulled a small key with a rope fob from her front pocket. "Safe-deposit box." She'd already begun planning our trip.

"You mean, I have to go to the bank."

She nodded.

"What's in the box?"

"Passport."

"What else?"

"You'll see when you open the box."

Steady had now crossed his hands across his lap and was smiling ear to ear. I returned to her. "Katie—"

"My name's not Katie."

"Okay, unnamed woman. I'll get the passport, but I can't go with you to France."

"Can't or won't?"

"Both."

"Please."

"Why can't you go alone?"

"Because you can go places I can't."

"I thought that was the point of you having this other identity."

"I need someone."

"You can hire someone there. It would be simpler. You don't need me specifically."

This time she turned. Eyes glassy. Voice softer. Pain surfacing. "Because—there's something there, and . . . I don't want to face it alone."

Now we were getting closer to the truth. I waited.

"I changed my name when I was about sixteen. I've spent my adult life becoming someone that I just buried in the Gulf of Mexico 'cause I don't want to be her anymore. So now, I'm trying not to be two people, not just one. That leaves me without many options. I don't know—" She was crying now. "Who is me now? How in the world would I know me if and when I met me? I'm not sure I'd know me if I bumped into me in the street. I just know I was born one person, I became a second, and now I'm trying not to be either one while I search the ocean floor for a third. How screwed up of a human being do you have to be to get where I am? I mean, how many more me's do I get before there's no more me? Can you answer that?"

This had just gotten a whole lot more complicated. "I cannot."

"Me, either. All I know is that unbecoming me is . . ." She shook her head. Tears dripped. ". . . Like dying every day. Over and over. I go to bed dead, wake up dead." She shook her head. "I'm caught in the middle, afraid to laugh for fear of resurrecting someone I can't be."

Quiet settled around us. Moments passed. I pressed her. "Can I ask you something and you give me an honest answer?"

She nodded. "I'll try. Right now I'm pretty deep in three-dimensional lies."

I stood, increasing the distance between us. "Are these tears real or are you acting?"

She wiped her face. "I think they're real, but

to be honest, I'm not sure I'd know if they weren't." Arms crossed. She stared through me, across the ocean. "I'm going to France to face something and I'm not sure I can face it alone."

Talking with her reminded me of the week I taught myself to drive a clutch. My neck was sore for a few days. Problem was that embedded between those lines was the truth. "Fair enough." A breeze pressed against the trees. I'm not quite sure what made me say what I said next. "I'll go."

"Really?"

"Yes."

She didn't know whether to kiss me, hug me, or shake my hand, so she did none of them. She brushed her face and wiped her palms on her cut-off jeans. "Well, thank you."

"You do realize, of course, that whoever flies us can't know that you are you."

"They won't."

"And neither can the customs people who check our passports."

She paused for effect. "You just worry about you and I'll worry about me."

"And you're sure you want to do this?"

"Positive."

"You'd better be, because if you thought things were bad before, let the world in on our little secret and . . ."

She let out a deep breath. One she'd been holding. "I know what's at risk."

If I had any illusion of being in control, it was over. I was now along for the ride and I couldn't see the track ahead. Space Mountain. And while I had several problems about to surface, only one was immediate. I had to find my passport and make myself look like the photo. I glanced past her. Way past her. Off my island and back a decade. And maybe, clinging to the edge and cracking fringe of my voice, lurked the anger and pain that time, oceans, sunsets, and tides had not washed away. "You better, because if you don't, you will shortly."

Chapter Thirteen

Katie said she thought we'd be gone a week. Maybe two. Given the uncertainty of a return date, I winterized the boats in my slip on the southeast side of Chokoloskee. Little more than a rickety dock where I moored *Gone Fiction* and raised *Jody* out of the water on a motorized lift. I left the batteries charging and paid a kid named Lenny, who lived in a trailer on the docks working the bait shack, a few bucks to keep the pelicans from crapping on either and to wash the boats when they did. He nodded and took my money.

I keep an old Dodge diesel truck in storage. I crank it enough to charge the batteries but really only use it to tow *Jody*. I raised the storage unit door and pulled the truck out. Katie and Steady climbed in. She wiped the dust off the dash, adjusted the AC vents and the thermostat. "Why do you drive a diesel?"

"I like it."

Another adjustment to the vent. "So you're one of those people."

"What kind is that?"

She fiddled with the thermostat, talking to herself. "Cold or hot, make up your mind." She turned back to me. "The kind that compensates by owning a big, hooked-up truck."

"Are you one of those rich actresses who compensates for their isolated loneliness by owning twenty cars?"

She lifted her feet onto the dash, tucking her knees into her chest. "That's not fair."

"No?"

Exasperated, she turned the thermostat all the way down. "Seventeen."

We could have hung meat inside the cab of the truck. "Seventeen, what?"

"Cars." She rested her head on her arms across her knees. "You're still compensating."

"Or I could be a guy who pulls a boat, who needs it."

She shook her head. "Nope. Compensating. You didn't make a big enough splash in life the first time around so now you've got to do it with an engine that sounds like a tractor."

She had a point so I said, "I'll bet you own a Porsche, don't you?"

A nod. "Four."

"And one of those black Range Rovers like they drive in James Bond movies."

"Two. Identical."

"Why two?"

"So I have one to drive while the other is in the shop." She reached for the thermostat again. I placed my hand on hers, stopping her. "Can I help you with the temperature in here?"

Steady was shaking his head, laughing to himself. He said, "You two will get along fabulously."

She shrugged him off and said, "Yeah, it's cold one minute, hot the next. I don't know what the problem is, but I don't have this problem in any of my cars."

"Well, maybe if you left the knob alone long enough, the temperature would settle somewhere rather than fluctuating between two extremes."

She twisted the knob, returning the setting to "snow," and looked out her window. "You got that right."

"What's that?"

"Somewhere between two extremes."

We rolled down Tamiami Trail with frost hanging off our eyebrows. Near the Shark Valley Everglades National Park she turned the knob to "sweat" and we did. Around the ValuJet memorial she rolled down her window and then twisted it back to "snow" in Coral Gables. As we turned onto the Mile, Steady muttered beneath his breath, "I don't think I was this cold at the Battle of the Bulge." A few blocks in and the otherwise calm Katie shrieked at the top of her lungs. I jerked, slammed on the brakes, and we both stared at her. She was pointing.

At Starbucks.

Steady tried to smile. "You'd like some coffee?"

She nodded.

I pulled into the driveway and spoke at the glass in front of me. "You could just ask."

She muttered a repentant "Sorry." She turned to me. "Okay, this is how I want it and it's very important that you say it just like this."

I nodded obediently, half listening.

She said, "I want a tall triple latte with seven shots of caramel, three shots mocha, one Splenda, half packet of NutraSweet, half shot of regular espresso, half shot of decaf, extra foam, upside down, and tell them not to burn the foam."

"Are you serious?"

"Extremely. We're talking about coffee."

"No. Coffee, I can order. This—this is something else."

I stepped out of the van. She hollered behind me. "If they can't make that then tell them I want a double tall nonfat, half caf, extra hot latte with whipped cream, vanilla, hazelnut, almond, raspberry, and toffee nut syrup, extra foam, two packets of Sweet'N Low, one packet of sugar, half pack of Equal, and three shots caramel sauce."

"Are you drinking coffee or baking a cake?"

"Hold on, I'm not finished."

"Really?"

"Really. Now pay close attention. Actually . . ." She grabbed a sheet of paper and began writing, talking out loud as she wrote. "I also want a venti seven shot, three shot decaf, and one and a half pumps amaretto, two percent, seven NutraSweets, extra whip, extra chocolate, extra sprinkles, java chip Frappuccino light blended coffee."

"Are you freaking kidding me?"

She waved me off. "Here, I wrote it down. Just get all three."

I walked inside, approached the counter, held up my sheet of paper, and said, "Kid, I apologize for what I'm about to do to you." Then I read verbatim the list she'd given me.

The guy said, "Are you for real?"

I slowly shook my head. "You have no idea."

He nodded knowingly and I handed him the sheet of paper. He reread it. "I feel for you, bro." He shouted something nonsensical back to some guy who returned with a "recall."

The guy behind the counter returned to me. "Anything for you?"

"Small coffee, please."

He smiled, poured the coffee, and handed it to me. "On the house." Another glance at the truck followed by a long look down the street. He rested one hand on top of the cash register the same way reminiscent men do at bars. "Katie Quinn used to come in here and order the same thing." He tapped his name tag. "Used to call me by my name." He nodded. "Once tipped me a hundred dollars." He punched a few keys on the cash register. "Nineteen dollars and seventeen cents."

I handed him a twenty.

In about six minutes, the guy baking the coffee concoctions placed Katie's three cups on the counter, along with a fourth small black for Steady. He slipped the little cardboard sleeve over each and then wedged them into a cardboard carry tray. Curious, I sampled one of hers. The stuff hit my tongue and I almost puked syrupy coffee puree across two walls. I passed on testing the second and third.

I slid a hundred dollar bill into the tip jar and returned to the van, where I found her foaming like Pavlov's dog. I set the tray in her lap and her entire body smiled.

I wound through the Grove. Steady talked as I drove. "I've arranged for a plane for tomorrow evening. Tonight, I've reserved two rooms at the Biltmore."

Katie took out a piece of paper, wrote, sipped, and sipped some more. By the time we got to the bank, her legs were bouncing, her head was on a swivel, and her eyes were darting left and right at a frantic pace. There was no telling how fast her heart was beating. She handed me the key, told me what to say, and I walked in. The people took absolutely no special notice of me. A man in a suit walked me to a room, inserted his key, asked me to do the same. I did. The man pulled out the drawer and left. I pulled the curtain and opened the drawer.

Katie Quinn was either stupid—which I seriously doubted—or she'd been considering door number three long before I ever mentioned it to her. On top lay her passport, which I didn't open. I wanted to but figured it really wasn't my business. Okay, so then I thought better of it and I opened it up to find a picture of a woman who showed a vague resemblance to Katie Quinn. Maybe just the eyes and the cheek lines. The woman called herself "Isabella Dubois Claveaux Desouches."

Beside it was a cell phone with a car charger. Beneath that lay money. And lots of it. Almost two hundred and fifty thousand in American dollars and nearly that much in euros. All in stacks of hundreds. In a small flannel bag next to that was jewelry—jeweled watch, a diamond ring, another colored ring, and a diamond tennis bracelet and necklace. Per her instructions, I extracted twenty thousand of each currency, grabbed the passport, phone, and the jewelry, and returned the box to its locked home. I stuffed my loot into a red bag they'd given me for my convenience and walked to the van, looking over my shoulder.

In the truck, I handed her the bag and said nothing. She took it then tapped Steady on the shoulder. "I need a few things from the costume store, if you don't mind." It struck me that she tapped his shoulder and yet I was driving.

A few miles later, I parked and left it running in front of Bozo's Party Store. Katie gave us each a list with specific instructions to get exactly what she'd written. "It's very important that you not deviate."

She slid me a hundred and raised both eyebrows. "And I want the receipt." I shook my head and we walked into the store with our assignments. Twenty minutes later, after having occupied the attendant for most of that time, we walked out with two bags of enough stuff to make one person look like six. Three different wigs of varying colors and lengths, fake eyelashes, false eyebrows, differing size things that women stuff inside their bras or wrap around their chest to make their boobs look bigger or smaller, peel-off tattoos, various colors and sizes of panty hose, four pairs of fake eyeglasses, and enough makeup to last her a year.

She rifled through the bag, smiling and nodding. When she came to one tube of lipstick, she shook her head and handed it back to me. "It's color sixty-four. Not sixty-six. In the red family, but not quite—"

I opened the door and said, "You are starting to get on my nerves."

She sat back, sipped one of her coffees, and crossed her legs. She then thumbed over her shoulder, smiling slyly. "Get in line."

I exchanged number sixty-six for number sixty-four and drove us to the Biltmore. In the ten minutes it took us to get there, she transformed herself into a blonde with big curly hair to her shoulders, wearing heavy makeup, an expensive-looking deep-red dress that revealed a fake tattoo, six-inch stiletto heels, and a Dolly Parton chest. Seemed like a lot of effort to walk through the lobby of the hotel. Steady laughed as I pulled up in front of the entrance to the Biltmore. I looked at her, eyeing her obvious enhancement. "Really?"

She shrugged. "If I don't want men to look at my face, then I give them something else to look at."

"Well, I'd say you've succeeded at that."

Steady handed us two keys. I said, "You're not staying?"

"I need to get back. Some rather talented reporters have put together a few of the pieces and it's believed that I was the last person to see or talk to Katie Quinn before she died. That means there are a lot of people wanting to ask me questions that I am obliged not to answer."

"Good luck with that." I handed him the keys to the truck.

He turned, beads draped over his other hand. "Luck has got nothing to do with it."

Katie and I rode the elevator to the fifth floor. Two rooms at the far end, doors facing each other. She unlocked her door and said, "You want a good dinner or"—her lip turned up—"room service?"

"You know a good place?"

She smiled. "See you in thirty?"

Chapter Fourteen

I donned my flip-flops, faded jeans, and a white button-down. Tied my hair back. I knocked on her door and the blonde I'd dropped off had been replaced by a brunette with a bouncy ponytail and titanium glasses. Gone were the big boobs, replaced by a relatively flat chest. Long trailing eyebrows. Dark eyeliner, eye shadow, high cheekbones, fishnet stockings. Short skirt. Long legs. She looked almost Asian and nothing like herself.

I checked the number to make sure I had the correct room. The lingerie model shut her door and began walking in front of me toward the elevator, sort of flipping her hips as she walked.

"What, you like Tiffany the bosomed trophy wife better?"

"No, I just wasn't expecting her—I mean, you."

We took a cab to the Mile and walked to a little restaurant called Ortanique. Unbeknownst to me, she'd made a reservation and requested a specific table. We waited while the servers prepped the table. People milled around us. Busy conversa-tions on all sides. Katie sunk her arm inside mine, completing the act.

They put us in a corner, her side to the room. This allowed her to look left if she wanted and view the room, or look right and discreetly view the reflection of the room in the mirrors. She'd done this before.

Before I had a chance to open my mouth, Ashley the Asian lingerie model had ordered for us. "Two mojitos."

The server noted this and said, "You ready to order?"

Katie pointed at me. "He'll have the mango salad. I'll have the Caesar. We'll split the brie. Then he'll have the double pork chop and I'll take the crab cakes."

The server nodded. "Good choices, all."

She continued, "For dessert, he'll have that chocolate decadence thing that makes you want to slap your mama, and I'll have the rum-soaked banana fritters." She smiled at me and brushed my hand. "Make you want to kiss your boyfriend."

The server looked impressed. "Sit tight. I'll get this in. Two world-class mojitos coming up."

He disappeared. "Boyfriend?"

"Acting is all about making others think something that may or may not be true. The truth of it lies with you." She glanced at the server typing in our order. "That guy's not thinking about"—she lowered her voice—"Miss Quinn. He's thinking about a couple having fun, about me being happy with you, and how a happy couple at his table means a better tip for him."

The mojitos arrived. We sipped. The concoction hit my lips, then my throat. Smooth would have been an understatement. She smiled, licked her lips, pulled out a mint leaf, and smelled it. "Good, isn't it?"

"No . . . 'good' is a gas station cup of coffee at two a.m. This . . ." I brushed the condensation with my thumb down the tall glass. ". . . Is the nectar of God."

She laughed. "Careful, it'll sneak up on you."

A pregnant silence. One, I guessed, she'd prepared. She held her glass to her lips. Pausing. Staring at me over the glass. "Tell me something."

"What?"

"Something nobody else knows."

I laughed. "I've never been here."

She sipped. "You said you were in 'manufacturing.' "

Another question posed as a statement. I

pretended my attention was spread across the room. "Yep."

"What did you manufacture?"

"Our target market was seventeen and under though we experienced considerable crossover into several categories above."

"That told me absolutely nothing."

Another smile. "I realize that."

"You play your cards close to your chest."

"Maybe, but not as close as"—I whispered—"Isabella."

Our food arrived and she changed the subject. We talked of likes, odd habits, what people were wearing, and why a second mojito was a good idea. My salad was good, but my double pork chop may have been the best piece of pork I'd ever put in my mouth followed closely by some colossal chocolate thing. We sampled from each other's plates as if they were our own and while her crab cakes were good, the rum-soaked banana fritters may have taken the cake. By the time I paid the bill, I was too stuffed to move. She pointed at the street. "Let's walk."

We reached the sidewalk, turned left, and she hung her arm inside mine, furthering the act. She surveyed the street, the shops, the people, and spoke just loud enough for me to hear. "Ever notice there are two Miamis? The one you see before sundown and the one you see after." Next door, a line of people stretched from the ticket counter of a small theater down the sidewalk and around the corner. The marquee read THE QUEEN LIVES. KATIE QUINN MARATHON. TONIGHT. 9 P.M. She stared up where the red and white lights reflected off her face. She whispered, less to me and more the memory of the place, "'That this huge stage presenteth nought but shows, whereon the stars in secret influence comment . . .' "

A good line. "Shakespeare," I said, surprised. "A sonnet, I think."

She looked at me out of the corner of her eye. "So you do come off that boat."

A slight nod. "Sometimes."

Her eyes reflected the white lights. Sparkling. "This is the theater where I got my start." A laugh. "At least, my start around here. They did stage plays before they converted it to a movie theater."

"What was it?"

"*Little Women.* Steady helped me get an audition. I played Jo." She laughed at herself. "That's back when I could get away with it."

"With what?"

She laughed and shook her head.

I pointed at the counter. "You mind?"

She stared at the line. Then down at the sidewalk to avoid any possibility of eye contact. Then at me. Weighing me. "No."

I bought two tickets and they opened the doors. I couldn't eat popcorn because I couldn't fit another thing in my mouth so we bypassed the candy counter and climbed the steps, getting two seats up in the back. We sat and within moments, the theater dimmed and the movie started. The title read *The Mountain Between Us*. She whispered in my ear. "Came out a couple of years ago. My third Academy Award."

I straightened. "You've won three—"

She put her finger to my lips. "Shhhh."

Maybe it was the mojito talking. I slowly uncurled three fingers and whispered, "You've won three Academy Awards?"

She tucked her knees into her chest, wrapped her arms around her knees, studied the crowd, and nodded.

She was mesmerizing. Tantalizing. In control of herself and everyone around her. When the credits rolled, half the audience was bawling. Oddly, while I watched the movie, she watched the crowd and chewed on a fingernail.

Every so often, I'd catch her mouthing the words before she said them on the screen. And the fingers on her left hand were like the puppeteer above controlling the stringed thing below. Every movement she made with her hand, she made on the screen. And with her right hand, she controlled her leading man. In the second movie, she played a homeless woman—Sam—on the run with her daughter—Hope—who writes letters to God. Both are rescued by a retired Texas Ranger who takes them back to his ranch in west Texas. At one point, the movie showed a scene in the river. Skinny-dipping. Brief nudity of the top of her buttocks. Just before the screen showed her wading into the water in her birthday suit, she slid her hand up and over my eyes.

Two movies later, the last credits rolled at five a.m. I sat there, spellbound. The audience around me stood and applauded, whistling, yelling, "Encore! Encore!" She tugged on me.

We walked the street to the rhythm of my flip-flops. She was quiet. Two streets off the Mile, we passed a bookstore. It was closed but the window displays were not. The front three windows, each eight feet wide, were covered with a single book: *The Ice Queen: What the Media and Katie Never Told You about Katie Quinn.* In the lower right-hand corner of the cover it read "The Unauthorized Biography." A poster of Queequeg sat to the left advertising a signing the following night. Undoubtedly, he would tell everyone about the new material he was working on. The bookstore must have had a hundred copies in the window display alone. It even got my attention. Someone had taped a printout of the *New York Times* best-seller list. *The Ice Queen* sat at number seven. Up three from last week. She shook her head. "Writers. Can't live with them. Can't trust them."

I stared at the book. "This guy really got to you, didn't he?"

"He took what I told him and turned it into what he wanted."

"So sue him."

She shrugged. "We didn't have enough of a case to stop the publication. So even if I were alive, where would that get me? It'd make him look credible and me petty." She turned, placing her back to the book. "Lies. All lies."

The smug look on his inked face mixed with the mysterious pose did not make him look like the mysterious writer. It made him look artificial. "He doesn't know it yet but he's a flash in a pan. A coattail rider. Here today, forgotten tomorrow. And his two seconds of fame are winding down, not up."

"It still hurts. I'm tempted to tell all to Steady and then let him pay someone to set the record straight."

As she finished speaking, two obscenity-laced, skateboarding, hoodie kids popping kick flips and grinding on the rail of the bus bench rolled past. One saw the book in the display along with a poster-size picture of Katie. With exaggerated hand motions and colorful epithets, he gave her picture the bird. " 'Bout time she died. Now maybe they'll shut up about how life was so tough for that rich bi—"

I tried to drown him out. "Don't pay them any mind."

She didn't even wince. Years in the spotlight

shone through. "It's tough to pity someone who has everything you wish you had."

My head was spinning and I needed sleep. "You want me to hail a cab?"

"No. It's not far."

We strolled the streets, arriving at the Biltmore forty-five minutes later. She talked of movies, roles played, lines spoken, loves lost. I listened, letting her talk. Once at the hotel, I walked her to her room. My curiosity surfaced. "Was that difficult for you?"

A shrug. Then a single shake of her head. "I finished filming that movie and then spent three months in a"—she made quotation marks with her fingers—" 'health spa' getting unhooked from Xanax and hydrocodone." She began walking into her room. "The amazing thing about movies is what's left on the editing room floor." She turned. "If they had seen those pieces, I wonder if they'd have clapped. Whistled. Handed me that statue."

France is six hours ahead of East Coast time so Steady had scheduled our plane to leave at six p.m., allowing us to arrive early in the morning. We had almost twelve hours before our plane took off. "See you tomorrow?"

"You mean today?"

"Yep."

Chapter Fifteen

I walked to my room, where the sight of myself in the mirror stopped me. I had a problem and needed help. I grabbed my passport, returned across the hall, and knocked on her door. She had peeled off Ashley and quickly become the frame upon which she hung these various personas. She stared without saying anything. I said, "I need a favor?"

She nodded. "Sure."

I opened my passport to the picture page and held it up. "I need you to make me look like him."

She ran her fingers through my hair. For one brief second she stepped out of character. "*Vous êtes fou.*"

"What's that?"

"French."

"What's it mean?"

" 'You're crazy.' " She took the passport and studied the picture. She looked at me without moving her face. "Is your name really 'Cartwright Jones'?"

I shook my head.

"Where'd you get it?"

"A character from one of my favorite movies as a kid—*Where Eagles Dare*."

"Ahhh." She smiled. "Sir Richard Burton. Now, there was a leading man." She studied the picture again and held it up alongside my face. "Shouldn't be too hard."

She shut the door behind me and I moved to her chair and sat down. "I don't really know how I want it cut."

She sized me up from across the room. "I do." She rummaged in her bags for what she thought she'd need. Then she crossed the room and stood behind me. She ran her fingers through my hair, stopping when she reached the end. Evidently, I grew rather tense.

She stopped. "You okay?"

"Yeah, it's just been a long time since anybody's done what you're doing."

"What, cutting your hair?"

"No . . . touching me."

She paused, turned away, walked into the bathroom, and said, "Come here."

I walked in and she was kneeling next to the tub, water running. "Sit." I did. "Lean your head back." I leaned against a towel and hung my head in the tub. Slowly, she began rinsing my hair with the attached sprayer. While most of the water ran into the tub, some ran off my head, down my shoulders, trickled down my stomach and onto the floor. Until that moment, I'd never had anyone wash my hair. And until the next moment, I'd never had anyone scrub it with their fingernails, rinse it, and then massage it with conditioner.

She handed me a towel and I dabbed myself, following her to the chair. She wrapped me in another towel, pulled a comb from her back pocket, and studied my head. She raised her comb, paused, half smiled, and said, "Hold still."

I tried.

She placed a hand on my shoulder. Control in her voice. "You're trembling."

"Sorry."

She spoke softly, eyes finding mine. "It's the stuff we bury that hurts the most."

I nodded slowly. "Yes."

She placed the comb in my hair and began pulling it down and outward. She moved her way around my head, combing out the tangles. She noticed my white-knuckled hands on the towel, tapped my fingers, and whispered, "Let go." I did. Finally, she leaned down. "Close your eyes."

I looked at her. She placed her palms across my eyes. "Close them."

I did.

"Now let out that breath you've been holding since you walked in here."

I did that, too.

For the next twenty minutes, she combed my hair, talking softly, telling me about her dressing rooms at trailers on locations around the world, lots in Hollywood, and locations on Broadway.

About the designers who styled her hair, their names, the way they laughed, how they smelled of smoke and what happened when one of them started smoking too much crack. She told me about one of the first movies she'd made, filmed in Spain, her first big role and what it felt like the first time someone combed—or in her case, brushed—her hair. What it did for her. How it made her feel. How it relaxed her. She finished by saying, "I've been in several places where they charge you a lot of money to get your act together, but I'm convinced I could open a get-your-act-together center and have a line out the door with only one service." She worked the comb through my hair, pulling gently. "Two chairs. One with someone standing behind it that washed and conditioned your hair. And a second where they combed your hair until . . ." Her voice trailed off. ". . . Your troubles disappeared."

I looked out of the corner of my eyes. "And bald people?"

A nod. Half smile. "Scalp massages. Pedicures." She waved the comb over the door. "Line would be down the street."

I didn't disagree.

She worked professionally. Arms extended. Like a dancer. Her shoulders were lean. Muscled. Arms toned. Working out had been part of her past. I stared down. At the floor. The pattern of the carpet around her feet. My hair clung to her skin.

She lifted my chin with the comb, eyeing my sideburns. Her face two feet from mine. I glanced. Sweat dotted her lip.

Forty-five minutes later, she stood in front of me, scissors snipping, a pile of hair at her feet. Head tilted to one side. Without explaining, she disappeared to the sink, made some noise, then came back with a cup spilling over with suds and bubbles. She lifted the mug. "You mind?"

"No." I raised a finger. "Just as long as you don't slit my throat."

She laughed, turned the chair, moving me closer to the wall, and leaned my head back. She laid the towel across my chest and one shoulder and slowly worked the suds into my beard. Given that I had not shaved in about two months, this took a while. Once lathered, she slowly worked the razor down my face. Then my neck. Then, she lathered my face again, shaving closer. She did it a third and final time. When finished, she stepped back and I toweled off the soap. She said, "Well, let me look."

I did.

She stared. Comparing me to my picture. Her head angled. Tilted like a dog. Finally, a nod. "Better. More Robert Redford. Less Larry the Cable Guy."

I stood. "Thanks."

She half bowed, said nothing, and began rinsing scissors, comb, and mug. I policed the floor, getting all the hair, then walked to the door. "See you tomorrow. Or today, rather."

She nodded, handed me her key. "I've been known to oversleep. If I don't answer by noon—"

I placed her key alongside mine in my pocket. "Okay."

I returned to my bed, turned on the TV, and flipped channels until I found her on the screen. She was laughing and riding a motorcycle through Italy. I pulled out my journal and scribbled a few notes. Several pages and one or two channels later, I drifted off to the sound of her singing a duet and playing the piano.

I didn't know she played the piano.

Chapter Sixteen

I knocked but she didn't answer. I knocked again. Nothing. I used her key, pushed open the door, and found her spread across the bed like a snow angel, a scarf over her eyes, some sort of plugs in her ears. I shook her toe.

She stirred, pulled the scarf off her face, and said, "What time is it?"

"Almost four."

"P.m.?"

I nodded.

She wrestled herself out of the sheets, shading

her eyes against the sunlight coming around the shades.

"Obviously, you're not a morning person."

She flopped back down on the sheets. "Not when I go to sleep with the sun coming up."

I laughed. "See you at the café."

"Let me get a shower."

An hour later, a third person appeared—a perfect match to her passport photo with no similarity to Katie Quinn. This was Isabella Desouches. A redheaded professional. CoverGirl hair to her shoulders. Notepad in tow. Black, wire-rimmed glasses. Matching suit-waist jacket and slim, tailored pants. Tasteful but low-cut silk blouse with lace trim. Black high heels. Short fast steps. The whole getup said, "I'm in a hurry and when I want your opinion I'll ask."

Isabella sat down, eyed the waiter, and tapped her juice glass. I leaned forward. "How many different people are you?"

A single shake. Half a smile. "Only as many as I need."

"Need? Isn't one enough?"

"If I always used the same disguise, someone could figure it out. I can't afford to risk that, especially now." She eyed me. "You have a favorite?"

I laughed. "I'm not falling for that. Not a chance. Where'd you get the clothes?"

"First-floor boutique."

"You shop quickly."

"Knew what I wanted." She caught me rubbing my chin and the sides of my face. "You missing something?"

I smiled.

After juice and two cups of coffee, we walked to the valet stand, where Steady was just pulling in with my truck. To complete her act, Katie stood off to one side. An executive, a business-woman, sharing a vehicle and little more.

Something in me didn't like it.

A young, half-dressed mother, smacking gum in the ear of the person on the other end of the phone, exited the hotel and pushed a stroller between us. The valet phoned a cab. Isabella, hidden behind designer shades, made no sign of noticing either the mother or the baby. Wanting attention, the baby plucked out her pacifier and threw it at Isabella. It hit and slid down her new pants, leaving a glistening trail of slobber, and came to rest on the toe of her shoe. Oblivious, the mother grew more animated in her retelling of last night's events. Fighting its straps, the baby reached across the space but fell a few feet short. Out of the corner of her eye, Isabella glanced at the mother, then the baby—then the pacifier. A long pause. Unnoticed, she stooped, slowly lifted the passy, and knelt next to the stroller, playfully tapping the kid's nose and then inserting it into the kid's snot-smeared mouth. The baby laughed, kicked its feet, and reached for her. Katie straightened her index finger and the kid wrapped four fingers around it. I watched without comment. A second later, she stood and her right hand came up beneath her glasses and patted the makeup below her right eye.

We climbed in my truck and Steady drove to the airport. He was chatty. We were not. I had one thought. Okay, two. Getting into France and past the customs people. And then getting back into the U.S. I didn't fear handcuffs and criminal accusation. It was something worse. Loss of anonymity. I'd worked hard to disappear and didn't want to sacrifice the life I'd come to live for the whimsical fancy of an actress trying to find something she'd lost.

And yet, I was sitting in my truck.

Steady kept looking at me out of the corner of his eye. He was smirking.

We parked at the private airport not far from Miami International and began walking to the plane. Katie kissed Steady on the cheek and went ahead. He tugged on my arm to stop me. I pulled my Costas down over my eyes. I said, "You sure you don't want to go?"

"No. Last time I was there, angry people were shooting at me. I'll pass."

He paused, squeezed my arm, and pulled within inches of my ear. Spittle in the corner of his mouth. His breath smelled of pipe smoke. "I told you I'd cut out your gangrene."

I nodded.

He glanced at the plane, then me. "The instruments needed can take many forms. Saw, scalpel . . ." I turned to walk away. He didn't let go. "The key . . ." He set my glasses up on my head. "Is sitting still while the medical professionals cut out the wound. And . . ." He shook his head. Sucked through his teeth. "You've got to let them get all of it. That means they've got to cut deep, into the stuff that's still living." He let go. Rested on his cane. "Peter"—it'd been a long time since he'd called me by my real name— "you're one of the more gifted human beings I've ever met. Maybe, the most." Another glance at the plane. "And I've met some very gifted people." He watched her climb the steps. "There are three of her and I'm not talking about the disguises. I'm talking about her. There's the one she gives the adoring public. The one she gives her friends. And the one she gives to no one." He shook his head. "I've known her more than twenty years and only met the first two." He looked up at me. "Find the third."

He let me go and I walked to the plane. As I began climbing the first step, he hollered from behind me, laughter in his voice. "Don't let her get you on a scooter in Paris. Don't go to the top of the Eiffel Tower at night. Drink wine at every meal. Anything from Saint-Émilion is good. If you go to Candes-Saint-Martin, check out the underside of the fifth pew from the front. And no matter what you do, don't by any means—" I climbed inside and the flight attendant shut the door behind me.

Katie buckled, leaned across the aisle, and waved at him out the window. She said, "You get the feeling he's been planning this?"

"Yeah. And for a lot longer than you have."

I glanced around at our camel-colored, plush leather surroundings and sniffed twice audibly through my nose. "You just never get used to that new-plane smell, do you?"

She laughed.

Using the funds at his disposal, and not having to answer to anyone, Steady had chartered a Gulfstream Jet that could cross the ocean.

Katie's papers said she was a high-end antiques buyer from the States. She made monthly, or bimonthly, visits to Europe to acquire inventory. A pretty good cover. It allowed her to deal in the world in which she was accustomed without being known. Clever.

Out the window, Miami grew distant. Smaller. As did the Ten Thousand Islands, the Glades, and the invisible world I'd carved inside. We sat in the quiet of thirty-nine thousand feet. Sliding through the air at a little over six hundred miles an hour. I thought about this fragile woman—the fingers of her left hand tapped the armrest, the others tapped her front teeth. I hardly knew her and yet I had agreed to fly to France with her. Why? Really? What was I really doing on this plane? I thought about what might await us and about Steady's words. About the fifth pew at Candes-Saint-Martin—whatever and wherever that was. About the many faces of Katie Quinn and his challenge to "find the third." Finally, I thought about his offer to me.

To cut out my gangrene.

I tried to shake it off, but the twitch in my side told me I might be too late. The discomfort grew. Below us, water ran to the edges of the earth. The only thing missing was a headstone.

I'd been running a long time. Something I was good at, comfortable with, and could keep doing for a lot longer. But the moment I'd stepped onto this plane, that'd changed. Clarity set in. In buckling my seatbelt, I'd given up control. Hand off the throttle. If I stayed with her, I became the puppet and Steady controlled the strings. What would happen when Steady the surgeon methodically picked his way around the wound, passing through the scars I used to protect me, and the scalpel cut into the stuff that was still living? With the wound laid bare, I'd have to deal with what it hid.

And, what I'd buried.

PART TWO

Summers and winters scattered like splinters
and four or five years slipped away.
> —Jimmy Buffett, "He Went to Paris"

I was a-trembling, because I'd got to decide,
forever, betwixt two things, and I knowed it. I
studied a minute, sort of holding my breath,
and then says to myself: "All right then, I'll
go to hell."
> —*The Adventures of Huckleberry Finn*

Chapter Seventeen

We landed, taxied, and before I had time to get nervous, customs agents boarded the plane and asked for our passports—in English. That's when an amazing thing happened. Isabella Desouches opened her mouth and spoke the most beautiful language I'd ever heard. And while I'm no linguist, she spoke it like she'd done it before. The French language rolled off her tongue like it'd been born there. In seconds, they were feeding out of her palms. Jibbering and jabbering, using their hands almost as much as their mouths. They barely glanced at my papers, more intent on the little dark Cindy Crawford mole on the corner of her mouth and the moist spray of perspiration just above her blouse's neckline. They stamped our passports, and wished us well on our way. The younger of the two slipped Katie a piece of paper with a phone number on it. She read it and shook her head. "French men. Predictable."

We walked through the private wing of the airport. Getting here had been a nonevent. My blood pressure returned to a normal level. I spoke without looking behind me. "Is it always that easy?"

"Yep."

Using her personal trainer–toned legs, and

ridiculously high heels, she hailed a cab, said something to the driver, then sat back, patted me on the thigh, and said, "You can breathe now." The cabdriver was adjusting his rearview mirror to see down her blouse but she didn't give him the pleasure.

The drive into Paris took about twenty minutes, as traffic was thin. The Eiffel Tower was the first landmark to come into view. Then the Arc de Triomphe. We routed around the arc and down the Champs-Élysées. Katie stared out the window, melting into the city. Or, maybe letting it melt into her. Just beyond a Nespresso store, the driver turned left, drove two blocks, circled right, zig-zagged through an area of restaurants and hotels, and dropped us in front of a bakery on a street marked mostly by storefronts covered with rolling garage doors. She paid the driver, walked into the bakery, ordered, paid, and was biting into a croissant by the time I walked in. The croissant, nearly the size of a football, was steaming, as it had just come out of the oven, and flakes were dripping off the corners of her mouth. Her eyes were closed and she was mumbling something about how she loved Paris. I sat and the lady delivered two really small coffees. Katie slid a croissant in front of me.

"Try it."

I did.

It might have been the best thing I'd ever put in

my mouth. The inside was filled with some sort of chocolate. My surprise showed. She sipped, took another bite, and lifted her eyebrows. "Welcome to Paris."

The window to my left gave us a view of city life in Paris. People walking to and from work, shopping, or home. Dogs on leashes. Hundreds of motorbikes. The smallest cars I'd ever seen stuffed to the brims with groceries and sofas and steaming baguettes. Women smoking. Men watching women smoke. Pigeons everywhere. Buses with Katie's picture plastered along one side. Kids wearing all black and drinking beer on the sidewalk. Old men dressed in sport coats and vests with Windsor-knotted ties and tweed hats, newspapers tucked under their arms.

A couple of things struck me. Paris was dirty. The buildings, streets, everything looked like it had been blown with exhaust or a brown spray. The street was littered with trash, most everybody had a small, fashionable dog, and dog feces dotted the sidewalk. Also, a lot of people smoked. Much more than in the States. While I was observing this, a man with a small Jack Russell walked in, ordered a coffee, and then sat with the dog on his lap, feeding him small pieces of a baguette.

She said, "What are you thinking?"

"I'm thinking I miss my boat."

She dropped a tip on the table. "Come on." We walked out, she checked her watch, tilted her head side to side, and said, "You in a hurry?"

"Lady, I'm with you. I have no idea where we're going, why we're here, or when we're returning. So, no, I'm not really in a hurry."

She turned laughing, reached in her purse, and slid on her glasses. "Follow me." We walked a block, turned a corner up a tight alley, and she stopped at the third garage door we came to. She fingered the combination lock, slid the lock sideways then kicked the door up revealing a garage of sorts. A car, several scooters, and a plethora of helmets closest to us, and then a rack of hanging clothes, stacks of faded jeans, piles of shoes, and two comfortable chairs. A sink, toilet, and shower filled one corner. She grabbed two keys out of a box on the wall, tossed one at me, and said, "Pick a helmet." While I found one that fit, she changed into some jeans, running shoes, and black leather jacket. She pointed at one of the scooters. "That's yours." It was something I'd never seen. The bike had two front wheels and one rear. She said, "You've ridden this kind before?"

I shook my head. "I've never really ridden any kind before."

She pulled on a helmet, then punched a button, and the black, tinted eye-shield popped up, revealing her eyes. "Don't worry. Thing almost drives itself." Her laughter told me she was lying. She pushed a button on the handlebars, it started, and she began pushing it out of the garage. I could still hear her laughing inside her helmet. We idled into the alley. I locked the garage door and then eased to the stop sign of the one-way street. I pulled up alongside her. Traffic moved in front of us, left to right.

"Keep up"—she flipped her shield down and her voice took on a garbled Darth Vader tone— "if you can." She kicked it into gear. She did not wait for an opening in the traffic. She just flicked her right wrist, launching her forward. The Apollo rocket was slower out of the gate. I followed, turned right, gunned it, and saw her three cars ahead. Steady's voice echoed: "Don't let her get you on a scooter . . ." We turned onto the Champs-Élysées, drove two blocks and then into the circle surrounding the arc. I saw her briefly on the far side where she looked back, blew me a kiss, and then she was gone.

I tried desperately to get out of the circle but people in Paris don't drive like me so I made three trips around cussing the absence of streetlights. Growing dizzy on the fourth lap, I gunned it, darted right, and popped up on the curb in front of a café after nearly getting crushed by a bus with a loud horn. A group of kids cussed me and gave me the finger. I'd interrupted their smoke. I parked the bike, dropped my helmet on the ground, and sat at a table. When the server spoke to me in words I didn't understand, I said the only

European-sounding thing I could think of that might result in something to drink. "Cappuccino?"

Halfway through a great cup of coffee, she appeared, screen up. "What happened?"

I pointed at the spaghetti-intersection of cars circling the arc. "That."

Darth Vader again. "Come on, rookie."

We spent the day zooming in and out of traffic and the only reason I kept up with her was because she held back. She could have left me at will. At one point she said, "There's no better way to see the city." I'm not sure about that but we did see a good bit of it.

She drove me through what turned out to be the Paris Flea Market—largest of its kind in the world. Hundreds, even thousands, of vendors, the market is not measured in square feet, but square blocks, and it is larger than some towns I've seen. She pulled to the side. "Gypsies started this. A share shop of sorts. Grew out of the idea that one man's trash is another man's treasure. Since then, it's grown. Some of the world's best antiques are right here. I've been coming here for ten years or so. Whenever I bought a new house, I'd walk through, buy every-thing I wanted, fill a shipping container or two, and then ship it to the new house where it'd be waiting on me when I arrived. Expensive, but"—she smiled—"fun. Used to drive my designers nuts, but"—a shrug—"I figured I was paying them so it was their job to figure out how it all fit together."

A shipping container filled to the brim with disconnected pieces. Somebody's discards. All traveling to a new home to be handled by a stranger.

It was a good image and I made a note of it.

Following brunch, then lunch, then another coffee, we stopped outside the Hermès store in the late afternoon. She pulled up next to the curb, eyeing the window displays. "One of my favorite places." She raised a hand. "And before you butcher the name, it's not 'her-meez.' It's pronounced, 'air-may.' "

"Glad you clarified that."

She surveyed the window displays.

I said, "Go ahead."

"They used to open at night. Just for me. No one else. I have, or had, about two hundred and fifty of their scarves." She shook her head. "Beautiful."

"How much are they?"

"The inexpensive ones are about three hundred euros."

I did the math. "Four hundred and fifty dollars?"

She nodded.

"And it's just a scarf."

"It's not just 'a' scarf. It's 'the' scarf."

I glanced through the window. "Does it come with a TV or something?"

She chuckled. "You should come in off the

water some time. There's a whole world out here just waiting to be seen." With that, she flicked her wrist. Within seconds, she'd become a speck in the distance.

Chapter Eighteen

At sundown we found a café beneath the shadow of the Eiffel Tower. She returned from the bathroom with a scarf covering her ears and forehead and large sunglasses covering the top half of her face. She topped it off with a second scarf around her neck. She blended in seamlessly—Patricia the Parisian painter. She ordered dinner, conversing with the server. Between the wig, scarves, and sunglasses he had no idea. I listened, watching her mouth. The way she formed the words. Unlike English, her heart was connected to these words. Hearing it reminded me of melting ice cream. Her mouth made the words but the transformation was in her body. Her facial expressions. She was in midsentence. She was excited, happy, and smiling. She waved her hand across the scenery. "You know how Tim McGraw sings that song about how you should live like you were dying?"

"Yes."

"Well, he should write one that talks about how to live like you were dead. It's much better." She was chatty. The excitement of the city had settled in her. "I like it here. People sit at cafés, drink beer, smoke cigarettes, eat desserts and taste them, like really taste them. They watch the afternoon go by." She shook her head. "Americans never watch the afternoon go by. It's silly to us. We think, 'Why would we do that?' We are always in a hurry, always on to the next minute and never enjoying the one we are in, and no one is a worse offender than me. I am, or was, always on to the next thing, never on this thing, never this right now. I used to send somewhere between a hundred and two hundred texts a day—and most were me telling somebody to do something. Giving orders. Success here is a bottle of wine, fresh flowers, or a loaf of bread just out of the oven. Sweet cream butter and a plate of olives. They get six weeks' vacation and work thirty-five-hour workweeks. They don't need three closets of clothes and four cars. They need right now. They live right now. Not tomorrow." She stood, walked to a corner vendor, bought a package of cigarettes, returned, packed them on her leg, and lit one, inhaling deeply. When she'd filled her lungs, she laid her head back and blew the smoke up and out.

"You smoke?" I said.

Another inhale followed by a smile. The smoke trailed up and out the corner of her mouth. "Only in Paris."

I whispered, "In your—" I looked over my

shoulder. "Did you play many French roles?"

She stamped the cigarette and shook her head. "None."

"Why?"

She stared up at the tower, now lit with a million lights. The memory rising to the surface. "My father used to bring me here." The full moon above the Eiffel Tower had her attention. "We rode the train."

The pieces fell together. "You're French?"

A sip of wine. "*Oui.*"

"That means 'yes,' right?"

The red wine colored the tip of her lips. She let the taste linger. "*Oui.*"

I paused. "Who else knows this?"

"Just you."

"What about that Richard Thomas guy?"

"I told him a few of my secrets, but not this one."

"Steady?"

She shook her head. "English was one of my favorite subjects in school, and I was able to speak it with very little accent by the time I met him." She spoke without giving it much thought. "About forty percent of English is actually of French origin."

"Get out of town."

"You don't believe me?"

She shrugged. The phrases rattled off her tongue like letters of the alphabet. "*Déjà vu, à la mode, pièce de résistance, bon appétit, à la carte, en masse, art deco, nouveau riche, au contraire, au naturel, au pair, au revoir, je ne sais quoi, fait accompli . . .*" She counted on her fingers as she made her point. Each finger popping up in unison with the words as she spoke them. "*Avant garde, bon voyage, RSVP, chaise longue, crème de la crème, café au lait, potpourri, carte blanche, laissez-faire, grand prix, cordon bleu, coup d'état, esprit de corps, crème brûlée, cul-de-sac, faux pas, double entendre, en route, art nouveau, film noir, Mardi Gras, nom de plume, papier-mâché, c'est la vie, raison d'être, tour de force, vis-à-vis . . .*"

She was still rattling when I cut her off. "Okay, okay. You made your point. You lost me about fifty words ago." I didn't say it but I loved the way the words rolled off her tongue. The way she made and formed the words. So much of the French language slipped by my ear before I had a chance to catch the slightest hint of a word, but the entirety of it, the way it all ran together seamlessly—it just worked. I'm no linguist but in my limited book, whoever said it was right, the French language has got the hands-down monopoly on the beauty of the spoken word.

Across from us, a bookstore sat facing the café. Given the foot traffic in and out, they experienced a brisk business. Thomas's book, *The Ice Queen*, filled the display—a newly translated

French version with never-before-seen photos from his personal collection. His smug enlarged picture stared at us. He was milking this for every cent. A banner above the stacks of copies announced #1 BEST SELLER. She glanced at it, shook her head, and said, "It keeps following me. And so little of it is true."

"You read it?" The fact surprised me.

Her eyes fell on the arc and the traffic circling it. The index finger on her right hand unconsciously began tracing the lines of the scar on her left wrist. "Yeah, I read it." She nodded over her shoulder without eyeing the book. "He's made the rounds of the late-night tell-alls, earned millions in royalties, and on what? My coattails and just enough truth to make it plausible." She looked at me. "You want to know the truth?" She didn't wait for me to answer. "The truth is that in the first hundred pages, he tells more than twenty-seven outright, bold-faced lies and he knows they are lies because he asked me and I told him they were. In many cases, I gave him the evidence proving they were." She smacked the palm of her hand. "I showed him in black and white." She shooed the idea of him like she was getting rid of a dog or a pigeon. "His book is nothing more than a tabloid cut-and-paste." She waved her hand across the bookstore. "What's amazing is that people read that crap." A shake of her head. "Number one! Who in their right mind bought that thing?" A shake of her head. "Some-body told me when I first got in the business that people believe what they read until somebody prints something that contradicts it. Then they believe both." She shrugged it off. Something she was good at. Maybe that comes with lots of practice.

I paid the tab and we began walking. I tried to make light of the book. "I don't like him."

"Who?"

"Queequeg."

She looked confused. "Who?"

"Thomas."

She smiled. "Good one. Wish I'd thought of it." After a shrug, she said, *"On n'apprend pas aux vieux singes à faire des grimaces."*

"I need a little help with that one."

"You cannot teach old monkeys to make faces."

Whatever I'd thought of Katie Quinn when I'd first met her was untrue. I'd jumped to wrong conclusions. And many at that. The last few days had proven that. What I was learning now, in these last few hours, was telling me I hadn't even scratched the surface.

Our path took us by the store. Once closer, we were able to see that a tabloid magazine had been placed in a plastic stand below the books. The cover of the magazine showed the book along with a not-so-flattering picture of Katie. The caption quoted an unnamed source as saying, "She

203

was a monster. Anyone who knew her, knew this."

Katie didn't speak for several minutes. When she did, her voice was quiet, as she stared through the window. "I don't even know that person. How do they know what I am?" Another moment. A nod. Crossed arms. She turned, looking at me through dark glasses. A tear fell from beneath her right eye. Despite her critics, Katie was human. Her tough veneer was paper thin. "But I am a monster, all right. Just not the kind he talks about in that book." She spoke almost to herself. "He hasn't got a clue."

Her ability to deflect was uncanny. She eyed the tower, hooked her arm in mine, and said, "Let's go up."

Chapter Nineteen

We bought two tickets and rode the elevator up while I marveled at her ability to shake off what sought to bring her down. One second she's talking about a man who betrayed her, and deeply, and the next she's marveling at the Eiffel Tower. We exited at the second floor, then took a second elevator to the top. When we stepped off, the wind pressed against us. Gentle, then a gust, finally calming. The Seine River stretched out from one end of the earth to the other. Paris lay all around us like a glowing landscape, electric sunshine poking through the carpet of the earth's floor, pinholes of light streaking through the weak places where the fabric had worn thin. "That red dot over there is Moulin Rouge."

"What's that?"

"You didn't see the movie?"

I just stared at her.

"How about the paintings by Toulouse-Lautrec?"

"Lady, I live on a boat."

She mimicked a few dance moves involving her hips that were actually quite good. "You've heard the song, right, 'Lady Marmalade'?"

"Lady what?"

A frown. "Honey, you need to come out from underneath your rock." More dance moves. She sang quietly beneath her breath. " '*Voulez-vous coucher avec moi ce soir*?' "

"I should probably know what that means, right?"

She shook her head, placed her index finger on her lips like she was reconsidering. "On second thought, probably not." A slight chuckle. Laughter at my expense.

"You're laughing at me, right?"

"Pretty much, but the fact that you don't know is cute so—" She leaned on the railing. "Moulin Rouge means 'red mill.' What *it is,* is the world-renowned Parisian cabaret. Home of the cancan. They put on quite a show. Many of the greats have performed there: Ella Fitzgerald, Liza Minelli, Ol' Blue Eyes."

"That little thing you did with your hips, where'd you get all the rhythm?"

A laugh. "Like everything else . . ." Her eyes wandered out across the city. ". . . I paid for it."

A pause. A slight breeze. "This your favorite city?"

She weighed this. "Close, but no."

"What is?"

She pointed southwest. "That way. A few hours. Town called Langeais." She pronounced it "lon-jay."

People milled around us. Taking photos. A kid next to her leaned against the railing and waited for the flash. Her friend backed up a few feet and held the camera to include as much of Paris in the background as she could. Ever cognizant of those around her, Katie turned slightly toward me, allowing the shadow to fall across her face. Incognito. She said, "Ever been to Paris before?"

"Once. Long time ago."

"Business? Work?"

Another gust. "Something like that. Although I loved what I did, so I wouldn't really call it 'work.' " I changed the subject. "I'm no linguist, and I can't speak a lick of French, but yours is very good."

"It should be." Her eyes wandered across the landscape below. "I used to get so homesick, even when I was filming, that I'd come here—even if I only had twenty-four hours, just to hear people speak, smell the bakeries, sip the coffee."

"Seems like it would have helped you to use it in a lot of movies?"

"When I moved to the U.S., and started over in—" She laughed. "Miami—"

"Why Miami?" I interrupted.

"It was where the plane stopped on the way to Kansas."

"What in the world would take you from Paris to Kansas?"

"Judy Garland."

"I'm not tracking with—"

"*The Wizard of Oz*." A shrug. "For some reason, I thought my future started in Kansas. Worked for Dorothy. Why not me?"

"So, why didn't you get past Miami?"

Another easy laugh, as if the memory was no longer painful. "Ran out of money when I got off the plane, so I went in search of a safe place to sleep. Exited the bus in front of this gigantic Catholic church, started wandering the sidewalks, and then I saw this man in flowing white robes smoking a pipe. I guess I did look a little lost. Steady took me in, found me a place to sleep with some of his parishioners, and then walked me to the theater. Introduced me. I auditioned, put my talents to work, and made a few bucks. I was saving money for a plane ticket when things started taking off and Kansas became irrelevant."

"And all because of *The Wizard of Oz.*"

She spoke without looking at me. "A story can be a powerful thing."

I waited. Said nothing.

She continued. "I didn't want folks to know I was from here. Didn't want to—" She shook it off. Glanced at her watch. "Come on, we don't want to miss our train."

I watched her move. Listened to her talk. Felt the easy, measured rhythm of her breathing. If anyone was ever in their element it was her, here.

We returned the scooters to their garage home, where she packed a backpack with a few items of clothing and then transformed back into another of her unrecognizable selves. We rode the metro to the train station to catch an 11:10 p.m. train to Langeais. Unlike almost anything America, it was exactly on time. We climbed on. The train was mostly empty. A couple of sleeping passengers dotted the seats. She glanced around, whispering, "I love the train at night."

We found our seats. Facing each other. Separated by a table. She stretched her legs out and sort of through mine. We had the entire car to ourselves.

The doors shut and the train left the station, gradually increasing speed to somewhere above a hundred miles an hour. Didn't take us long to leave town and enter rolling hillsides. The moon had risen higher, grown larger, and shone brighter since we left the Eiffel Tower, throwing long shadows across the French landscape. She stared out the glass and, from what I could tell, was watching old memories more than French countryside.

Chapter Twenty

We slept a few hours on the train. Off and on. Me more than Katie. At three a.m., the train pulled to a stop at the Langeais station and the door slid open. We exited onto the platform next to a bright red wooden train car that looked to be a hundred years old. Freshly painted, brass plaques; a star of David covered one side. She ran her fingers alongside the edge, finally dipping her fingers into the brass letters, tracing the words. She read out loud. " 'This car ferried more than a hundred and forty thousand "prisoners" to the death camps.' "

We crossed the street and began the walk through town. Two main streets. Shops on either side. Cafés. Bakeries. Butcher shops. A shoe store. Hair salon. Candy maker. Several bars. She almost skipped as she walked. "About twenty-five hundred people live here."

She stopped at the end of Main Street. "In World War II, the Gestapo occupied this area." She pointed to an enormous castle rising up, over, and out of the town like the rock of Gibraltar. Château de Langeais. Lit from every angle. "French resisters were hung from those walls."

"You like history?"

She weighed this, choosing her words. "I value it."

I shouldered my backpack and offered to take hers, but she waved me off. "No, I'm okay." We began walking through the medieval town, winding through the narrow streets. She walked slowly. A sailor on dry ground after months at sea.

I said, "Is it far?"

She smiled, jumping over the cracks in the sidewalk. "Is what far?"

I pointed into the darkness. "Wherever we're going."

She shook her head. "A mile. A little less."

The cobblestone road serpentined and rose upward slightly. Shops gave way to a small creek, a cemetery, a church. She pointed to the last. "That's more than a thousand years old."

The road had been carved next to the church so the doors of the church literally poured out onto the street. We stopped and she ran her fingers through the intricate carving on the thick, twelve-foot doors, darkened by exhaust.

"How old were you when you left here?"

"Just shy of sixteen."

"Why 'Katie Quinn'?"

A shrug. "Has a good ring. Rolls off your tongue."

"You picked a name because it has a good ring and rolls off your tongue."

A nod. "And because it was nothing like the name my father gave me."

"Which is?"

"Isabella."

"Isabella is your real name? I thought it was just the name of the woman you're pretending to be right now."

"Well, it's both. When I was sixteen, I left Isabella behind, only to dig her back up when fame and fortune drove me to resurrect her. So now, Isabella is the woman you see and the one that allows me to fly back and forth unnoticed." A long silence. "My father said it was his mother's name. Said she held me once before she died. Whispered my name in my ear. In public, he called me 'Bella.' It means 'beauty.' " She shook her head. "Which I needed to hear because, despite what you and others see, and what I've spent a small fortune obtaining, I wasn't."

"You're kidding."

She turned and led me uphill. "I was a fat, zit-faced kid with thick glasses, braces, and slight strabismus."

"Stra-what?"

"Bismus." She looked at me; her pupils both fell inward toward her nose. "I was cross-eyed."

"You're lying."

"Surgery fixed it, but . . ." She allowed her eye to naturally go lazy. It turned slightly. "Every now and then, when I get tired . . ."

"I never knew."

"No one has ever known."

"Well, lots of kids are a little heavy, wear glasses, and have crooked teeth."

She nodded. "Yep, and that was to my benefit as I got older."

"How so?"

"I had blended in and was so unremarkable for so long, that when I became 'remarkable,' no one recognized me. No one put the pieces together."

We approached a tall gate. She punched a code into the electronic keypad and it slowly opened. Electronic lights, strung along the driveway, automatically lit like dominoes climbing the hill, outlining a quarter mile path up through the trees to a building large enough to suggest either a hotel or a castle. She crossed her arms. Warmed by a memory of which she did not speak.

I followed her up the drive. Her step quickened. She spoke as she walked. "There's been a structure on this property for over a thousand years. The first was wooden. Later, stone." She waved her hand across the rolling lawn to the right. "Using a metal detector, I found spent U.S. rifle casings out there in the dirt." She pointed in another direction, off to one side of the house. "Found a gold Roman coin over there."

We wound through the trees and up the drive. When we reached the top, she waved her hand across the spiraled, four-story structure in front of me, the pool to our left, the gardens on the hill behind, and the four other buildings scattered throughout the property, each lit both from the ground up and from the trees down. Set on a hill, it was an enormous estate. I'd never seen anything like it. "Welcome to Châteaufort." She turned around. Several acres of tightly manicured lawn rolled out before us. It looked like the Masters in April. Beyond that, Langeais spread in the valley below.

"This is yours?"

She eyed the expanse of the building, the acreage beyond. A nod. An honest admission. "It's my home."

Both eyebrows raised. "Your family owned this?"

A chuckle. "I didn't say that. I said, 'It's my home.'" She pointed at the intersection of the driveway and the sidewalk. The remains of a tree trunk rose up through the mulch alongside the sidewalk. She pushed her sleeve above the elbow, exposing a small scar. "Fell out of that tree. I held it together until I saw the bone sticking through."

"What were you doing?"

She glanced at the second-story window above

us. "Climbing out of my bedroom window about this time of night." She tugged on my arm. "Come on."

She unlocked a side door and let me into a wood-paneled and carved foyer. A large fireplace to one side. Grand stairwell in the background. Painting of an older woman above the mantel. Green velvet dress. Diamond necklace. Probably in her late seventies when she sat for the portrait. She pointed at the mantel. "The countess. She owned Châteaufort when the Gestapo knocked down the front door, demanding that she leave. At the time, her husband's portrait sat above the mantel. A German duke with a chest full of medals. She stood on the stairwell in her best dress and pointed at his portrait. The German officer saluted the portrait, turned around, and Châteaufort was spared the ravages of World War II."

"How do you know this?"

A longing look. Her tone of voice shifted. Gentler. "She told me."

She grabbed two flashlights out of a drawer and glanced at her watch. "We have a few hours until the staff discovers I'm here. How about a tour?"

"Staff?"

More laughter. "Come on."

Chapter Twenty-one

The oldest portion of the château was over five hundred years old. Twelve-foot ceilings. Dark wooden floors, each plank a foot wide. Walls of stone upon ancient stone. Covered in wood panel or paper or velvet or some type of silk. A fireplace in every room. The music room had ebony walls with acoustic tiles centered around a Steinway. The circular staircase that wound up four floors had settled and leaned in toward the middle. She ran her hand along the railing and stared up. "I used to get dizzy riding this thing." The dining room table would seat a dozen—on either side. The room sparkled with crystal and china. She pointed. "Those are faiences—china made here from the 1880s on into this century. The brown and red are the most desirable. The color comes from the soil." She shook her head. "Nowhere else in the world." We climbed to the second floor. "At its peak, it had sixty-four rooms." She began opening doors. "I thought they were small, so I converted them into thirteen suites."

"Why thirteen?"

"It's just the way the layout and architecture worked."

"You ever entertained? Had guests?"

She shook her head. "No. Just me, and the memories I keep."

Each room had a different theme. One was blue, another red, another stripes with airplanes. She led me to the third floor and down to the corner room at the far end of the hall. She pushed open the door. "You may sleep in any of them, but I thought you might like this one."

The room was enormous. A king-size bed. Two different sitting areas. The bathroom was connected via a hallway and larger than some bedrooms I've slept in. I walked to the windows. The view spanned from the garden on the hill behind to Château de Langeais and all of the town. She opened two opposing windows, allowing the air to circulate. "I thought the breeze might remind you of your boat."

My boat seemed a world away. I tried to make light of it. "I own a boat?" She smiled. I said, "Thank you. This will do just fine."

She walked to a painting on the wall, gently running her finger along the gold frame. "Sometimes I come up here, sit, and just stare."

I looked closer at the painting. An older woman, no teeth, wrinkles, gnarled hands, a dirty apron, laughter in her eyes. She stood back, taking in the painting. "Isn't she beautiful?"

"Is that really a Rembrandt?"

She waved her hand across the room. Eight

paintings hung on the walls, subtly lit by overhead lights. "Several are."

"You own a Rembrandt?"

A shrug. "And Gauguin."

"Sorry. Don't know him."

"He's the guy that Van Gogh was arguing with
just before he cut off his own ear."

"Sounds like a great friend."

"Other than deep bouts of depression and the
occasional tendency toward suicide, he was
probably a great friend."

"Why these?"

She walked by each. Hands behind her back.
"Two reasons: In an era when artists edited
reality, painting people as they wished they were,
they painted them as they were. Warts and all.
What the French call '*d'un beau affreux.*' "

"What's it mean?"

" 'The beautiful-ugly.' " She returned to the
toothless woman. "Somehow they found the
beauty they were born with and made it rise off
the canvas." She traced the frame with her fingers.
"They are my reminder."

The two styles were different. One more
detailed—it made more sense up close. The other
more loose. It made more sense the farther
away you stood. "Of?"

"Gauguin called it '*le laid peut être beau.*' Or,
'the ugly can be beautiful.' It's the idea that what
we are is worth painting." She nodded. "That

we're good enough before we try to be. Before we open our eyes." A longing look. "I've never done a portrait. Been asked a lot. Been offered a lot of money, but never did it." An assertive nod. "But I'd sit for either of those guys."

"What's the second reason?"

She paused. Glanced up. "Because no matter how screwed up the artist might be, there's still the chance that they can produce art that people like us hang on our wall and talk about long after their death. That the sum is greater than one part. That maybe one incident does not a life make." She rubbed her face with both hands. Tried to hide a yawn. "I've hit the wall. I'm off to bed. See you in the morning."

I glanced at the gardens. The other buildings. I was having fun. "What about the rest?"

"Some other time. See you at breakfast?"

"Sure."

She walked to the landing at the top of the stairs, turned a knob that looked like it was part of the curtain, and a door I had not seen opened behind her. A door hidden behind a large painting of the château, completely concealed. The door swung open and revealed a small, wooden spiral stair-case to what would be the fourth floor. She put her foot on the stair, and spoke down behind her. *Mi casa es su casa.*

"Seems like I've heard that before."

She waved her hand across the house. "Make

yourself at home." She smiled. "Good night." And pulled the door closed behind her. The door completely disappeared.

I sat in my room, on the end of my bed, staring at all the eyes staring back at me. I thought about the château. Hard to imagine that something so beautiful was not lived in. Thirteen empty suites? Not shared, known, or enjoyed. The enormity of that struck me.

I got in bed, opened my journal, and followed her movements via the sound of creaking floor-boards above me. An hour later, somewhere close to four a.m., I heard a door shut and she slowly descended the stairs. Below, a few doors opened, closed, and then rising out of the far end of the house, I heard the piano. Quiet. Soothing. Gentle. Longing. I sat at the top of the stairs, listening. A pencil in my hand. She played one song, then another, then climbed the stairs.

Unable to hold my eyes open any longer, I climbed back into bed, my journal spread across my chest, and slept.

Chapter Twenty-two

An hour and a half later, she shook my shoulder. "I think I have something you're going to want to do." She wore no disguise. Just the framing.

I sat up. Rubbed my eyes. "Don't you ever sleep?"

An empty mug was wrapped in her hands. "Not much. Come on."

She led me to a room in the back of the house that I'd not yet seen. Four fly rods hung on the wall. I pulled one down. "I'm impressed. Thought you didn't know how to fish."

She shook her head. "I don't, but I paid a consultant who told me that if I took up fishing, and if I got real good, that I'd appreciate these and the day I bought them. I keep promising myself I'll learn—"

"Loomis." I surveyed the rod. "You have good taste." She grabbed a scarf and her bug-eyed glasses, and we walked out the back of the house and down a scarcely worn trail through the trees that led away from the house. Her flashlight showered the ground below her. She waved her hand across the hillside opposite the château. "I own a couple hundred acres that way. And that way." Another wave. "And I own the stream down there. If we bump into anybody, they're trespassing and you get to handle it."

We walked a half mile to a stream about the width of a road. We approached slowly. She whispered, "I have it stocked every spring."

"But you don't fish it?"

"Nope."

I began stripping line.

I walked her to the stream's edge, stood behind her, and placed the rod in her hands. The grass bank was open, and looked like it flooded occasionally, which explained why the trees were pushed back off the bank. Made for easy fly casting. Working together—her back pressed to my chest—I showed her how to begin throwing the line, making smaller loops, then larger. Finally, large figure eights.

She stood next to me. Bumping my shoulder. She had gotten playful with me. At ease. Comfortable. Which I didn't mind.

The pretense, the walls, the measured self—all were coming down. Peeling away. Shedding. The best word I could think of was "sobering." She had been sobered. Or, stripped. Unloaded. Absent baggage. Traveling lightly. The woman I'd first met in the fifteen-million-dollar penthouse condo had given way to someone I'd not anticipated. A person I found myself not disliking.

The fish were hungry, had never been "fished," had never seen a fly, and jumped at anything she threw at them.

In less than twenty minutes, she'd caught nine fish. She'd catch, reel it in, I'd unhook it, release it, and she'd start fishing again. A half hour later, she was giddy. Over the next two hours, we walked the length of her stream, nearly a mile, and caught over eighty fish. Most were less than twelve inches but eighty fish is eighty fish.

Toward nine a.m., she lay down on the bank, a snow angel in the grass. She was laughing. Smiling. Rubbing her sore arm. "That was the best day of fishing I've ever had."

I studied the stream and the twelve fish on a stringer in my hand. "Yeah, it might be tough to beat that one."

She picked a flower. Turning it. A berry encased in a cup or an orange-red lantern. An incredible creation of nature. It reminded me of a dogwood bloom. She said, "It's called '*l'amour en cage.*' "

"What's it mean?"

" 'Love in prison.' "

"Strange name for a flower."

"Not when it's the only name you've ever known."

I didn't answer. She didn't hesitate. She caught me off guard, which was how she planned most of our interactions. "What do you miss?"

"What do you mean?"

"Is there something in your life that you used to do that you don't do anymore that you miss?"

That was easy and the answer didn't reveal too much. "I miss making people smile and being the reason."

She turned and started walking uphill toward the house.

"Bring the fish. You're cooking breakfast."

We returned to find the staff had stocked the kitchen with fresh produce in our absence. Katie slipped upstairs to change into Isabella, then cooked breakfast, which was an odd combination of the sautéed fish, and crêpes soaked in butter and Grand Marnier. I offered to help but was met by a stop-sign hand. "Out." Evidently, the French are sensitive about their kitchens. Or, at the least, protective. When I noted to Katie that we were drinking at ten a.m., she shrugged. "Let your hair down a little. This is France."

Which seemed to be her response to most everything since we'd arrived.

After breakfast, I sat down in a lounge chair next to the kitchen and the combination of no sleep mixed with pancake carbs mixed with butter mixed with Grand Marnier made for a deep and fantastic nap. Next thing I knew a noise woke me. I could hear the hum of a vacuum cleaner some-where down the hall, and a woman outside talking with a man. I checked my watch. 11:45. I rubbed my eyes. It still said 11:45. I walked to the window. The woman was older. Maybe fifties. Silver hair in a clip. A crumpled straw hat. Over-alls. Dirty hands. Slight curve to her back. A limp. Fresh flowers in pots next to her. Several had already been planted. The woman was kneeling, digging in the dirt, not afraid to get her hands dirty.

When I appeared at the window, the woman gardener shaded her eyes, winked at me, pointed at the kitchen, and then opened her hand, extending all five fingers. I climbed into the shower mumbling to myself, "How many different women is this woman?"

I shaved, dressed, and found fresh coffee waiting on me when I got to the kitchen. Gretta the gardener greeted me in the kitchen.

Gretta smiled at me. I shook my head, grabbed a cup of coffee, and sat at the table. She whispered, "The locals and the rest of staff think all of this is owned by a wealthy hedge-fund owner out of Connecticut." A shrug. "Which is partly true. I set up a Connecticut-based shell of a company called Perrault and Partners, Inc., which, after you jump through a bunch of technical hoops and wild-goose chases, shows that Isabella Desouches is the sole shareholder. The company owns this and"—another shrug— "other assets." A smile. "Perrault employs several full-time staff here, so I 'play' various roles as needed, but I have two regular characters. A distant relative of the owner who lives in a flat in Paris, but loves to garden and comes here on occasion to do so." A smile with a slight curtsey. "And the redheaded Isabella woman with whom you flew here."

When Steady said there were three of her, he wasn't kidding. There was no telling how many faces this woman had.

"Sometimes I choose just one when I'm here, sometimes several. I've even played Isabella's assistant and Isabella on the same trip. Depends on how long I'm here, who I'll see, what I need to do. There are a few part-time employees who work in the house—cleaning, maintenance, stocking the kitchen. And it's a small town, so being several characters keeps people from getting too inquisitive about any particular one."

She pointed out the window. "The other employees work over that hill at the vineyard."

I almost choked on my coffee. "Vineyard?"

A smile. Both eyebrows lifted. "Would you like to see?"

"Lady, I'm so confused right now I don't know if I'm coming or going and I certainly don't have any idea who you are, but yes, if you have vineyards, I'd like to see them."

"Good." She wiped her hands on her apron and served me a frittata, sliced fruit, fresh-squeezed orange juice, and fresh croissants. "Isabella will be your tour guide shortly."

As she was walking off, I asked, "Is this exhausting?"

A look around, followed by a shrug. "What's the value of anonymity?"

I shrugged. "I suppose it's worth a good bit more after it's been lost?"

A chuckle. "You might say."

She disappeared through the door and I mumbled to myself, "I feel like I'm traveling with the female Scarlet Pimpernel."

She hollered down from the stairs. " 'We seek him here, we seek him there. Those Frenchies seek him everywhere. Is he in heaven?—Is he in hell? That damned, elusive Pimpernel.' "

Chapter Twenty-three

Carrying her clipboard and best don't-mess-with-me expression, Isabella and I left the house, walked to the garage, and hopped into a golf cart with knobby tires. She drove me around the house, up a hill, down a long dirt road and to a small summit, which turned out to be the highest point for miles. We could see the roof of the château behind us, Langeais beyond, and pasture around us. She drove slowly forward, revealing the other side of the hill. Or, hills.

Vineyards, as far as the eye could see.

I guess my jaw opened slightly because she reached up and touched it with her index finger. "Careful, or you'll catch flies."

"That's yours."

A nod.

We drove down through the vineyards. The thick vine bases rose two feet out of the ground and new shoots were already climbing along taut wire stretched between what seemed like miles of symmetrical rows. I pointed. "How do you have time to manage this?"

"Well, I don't. I hired a guy who does. We're a relatively small vineyard. Boutique, really. We make a small profit. I pay him well, give him incentives, and he's all too happy to help Perrault and Partners make good wine." A sly look. "Would you like to taste it?"

I nodded and we drove down the hill. I pulled my Costas down over my eyes. "You get more interesting the more I get to know you."

She laughed. "Which one of me?"

She drove to an old barn lined with metal-looking barrels and computerized modern machinery. She motioned to the barrels. "We don't use oak anymore. Just aluminum."

From the far corner, a tall, midfifties, freckled man with wild carrot-red hair walked out of an office. He looked like he'd just stuck his finger in an electrical outlet. His top lip was taut, his accent was thick Australian, and his smile spread ear to ear.

He bear-hugged Isabella. Then me. She spoke in French to begin with, then transitioned to English. When she finished, he responded to her in French, then turned to me and spoke in English. "Welcome, mate." He stuck out a callused, thick, muscled hand. "Ian Murphy. If you need any-thing . . ." I liked him immediately.

Isabella led me to a table where he uncorked several bottles. Two white. Two red. One sparkling. He handed me a glass. He turned his, spinning the wine. He called it "aerating." Then he gulped, swirled it around his mouth, gargled, and spat in a spittoon-looking thing at his feet. Oddly, Isabella did the same. She gulped, swirled, gargled, and spat with some precision. She motioned for me. I sipped, swirled, and swallowed.

She said, "You're supposed to spit it out."

I held up the glass. The wine was really good. "I'm not much of a wine person, but I'm not about to spit that out."

Ian laughed deeply, welcoming my comments. He talked freely about the wine, and the process. He used words like "volume," "sticks to your cheeks," "muscular structure," "aerobatic something-or-other." I didn't understand a word he said, but in five seconds I was pretty well convinced that he knew more about wine than I'd ever known in my life. He poured a second, then a third, a fourth, and finally a fifth. He smiled, proudly. Holding the bottle to the sunlight. "A 2005. Best wine year on record. Maybe ever. Ninety-nine points." He poured. "It's firm in the mouth. You can taste the complex body of flavors." I didn't know anything about firmness or complex flavors but it tasted like really good red wine to me. I nodded. A young man's French voice hollered from the back of the barn. He set down his glass. "Great to meet you, mate. If I can do anything—" He shook my hand and returned to the barn.

"What did you tell him?"

"You mean, as in 'Why are you here?' "

"Yes."

"I told him you were a buyer from a distributor in the U.S."

I could imagine how convincing I was. But if Ian thought I was someone else to Isabella, he gave no indication.

She looked at me, a long few seconds. Considering something. Considering me. She tucked her clipboard under her arm. "Come on. I want to show you something."

She drove me back toward the château, taking another road. We skirted the hillside and came upon another barn-garage-looking structure and several doors that led into the rock wall below the château.

She stepped out, waving her hands across the iron doors that led into what looked like caves dug into the rock. "More than a thousand years ago, the people that lived along the Loire River —called Troglodytes—came up here and dug, for lack of a better word, 'homes,' into the rock walls. Those caves grew over time." She unlocked the first door and clicked on a series of light switches on the wall. The cave lit up to reveal it wound deep into the mountain. The entrance was large enough to drive a tractor-trailer through. We followed the primary cave, lined with smaller caves on each side. She pulled a flashlight off its charging post on the wall and shone it into the smaller caves. Each was lined with bottles of wine. Labeled by year. The farther we got back into the cave, the older the dates became. Finally, maybe some two to three hundred meters into the mountain, she walked me to a set of steps, cut into the rock, leading down. She flicked another switch and lights, hung along the wall, shone yellow and dull. At the bottom, she unlocked an iron gate and swung it open. It creaked. Another light switch. This cave was smaller. Low ceiling. Barely tall enough for me to stand in. She pointed her flashlight at a hole in the ceiling. Two bats hung sleeping. She pressed her fingers to her lips, turned left, and walked to another iron door. Like the other caves, the walls around us were lined with numbered bins all stacked high with bottles. "The temperature stays constant at fifty-two Fahrenheit, year round. Perfect for wine." She unlocked the large iron door, pulled it open, another light switch, and we stepped in. She said, "My father's room. Where he kept his Reserva." The room was filled with thousands of bottles of wine. She pointed at a bin labeled "1977 Isabella." "He bottled that the year I was born. Set it aside for my wedding." The dates went back to the 1920s. She continued. "Some of it's gone bad. Some"—a confident shrug—"hasn't."

She looked at me. "My father was the head gardener. Eventually, once he'd won the confidence of the countess after her husband died, he oversaw the vineyard as well." A look away. Then another look at me. Into me. "He was what the countess liked to call a 'purple-tinted-finger, eccentric genius of the vine.' My mother cleaned the house, washed linens, and left when I was less than a year old. I have no memory of her. I—" She ran her fingers along the dusty bottles. "I was the ugly kid with glasses and hair down over her face. Dad couldn't afford childcare so I ran to town, the market, bakery, washed floors, and tried to make myself both useful and invisible."

She looked around. "By the time the countess died . . ." A shrug. "I'd been gone a decade and made a little money. Was over here on a vacation of sorts. Saw a sign on the front gate about it being sold at auction. It was run-down. In disrepair. The countess was a widow, had no family, and through the years she'd sold bits and pieces because she needed the money. Châteaufort was a shadow of its former self. I walked into the bank and bought it that day. As I made more, I bought more. Putting it back the way my father would have known it." A glance around. "I thought he'd like that."

The underground was a maze of one cave after another and more wine than I'd ever seen in my life. "About a quarter of this wine was down here when I bought it. Much of which was my father's."

"You all have been working hard."

"Ian has. Not me." A fun smile. "I just sign the checks." She reached in her pocket. "Speaking of checks—" She handed me a wad of euros. "In case you get lost."

"Thanks."

She smirked. "Consider it payment for services rendered."

I laughed and pocketed the money.

It was late afternoon when we exited the caves. Sun going down. Coolness in the air. She turned to me, pointing at the château. "Think you can find your way back?"

I nodded. She turned. Almost said something. Didn't. Then spoke over her shoulder. "I need to do a few things. Can you entertain yourself a few hours?"

"Sure."

"I won't be gone long. How about you let me cook you dinner? Say, eight?"

"Can I help?"

Another fun smile. "No, but you can watch." She waved her hand across the world. "This is France. Food is an experience." She walked off, then turned. "If you're nice, I'll let you open a good bottle of wine. And if you don't turn your nose up at my cooking, I'll let you actually step foot in the kitchen—which is a big deal."

Chapter Twenty-four

— I waved, watched her walk to the garage and climb into a silver Mini Cooper with tinted windows. She pulled up next to me and rolled down a window. "If you go into town, you'd do well to remember three very important words: '*s'il vous plaît.*'" She pulled her sunglasses down over her eyes, shifted into first, let off the clutch, and exited a driveway that led out through the trees opposite the front entrance. Through the trees, I heard the engine whine, and she shifted into third before fading behind the hill.

I turned around and looked at the château towering above me at the top of the hill. That enormous shell of a house that housed no one. Where memories walked the halls. Something in my gut started to hurt. Pain is not an accurate description. But I don't know what else to call it. I wanted to call Steady and ask him what he'd gotten me into but I had an idea he knew all too well. That's why he sent me. And make no mistake about it—Katie, or Isabella, might have thought she was inviting me or ordering me or whatever, but she and I were little more than puppets.

If I thought I was screwed up, I had another thing coming. I lived one lie. This woman lived multiple. Simultaneously. She was probably a genius, illustrated by the fact that she kept it all straight. No wonder she'd won three Academy Awards. If they knew what she was really like, they'd give her one for each persona—Daisy the well-endowed ditz, Ashley the long-legged Asian lingerie model, Isabella the don't-mess-with-me-I-don't-have-time-for-you CEO, Gretta the haggard, arthritic gardener. There's no telling who would be in the kitchen tonight. And while anonymity explained some of them, it did not justify them all. One or two would get the job done. This many had its roots in something else. Something about the number of them bothered me. As in, Katie was trying really hard *not* to be someone in particular.

I had a few hours, so I grabbed my wallet and walked down the drive and into town. Maybe I could order a cup of coffee. I walked the mile to town, past the thousand-year-old church, around the rock-of-Gibraltar Château de Langeais, and into the center of town, where my nose led me to a bakery. I sat at a table and a server approached me. "*Bonjour.*"

I held up one finger. "Coffee?"

She said, "*Americain?*"

I nodded, figuring if she was offering, I was agreeing.

She smiled, nodded, and disappeared inside. When she returned with what looked like a cup of coffee, I pointed at the window and the many croissants displayed in the glass. "Croissant?"

She said, "Shoco-lott?" The word exited her mouth emphasizing all the wrong syllables.

I thought about it. The syllables rolled inside my head, finally registering. "Yes." Then I tried to remember what Katie had told me. I racked my brain, finally speaking. "See view . . . place."

She laughed, grabbed a croissant from the tray inside the window, and placed it on my table. She left me with my coffee and my bread. I was quite proud of myself. I'd just navigated ordering. If I found myself alone, I wouldn't starve. I looked around and realized it was a good thing I didn't have to ask for a bathroom because I'd either be looking for a tree or sitting in a Langeais jail after having made misinterpreted hand gestures that landed me there.

I drank my coffee, which was quite good, and nibbled my chocolate croissant, which had been dipped in butter, baked, and infused with chocolate. After a second cup of coffee and a third croissant, the girl left the check. I left a twenty-euro bill on the table, thinking it would cover my check and her tip. It did. She tried to bring me change but I said, "No," and she smiled.

I figured I'd pressed my luck with the language enough so I stood and began making my way home.

The sound of the engine and the flash of silver caught my eye. A Mini Cooper, tinted windows, wound a serpentine road higher up on the hill. Surely there was more than one. Then she stopped, stepped out, flowers in tow, and began walking across the lawn on the hill above. She was a half mile from me but didn't see me. She was intent on something else. I wound through the streets, up a series of steps, and exited into a cemetery. A very old cemetery. Isabella, covered in a scarf and sunglasses, knelt in a far corner. I held back. Hiding behind old stones and a mausoleum. She brushed the grave, setting the flowers in the brass fixture, and knelt there a long time. I heard her. Talking first, then sobbing. Occasionally, she would say something but I couldn't make it out. The distance garbled it. I'd not seen this side of her. This was unabashed. Unedited. Torn open. Laid bare. Whoever this woman was, this was her.

An hour later, she left. I watched her load into the car and slowly wind around the town toward the château. When she was out of sight, I walked up to the grave. The flowers were fresh. Tears still wet on the marble.

My insides hurt. Like they hadn't hurt in a decade. Old wounds, picked open. The scab and scar, peeled back. I turned, looked away. Pain is pain whether it's yours or someone else's. It's one thing to know it as your own. It's something else to watch it crack someone down the middle.

I wandered back to town. Window-shopping. Part of me wanted to run. Leave this woman and her problems and her pain and skirt back across the ocean. And part of me did not want to do that. My mind raced. Questions I couldn't answer. I felt like Steady was walking alongside me. Heard his heels shuffling. Before long, I was talking with him. Out loud. Or, at least, the idea of him. *Why me? What can I do? What should I do? What would you do? No, don't answer that one.* A woman and her daughter approached, then crossed the street and passed on the other side— keeping a safe distance. Evidently, my conversation had grown animated. An hour later, I found myself staring through the window of a used-bookstore. Katie's biography sat in the display staring back at me. The proprietor had both French and English versions.

I gave in to my curiosity, paid the man, and stuffed the book under my arm.

Chapter Twenty-five

The Ice Queen was a quick read. Easy to get into. He'd cobbled together tabloid rumors and Katie's story with a good dose of his own invention. It began with a scene designed to hook the reader, made as melodramatic as possible. It was about ten years ago, when she had "hit rock bottom."

Yes, some of it was true—Katie had admitted as much—but much was fabricated, and its tone and intent was nothing short of cruel.

By page ten I was ready to put it down. The guy was a gold digger and she was his golden goose.

The sound of banging pots and pans mixed alongside the Allman Brothers drew me to the kitchen. The woman I'd witnessed at the graveside was gone. Someone else had taken her place. This woman was singing, "And I got to run to keep from hiding." Unlike everything else about her, she did not have a good voice. When I poked my head around the corner, she looked like she'd been dipped in flour from ear to elbow. She sneezed, wiggled her nose, waved me forward with a white hand. "Come here. Quick."

I obeyed. She sniffled, pressed her nose against my shoulder, rubbing hard and smearing flour and snot across my shirt. "Thanks," I said.

She sneezed. Then sneezed again. Louder. Finally, she arched her back, took a deep breath, held it, and—drawing the force up from her toes—sneezed a third time. Having sprayed spit across the kitchen and what looked to be our dinner, she shook her head and said, "Wow!"

"You better?"

"Yep."

I thought to myself but spoke out loud. "How can someone so small make such a loud noise?"

"Cheap seats."

"What?"

She pointed to an imaginary row of seats somewhere beyond the kitchen. "Cheap seats. Back row. If you want to reach them, you've got to project."

"Got it."

She was as close to her physical self—whoever that was—as I'd seen her since we left my boat. No wig. No makeup. No fake eyelashes or fake boobs or fake teeth. This was woman stripped bare. I didn't know what to call her. So I started there. "What should I call you?"

She was kneading dough. She smiled, didn't look at me. "Sort of difficult not knowing what to call someone, isn't it?"

I nodded. "Touché."

She motioned to a small bottle of vanilla extract. "You mind?"

I picked it up, screwed off the cap, and handed it to her. "Peter."

She stopped. Her eyes found mine. She considered this, her wheels turning. Maybe a slight recognition. A question surfaced. Or was that just me, reading something into nothing.

I shrugged. "It's my real name."

"And 'Cartwright Jones'?"

"I bought him. Or rather, paid some guys to make his name mine. I thought it'd be good to have if I needed to run farther than I'd already run. I've used it a couple of times to get in and out of Canada."

"Fishing?"

"No, I just wanted to know if it'd work."

"You drove all the way up there to see if your fake passport would let you into Canada?"

A shrug. "Well, yeah, but I was also curious to see if, once out, they'd let me back in."

"A bit paranoid, aren't we?"

"No. Maybe." I smiled. "Okay, yes."

She returned to her ingredients. Smiling. I noticed in moments like these that she talked much like some of the NFL's great running backs played football—she could change directions on a dime. Catching people off guard was her version of a truth serum and a guarded attempt to communicate beneath the surface but only on her terms. "And how far have you run?"

I considered my answer—and its ramifications. I erred on the side of vague honesty. "A long way."

She accepted my answer then scribbled on a piece of paper and handed it to me. "Flashlight in that drawer right there." She pointed to the back of the kitchen. "That door there will drop you down into the wine cellar. The first two are in bin thirty-seven. The third is in forty-three, I think. Maybe forty-four. I get them confused."

I clicked on the light and made my way down into the dungeon, talking to myself. "Yeah, my wine cellar below my château always confuses me, too."

I wound down the stairs, down a hallway lit with a string of lights, down another set of stairs, and eventually into the first large cave we explored that morning. I got my bearings, then descended down the second set of stone steps, and landed in the Reserva. I opened the iron gate, searched the labels, matched them with her note, and began walking out.

The flashlight created the shadow that caught my eye. Small steps carved into the stone at my feet led up and to a small round opening over my shoulder, large enough to turn sideways and wiggle through. I set down the wine, climbed up, and shone the light. It was something of a loft to my current cave. Someplace you had to know about to get to. Get into. I wiggled in, and stood hunched over, my back pressed against the ceiling. The empty room was eight by eight. The entrance was worn where someone—or some-ones—long ago, had slid in and out. The only sign that anyone had ever been here was a hand-carved date on the wall: May 5, 1992. Some twenty years ago. The numbers were curved and not too deep, suggesting a girl had carved them. I traced them with my fingers, doing the math in my mind. If Katie Quinn or Isabella Desouches had carved them, she would have been fifteen. Meaning, a year later, she would land in Miami.

• • •

I returned with the wine and she put me to work setting the table in the smaller of the two dining rooms, which I found down a short hallway from the kitchen. The back of the château sort of bled into the mountain, or hill. That meant that the dining room we were eating in had been shaped into the mountain. A cave itself. Low ceiling. Fireplace. Dark wooden table. Candles on the wall. I set the table, and because the temperature was a constant fifty-two degrees Fahrenheit, I built a fire and lit the candles. No one has ever accused me of being romantic, or even understanding what romance might look like, but I had a feeling that room fell into the category.

Three hours later, we finished the best dinner I'd ever eaten. Three courses. Starting with tomato soup. Three different types of fresh-baked bread. The best butter I'd ever put in my mouth. Lamb. White asparagus topped with parmesan cheese. Some sort of cheesy potato thing. Salad with strawberries and walnuts. And one more thing—the French are serious about their wine and they don't just drink one bottle with dinner. They drink all or part of a bottle with each course. We drank three different bottles: Blanc de Lynch-Bages 2007, Château de Liscous 2005 Saint-Émilion Grand Cru—my favorite—and Château Lafon-Rochet Saint Estephe 1993. I know their names because I wrote them down.

I also learned that French folks do dinner backward. Soup. Main course. Then the salad. And along with the salad comes a selection of what they call cheese. Notice I said *they* call cheese. I didn't say that's what I'd call it. She served the salad, then passed a plate. The smell nearly made me vomit. I gagged. She tried to suppress the smile and look surprised. "What's wrong?"

I turned my head. "*What* is that?"

"Goat cheese?"

It was all I could do not to retch. I handed the plate back.

She proffered again. "Try it."

"No, thank you."

"Really. You'll like it."

I pointed. "That could gag a maggot."

She cut a slice and ate it. Savoring it. "Suit yourself."

She chewed and swallowed.

"How do you eat that?"

"It's a French thing."

I shook my head. She took a bite from a different roll of cheese, this time using a spoon. My lip curled. "You might want to use some mouthwash after that."

The words had just exited my mouth and she was in the process of laughing when we heard a loud and purposeful knock on the door. She stopped chewing, turned white, and began looking around. As in, looking for a place to hide. I asked, "You expecting someone?"

"No."

She looked at herself, shook her head. "I don't have time."

I stood. "I got it."

"What if they speak French?"

"Follow me. Climb the steps to the second floor. If they don't understand me, you can yell down and tell them you're on a conference call."

She followed behind me, holding on to my shirt, hiding behind me. "You're good at this."

"I've had some practice."

We slid through each room, I turned off the lights as we walked. She climbed the steps. A man's shadow stood outside the front door. I stood to the side, clicked on the porch light, and saw Ian Murphy standing on the porch, a bottle in his hand. I pulled open the door. He said, "*Bonjour*, mate."

I still had my napkin in my hand. "Oh, hello."

He leaned his head forward but didn't step inside. "Is Madame Desouches available?"

I was about to open my mouth when she hollered down from the second-floor balcony. The sound echoed through the foyer. "Ian, I'm on a conference call with people in the U.S. Can it wait 'til tomorrow?"

"Oh, right then. Sure thing. Well—" He offered

the bottle. "This is for you. Some of our best. Cheers." He shook my hand.

"Good night."

I stood at the window and watched his red tail-lights disappear down the drive. I felt her walk up behind me. She put a hand on my shoulder. I felt her breath on my neck. "That was close."

I nodded.

She tugged on my shirt. "Come on. Soufflé's getting cold."

"Soufflé?"

We returned to the dining cave. She shook the intrusion off quickly, pulling the soufflés out of the oven and telling me to have a seat and close my eyes. I did. She set it in front of me. As if I could eat another bite. A swollen tick had more room than me. The smell wafted up to my nose. My mouth began watering. She sat. "Okay, dig in."

I opened my eyes. It was a chocolate soufflé covered with some sort of raspberry sauce and dusted with powdered sugar. A scoop of cinnamon ice cream sat along one side.

The mixture of hot and cold, chocolate and raspberry, cinnamon and sugar was celestial. Five minutes later, I set my spoon down. Plate empty. She stared at me over her spoon. "Good?"

"Hands down best dessert ever."

She nodded. "Thank you."

We sat, each painted in reddish-orange firelight and golden candle flame. I was sleepy. The moment was perfect and I tried not to think past it but it was difficult. Pictures of her raced across my mind's eye: covered in flour in the kitchen, standing on my bow casting across the current, seated on a scooter zipping through Paris, weeping at the graveside, standing in the caves beneath us, the various personas. I couldn't shake the thought of the life she had in front of her. How long could she keep it up? How long would she last? And when she let down her guard, who would be there to answer the door?

The candles burned down, the fire died. I pushed back, wiped my mouth. "I think that was the best meal I've ever eaten in my life."

She was lost in the firelight. She spoke without looking at me. "Thank you."

She yawned. I stood. "You cooked. I'll clean."

"Thanks." She dropped her napkin on the table. "I'm going to take a bath and go to bed."

"See you in the morning."

She walked to the door, leaning against the frame. Her toes swept across the floor. "I know you're probably missing your boat about now and . . . I just need a few more days here."

I began collecting our plates. "My boats will be okay without me." I rubbed my swollen tummy. "I'm just starting to get used to the food."

"I guess I should've asked this before. Would you like to see any of the countryside? Maybe a tour before we head back?"

I sensed she was stalling. Needed more time. "I'd like that very much."

"Really?" She seemed surprised by this.

"Really."

"So, you're not in some great hurry to get back?"

"The tarpon don't start running for a couple of weeks. I've got time."

"Must be nice planning your life around the fish."

A shrug.

"Tomorrow morning then?"

"See you in the morning."

I retired to my room and *The Ice Queen*.

Chapter Twenty-six

She appeared bright-eyed at breakfast. A new persona. One I'd not seen. She looked midsixties. White hair pulled back. Pants suit. Narrow waist. The jewelry I'd taken from the bank lockbox in Miami now displayed across her body. Watch. Ring. Necklace. Diamonds were the color of the day. "It's going to be tough for me to take you seriously. I mean . . ." I looked around the kitchen. "At your age, do we need some adult diapers?"

"Funny." She slapped my shoulder and handed me a set of keys. "Hush and go get the car. Black Range Rover. You're the driver."

"Who am I driving?"

"Mrs. Claremont. A wealthy widow, and dear friend of the owner of this château. She always stays in the blue suite when she visits. She likes to redecorate her house in London, and Isabella advises her on where in the area to find the best antiques."

I pointed at the jewelry. "How much is all that worth?"

"Couple hundred."

"Define 'couple hundred.'"

She figured, adding it up. "Six-fifty to seven."

"That's what I figured."

"What do you mean?"

"Now I'm a bodyguard, too."

We pulled out of the drive and exited the gate. She waved her hand across the windshield and the valley beyond. "They call this the 'Valley of the Kings.'"

I laughed. "Well, you'd fit right in."

She smirked. "Are you going to do this all day? If you do, we'll never get through everywhere I want to take you." She was trying not to laugh. "Now, hush. We have a lot of ground to cover."

Another wave. "They say it's the cradle of the French language and, given the vineyards, the garden of France. Hence, beauty is spoken, and grown, here."

"Who's they?"

A smile. "People who know better."

I spoke without looking at her. "Well, they certainly got that one right."

She liked it here. A tulip at daybreak. She laid her head back against the headrest, staring out the window. Her finger pointed directions while her mouth gave the history. "This is the Loire River—the longest river in France at a thousand kilometers long. Today, more than four hundred castles exist along the river. Most private." She swung left. "That large black-and-white bird is called a 'pie.' " She pronounced it "pee." "Looks a lot like the American magpie." She swung right. "Those huge, gorgeous trees are cedars of Lebanon planted sometime in the nineteenth century. You may have heard of them—Solomon used them to build the temple."

"Wow. You really are good."

She shook me off. "Leonardo da Vinci moved to Ambois—which is that way—late in his life, bringing with him three unfinished paintings, one of which was the *Mona Lisa*. He's buried in the chapel at Ambois. We can go there if you like."

I tried to say something cute but she cut me off. "Now, listen up because this is important."

"I am engrossed."

A smile. "Hush. My father used to tell me that the most important date in all of France was November eleventh because three very important things happened."

More bait. I nibbled. "You don't say."

She spoke through her chuckle. "First, it was the date we signed the—"

" 'We'?"

"Yes, we."

"Wouldn't Mr. Thomas be surprised to hear that?"

She shushed me with another wave. "Let me finish. This is important."

I smiled. Saying nothing.

A deep breath. Lecture face resumed. "We signed the armistice with Germany ending World War I. Second, it's St. Martin's Day. St. Martin was a Roman soldier who became a monk and later bishop of Tours. He died in Candes-Saint-Martin on November eleventh, 397."

"Candes-Saint-Martin" echoed in my mind.

She continued. "When he died, mourners took his body upriver to Tours for burial. As his body reached Tours, the flowers in the fields alongside the river bloomed—in winter." She spoke with certainty. "A documented miracle—it's called the 'Summer of St. Martin.' "

"You know if the whole acting thing doesn't pan out, you could hire out as a personal tour guide. You're pretty good. I see real potential."

She ignored me. "And lastly, and, according to my dad, most importantly . . ." Another smile, which she was doing a lot. "It's my birthday."

"I don't suppose Queequeg knew that date, either."

"He knew the date I gave him."

"And your dad?"

A shake of the head. Long silence. "Died when I was fifteen."

"What was his name?"

"Diddier. Diddier Andrais Maximilien Beaunier Claveaux Desouches." A moment passed. A finger in the air. "When it was just us, Papa called me '*ma cherie.*'"

I waited for the translation.

She tasted the words. "It means 'my love.'"

"It's . . . tender."

A nod. "Even more so when it's aimed at you."

We drove for hours. Places named Chenonceau, Villandry, Azay-le-Rideau. She understood the architecture, the gardens, the history. At some locations—depending in large part upon the crowd—we bought a ticket and entered, while others we simply drove by as she explained the who, what, where, when, and why. Her knowledge was encyclopedic.

Late in the afternoon, we stopped at a café alongside the river in Candes-Saint-Martin, the medieval town where the saint was said to have died. The Church of St. Martin rising up above us. More than a thousand years old, its edges were worn and smooth. She pointed at the dozens of headless statues that had been carved high into the walls of the church. She said, "One way to win a religious war is decapitate the things your enemy holds dear."

The café was little more than a bait shack at a boat ramp at the foot of the town. I felt rather at home. The river flowed below us. Old wooden boats, a kind I'd never seen, floated upriver. She sipped cappuccino and waved her hand across the water. "The river is shallow. Swift currents. Lots of undertow. Those boats are very old. The smaller ones are called '*thoue*' and the larger are '*garbarres.*' They've been used on this river for hundreds of years."

I nodded. "The original flats boat."

She smiled.

After coffee, she ordered two crêpes dipped in Grand Marnier.

They arrived and as I was stuffing one in my mouth, she held her hands up, made a square, and framed me as you would in a photograph. A mixture of butter and liqueur was dripping off my chin. "You go good in France." She sat back. "You're good at watching the world spin by."

"I've had some practice." I stopped midbite. Something was nagging me. "Tell me again the name of this town."

"Candes-Saint-Martin."

There it was again. I repeated it out loud. Then again. Finally, Steady's words returned. "Fifth pew . . ." I grabbed her hand and dropped money on the table. "Come on."

"What? Where are we going?"

We began running uphill. "Church."

We stepped along the cobblestones uphill. "You want to tell me why?"

"Just keep your shorts on."

"But you've never been here."

"Right. But Steady has."

She held my hand as we climbed the steps into the church. Stained glass. Cathedral ceilings. White stone. Lined with pews. Deep, dark, hand-worn wood. The tops and backs were darker due to centuries of hand oil. It would seat several hundred but, at the moment, the church was empty. Our steps and whispers echoed. I walked to the fifth row and began crawling along the ancient marble floor. Left to right. Glancing beneath each section. She leaned down. "What are you doing? They'll throw us out of here."

The words were over sixty years old yet they weren't too tough to find. Weathered, but he'd carved it with his bayonet so the letters were deep and not going anywhere. I rolled over, lay on my back, and beckoned her toward me. She knelt, eventually rolling over and lying along-side me. Shoulder to shoulder. I pointed. "During the war, Steady spent a night here when his unit marched through."

She read the words. Smiling. They were classic Steady. "If you let me survive this—I will be your priest. Carrying both stretcher and blade.

Whose robes are stained. I will walk back across the battlefield. Rescuing the wounded. Offering to cut out gangrene. What happens after that is up to you."

She ran her fingers through the carved letters. Whispering, "Even here—"

I tore a sheet from my notebook, laid it across the neatly carved letters, and began making a charcoal rubbing with my pencil.

We lay there several minutes, reading and rereading the words. I slid the impression into my notebook. When we heard footsteps shuffle near the front door, we sat up, exited the church, and strolled back down the street. It had been a good day. A real good day. I turned to her. "Thank you for today. I really enjoyed it."

She said, "You got time for one more place?"

We had at least an hour of daylight left. "Lady, I'm just the driver."

Chapter Twenty-seven

We backed the Range Rover out of the parking lot across from the bait shack and drove across the cobbles through town. We intersected the river and turned onto the two-lane road that paralleled it. The countryside rolled by. Hillsides and old homes and even older towns passed on either side. The Loire River lay just below us on the left. A sign read CHÂTEAU D'USSÉ with an arrow pointing right.

In the distance, a large castle sat on a hill. Spirals and walls. It said "fairy tale" without saying it.

The road neared; the Château d'Ussé sat enormous and unavoidable in the distance. She pointed and I turned, which placed the château directly in front of us a mile away. Halfway there, she pointed again and I pulled into a parking lot made for viewing the château. A young couple stood on the picnic table, the château behind them, a friend with a camera telling them to do something in French that I took to mean "Smile." I put the Range Rover in park and we sat quietly, staring. I kept thinking I'd seen this château before in a picture but I couldn't place it. Unlike the rest of the day where the story, or history, rolled off her tongue long before we arrived and sometimes after we left, now there was only silence. Moments passed. When she did speak, her voice was a whisper. Cracking. She tried to clear her throat. "Many great writers have come out of France: Rabelais—he wrote novels in the sixteenth century; Alexandre Dumas, who wrote *The Count of Monte Cristo*, *The Three Musketeers*, *The Man in the Iron Mask*, and *The Nutcracker*; Honoré de Balzac; Pierre du Ronsard; Gustave Flaubert, who wrote *Madame Bovary*; Victor

Hugo, who wrote *Les Misérables*; but the greatest French writer of all time . . ." She eyed the castle. "Lived right there. Château d'Ussé was the one-time home of a guy named Charles Perrault. He lived in that tower around 1640. The time of Louis the Fourteenth." She paused. "He lived here a year. Experts say the time here influenced his life's work, one piece of which was called *La Belle Au Bois Dormant.*"

—She glanced at me—I found her disguise less distracting when I could see her eyes—and translated. "*Sleeping Beauty.*" The picture in my mind came into focus. The château looked like the Disney castle. The couple hopped off the picnic table and drove away. She exited the car, walked to the table, and sat facing the château. She patted the table next to her. "When I was eight, my dad brought me here. This parking lot. I was just starting to pick up on the fact that I wasn't too . . . desirable." She palmed away a tear. Blew her nose. "He put me on this table and read the story. At least the first half of it. I memorized it. Knew every word by heart." She tried to laugh. "Strange how one writer, long since dead, could bring such hope to an ugly duckling like me."

I remembered our exchange over Pascal and about dead writers and their words. I had thought then there was more to it. I was right. I'd found it. The words pierced me.

"He used to brush the hair out of my eyes and

say, '*Ma cherie*, your prince will find you.' Then he'd smile and say, '*Le seul vrai langage au monde est un baiser.*' " A long pause. "It means 'The only true language in the world is a kiss.' " The tears ran alongside her nose, off her chin, and onto the stone bench below. "I thought he was right so I let a lot of men kiss me, but—" She shook her head. A long glance at the château—and into the years behind it. "I've been asleep my whole life."

She was quiet on the drive back. She napped much of the way. The GPS served as my guide. It was nearly dark when we pulled into the drive. She woke and said, "I'm going to take a nap. Wake me around eight and we'll make some dinner."

"Sure."

She made her way upstairs and I glanced at the lights of Langeais below. Then my watch. I didn't have much time.

The proprietor of the bookstore was about to flip his OUVERT sign to FERMÉ when I ran to his door. He smiled and opened it. I stepped in, and waved to the man. He said, "*Bonjour, monsieur.*"

"*Bonjour,*" I said followed by, "Hello."

"You finish *The Ice Queen*?" he asked in French-thick English.

"Not yet, I'm about halfway."

"Good?"

I didn't know how to answer without offending.

"Don't know yet. I'll let you know when I finish."

He smiled. "Do you need help?"

"Yes, do you have an older book? Maybe fifteen years old. *Pirate Pete and the Misfits*?" He nodded knowingly, turned, and led me to a shelf. There were several editions. Hardcover. Trade paper. Spanish, French, German, and English editions. Some more used than others. He pointed at two, one English, one French, touching them gently. "These two are first editions. Very valuable to the right person."

I bought them both.

He asked, "Would you like them gift wrapped?"

"Please."

He spoke while he wrapped and looked at me over his reading glasses. "You have read this?"

"Yes."

"You have read all five in this series?"

I nodded.

He ran his finger across the title. "My wife and I, we have four boys. We have read them all many times." He sucked between his teeth. "Books like this—" He shook his head. "They come around maybe once in a generation."

"A shame," I said.

"Yes, very big shame." He handed me the package, tapping the books inside.

I paid, thanked him, and walked back out into the street, where the discomfort in my side was growing.

•••

I built and lit a fire and finished *The Ice Queen.* It was authorial malpractice. If I wasn't against book burning, I'd burn it. Problem is, I think we're better off knowing the truth of what someone thinks. Burning the book doesn't kill the truth or the lie that resides between the covers. Maybe I first learned that from *Fahrenheit 451.*

I climbed the stairs and woke her at eight. She was tired, had a tough time waking up, and leaned on me coming down the stairs—even holding my arm. An unusual dependence. We heated left-overs and ate in the same cave where we'd eaten the night before. I fed and stoked the fire and we grew sleepy in its warmth. We were tired so conversation was thin. After dessert, we turned our chairs to face the fire and soaked. Sleep pulled at me. She spoke quietly. The words rolled off her tongue. *"Belle journée."*

"It sounds pretty. What's it mean?"

The firelight danced on her face. " 'Beautiful day.' "

"Yes. It was." I stood, began gathering plates. She looked tired. "I've got the dishes."

She looked surprised. "Two nights in a row?" She wiggled her nose. "If I didn't know better—"

I cut her off. "It comes from living alone. If I don't do them, they don't get done. Really, I got them. See you in the morning. Thanks again for today. I really enjoyed it." She nodded, stared at me a second, then walked upstairs.

An hour later, I'd finished cleaning the kitchen. I was scrubbing the countertop. I turned and found her watching me. Wet hair. Woman's pajamas that look like a man's. The smell of lavender. "How long you been there?"

She leaned against the door frame. "Can I show you something?"

She took me by the hand and led me up the steps. When she reached the third floor, she turned, opened the hidden pocket door, and led me up the spiral staircase to the fourth floor, where she clicked on the lights. The ceiling was gabled, huge, with exposed beams. I could only stand up straight in the center. Worn wooden floors, a twin bed along one wall below a window, bathroom at the far end. I studied the room. Life-size, hand-painted murals covered the walls from floor to apex. Scenes of a wooded land, a king's chamber, a castle ballroom. A prince on a white horse. A sleeping princess. Characters from fairy tales covered every square inch of every wall. A near identical rendition of Château d'Ussé covered the entire wall above the bed.

The paint was faded and cracking. She said, "Given my physical appearance, and the fact that I had no friends to speak of, my father created a world where I'd be safe and read me fairy tales, inserting my name into the story. He painted these—painting me into the stories." She pointed at one picture. Maybe Cinderella at the ball. "That's me. The countess had arthritis so she never left the first floor. She never knew about this." A rack of dresses lined one wall. "Dad didn't make much but what he did, he spent on me. He bought some fabric, and that sewing machine, and we made these." She ran her fingers through each. An old sewing machine sat in a corner. Rolls of thread next to it. "He bought books and taught himself and me how to sew." She laughed. "Pretty crude to start but he improved." A makeup stand covered in piles of makeup, wigs, a pair of clear plastic slippers, and every nature of things needed to transform one person into another. "We didn't have the money to fix my eye so I hid up here where it was safe. Where the laughter didn't follow and couldn't find me." She shook her head. "And ever since, every role, every character, every rehearsed line —I was hiding where I thought it was safe." A tear welled. She twirled. Her hands holding the edges of a dress she wasn't wearing. "Up here— this is where I'm most me. Whoever she is, I am her, here."

She walked to a window and looked out across Langeais. Lost in a memory, she leaned her head against the window frame. "At night, after rehearsals, and everyone had gone home, I'd walk out on that stage—no spotlight. Just me, my echo, and the hot tamale glow from the single exit sign. All the world was Technicolor, panoramic, and 3-D. And there, somewhere over that Judy Garland rainbow in a yellow brick and emerald world, I would open up and pour out. Share it with worn seat backs, roped balconies, and empty velvet cushions. When the pleasure was simple and complete . . . In the offering. Then—" Katie's complexion changed. The memory soured. "They used to say I was 'the One.' " A forced chuckle. "Now, I'm just one of many. A statistic. Once a meteor shot and bright, shining star, I'm the poster child for the crash and burn." Tears streaked her face. She looked at me. "The measuring stick for the fallen."

I studied the room, looked for something—anything—to say and found nothing.

She ran her fingers along the edge of a painting. "Tell me about your parents."

A shrug. "Can't."

She looked at me suspiciously. "Can't or won't?"

"Can't." She didn't ask me why so I answered her anyway. "My record, or at least what I've read about myself, says that I was born somewhere in Florida, and after two days of not nursing me, my mother left me in a deserted trailer where I picked up fleas, lice, and scabies. I was found two days later by a homeless guy jacked up on something and looking for a place to come down."

Her complexion changed and I was not ready to have the conversation that would soon follow so I cut her off. "So, I can't. And won't." She studied me. I said, "I got you something today."

She looked surprised. "You did?"

"Wait here." I went to my room, picked up the package, and found my hands shaking and my breath shallow.

I returned and stood, holding the package. She stared at me suspiciously. I said, "A long time ago, I found something—something valuable. For a time, I shared it."

"What happened to it?"

I didn't know how to answer so I handed her the gift. "I used to give this to people—like you."

"Like me?"

A nod. "People in pain."

"How many people did you give it to?"

I turned away, shook my head. "Directly, or indirectly?"

"Both."

"It started with one, a girl named Jody. Then grew to tens . . . of millions." Her eyes fell to the gift in her hand and her lips parted slightly.

I stepped out and down the first few stairs, and heard her slowly tear the paper. I spoke over my shoulder. "I signed it for you." She opened to the title page and brushed her fingers across the name, "Bella." I held on to the railing, afraid to look behind me. "You were right about writers."

Her voice was a whisper. "How's that?"

"They die. Their words don't."

I descended four flights of stairs, my knees weak. I wanted to run but didn't know where to go so I walked outside and threw up in the bushes. Once that wave had passed, I threw up again. Empty, I wiped my face on my sleeve, shoved my hands in my pockets, and meandered through the gardens—trying not to think about the transaction occurring inside. Those thoughts took me through the pasture, then the vineyard.

It was a long, long walk.

After midnight, I returned to my room, and lay on my bed, my journal on my chest. My heart pounding. The window was open and the breeze rolled the curtains. Around three a.m, I turned out the light but didn't sleep. Every now and then, the boards above me creaked, suggesting she was still awake. Still reading. Throughout the night, I heard laughter and muffled sobs. For the last hour, she hadn't made a sound.

Somewhere after five a.m., the stairs creaked. I turned to find her standing in the doorway, clutch-ing the book to her chest. A tissue in her hand. Slowly, she approached the bed, walked around it, and sat on the edge. Her eyes were red and face puffy. Several moments passed before she spoke. When she finally did, she didn't use words.

She lay down next to me, placed her arm

around my waist, and kissed me, her tears running down my cheek.

In my previous life, I learned something. I remember seeing it painted on the faces of the kids in the hospital. It is this: All hearts have but one request. One simple, unspoken, undeniable need. One undeniable fear.

To be known.

You can stamp it out. Kill it. Box it up and hem it in. Numb it and close the door. Bury it and nail it shut. Encase it in stone. But eventually, the needs of the heart will tear the door off the hinges, unearth it, and crack the stone. No prison ever built could house it. Those of us who think we can are lying to ourselves. And those next to us.

Hope never dies.

She moved closer, her back to my chest. Moments later, she was asleep, and I was not.

Chapter Twenty-eight

It was nearly noon when I opened my eyes. Her face sat inches from mine and she was looking at me. My hands were folded across my chest. One of hers lay across mine. Her fingers intertwined with mine—two young vines trained by the gardener. She pulled them to her chest, and whispered, "Hi."

"Hi."

She turned, pulled on my arm, and pressed her back to my chest, squeezing my arm around her. More spooning. "I can't believe it's you. I mean, you're really you."

I chuckled. "It's me all right."

She spoke over her shoulder. "There are some—mostly those who believe Elvis and Marilyn are shacked up in the Austrian Alps—who think you're still alive. Never died."

"Those same people are probably starting to say the same thing about you."

She shrugged. "No wonder you knew so much about door number three."

"Yeah, well . . ."

She was almost giddy. Like the revelation had put us on an even playing field. Partners in crime. "I can't believe it's really you." Another squeeze. "I mean, it's really you. Peter Wyett right here in my bed. Sleeping under my roof."

"You already said that."

"Look at me—my palms are sweating. So this is what it's like when you meet somebody famous?"

"Not sure I'm all that famous anymore."

One hand on her hip. "Whatever happened to that last book? The one the whole world was going crazy over? Your 'lost masterpiece.' "

I shook my head. "Don't really know."

"You wrote it, didn't you?"

"Yes."

"Did you lose it?"

"Something like that."

"Well, can't you just rewrite it?"

I shook my head.

"Why not?"

"The reason I wrote it—was taken from me. And, then or now, I couldn't—can't—understand why."

She smiled. "Guess I'm not the only one with a secret."

"Guess not."

She pressed her back against me. The smell of her hair under my nose. She smiled. "Can I tell you something? An honest confession."

"Better save that for Steady."

"I'm serious. This is important."

"Sure."

"And you don't mind if I'm brutally honest with you?"

"No."

"This is the first time I've ever been to bed with a man and woke up clothed."

"Can I tell you something?"

"Yes." She was smiling.

"And you don't mind if I'm brutally honest with you?"

"No."

"This is the first time I've ever slept with a woman."

A chuckle. "Seems like I remember you saying something about that." She squeezed my arm beneath hers. "Well, there's more to it. I mean, it gets better."

"So I've heard."

She sat up, facing me, and crossed her legs. Hands in her lap. She searched for the words. "Okay, another honest admission. I was wrong about something." She shook her head. "You're not compensating."

"What?"

"Your truck. I told you that you owned a big hooked-up truck 'cause you were compensating. Trying to be someone you weren't. 'Cause you didn't make a big enough splash the first time around. But now I think you drive it 'cause you need it."

"Thank you."

A shrug. "I, on the other hand, own four Porsches for reasons we won't go into."

Her self-reflection was confusing me. I sat wondering where this was going. "Okay."

She was all over the map. Her fingers tapped the cover. Changing direction on a dime. "Beautiful. Just . . . how you do it?"

"People say the same thing about you."

"Yeah, but this, I couldn't begin to— Wouldn't know where to— What I do is acting. It's all pretend. Totally scripted. A shield between them and me, but this—this is real. It's perfect. Every word is—honest." A shrug. "Listen to me. I'm all thumbs. Just like my fans, I get in the presence of somebody great and fall to pieces." She turned, clutching my book. "Thank you. I treasure it."

"I'm . . . glad you, well, it's been a long time."

She wrapped her arms tighter. "Your secret's safe." A pause. The beginnings of a smile. "Did you know your Facebook fan page has over four hundred thousand fans?"

"Didn't know that I had a Facebook page."

"Well, you do."

"You have one?"

A nod.

"How many fans do you have?"

"You mean before the ship caught fire in the gulf?"

"Yes."

"A little over twenty million."

It was almost evening. Darkness had fallen. Her giddiness reminded me of grammar school show-and-tell. The questions I thought would follow, the how-comes and what-happeneds I was prepared to dodge, did not.

Her dealings with me reminded me of the kid who forever shook the presents under the tree, even hefting their weight and holding them up to the light but never tearing at the paper or pulling back the cardboard because she'd been let down too many times—the gift never measuring up to her hopes. Unsure of the contents, and afraid of one more disappointment, she stood content to just pick at the edges of my wrapping. She looked at me out of the corner of her eye. When she finally dove beneath the surface, she did so tenderly. "You didn't like the world you were living in so you checked out, didn't you?"

"Yes."

"What was wrong with it?"

"The pain outweighed the joy."

She wrapped her arms tighter about my book. "Given your gift, some might accuse you of being rather selfish."

I nodded. "I didn't used to be."

"What if the world needs your gift?"

"I'm still wrestling with that."

"Your honesty is disarming."

"I'm aiming for honest. That's all."

"I know the world looks at me and thinks, 'all together,' but what if I'm not? I'm on display for all the world to see and show them this perfect image, so what . . . so a bunch of people can make money off their wanting to be like me. But those girls . . . they shouldn't want to be me. I want to tell them all that the guys . . . once they've had you, all they want to do is brag that they did. They want to know they conquered me. But so what? What have they gained? Certainly not my heart. And more importantly, what, or what else, have they lost? Have I lost? Is there a limit? I mean, to how much we can lose?" Finally, she got to the question she really wanted to ask. Her pupil filled the corner of her eye. "Do you think your checking out pissed off God?"

"You should ask Steady that question."

"I'm not asking Steady. I'm asking you."

The truth was tough to come by. I whispered, "I don't think I pissed Him off as much as I broke His heart."

"How do you know?"

" 'Cause it took me a long time to stop crying." I stared out the window, finally speaking softly. "Stories order the pieces. They begin as seismic shifts, then they surface, becoming ripples that lap upon foreign shores. They are the echoes that resonate in this world and the next."

She stood next to me at the window, studying the same stars. My book still clutched to her chest. "You think God reads this?"

A tear climbed down my face. "I hope so." I stared at her. "I wrote it for one of His angels."

She tapped the book. "I want to say something to you but when it comes to things that matter, I'm a lot better when someone else writes the words." An honest smile. "I want you to know—" She squeezed the book tighter, then shook her head and offered her hand.

I took it.

She walked me the length of the house to a room I'd not seen. She pushed open two tall doors leading into a cavernous ballroom of sorts. The ceilings must have been twenty feet high. Four crystal chandeliers the size of her Mini Cooper. Fireplace large enough to sleep in. Floor to ceiling windows with floor to ceiling curtains. Black-and-white marble floor. Each stone was eighteen inches square. A long Steinway sat angled in a far corner. She opened a door, clicked several buttons lighting what looked like a sound system built for NASA, and then began slowly walking the perimeter of the room. The music began playing from more surround speakers than I could count. She eyed the speakers.

" 'The Waltz of the Flowers.' " She walked into a memory and twirled once in the corner. She spoke without looking at me. "The countess had been a dancer before the war. She loved to dance." She walked to a curtain and pulled it around her leg much like a matador. "I used to hide and watch the highest of society turn and twirl out here. I'd imagine myself getting asked by the most handsome of eligible men who would lead me to the floor and then every few minutes another man would tap my partner on the shoulder. By night's end, I'd danced with them all."

She turned to the piano. "The countess taught me. Said I was 'a natural.' Told me I could play Vienna. Melbourne." She twirled in the middle. "Some of my fondest memories took place here." The music ended. Another piece began. She pointed again. "Pachelbel." She walked to the piano, sat, and played along. Midway through, she stopped and set her fingers in her lap. She surveyed the room. "My memories of this room are like"—a glance at me—"reading your story—taking half a deep breath. Always breathing in. Never breathing out."

She walked to the middle of the room, studying the floor and dancing with a partner who was not there. She raised her arms and danced beautifully, resting her hands on the shoulders of a memory. She spoke as she danced. "It was the first time the countess had ever invited me to a social gathering. Often people would play, there would be dancing, maybe someone would sing . . . the wine sparkled, the women sparkled, men laughed, a grand evening." Another twirl. Another turn. "I was almost fifteen. She had paid to have a dress made that fit me just . . ." She trailed off. "She did my hair. My father sat back in amazement as she transformed me before his eyes. She had invited all of Langeais. Said she wanted to make sure I had 'options.'" Arms extended, another twirl. "I danced with every boy. Went to school with many of them but few had noticed me until that night. It was, without a doubt, the best night of my life. My own fairy tale . . ." She trailed off. "I woke the next morning with blisters on my heel. I returned to school and found that six boys were vying for my attention, which I freely gave. I'd never known such . . ."

The dance slowed. "For a few weeks, I lived in an enchanted place. I was so happy. Of the six, I liked one more than the rest and to my great pleasure, he had promised that he liked me." A change in the music. "Mozart." Her tone changed again. The memory both fond and growing cold. "We went on walks, ate ice cream, dinner in town, cappuccinos after school. I fell so hard, so fast, so . . . We made it all the way to May . . . and I finally . . . gave in." The dance stopped. Her voice turned cold. She crossed her arms, and stared at the floor. Cold and alone. "My father had warned me. Begged me. Tried to—" She shook her head. "He, the boy, led me into the caves. I willingly followed. We were—exploring." Her tone dropped lower. "When he was finished, he left without so much as a word." She stared up, tears falling down. "May fifth, 1992." She walked to a window and stared into the night. "At school the next day, word had spread. All eyes were on me. I learned I'd been the subject of a wager. A wager placed that night of the dance—here in this room. While I thought they were fighting over me, they were placing bets. Each boy put in some amount of money, which the winner 'won' as soon as he—" She didn't finish the sentence. "My 'conqueror' was quite proud of himself. I was told he bought himself a new watch."

Chapter Twenty-nine

The night was dark. No moon. She walked out of the ballroom and to the front door. I followed. She wrapped herself in a scarf, put glasses on her face, and looked at me. She was trembling. No disguise. Woman laid bare. She had no script for this role. No exit stage left. She asked. "Will you walk with me—please?"

The tortured look on her face told me this was the reason we'd come to France. "Yes."

We walked down the drive, past the old church and into Langeais, and started up the hill on the far side.

We followed dark streets, turning left and right, following no apparent pattern until I saw the signs that led to the convent. The large iron sign said that the Lady Mary Convent had been built several centuries prior. It started out as caves in the high walls above the river. Napoleon had lived here for a time. Later he sent prisoners here. The nuns took over after that. The buildings grew out from the cave and had been added onto several times. The complex was quite large. Orphanage. School. Indigent hospital.

We turned one last corner and the single light above the doors to the convent shone orange in the distance. She stumbled and I caught her. She was leaning heavier now. As if a gut-level ache had returned. Two oaken doors faced us. The door on the right was a large wooden door that had seen centuries of traffic. Maybe twelve feet, crossed with iron straps, a large knob. Whoever opened it would have to put their weight into it. The second door sat to the left. It was maybe five feet tall and more like a revolving, two-sided lazy Susan than an actual swinging door. The door revolved, or spun on an axis. A shelf had been built into the side facing us. The only way to get inside was to sit on that shelf while someone on the inside rotated the door. The wall on the right curved around the axis of the door making it impossible to see inside while the door was turning. The walls seemed to protect each side from the eyes on the other side. I ran my finger along the shelf. It was well worn and just large enough for a laundry basket.

She was clinging to me. Leaning heavily. Hiding behind me as we approached. She said, "Father was so ashamed, as was the countess. In America, it may not have been such a big deal, but this small village was not America, and everybody knew. The countess was of another generation, and because she'd done so much, had introduced me to everyone she knew . . . Feeling disgraced and ashamed, she fired him and told him to get off her property. I wanted to talk to her, to explain, but she wouldn't see me so I dropped out of school and we lived in a rented house in the country not far from here. Father worked three jobs, contracted pneumonia, and died three months before the baby was born. Six months pregnant, I didn't have enough money to bury him, so I snuck into the countess's house, and stole whatever I could find. I lived alone for three months, and then my water broke. I thought I could deliver at home, but—" She shook her head. "I made my way to the hospital, collapsed in the emergency room, and delivered a few hours later. Given the difficult delivery and the fact that I was a young girl with no family, they kept me a few days trying to figure out what to do with me. Four days after delivery, I walked out of the hospital, and wandered around town until almost midnight. Finally, I walked down here, wrapped him in a blanket I'd made, and placed him on that shelf. I had a piece of paper from the hospital that wasn't a birth certificate but more like a statement of live birth. It had his name, date of birth, weight . . . I tore off the section that gave my name and stuffed the statement inside his blanket. Then I rang that bell and walked to the shadows. The door turned from the inside, counter-clockwise. Sometimes, when I hear a door squeak, I— The door turned and I watched my son disappear. He was crying and reaching upward. I remember my milk was letting down and I didn't have a nursing bra. The door closed as my milk trickled down my stomach. That was March first,

1993." She paused, closing her eyes. "I walked to the train station, rode the train to Paris, used some of the money I'd stolen from the countess to buy a ticket to the U.S., landed in New York with the passport my father had given me for my twelfth birthday, bought one last ticket to Miami—because it was cheap—and walked off the plane with three dollars, one severely crossed eye, and the name of Katie Quinn. I lied about my age, my history . . . I lied about everything. I took three jobs, saved up enough money to straighten my eye, and then did the only thing I knew to do to help ease the pain . . . to help me pretend that I wasn't who I was." She looked at me. "I walked up on a local stage, pointed my voice and talent at the back row, and acted my way out of the hole I'd dug. It took a few years, but when I had enough money, I moved to L.A. I got a lucky break. An independent film that turned out to be the role of a lifetime. My career took off. I could do nothing wrong. I could barely keep up with it all. Everybody wanted me." She turned again to the door. "Quinn. Quinn was my son's name.

"I was twenty-two when I was able to come back here the first time. He was seven years old. I saw him once, out with some children in the village. He looked happy. Had my eyes." A pause. "For the next three years, I came back here every chance I had, always hoping to learn something about him, or better yet to see him again. I couldn't be Katie Quinn, so I became other people who had reasons to interact with the people around him. I almost touched him once. He sipped water from a fountain next to me where I was spying." A pause. "Given what I'd done, I couldn't bring myself to claim him. I thought he was better off . . . I blamed the exposure of the paparazzi. The truth is I was ashamed and afraid of the consequences, of what people would think. Any strength I had was an act. I wasn't the person I pretended to be. Katie Quinn was just another role. But I had time to make it right. Or—thought I had time . . ." She closed her eyes and stood behind me. Speaking over my shoulder. "One day, he stopped appearing in the playground so I hired an investigator." Her voice cracked. Her finger trembled. She held the rising wave at bay. "I know when—I just don't know how." She stared at the door. "I've been here a hundred times. Stood right here, but I've never rung that bell." She held my hand and looked at me.

I walked to the bell and softly rang it. She followed behind, wrapping her face in the scarf and putting her glasses on. When no one answered after five minutes, I rang it again. This time louder. Moments later, we heard shuffling behind the door to our right where people entered and exited the convent.

The huge door opened and an older woman,

maybe in her late seventies, stepped out. She wore a habit and the residue of deep content, now disturbed sleep. She was tall and slender—not what I was expecting. She looked at me. *"Puis-je vous aider?"*

Katie hid her face behind my shoulder, her arm hooked inside mine. I answered, "I'm sorry, I don't speak—"

She stepped closer. Her voice was kind. Not bothered. "I speak English."

I stepped into the light. "Ma'am, a long time ago a boy was dropped off at this door here. I'd like to know what happened to him."

She stared at me. "Please understand, we don't give out that information."

"I realize that, but if I could give you a date and time, could you just tell me anything?"

"You have a date?"

"March first, 1993. About this time of night."

"Boy or girl?"

"Boy."

She stared at me, then Katie. She stared at Katie a long time. The corners of her eyes rolled down. Empathy without words. Katie turned, hiding more of her face. The woman half bowed and said, "Please, follow me."

We followed her inside, where she leaned against the door and locked it behind us. We walked down a long arch-covered path lined with large, well-worn wooden doors. She touched one of the doors and waved at the others, speaking softly. "Our school."

We crossed through a courtyard, then began climbing a long series of winding steps numbering more than a hundred. When we reached the top, the steps ended beneath towering trees with leaves the size of a sheet of paper and carpet like grass. She took off her shoes, and held open an iron gate, motioning us to follow. We slipped off our shoes and stepped through the gate, following her through the grass.

The grass of the cemetery.

Katie wrapped her arms around herself and her steps slowed. We weaved between several tombstones. Some old. Some not. The woman opened another gate, this one smaller, and led us through. A glance around told me that this portion was for smaller people. The length of the graves was less, as was the space between the stones. The color left Katie's face.

Finally, our guide stopped, clicked on a flashlight, and shined it in a section of grass beneath us. The grass was green and had been freshly cut. The yard was immaculate, empty of cuttings. Each stone perfectly manicured. She spoke softly. "I had only been here a few years. I was in the chapel when I heard the bell." I looked at her in disbelief. She stared at the stone and told the story as it returned. "I pulled the rope, turning the door. This beautiful baby boy appeared, wrapped in what looked like a handmade blanket. I picked him up and the certificate of live birth had been tucked alongside his chest." She motioned with her fingers. "The name of the mother had been torn off." She stared upward. "He would be almost twenty now." The words "would be" echoed off the underside of the trees. Katie stepped up alongside me, looking down. The woman paused, choosing her words. "I took him in. Fed him. We—all of us—raised him along with the others." She shook her head, a slight smile. "He had the most beautiful aqua-blue eyes I'd ever seen. Almost not natural—" She brushed off the top of the stone with her palm. "He was fine until the age of two when he developed asthma. A rather severe case. There were times when"—she touched her throat with her hand—"his throat would swell up, and his lungs would spasm, rendering him unable to breathe." She fell quiet. Out of the corner of my eye, I noticed Katie's hands had begun shaking. The woman continued, "I moved him into my room, so I could keep an eye on him. We tried everything. I tried every-thing. Doctors, medicines, remedies. I used to lie awake nights asking God why he didn't let this poor child breathe. Why he didn't pour air into his life. Open his throat. Open his lungs. I'd never seen a child suffer the way he suffered. As he got older, he fell in love with football. Or, soccer as you call it. Reluctantly, I let him play. He was sick a lot. Often, pneumonia. So, he played little."

She stopped talking, and waved her light on a small tombstone below us. Katie froze. The nun stepped back. Her light flashed across the stone. I read the word "Quinn" as did Katie because she sucked in deeply, covered her mouth, and began to moan. Katie fell to her knees; her index finger had a barely perceptible tremble as it traced the dates. He had been ten.

The woman stepped back into the shadows, clicked off her light, and continued, "He died"—she closed her eyes—"alone in his bed. Unable to breathe."

Katie crumbled. She ripped off her scarf and glasses, clung to the stone. There was a long moment when she did not breathe and made no sound. The woman watched, head bowed, unmoved, and unmoving. Katie rocked back and forth.

When she did breathe, it brought with it a sound I'd only heard once in my life. It was deep, primordial, and laden with pain.

I stood behind her, listening to her soul empty itself. Tears, cries, decades of pain. After several minutes, she retched to the side and vomited. Then again. Then a third time. When empty, she dry-heaved. Katie had no persona for this. No wig. No makeup. No act. Clinging to the marble, her fingers tracing the letters of her son's name, a lifetime of torment exited her body. And it did so violently.

The woman disappeared behind us.

I knelt, placing my arms around her. Katie's body was drenched in sweat, torquing in spasm. She collapsed. Breaking. All the king's horses and all the king's men could never put her back together again.

After an hour, I lifted Katie to her feet. A spent ragdoll. She clung to me as we descended the steps. Every few minutes, a sound would exit her body. Part moan, part wail, all torment, unsurpassed pain.

I walked her through the columned courtyard and past the school. Candlelight caught my eye. A stained-glass chapel sat in a corner of the courtyard. It was small. Maybe a prayer chapel. The woman who'd let us in was kneeling at the railing. Hands folded. Head bowed. Katie stopped me, took off her watch, her diamond ring, and diamond necklace and piled them all in my hand.

I walked to the chapel and cleared my throat. The woman turned but said nothing. I walked forward and held out my hand. She extended hers. I emptied mine. She stared at it and was about to speak when I turned and left.

We exited through the same door and back into the shadows of the street. Halfway home, Katie fell. I caught her, lifted her, and carried her up the street to the château.

I set her on the bed, wet a hand towel, and wiped her face and mouth. I did that a couple of times, rinsing the rag each time. Finally, I wrapped ice inside the rag and placed it on her forehead. Her head shook and her lips moved but she never spoke. She lay still, staring at some object beyond the window. When the ice had melted, I replaced it, and placed another rag on her head. She touched my hand and whispered, "I want to die now."

Chapter Thirty

I thought back through the last several weeks. From our meeting on the balcony to the explosion in the gulf and everything since. The blame set in—I was an accessory. I'd rigged her boat, set fire to it, created the illusion. I'd helped kill Katie Quinn. I thought I was helping her. Thought I had some notion of what was best because I'd been there.

I had not.

Sweat soaked the sheets beneath her. She was played out and she could never be me. She couldn't live the life I lived. The solitude. The constant hiding. The separation and isolation. The time left alone with her past. It'd kill her. Or, it'd kill what little remained. My reason for being in the spotlight had been taken so I retreated to the shadows, while she stepped into the spotlight to escape the pain of the shadows.

She'd already attempted suicide twice. Had the scars to prove it. The third time would be different. She'd leave nothing to chance. No doubt. The night passed. I wondered how she'd try it this time. Rope? Knife? Gun? Pills? Moving train? Or, would she just die in her sleep. Death by broken heart.

The sun came up across her face. A single blue vein throbbed on her temple. I watched her and found myself holding my breath. Four words echoed up and out of the ground. *Tell me a story.*

Faces I'd not seen in a decade flashed across my mind's eye. Hope-filled faces. Jody's face. There was a time when I thought stories helped fix broken people. When nothing was more powerful than a story. When stories were the antidote.

I looked at my hands. Wrinkled. Spotted. Too many hours in the sun.

I looked at my journal. White pages staring back at me.

The truth set in. If I had any chance of saving Katie, I had to tell her my story. It was an exchange.

My secret for hers.

Sweat trickled down her forehead. Her eyes darted left and right and her body twitched. The vein on her temple throbbed. Attempt number three was not a question of if but when.

Steady came to mind, white-robed, pipe in his hand, spittle in the corner of his mouth, lip quivering. His words echoed across the ocean. "I'm offering to cut out your gangrene." When he'd said it, I'd believed him. I just had no idea that he'd use my own pen to do it.

I stared at my journal. The truth stared back. If this got out, if someone other than Katie read this, if she shared this or passed it along, then life would change.

Unbecoming Katie meant unbecoming me.

Chapter Thirty-one

When I woke, she was gone. Tear-stained sheets remained. I searched downstairs but did not find her. Searched the gardens, the ballroom, the entirety of the house but found no Katie. Finally, I climbed the stairs and spiraled myself into the attic. She sat on the floor, staring out a window. Lost somewhere beyond the edge of France. I backed out, spent the day below her in my room, listening to any creak in the floor above me.

I heard none.

The next morning, I took her breakfast. When I spoke, she made no response. She lay on the floor, arms wrapped around her legs, eyes open, lost beyond the window. Dinner followed, then breakfast, then more dinner and more breakfast and two more days with no change.

I sat below her, my knees tucked beneath the desk, writing furiously. Never before had I written so much so fast. Determined to lay myself bare, I cracked open the walls, opened up, and Niagara poured forth. Into the third day, I looked up, my hand cramped, and realized that I'd written the last twenty-seven hours straight.

Two ladies came to clean the house. They didn't seem bothered by my presence. They also went nowhere near the fourth floor. I suspected they had no idea it existed. They left in the afternoon.

Five days passed from the night at her son's graveside. I had slept little and written much. Finally, I laid down my pen and let the sleep take me.

Heavy footsteps woke me as did heavy automobile traffic down the hill. I stared toward town. Cars lined the streets. Media trucks were parked near the center of town at the farmers' market. Each antennae had been telescoped into the air. Noise from a television downstairs caught my ear.

I walked into the kitchen. The TV was on. A French reporter sat at a news desk. A picture of Katie flashed above his right shoulder. Above his left flashed two pictures. One of Steady. The other of Richard Thomas. I couldn't understand a word the reporter was saying, but as she talked live video of Langeais, which was no doubt being fed from one of the trucks near the center of town, rolled across the screen. The last screen shots were a photograph taken of documents for the Connecticut-based company, Perrault and Partners, and a handwriting comparison of several of Katie's signatures next to the signature on the Perrault and Partners documents. Thomas might not be much of a writer, but he was turning out to be a heck of an investigator.

It was only a matter of time.

I climbed to the fourth floor and Isabella emerged. Her face, posture, and body language had changed. The walls that had crumbled in the last several days and week had been rebuilt and fortified. The woman before me was the woman I'd met on the patio of Sky Seven, just after she'd launched herself over the railing. Deep black circles surrounded her eyes. She brushed past me and started descending the stairs. "You have five minutes."

"But, Katie?"

She froze. A finger in the air. Spittle in the corner of her mouth. "Don't call me by that name. Not any name."

"Okay, but where're we going?"

She was terse. Protected. "Not here, and not France."

Six minutes later, I stepped outside, my backpack over my shoulder, and found Isabella sitting in the car, engine running, one thumb tapping the wheel. I climbed in, and she spun gravel out the drive before I'd closed the door. She exited the town on dirt roads. When we pulled onto the highway outside of town, she had red-lined the Mini and was shifting into fifth gear. We weren't headed to the train station and, according to the signs, not to Paris. I didn't ask questions and she didn't offer answers.

Thirty minutes later, she pulled off the highway and wound down dirt roads to a small private airfield. A jet sat waiting. She parked the car, left the keys in it, and began walking to the plane. I followed.

We boarded. She spoke to the pilots. They checked our papers and eight minutes later, we were airborne and climbing. I grabbed two cups of ice, a can of Perrier, poured her a glass, and set it on the table next to her. She backhanded it, sending water, ice, and plastic slamming against my side of the plane. One of the pilots turned around. She spoke without looking. "If I want something, I'll get it."

I buckled in. I'd lost her.

We landed in Miami five hours later, during which time she stared out the window and spoke not a word to me. Customs boarded the plane, checked our papers, our luggage, and stamped our passports. We walked across the parking lot and into a parking garage. She pulled an electronic key fob from her purse, pushed one of the buttons, and an alarm sounded. Over my left shoulder, a black Range Rover barked to life, flashing lights and horn honking. She corrected course, and silenced the alarm.

We loaded up and drove in the same shrieking silence in which we'd been living for the last several hours. We drove out of the terminal and onto the highway. A billboard rose up on our left. Her picture emblazoned across it. The sign read: KATIE WE LOVE YOU. LONG LIVE THE QUEEN. She changed lanes, punched the accelerator, and climbed the ramp onto the turnpike. The supercharged engine roared. We passed a hundred and thirty before she eased off. She exited at Tamiami Trail and pulled into the parking lot of a Miccosukee Indian casino. She skidded to a stop but didn't bother putting the car in park.

The fragrance and feeling of France seemed a lifetime away. She spoke without looking. "Out."

"Why don't you come with me?"

Her thumb tapped the wheel.

"You have any idea where you're going? What you'll do?"

Still no answer.

"Katie—"

She raised a finger and shook her head once. A single tear welled, broke loose, and trickled down.

I opened the door, stepped out, and pulled the journal from my backpack. I hefted the journal. An offering. I laid it on the seat and slowly removed my hand. She wouldn't look at me. I held on to the door handle, finally speaking. "This was once me."

She spun the tires, and the engine whined. The Range Rover became a black speck, then disappeared. I shouldered my backpack and began walking to Chokoloskee. In my mind, I reread the cover letter, wondering if she'd read it:

Dear Katie,

I used to think that a story was something special. That it was the one key that could unlock the broken places in us. What you hold in your hand is the story of a broken writer who attempted to kill himself and failed who meets a broken actress who attempted to kill herself and failed and somewhere in that intersection of cracked hearts and shattered souls, they find that maybe broken is not the end of things, but the beginning. Maybe broken is what happens before you become unbroken. What's more, maybe our broken pieces don't fit us. Maybe all of us are standing around with a bag of the stuff that used to be us and we're wondering what to do with it and until we meet somebody else whose bag is full and heart empty we can't figure out what to do with our pieces. And standing there, face to face, my bag of me over my shoulder, and your bag of you over your shoulder, we figure out that maybe my pieces are the very pieces needed to mend you and your pieces are the very pieces needed to mend me but until we've been broken we don't have the pieces to mend each other. Maybe in the offering we discover the meaning, and value, of being broken. Maybe checking out and retreating to an island is the most selfish thing the broken can do because somewhere on the planet is another some-body standing around holding a bag of all the jagged, painful pieces of themselves and they can't get whole without you.

There was a time in my life when I unselfishly offered my gift. Risked everything. Emptied myself. And, when I did, I found that more bubbled up. The well never ran empty. But then, life tore my heart in two and I swore I'd never offer it again. That I'd never risk that.

Maybe love, the real kind, the kind only wished for in whispers and the kind our hearts are hardwired to want, is opening up your bag of you and risking the most painful statement ever uttered between the stretched edges of the universe: "This was once me."

Maybe that in and of itself is the story.

THE LIFE AND DEATH OF PETER WYETT
BY PETER WYETT

I have no memory of my mother. Or father. My records state that my mother was raped by an old boyfriend. The rape produced me. My mother kept me around for about forty-eight hours and dumped me in a trailer where I was found by a homeless guy looking for a roof. After that, I did the foster home dance where I ingested mostly cigarette smoke and fast food. At the age of two, I was found malnourished in a soiled crib so they placed me in a different home—either my fifth or sixth—and circumcised me. For reasons I can't explain, I developed a stutter about the age of four, but I have no memory of ever not having it. While I was "fostered" and moved around a good bit, and occasionally held by well-meaning and well-intentioned people, I have no memory of being wanted. Or, needed. Because in the end, I wasn't.

Nobody picked me.

I was a daydreamer. Quiet. Unseen. Stages scared me. Shadows did not. I sat in the back and watched the world out of the corners of my eyes. What I saw and heard entered through my senses then bounced around inside, looking for a place to attach. To settle. To mean. But that was the problem. I didn't know how—or couldn't—assign meaning. What something "meant" wasn't always clear. I'm not sure but I think parents are a big part of this equation. I think they're supposed to lead us in figuring out how to understand what something means. It's as if meaning is a baton passed down. It's like fishing—you can read the maps until you're blue in the face, but the fine print is what really matters. On the bottom of every fishing chart I've ever read, it states: "Local knowledge is necessary to avoid holes and find exact fish locations." This is why people pay fishing guides to take them fishing. Local knowledge.

As a kid, I didn't have a guide and little local knowledge of how to make sense of the world. What I did have, I stumbled upon. This made conversations tough. Sarcasm and humor a complete mystery. Multiple choice tests a disaster. I lived in a world without terra firma. Nothing to stand on. To push against. If I asked myself, "What does that mean?" once, then I asked myself a thousand times. Sometimes at night, I'd close my eyes and cover my ears to slow the world. Make the bad man stop.

A growing cloud with no way to rain.

In school, I sat in the back, seldom raising my hand and never raising my voice. But the absence of verbal expression did not mean I was dull to the needs of others. Didn't mean I couldn't think and feel. Didn't absorb. I thought and felt just fine. Absorbed like a sponge. My peripheral vision was twenty-ten. I cried when strangers hurt. Laughed when others smiled.

It's what entered the heart that muted it.

When nobody wants you, all you have is hope. Hope that somebody might. This thought alone got me out of bed for the first eighteen years of my life. It was the stuff I fed on. We all did. We could skip food and water but not hope.

The inability to make sense of my life made childhood a bit rough. 'Course, the stutter didn't help, either. For the most part I kept my mouth shut and seldom spoke, even when spoken to. But that doesn't mean I didn't want to talk. I did.

I developed two habits. Since I had no real home and had no one waiting on me, I went where I knew I'd never be alone. The library. And since I was a kid, I started in the kids' section. I read everything I could get my hands on. Anything that would take me some place other than where I was. *Winnie-the-Pooh, Peter Pan*, The Chronicles of Narnia, *The Wizard of Oz, The Velveteen Rabbit, Peter Rabbit, Where the Wild Things Are, The Polar Express, Charlie and the Chocolate Factory, Little House on the Prairie, The Secret Garden, The Boxcar Children, The Indian in the Cupboard, The Giver, The Wind in the Willows, James and the Giant Peach, Anne of Green Gables, Stuart Little.* I even read *Heidi* and *Little Women* when nobody was looking. As I got older, I moved up to thicker, longer books with smaller text and fewer to no pictures. *Where the Red Fern Grows, The Hobbit, The Call of the Wild, To Kill a Mockingbird, Huckleberry Finn*, and *Tom Sawyer*, then *Great Expectations, Les Misérables, The Sacketts, Moby-Dick, The Count of Monte Cristo, The Three Musketeers, Le Morte d'Arthur, Robinson Crusoe*.

The library was magical because every time I walked through the door, there were literally thousands of voices ready and willing to have a conversation with me. I walked through the door, stared at all those stacks and bindings, and whispered, "Tell me a story."

And they did.

I found that I belonged at the library. My dream became to add my voice to the hundreds of thousands I heard around me. Which meant I read even more. Every day I made a new friend.

And none of them rejected me.

I stayed until dinner, walked to the orphanage, ate amid conversation that never included me, then retired to my bunk—or the hammock on the porch if it was available, and continued right where I left off. I joined the conversation and never had to open my mouth. I imagined my own fantastical stories cut from the same cloth as those I read daily.

Because of this, I never felt alone.

The orphanage sat blocks from the water. At night, when the breeze moved in off the ocean we could smell the salt and hear the bells of the shrimp boats going and coming. When I got old enough, I walked down to the docks and tried to make myself useful. I did anything. The fishing guides always needed help washing down their boats, spooling reels, catching baitfish. I was too young to get hired on officially so I worked for tips. I didn't care because tips meant books. Soon, the guides grew to trust me. That meant they talked to and with me. Sharing their secrets —which could come in handy later.

Every quarter the library would have a sidewalk sale, so for pennies on the dollar, I began collecting the stories that had fed me as a kid. Many first editions. Finding these stories was like discovering Incan gold. My stack of books grew, taking up one shelf, then another, and another. With every new book, the house mother would look at me and laugh. "You've got to be kidding?"

No, I wasn't.

Naturally, reading led to writing. The opposite side of the same coin. I created worlds with my pen where people didn't giggle and point when I spoke. Where my parents tucked me in. Where I didn't stutter. Where I had chores assigned by a chart on the wall with my name on it. Where the seat at the table was mine and I was missed if the bell rang and I didn't fill it. Where I was always the prince who rescued the princess, the Hobbit who destroyed the ring, the boy who saved Narnia. Where I was Pip.

Sometimes I wrote all night. Filling pad after pad. True or make believe mattered little. Life was in the telling. In the exhale. Writing became the outlet for the one-sided conversation inside my head. The only place I knew complete expression. A thought encapsulated. A breath deep enough to fill me. Punctuation with certainty. Writing was how I worked out the goings on inside. The act of making story made sense of what I couldn't make sense of. Like being an orphan and never being adopted.

People with parents who claim them have a tough time with this, but it's simple: Being an orphan is illogical. The brain never makes sense of it. Ever. It shelves it in the "miscellaneous" file. It's like a book with no place on the shelf, forever relegated to the cart that circles the library, never stopping to slide between two worn covers.

Writing became my therapy and allowed me a revolutionary thought: Maybe I'm not crazy. It also allowed me to ask myself a universe-rocking question: What if I'm of value? Or better yet, What if I matter? It was rather simple: The people in the stories I read mattered. If they didn't, then why were they on the shelf? And if they mattered, and they included me in their worlds, then why didn't I?

At eighteen, I became my own. I checked myself out with a suitcase and sixteen boxes of books. I graduated high school in Jacksonville, took an un-air-conditioned room above a garage next to the docks for twenty-five dollars a week, and since college was out of the question, I began putting in some serious time at the docks. Where guys who worked hard could make good money. The guides would come in, their clients and lines in tow, and I'd offer to wash down their boats or clean their fish. Most of them knew me, 'cause I'd been hanging around for years. Cleaning led to building rods, repairing reels, working on boats, whatever the guides got tired of doing and would let me do. I worked daylight to long after dark, keeping my head down and building more shelves in my apartment. Before too long, I lived in a library I'd built myself. My greatest fear was not death or sickness, but fire.

Eventually, I bought a used skiff off a guy, rebuilt an old two-stroke, and began learning the backwaters. Because I'd hung out around so many fishermen for so long, I knew some of what and how to fish long before I could actually get out there and do it. Once I hit the water, I put my head knowledge to work and acquired local knowledge. A year or two passed, word spread about "the quiet guide," and before too long, my schedule was full and booked six months in advance. Fortunately for me, clients don't care if their guide can talk, only if he can put them on the fish. And I could. Rain, heat, storm, or calm, I learned where and how to catch snook, tarpon, reds, and more trout than folks could eat. I figured my career was set.

I hadn't even scratched the surface.

It was a Saturday. Late afternoon. Conditions perfect. My client was an attorney. Jason Patrick. Good guy. He'd hooked into a large red drum. Nearly forty inches. Got it to the boat. I'd dropped the power pole in the ground to hold our position and knelt to lift the fish. When I did, the red decided he wasn't finished fighting. With a snap of his head, he spat out the Top Dog and my client, still applying pressure to the rod, sunk that treble hook deep in the meat of my palm.

Ordinarily, I'd push the hook through the skin, snip it beyond the barb, and keep going. Clients pay for a full day and they expect to get it. But this one was a little different. Down in the nerve. Sooner or later, this would need a doctor. And, given that we were nearly sixty miles in the backwater, it was going to be later. Two hours later, I got Jason back to the dock, paid a kid to clean his fish, and made my way to the River City Hospital—Jacksonville's riverbank hospital.

It was nearly nine o'clock and my hand was good and stiff and swollen and getting toward purple by the time the doctor saw me.

The doctor cut out the hook, stitched me up, gave me a shot for the infection, and asked for my card. Said he wanted to catch a tarpon. I said I knew a few spots.

Walking out of the hospital, I took a wrong turn, got lost, and ended up in what I soon learned was the children's wing. It was nearly midnight, I was tired, and needed to be back at the docks at five to meet Sunday's client but there's something about a place just for kids.

I turned a corner and saw a slippered kid standing in the middle of the corridor wrapped in a blue blanket. He looked like he belonged there. His pajamas were covered in tigers and air-planes and hung loosely. A stainless-steel pole on wheels stood next to him. A bag of clear liquids hung from it. A plastic tube ran out the bottom of his shirt sleeve and tethered him to the bag. I said, "Hey, p-pal, which way out of h-here?"

He turned and began pushing that pole so I followed him. We walked the length of the corridor. When we reached the end, he turned and pointed at an exit sign at the far end. I said, "Th-thank you."

He nodded and stepped into a brightly lit room just off the hall.

I can't quite remember why I walked into that room. Curiosity, I guess. The walls were covered in scenes and posters from kids' movies we've all seen. *Star Wars. Indiana Jones. Robin Hood.* The furniture was plush, comfy, and made for lounging. Shelves of books with tattered bindings lined one wall. The opposite wall was filled with Lego, puzzles, wooden train sets, and every imaginable toy that might occupy a child's time and take their mind off the pain ravaging their bodies. Two large wide-screen TVs lined the far wall. Each was hooked up to a different gaming system.

I'd never seen anything like it.

The kid walked to one of the gaming systems, punched a few buttons, and the TV screen lit. Within seconds, he was controlling the BMX rider on the screen. Didn't take me long to realize that he was pretty good at that game.

I inched forward, wondering, where were this kid's parents? His nurses? Doctors? Who in the world was watching over this kid? Eight security cameras on the walls told me that somebody in some booth was watching our every move, but "watching" and "caring for" are two very different things.

I know.

The kid turned to me and offered me an identical remote control. I shook my head, "I . . . I've n-never."

He offered it again and said, "It's easy. I'll show you." To my left hung a framed life-size poster of the 1939 version of *The Wizard of Oz* starring Judy Garland.

Over the next two hours, he beat me eighteen races in a row.

His bag empty, he stood to leave. He turned to me, extended his hand. "Randy."

I smiled and offered him the hand that was not wrapped in gauze and tape—my left. "P-Peter."

He stared up at me. "You coming back tomorrow?"

I shook my head. "No, I j-just—"

He turned and walked away.

Sunday arrived, my client caught a fair amount of fish, and I kept thinking about Randy. Throughout the day, I caught myself looking at the plastic hospital bracelet hanging on my wrist.

Sunday night found me in my den, staring at a blank TV screen trying to chum up the courage. Talking to myself—*What kind of weirdo goes up to play video games with kids he doesn't even know . . . ? They'll put you in jail. Pervert.*

Monday was my self-imposed day off. When I repair and respool my reels, clean the boat, and generally fix what's broken. Spend enough time on the water and most everything will break. Even the good stuff—although it has a tendency to break less.

At seven p.m., I arrived at the hospital carrying a stuffed tiger, and a model airplane in a box, and looking stupid. Think "fish out of water." I wound my way back to the kids' wing, and walked down to the game room trying to look like I knew what I was doing and that I belonged. The room was empty. I stood scratching my head. A nosy nurse asked me, "Can I help you?"

"I'm l-looking for Randy."

Both eyelids lifted in sympathy. "Simmons?"

"To be honest, ma'am, I d-don't know. I was here Saturday night, he taught me to p-play a game, and invited me b-back. He had on tiger and airplane p-pajamas and had a b-bag of stuff dripping into his arm."

She nodded. "The funeral is this weekend."

I stood staring around the room. Life's impermanence struck me.

She pointed at the items in my arms. "If you have no use for those, we have about fifteen more Randys here—all shapes and sizes. We'll put them to good use."

I handed them to her and began walking down the hall.

I'd almost made it to the exit when she spoke from behind me. "The kids usually start showing up about eight. Sometimes nine. After rounds."

I nodded, walked outside, and threw up in the bushes.

Chapter Thirty-two

Two months passed. My hand healed up, the tarpon arrived en masse, and my schedule got busy. I fished seven days a week for seven weeks straight. I used to do what I call "work" but we all know better than that. It could be with the wrong clients but I weeded those guys out long ago. I was selective, didn't have a large overhead, and wasn't interested in making a million dollars. That allowed me to fish with who I wanted. Made for a better life. On more than one occasion, I've idled out of the docks only to return and unload my client thirty minutes later because he was of the idea that his money buys me. Don't get me wrong, I don't mind serving people. It comes with the job. I bait hooks, serve sodas, clean up spills, you name it. The difference comes when someone expects it rather than appreciates it for what it is. It's an attitude. A looking-down-upon. And I didn't let you step foot in my boat so you could assume an air of indignation around me. If you were better than me, you wouldn't hire me to take you fishing. It's not arrogance. It goes back to value.

August rolled around. My client and I were headed back in. The sun going down. My client, a radiologist, looked at my wrist. "What happened?" The plastic had yellowed.

"Treble hook attached to a forty-inch red." I showed him the scar.

He nodded. "You know, you don't have to keep wearing that thing. You can take it off."

I smiled, and nodded.

At nine p.m. that night, I stood next to the nurses' station looking for the woman that I'd met months ago. To my surprise, she turned the corner. "Can I help you?"

"Yes, ma'am, I . . . um, I w-was here—"

She nodded. "I remember. Tiger. Airplane. You were looking for Randy."

I smiled. "That's r-right." I set the box I was carrying at my feet. "I was w-wondering if maybe I could get h-hospital approval to h-hang out with the k-kids." I tapped the box at my feet with my toe. "Maybe p-play a few video games . . . just whatever they wanted to d-do."

She raised a single eyebrow. Her lips tightened. "Can you pass a background check?"

I nodded. "Yeah . . . And I w-wouldn't b-blame you for doing one. Just don't ask me about my p-parents or my real name. I've never kn-known, either."

Her head tilted sideways.

"I was orphaned."

"Oh, you were adopted."

"Nope. J-just orphaned."

She nodded. "If you leave me your information, let me make a copy of your ID, I'll run it by admin and they'll be in touch."

Something had been bugging me since I'd walked onto this floor. I waved my hand down the hall. "What's the story with this place?"

She pointed to a picture of a genteel lady on the wall. "See her?"

"Yes."

"On August eighteenth, 1972, her daughter gave birth to twins who were a couple months premature. Both girls weighed about a pound. They would fit in the palm of your hand. Neither one's lungs were developed and the hospital wasn't prepared for preemies. We only had one incubator so the girls took turns." She pointed to another picture on the wall. "He worked on them both for eight days. When one of the girls started failing, the other went into cardiac arrest. He was only able to save one." Her finger waved at the first picture again. "That made her rather angry. Hence, River City Children's Hospital."

"Where are these k-kids' parents?"

She tilted her head. "I thought you knew." She weighed her head side to side. "They don't have any." A shrug. "Least not any that claim them. Most of them come from facilities around the Southeast. Most all of them are past the age of two so their chances of getting adopted are slim.

Add in sickness or disease and . . . well, those chances don't get any better. Through some private grants, we're able to care for them. Give them a chance they might not have otherwise."

I knew there was a reason I liked this place.

"Thanks." I handed her my ID. She made a copy, handed it back, and said, "Somebody'll be in touch." Her voice softened as she glanced at the game room. "They're always looking for somebody to hang out with. If you come up clear, then I'm sure someone will be calling."

I handed her the video game console in the box. "H-hold it 'til I get back."

She lifted an eyebrow. "And if you don't get back?"

I shrugged. "En-enjoy."

She laughed and accepted the gaming system. "Thanks. We've been needing another. They're pretty rough on these things. Seems like they wear one out about every six months."

Two weeks passed and I'd almost written it off when my cell phone rang. It was a male voice I did not know. "Peter Wyett?"

"Sp-speaking."

"This is Ward Stevenson. I'm the administrator at River City Hospital. I was given your name by some folks who coordinate activities with our kids."

"That's correct. I was j-just hoping to

maybe . . . come up and sp-spend some time . . . whenever it was okay with . . . with you all."

He paused. "Do you know someone up here?"

"No. Do I n-need to?"

"No. It's just that your request is the first I've received in fifteen years in this hospital."

I smiled. "Well, if it makes you f-feel any better, it's the first time I've requested it in twenty-five years of l-life."

"We can't afford to pay you."

"N-no bother. Long as the fish keep b-biting, I'll be all right."

He laughed. "Your background check came up clear. Says here you run a guide business."

"That's . . . correct."

"You any good?"

"I've been known to c-catch fish when others don't."

He laughed again. "If you could get to the hospital any weekday afternoon between four and seven, ask for Judy Stanton. She's in charge of kids' activities. She'll get you an ID, and show you around. Get you started."

"I'd like that."

"Peter?"

"Yes, s-sir."

"In my experience, people who do what you're asking to do don't last very long. It can be . . . rough."

I paused. "I understand your con-concern."

"Good luck to you."

"Yes, sir."

Two days later, I parked in the garage and began climbing the stairs to the kids' wing.

Judy Stanton was not the nurse I'd originally met. She'd transferred. I was not told why although I can imagine. Judy was late fifties and spunky. Colorful, too. She looked like a walking color wheel. Today was primary-color day.

She met me at the door, hung a temporary ID around my neck, and then led me on a power-walk around the hospital, her shoes squeaking on the clean floors, ending at the kids' game room. She turned to me. "Well . . ." She stared at her watch. "Kids don't arrive 'til after eight but you can come and go as you like. Let me know if you need anything."

"Thank you."

The gaming system I'd left had been plugged in and was looking well used. As was the James Bond 007 and BMX disks I'd bought to go with it. Cords snaked out of the front of the TV, ending in two controllers that sat upright on the floor. With the room empty, I walked down to the cafeteria, ate a turkey dinner, and made it back to the room by eight.

When I was a kid, our favorite Christmas movie was *Rudolph the Red-Nosed Reindeer* but not for the reasons you might suspect. Yes, we loved Rudolph and his red nose but we wore out the tape because of the Island of Misfit Toys. And because they were not forgotten.

Which should be self-explanatory.

At eight thirty, they began shuffling in. And when they did, I thought about that island.

They came in all shapes and sizes. Tall, short, boy, girl, freckles, glasses. By nine p.m., twelve kids were sitting in the room, in various stages of game, puzzle, toy, and book. Several were dropped off by their nurses, who didn't stay. The kids were quiet, not too rambunctious. Even the Ping-Pong table was muted.

I stood, looking for an entry, but realized that Randy had helped me more than I knew. I scratched my chin and something poked me in the ribcage. I looked down. She was short. Maybe four feet. Coke-bottle glasses. Braces. Light brown hair. And she wore a robe that covered up most of her. The rubber bands on her braces made her speech sound thick and garbled. She poked me again with the book. "Read me a story?"

I looked around. No one seemed to mind. "S-sure." She turned and began walking toward a large chair, exposing the fact that the braces weren't just in her mouth. Strips of metal hugged the outside of her legs. The waddle reminded me of a penguin. The only thing missing was Morgan Freeman's voice telling me how bad things were about to get.

Her legs came out of her hips at twisted angles. The shiny silver braces sought to help with that. They were clumsy, heavy, and noticeable. The Tin Man walked with more grace. She couldn't climb into the chair so she plopped down on the floor and patted the chair for me. Her legs clanked, and flopped straight on the floor. Raggedy Ann stared up, waiting.

I sat. She stuck out her hand. "I'm Jody."

That hand cracked a fissure in the universe. I held her hand. "P-Peter."

"Nice to meet you."

"It's n-nice to m-meet . . . you."

Her head tilted sideways. "What's wrong with your mouth?"

"I have a s-stutter."

"Does it hurt?"

I laughed. "No. It's j-just that sometimes when I try to s-speak, the thought leaves my brain but gets h-hung up in my mouth. Not sure wh-why."

She nodded. Scooted closer to me. One side of her lip curled up. "Do you take medicine for it?"

"No."

"Can they operate?"

"No."

"Okay."

She turned her attention to the book. I turned

the first page. I couldn't speak in clear sentences to save my life. Sounded like a broken-mouthed fool, but give me a story, something I could read, something where the words weren't mine, and . . . all bets were off. The same was true of Mel Tillis. Only difference was he sang. I read. "One fish. Two fish. Red fish. Blue fish."

She stared up at me. Listening. Halfway through the book, she poked me in the shoulder. "Hey, your mouth." She pointed at my face. "It's fixed. You're all better."

"Well, wh-when I r-read stories, it sort of f-fixes itself."

She nodded. "Then . . . you should read stories."

Some things were just so simple. "Okay."

As I read, more kids appeared. The hospital library was pitiful and sorely lacking, but by our fourth book, there were five kids sitting cross-legged in front of me. Every time I finished, Jody climbed off the floor, walked to the shelf, pulled another, and I read. An hour in, I looked down at the six faces looking back at me. Mall pet shops make me feel the same way.

At eleven o'clock, a nurse walked in, gathered the kids, and mother-henned them off to bed. The kids filtered out. The last to leave, Jody pulled herself up on the couch, muttering to herself, "Weebles wobble but they don't fall down." I stood, not sure what to do. I put my hands in my pockets. Took them out. Put them back in.

She smiled, stuck out her hand. "Hold my hand?"

I took it.

She leaned to one side and sort of threw the opposite leg in front of her. Willing it up and onward. She looked up. "Sometimes . . ." Another step. "I fall down."

I walked her to her room. She stood in her doorway. "You coming back?"

I nodded. "Yes."

"When?"

"T-tomorrow."

She smiled. "Okay."

She turned, walked into her bathroom, and shut the door. I stared through the glass, on the far end of the room, and decided right then and there that I would read her ten thousand stories if she would but ask.

Chapter Thirty-three

– In six weeks, we read every book in that library and many from my own to fill in the gaps. The kids were voracious listeners. Once we made it through their limited library, we moved into chapter books. And chapter books are an entirely different ball game than a book you can read in one sitting. Chapter books require you to dog-ear the page. Which is a marker. It's not just holding your place in the book. Not simply a crease in a piece of paper. It is a promise. An oath. One they need kept. It says, "I will be back, and we will continue this later."

Reading became an event. At first, I started on the couch. The kids before me. But, wanting to be near me, they pulled me down with them. Knee to knee. When the room was full, which was most of the time, it looked like God had played a game of pick-up sticks with kids. They were piled alongside, over, and across one another. Logjams on rivers have more order. And our knees always touched. Everybody's knees. It was the connection between us.

We read a lot of my favorites. I often read for four hours at a sitting and the kids never blinked. We'd started other books but if they didn't like it—which their body language communicated better than their mouth—by the end of the second chapter, we'd pitch it and start another. That taught me something. You live and die by the hook so hook them early. If you don't, you won't reel them in. Funny how life mirrors fishing.

Kids came and went—as varied as the ill-nesses that had brought them there. Some hung around a week. Two. Maybe three. A few were long-timers. Jody was one of those. She'd been in a car wreck as an infant. No car seat. The wreck had broken both legs, her pelvis, and several other bones, which was made more complicated by poor medical treatment following the accident. Bones had grown back incorrectly. The work to correct her legs would take several surgeries over several months and the hospital had committed to it. However long it took.

Critics say the medical system is broken. I'm not convinced.

Being around the hospital, I got to know the staff, the administration, even some of the doctors. Each welcomed me and what I was doing, which really wasn't that much. A C-average high school graduate with a pretty mean stutter reading to the kids. It wasn't rocket science. Since I couldn't be there full time, and the kids were, I asked if I could donate some of my books. They asked, "How many do you have?" At the time, my library numbered about ten thousand.

They were more than happy to accept them.

Every night, I'd appear with the book I was reading and then several more for the kids to take back to their rooms. To keep, if they liked. Most passed them around. Shared them. Or put them back up on the shelf in the hospital's growing library. Giving away books served another purpose—one I selfishly admit. Living near the docks meant constant humidity and the ever-present possibility of fire. Besides, most sat unread as I could only read one at a time. Giving them to the hospital meant they sat 24/7 in a temperature-controlled environment, and they were available for far more people to read them. And while that may sound like a lot of books, and it was, I often had several copies of the same book. At one time, I owned forty-two copies of *Great Expectations*. Twenty-seven of *Robinson Crusoe*. Thirty of *The Hobbit*. Seven of *Winnie-the-Pooh*. Seventeen of *Huckleberry Finn*. Some people can't turn away stray cats. I couldn't turn away stray books.

The transfer of my library took months, but before long I began arriving with boxes. The library dedicated an entire room off the kids' game room. They lined it with shelves, installed plush carpet on the floor, beanbags big enough to curl up inside, and large reading chairs that were two and three kids wide. Soon, the game system was dusty and not the books. Jody became the self-nominated librarian and, together, we developed a system to catalog and shelve the books.

If Jody's hand had forced a crack in the universe that surrounded me, the kids alongside her hammered in a wedge. Widening it with every broken smile. Every quiet request. As a kid, I'd turned to stories—helping me fight the pain that was my life. The characters I met had become my closest friends. Now, as I sat on the floor, knee to knee, kids piled around me, I introduced my new friends to my old friends.

I'd found my place in the world.

While all were orphans, Jody actually had a chance. A young couple, Rod and Monica Blue, was actively working to adopt her. Due to a high fever when he was a kid, Rod could not have children. That brought them roundabout to Jody. After the third surgery, while she was confined to a wheelchair, I was invited to the courthouse to watch Rod and Monica become her parents. The judge uttered the words "irrevocable right" and tears dripped off my chin. It was a good day. The island lost one of its own—which was good.

Jody said she wanted to go fishing so I took them. I retrofitted the boat so her wheelchair could be locked down and not bang her around in the chop. We caught reds, trout, a few sheephead, and Rod caught a small but nice tarpon. Monica hung back and shot pictures and video. I baited hooks, tied knots, and served sodas and sandwiches. It was one of the best days I'd ever known on the water.

As the months passed, and one successful surgery was followed by one more, and Jody's steps quickened and her smile spread, we all forgot about what might happen. What could happen. Being together, hanging out, we leaned on each other and our hope was built.

Didn't take much to bring it crashing down.

Her fifth surgery had gone well. Doctors were pleased, but germs and viruses are tough to see. Even tougher to fight. She developed an infection deep in the bone of her hip. Took them a while to find it. She started running a fever. It sat at 104 for days. Started taking its toll on her. She got weak. Doctors started muttering the word "amputation." I canceled my clients and hung out at the hospital, wringing my hands. Threw a blanket on the cleaning room closet floor. Rod was stoic. Quiet. Monica was a mess. The doctors gave her something to help her sleep.

It was Monday night. Two a.m. Rod woke me. "She's asking for you." He looked tormented.

She was pale. ICU. Behind a plastic curtain. I reached out, placed my palm flat against hers. The plastic between us. The fever had ravaged her. Jody knew about my journals. About my writing. I'd shown her snippets. Too tired to open her eyes, she whispered, "Tell me . . ." She pointed at me. "Your story."

One of my favorite stories as a kid was *The Wonderful Wizard of Oz*. I read all of the Oz books, but I kept that one under my pillow for reasons I cannot explain. Maybe it had something to do with the wizard . . . or the fact that there was one someone in some world some-where who controlled the levers that controlled me. Anyway, I must have read it a thousand times. The last time I saw that book the green cover had faded white, several of the pages were missing, and the binding had been duct-taped more than once. I didn't know it as a kid, but the author, Frank Baum, used to tell whimsi-cal stories to kids, which later became the fodder for Oz. I've read that C. S. Lewis, A. A. Milne, Lewis Carroll, James Barrie, Kenneth Grahame, and J. K. Rowling did the same. Folks used to ask me where my stories came from. Psychoanalyzed me ad nauseam, trying to discover the place from which my stories grew. It's a simple picture really: an orphanage, a bunk bed, a flashlight, Oz, and me. It doesn't get any more complicated than that. Or, if it does they're just smarter than me and I'm too stupid to understand what they're saying.

When I wasn't fishing, or reading to the kids, I was penning scenes in a notebook I carried in my back pocket. Jody knew this. She also knew that I'd put her in my book. To make it more interesting, I'd inserted her as a character in my story. Absent her handicap. She was giddy with expectation.

I ran to my truck. Pulled out the pages, and scooted up a stainless-steel stool next to her bed. The book was several hundred pages. No short read. It was the story of a one-legged, time-traveling pirate named Pete who lived in an old ship named *Long Winded*. Pete was flamboyant and wore ruffled shirts and a large purple hat with a peacock feather. He also wore a magical brass monoscope around his neck that could transport him back in time. A time line of years was etched onto the side of the brass—from present to several thousand years B.C. The farther out he extended the monoscope, the farther back he could see and travel into time. He, his ship, and any mates who traveled with him could travel back to any place or time in history. They could also travel back into places depicted in any of the books shelved in the cavernous library aboard his ship. This made for limitless adventures. Given my love of the ocean and all things seaworthy, the villain was the real-life seventeenth-century Dutch privateer, Piet Hein—the first and only captain to capture the entire Spanish treasure fleet. Doing so disrupted the European markets and threw life into chaos. Not too worried about Europe's markets, Hein took the plunder to Holland, which pleased King Philip III even less. The problem with the plunder was that while it made him infinitely rich, it did not include one very important item. Yep, you guessed it. A magical monoscope. In the beginning of my story, Pete is sailing up the

St. Johns River, where he moors at the docks alongside the River City Hospital and begins looking for a crew. Chapter one begins with the sound of his pegleg echoing down the halls of the children's wing—just outside Jody's door. Through the window, the moon casts a shadow across Piet Hein's main sail silently coursing upriver. They didn't have much time.

I said, "This might take a while."

She smiled. "I have time."

So, for the first time, ever, I opened my mouth and told a story that I'd written. And told it to someone other than myself.

For all of my life, I had stored my love in a place down inside me that had no outlet. I contained it there. Kept it to myself. Afraid to let it out. Thought if I did, it'd seep out and I'd be left with none. I didn't have much to start with. Then I opened that book, tilted the pitcher that contained my small reservoir, and started pouring out. First, sparingly. A drop or two at a time. Then a trickle. Then a flow. The more I poured, the more I had to pour. The cup that never ran empty. Strange how that worked.

Three hours in and she opened her eyes. By daylight she was sipping water and they'd propped up her head. Rod and Monica sat and listened. Some of the nurses and doctors had taken their breaks, ate their lunch within earshot.

This event—reading a story to what might be a dying girl—had never been done before in this hospital.

Twenty-four hours later, I was still talking. A competing band of pirates had captured Pete, and demanded to know where he'd hidden the monoscope. The crew of Misfits had just landed on the island where Pete was being held and soon to be tortured. Jody was sitting up. Her fever had dropped. When she drifted off and slept a few hours, I did, too. Right next to the plastic that surrounded her bed. When she woke, I picked up where I'd left off. That night, she ate for the first time in a week. Two days in, her temperature was sitting at ninety-nine and holding.

Two days later, I finished the story. A story that was part fairy tale, part love story, part quest. It was inspired by Tolkien, Lewis, McDonald, and L'Amour all thrown into one kitchen sink and Jody played the lead—having risen from lowly crewmember to first mate. When I stopped, story completed, nurses and doctors stood and clapped. Some crying. Some smiling. Monica kissed me on the cheek and Rod hugged me. He was shaking. Jody stood inside her plastic wall and bowed for the audience surrounding her bed.

Jody recovered. They moved her back to her room, where she promptly asked for a purple hat with a peacock feather. She wore it every day. Pretty soon, we found ourselves back in the game room and word had spread. All the kids wanted to hear the story. She had me read it again. The place was packed. Nurses took their breaks. Doctors even filtered through.

That started two trends. The first had to do with hats. Everybody, doctors and nurses included, started wearing hats. Second, every kid now wanted to be in my story. Play a part. Become a character—a crewmember. I had lots of stories so it was rather easy. I simply inserted their name for a character's name. To make it fair, we passed a hat filled with slips of paper. "Winners" got their name in the story for the entire reading, but once in, they had to sit out the hat passing until everybody got in their story. Smaller parts, where maybe a character only appeared for one or two scenes, I "assigned" on the spur of the moment, giving kids the expectation that they might cameo in a story. The formula worked and the logjam spilled out of one room and into another, prompting the hospital to blow out two walls and expand the library.

Somebody told somebody who told somebody else who told somebody at the local news station. They showed up. Cameras in tow. Jody was sitting up, eating, talking about running and playing soccer. They got to me, shined the light in my face. Then they interviewed the doctors. They shook their heads. "I've never seen anything like it. That girl was at death's door and then he walked in there, started reading that story . . . and then walked her out." One of the networks picked up on it. Sent their morning anchor. Ran a story.

The phone started ringing from there.

Chapter Thirty-four

Jody began walking laps around the hospital, albeit with the help of crutches, but the fact that she did anything under her own power was powerful enough. She spent hours in therapy every day. Rod and Monica never left her side. I fished during the day and spent every night at the hospital. And while I was more comfortable reading others' stories, nobody wanted to hear those anymore. They wanted me to tell the stories I'd written.

I was on the water when my phone rang. "Peter Wyett?"

"This is P.W."

"This is Jud Rollinger. I run a publishing house in New York. Heard you've got a story that kids like to hear."

"They s-seem to s-sit still while I'm t-telling it."

"Way I hear it told . . . they're glued."

"S-some."

"Has it got a title?"

"Not that I know of."

He laughed. "You mind letting me read it?"

"No sir, I d-don't mind."

When he'd finished it, he called and said, "Son, I think you'd better find a title for your book."

"I can do that."

I called Jody. Asked her if she had any ideas. She thought a minute and then said, "Call it *Pirate Pete and The Misfits—Book One*."

"Book one?"

"Well, sure. How else are you going to title the other stories?"

For a ten-thousand-dollar advance, the New York house bought *Pirate Pete and The Misfits*, printed five thousand copies, skipped sending me on a book tour, and placed the story on the shelf, somewhere near the back of the store because the publisher had second-guessed himself and didn't want the hassle or the embarrassment of a failed book. While he liked it, he didn't know who the audience might be and therefore couldn't predict who might actually buy and read the story. He thought the story of me reading to the kids was engaging, but he wasn't sure that the story I'd written was. On second thought, he simply wanted to recoup and save face. Before it printed, the lady assigned as my editor asked me who I wanted to dedicate the book to. That was easy. It read: "For Jody. The bravest kid I've ever known." I walked into the bookstore and saw my book, spine-out, wedged between a million other books.

I'd joined the conversation. Found my seat at the table. Joined my voice with the chorus of the thousands who'd come before me.

Unfortunately, buried between two other stories is where it sat. Collecting dust. Dead on the vine. But life has a funny way of bringing about the intersection of the known and the unknown. The living and the dead.

The wife of an actor stumbled upon it. The title caught her eye. She was adventurous. Read it in one sitting. Then read it to her kids. Their response surprised her. She commented to a friend of hers about it—an anchor on an L.A. evening news show. She read it and mentioned it to the friend of an editor at the *Miami Herald* who suggested it over wine to a guy who produced commercials for cosmetics companies who suggested it to a lady who could care less and couldn't figure out what the big deal was. But, somewhere in that, something happened. And the one and only thing that sells a book began to build and spread—word of mouth.

I fished during the days. My clients were

oblivious. Had no idea. At night, I read to the kids—more installments of other stories I was writing. After almost a year in the hospital, Jody was released and moved home with Rod and Monica. They had me over for the party. Said they wanted it to be just family, so it was the four of us. We had cake and then burgers, in that order—just the way Jody wanted it.

Months passed. Whispers on the street mentioned a writer who'd managed to pen what so many kids wanted to hear. Took them places they wanted to go. Through characters they hoped for. With a voice they believed. While marketed mainly at kids, parents were having trouble putting it down. One of the early reviews said the book sat "outside genre."

You've heard of the tipping point?

I didn't believe it so I drove to the bookstore, sat in the shadows with a bottle of water, and watched readers out of the corner of my eye. One by one, I measured their facial expressions. Wasn't too hard. Maybe I shouldn't have been so surprised; *Peter Pan* and *The Wonderful Wizard of Oz* and The Chronicles of Narnia grew out of similar circumstances— some man telling stories to a bunch of kids. Then I watched an amazing thing. A father walked in with three kids. Each holding hands. They ran to the shelf. Pulled it off. Then pleaded. "Read, Daddy!" He sat down, they followed suit, cross-legged and wide-eyed, and he read, inserting their names for mine, turning page after page after page. I sat one aisle over, leaning my head and back against the shelf, listening. I sat there, shaking my head. No other thing or power or force in the universe does that.

Six months passed. The fire spread. No one really knows the one single straw that broke the camel's back, but one thing is certain. Life changed.

The critics raved. "A stunning achievement." "Mesmerizing." "Monumental." "Not seen since Tolkien and Lewis." "The measuring stick . . ." The comments left me scratching my head. Although I will say that I smiled when they said, "The reincarnation of L. Frank Baum."

In truth, I had no idea what these people were talking about yet readers devoured it and a literary star, i.e., me, was launched into the stratosphere. My publisher was pleasantly pleased with sales. He called. "Do you have another book?" I had many. Book two released soon thereafter. Jody titled it *Pirate Pete: Return to Misfit Island.*

They put me on a book tour and if I signed one I must have signed ten thousand books. As a result of the book, the hospital got noticed, and so did the kids. Santa came to the island and I got to go to the courthouse four times that year and hear the words "irrevocable right." It was a good year.

A Hollywood studio bought the movie rights to books one and two, so winning the National Book Award seemed after the fact. When they asked me to attend the dinner, I, with Rod and Monica's permission, took Jody as my date.

She walked up on stage with me and accepted the prize. Her carbon-fiber braces snapping, clapping, and her double-thick oak-leather soles scraping the stage. Peacock feather waving. The audience stood and clapped for ten minutes. The noise was deafening. Rod and Monica hugged each other and patted me on the shoulder. Monica's mascara was running everywhere. The emcee asked her why she wore the hat. She responded, "Because, like Pete, I live in a world without limits." Funny how three words can change things. The *New York Times* ran the story the following day. Front page. The headline read: WORLD WITHOUT LIMITS.

Overnight, Jody became the poster child for hope. Her purple-hatted, peacock-feathered picture hung in hospitals and on magazine racks across America.

The kid who'd never been picked had found his place in the world and as a result I poured out all the love, and words, I could find.

Interviews, articles, talk shows, people wanted to know me. Touch me. See me. Know my opinion. What I thought. Hold up my books and ask me, "Where does this come from?" I just shrugged. I didn't know. They kept calling me a "writer." I told them they should reserve that term for someone who deserves it. I was a fishing guide.

My critics confused my pitiful answers for arrogance and poked fun at what they didn't understand and could never be. It wasn't that I didn't want to answer their questions. It was just that I couldn't. I squirmed in my seat. Such big questions for so small a man. So insignificant in the span of time. They said I'd written a story that "spoke to a generation." One night, Larry King asked, "How'd you speak to so many?"

I shook my head and offered a tepid whisper. "I d-didn't speak to many. I spoke to me . . ." I pointed to Jody. "And a little g-girl named J-Jody. And it just so h-happens that several million m-more liked it." I was quiet a minute. "I w-wasn't telling a story to the millions, I was t-telling it to a little girl who might have been d-dying and certainly about to l-lose her leg— and maybe I was telling it to the b-boy I used to be."

From there the book flew off the shelf.

My third book, *Pirate Pete and The Misfits: The World Is Flat*, spent forty-two weeks at number one. When the movie version of the first book was released, the top three spots on the

New York Times hardcover best-seller list were my three books. I am told that Academy Award–winning producers, directors, and actors called studio heads requesting my stories, explaining why they desired the roles. My publisher hired a staff of people to handle my mail. I certainly couldn't. I was too busy fishing. I bought a sixty-thousand-dollar flats boat, a passel of new Shimano reels and St. Croix rods, several pairs of Costas, and set off for the backwater. When it came to tackle, I spared little expense. I fished during the day, taking my clients same as always, and told stories to a roomful of kids at night. Never had my heart felt so alive. So full.

The expanded library had grown too small. Folks from all over the hospital came to hear me read. The sick, infirm people hooked up to chemotherapy drips, women with no hair, men with swollen prostates, kids with scars on their chest—all shapes and sizes, all sicknesses and illnesses. I was seldom happier than when I was reading a story I'd written.

'Course, a good tarpon run was a close second. As was catching snook or a forty-inch red. But the thing that gave me value was reading a story I'd told.

Five years. Five books. Dozens of languages, over sixty countries, more than seventy million copies sold. They said my career trajectory had been unlike any they'd ever seen. All because I opened my mouth and told a story.

And then there was the money. I made more money than I could ever spend, and paid more in taxes than most make in a lifetime.

And while all this exceeded my wildest imaginations, I learned something and I learned it the hard way. Words can make people hope. And they made me rich and famous in an odd sort of way. Put my picture on the cover of *I* magazine. There is one thing words cannot do.

They can't bring people back to life.

Chapter Thirty-five

I'd finished final edits on my latest book and was spraying the boat with water while I thought about where I was going to fish tomorrow. It was how I let my mind unwind. My editor and publisher had been chomping at the bit to get their hands on it. They had big plans. I'd planned to read it to the kids first. Always did. They were the litmus. The only person I'd given it to was Jody. She had the only copy of the manuscript and from the message she'd left on my machine the night before, she'd finish it that day.

I'd told the kids and they were excited. We'd start that night and I'd finish in four or five nights. The hospital loved the exposure. The excitement. They'd called and asked if we could move the "reading" to a nearby auditorium. Include a couple hundred people. I said no.

I was moments from driving to the hospital when the phone rang. It was Rod. His voice was trembling. "She's asking for you, and . . . hurry."

About ninety seconds later, I looked down at the speedometer. It read "110 mph."

She was sixteen now. A beautiful young woman. When I arrived, they briefed me. She'd been leaving school. Standing on a street corner. Chewing grape bubble gum. Headed home to get all gussied up for the homecoming dance. She was on the court. They said she never saw the bus that blindsided her. They also said she was reading. Engrossed.

A honeybee distracted the driver of the bus, she swerved, jumped up on the curb, and caught Jody at over forty miles an hour.

Nurses were sobbing in the hallway.

I slipped my hand beneath hers. "Hey, kiddo."

Her eyelids flickered. Her body lay twisted. Canted. Her lips were caked in blood. She tried to speak. Tried again, swallowed. Her eyes were focused midway between this world and the next. "Tell me a story." She squeezed my hand. "Read me—"

She slipped into a coma. Breathing tube. Life support. A nurse handed me a plastic bag filled with my manuscript. They'd gathered it from the street. I put the pages in order and read to her around the clock for ninety-seven hours. When the monitor above me flatlined, the cup inside me, the one that held my love, shattered into a million jagged pieces—the slivers embedding deep within me.

We buried her a few days later. I stood next to her casket, listened to Monica make noises I'd never heard a human make, and watched my tears streak down the wooden grain of the lid. I stood there hurting. Pain I'd never known. Of the six billion people on the planet . . . why her? What kind of a God would do this? I swore I'd never tell another story. Never dog-ear another page.

Victor Hugo once said that hope is the word that God has written on the brow of every man. Really?

Then to hell with hope.

Days passed. My phone began ringing off the hook so I walked down to the dock and fed it to the fish. I didn't want to read to the kids. That night. Or any other night. And I didn't care if anyone ever read anything of mine again. I didn't eat, and didn't sleep. To medicate the pain, I crawled inside a gin and tonic and stayed there a month. I did not want to fish. Did not want to talk. Did not want to live.

Alcohol and isolation fed my anger. And I was very, very angry.

The word "recluse" didn't scratch the surface. I disconnected my heart from the body that fed it. I saw no one and no one saw me. A year passed with no book. Speculation grew. A persistent reporter paid a minimum-wage employee at the mail-it store where I rented the P.O. box to call her when I picked up my mail. He did. I emerged and she stuck a microphone in my face. The camera light blinded me. "Are you writing?"

My answer was not unkind. "N-no."

"Then, you've finished it? Book six in the Pirate Chronicles is finished?"

A shrug. A nod.

"Do you like it?"

I pushed my Costas up on my head, squinting from the glare off the water. I tilted my head to one side. Stared at some indiscriminate point far away.

"Can you tell us anything about the story?"

I found her smile attractive. Her eyes warm. Not too over done. She was pushy but also just doing her job. I'd known worse. I wondered for a brief moment if she'd like to get a cup of coffee. But what was the use? My mind never stuttered. She proffered the microphone again. "Would Jody like it?"

"Yes. V-very much."

I stared at her. The tears soon followed. I climbed into my truck and disappeared.

The *New York Times* proclaimed, THE RECLUSE REAPPEARS: PENS HIS MASTERPIECE. I never understood the fuss. I didn't understand most of it. Six months before my September release, preorders on the web placed the untitled manuscript at number one.

September came and went but the book never showed. That's not to say it didn't exist. Rather, it just never appeared. Reporters exhausted every detail. Every lead. My P.O. box filled, overflowed, and I never checked it again. No matter how many times I changed my phone number, they always got it. I stopped answering.

A tabloid published a rumor that I'd met a girl. Married. But she'd left me after only a year. Speculation grew. Someone whispered, "Tragedy." I had no idea what they were talking about.

A couple years prior, when my books had sold beyond my wildest imagination, my editor gave me a gift—a Mercedes. Fastest one they made. Shiny black. An S65 AMG. More than six hundred horsepower. Manufacturer's suggested retail price was over $210,000. A little flashy for me, so I didn't drive it much, but it was fast, so I backed it out of storage.

I left Jacksonville at noon. The manuscript beneath a bottle of Bombay Blue and a liter of tonic, wrapped and tied up in a trash bag because that's where it was headed.

I called my editor and said, "Thank you . . . r-really." I called my accountant and told him to record the phone call, where to put the money, and what to do with the remainder of my library. I called my agent and said, "G-good-bye and th-thank you." Soon as I hung up, my phone rang. A South Florida news affiliate had tracked me down. I took the call. With little introduction, the reporter asked: "We understand the parent company of your publishing house has sued you in order to force the release of your next book."

"Th-that's true."

"Have you finished it?"

"Yes." The less words the better.

"Where is it?"

I glanced in the passenger seat where book six, *Pirate Pete and The Misfits: The Last Sunset*, sat wrapped in the plastic bag. "H-here."

"What are your future plans for it?"

When I answered honestly, the nature of the interview changed. My response caught everyone off guard. The local story abruptly became national and they patched me through to the anchor during a live broadcast.

"You have the manuscript? Why final? Where

are you right now?" I swigged from the bottle and answered her last question by telling her not where I was, but where I would be. Then I tossed my cell phone out the window where it shattered on the asphalt at eighty miles an hour. I sped up, unbuckled to make sure that nothing would prevent my head from impacting the glass, and opened the sun roof so that there'd be plenty of oxygen to fuel the fire I was about to light.

My blood was already on fire. Three-quarters gin, one-quarter me.

I'd picked the time and the place—now, and Card Sound—for two reasons: First, by a fluke of luck some years back, I'd had the best day of tarpon fishing there that I'd ever had. I figured that'd be a good place to end things. Second, I wanted finality. The Card Sound Bridge spanned the waters I'd fished and provided an adequate launch. As a bonus, pedestrians were not allowed and it was very tall. Sixty-five feet above the water. More than enough.

I switched lanes and wondered if anyone would show. Would anyone care.

They did.

Cars had stopped. A long line of taillights. Traffic was backed up. A crowd had gathered. Video cameras shone in streetlights. One news van had arrived and telescoped its receiver. The reporter stood in front of the camera, framed against the backdrop of the crowd, bridge, and toll plaza. I was glad. Witnesses meant no doubt. I lit the end of the rag dangling from the gas can on the backseat, then laid on the horn and flashed my lights. The cameras swung. The crowd waved. A few waved my books. I eyed the bridge, pushed the accelerator through the floorboard, crashed through the toll plaza gate.

Then I drove the car up, and off, the Card Sound Bridge.

Eyewitnesses—of which there were many—said the crash was horrific. Reports described my car crashing through the railing, spewing glass, concrete, and twisted pieces of a light pole. The high-performance engine red-lined, sending the vehicle arcing out into the dark-ness. It rolled a quarter turn and dove vertical to the surface. Some said the car hung briefly in the air, almost pausing, while others swore they heard me, locked inside and screaming—burning alive. Because darkness shrouded the water's surface, the impact was sudden and loud but not as loud as the silence that followed.

Eyes wide, the crowd held their breath as the fast-moving water below the bridge enveloped the car and dragged it, and me, to the bottom of the channel, leaving nothing but bubbles. Over a hundred stunned people simultaneously dialed 911, several shined flashlights and searched the water's surface, while a few others jumped in only to need rescue moments later. Emergency personnel boats were summoned and divers were dispatched but the channel current was too much. They shook their heads and stared east. "Probably washed out to sea." Much like my life. Grief counselors arrived and consoled those affected by what they saw. Two days later, beachcombers found my torn shirt along with my pants and one shoe. A half mile downriver, the car was discovered in eighty feet of water and hauled to the surface. Articles were removed. A gym bag containing half a bottle of gin, an empty bottle of tonic, Costa Del Mar sunglasses, a spinning rod and reel, a fillet knife, sunscreen, a five-gallon gas can, and several laminated maps. DNA tests confirmed it was my car.

While some of the country was immune to my death, much was not. A memorial service was held a week later. Crowds of mourners, gawkers, and the just plain curious filled the beach east of the bridge, stood in the rain holding tear-stained books, pressing ever closer to an impromptu and growing shrine. The national media were in full attendance. A local priest officiated. He regretted that he had not met me and said something about "beauty for ashes." If there was beauty, it escaped those standing on the beach.

In the months that followed, news agencies milked the story for everything it was worth. Documentaries, hour-long features, two- and three-part investigative pieces. Conspiracy theories abounded. An unauthorized biography, "years in the making," hit the shelf three months after the crash. My backlist titles climbed the bestseller lists once again. A concrete marker was erected on the beach, giving permanence to the shrine. A local vendor, claiming to be an eye-witness, sold T-shirts, cups, mouse pads, coolies, and paperback copies of my books. "Signed" first editions that I don't ever remem-ber signing popped up for sale from collectors. A local university endowed a writing scholar-ship for the verbally challenged. Another endowed a chair in the writing program. On the first anniversary of my death, the movie of the story of my life was released in theaters across the country. One of my favorite actors played me. Did a good job, too. Fans stood in line. At the end of the day, I became far more famous in death than I'd ever been in life. In the five years that followed, journalists, commen-tators, bloggers, prognosticators, and anyone with a voice and the energy to broadcast it exhausted every detail of my gifted, tragic, and short-lived life, leaving no stone unturned.

But . . . they never found the book.

Chapter Thirty-six

I woke on the beach. Naked. Cold. Sea foam clouding my face. A fiddler crab nibbling at my nose. I knew a couple of things: I did not know how I got there but to get anywhere else was going to require help. I knew I was alive not because of the blinding sunlight, smell of salt, or sound of seagulls but because of the searing pain in my chest and throat.

I lifted my head, looked around. Beach left curving out of sight. Beach right curving out of sight. White sand. Lots of trees. Noisy birds. No people. My thoughts were thick, garbled, and slow in coming. Must be something of an island. Oddly, when I closed my eyes I found the same condition.

I did not want to be alive and wasn't quite sure how I'd managed it. Evidently, I swam a distance farther than people thought to look. I heard footsteps. Crunching sand. Then he appeared. Dressed in white. Robes flowing. He stooped down, shading my face. My eyes took a second to focus. He said, "There are a lot of people looking for you."

I nodded.

He paused, stared down the beach, then back at me. "Do you want to be found?"

It was a simple question. It was the answer that was complex. ". . . No."

He nodded. Another pause. "For how long?"

There used to be a British rock band named Queen. Maybe there still is. Anyway, I think I remember them singing a song called, "Who Wants to Live Forever?" I think it was part of the sound track to a movie, *Flash Gordon*, about a guy who died. Woke up in another world. I heard the song in my head and knew it was not me. For the first time my eyes focused on his face and I was quite certain I'd never seen eyes that blue. I whispered, "F-forever."

He stood up. "Well, come on then. If you stay here you really will die."

I stood up, then fell down. Stood again, and fell a second time. Stood a third time and he caught me. I leaned on him. He said, "You can't very well go walking around like this." He lifted his outer robe over his head. Beneath it, he wore black slacks, black shoes, black shirt, white collar. He slipped the robe over my head and shoulders, helped me feed my arms through. It draped about me.

One foot in front of the other.

We walked through the woods to the other side of the island, where he'd beached his boat in a protected cove. A twenty-four-foot Pathfinder with a Yamaha 250. Turns out, he was a priest with a fishing addiction. I fell into the bow. My head was spinning. I wasn't sure if it was the gin, or the crash, or both. I scratched the back of my head, where I discovered that most of the hair was missing. Singed short. I tenderly touched the skin on the back of my head and shoulders. It was tender. I remember seeing flames wrap around me but nothing after that.

I said, "H-how long ago did I . . . ?"

He lifted the power pole, cranked the engine, and spoke without looking at me. "Three days ago."

It was not the gin. Dehydration maybe. "D-do you h-have any water?"

He handed me a bottle. It was cold. Condensation dripped down the side. I drank it. Then another. And another. Focus became easier.

He put the engine in gear and began idling out of the shallow water. He turned to me. "What shall we call you?"

I hadn't thought about this. I hadn't thought about any of this. The thought of not dying had never occurred to me. My mind was reeling with the question, What do I do now? I didn't want to be called anything because I didn't want anyone to call me. I shrugged, shook my head.

He nodded, pursed his lips, considered this. A moment passed. "How about 'Sunday'?"

"What?"

"Sunday."

"You mean l-like the d-day of the week?"

He nodded. "Yes."

The world was still fuzzy and not much was making sense, but this made no sense at all. "Why . . . S-Sunday?"

"It's my favorite day of the week."

That made even less sense. I guess my blank stare convinced him of this. "What . . . ?

"It marks the beginning. A fresh start."

I suppose there was some method to his madness. The word "Sunday" rattled around the inside of me. I looked at him. He'd slipped on some sunglasses. I stood, squinting. He flipped up the seat behind him, grabbed a second pair, and handed them to me. "Here, this'll help with the glare." They did. Muting the pounding in my head. He pushed the stick forward and quickly shot us up on plane. The wind tugged against the sheet I was wearing. I turned to him. None of this made sense. "Wh-what do I call you?"

"Steady."

I shook my head and grabbed the stainless-steel bar that framed the center console. "No, I'm n-not feeling very s-steady."

He smiled. "No, that's my name."

" 'Steady' is your n-name?"

He nodded.

I stared across the water. The world had changed since I'd left it. Little made sense. I shut my mouth, moved to the front of the boat, closed my eyes, and let the breeze press against me. I thought about the kids. The hospital. Jody. Rod. Monica. The orphanage. My bunk. Life as I once knew it.

A lot changed that day. Everything changed.

Well, almost.

With no spouse and no children, Steady had one hobby. One addiction outside of the church. Fly-fishing. He was a tarpon fanatic. And I thought I knew a lot about fishing. Years back, he'd bought a small island and fixed up the cabin on it. It was his retreat. His quiet place on stilts. His waterfront view of the world. He took me there. "This island has an odd history. Folks used to make moonshine here during the Depression. Then, others used it to store dope when they were running it up from Cuba. Then, still others moved cocaine through here from South America." He waved his hand across the mangroves and mosquitoes. "Make yourself at home."

I didn't know much about its history but people who do those things don't do them in places that are easy to find. They pick places that are tough to get to. That don't appear on maps. This place was one of those.

My life changed. No phone. No address. No expectation. I changed the way I slept, ate, drank, and how I spoke. Folks once told me that I couldn't overcome my stutter; well . . . they hadn't lived my life and didn't drive off a bridge at a hundred and forty miles per hour. If my thoughts don't stutter, why should my mouth? At least, that was my thinking. The only thing that did not change was the way I thought. I could not change who I was before I opened my eyes. I studied the water's surface. Read fish movement. And told stories. The thing that told me I wasn't dead was a broken heart. I could still feel that. I retreated into the Glades, the Ten Thousand Islands, the waters of the gulf in and around Florida, and I've been there ever since.

Once I recovered, I started remembering in bits and pieces. I remember feeling the car break through the concrete, vault over the side of the bridge, dive, and rotate slightly. I remember the shatter of glass, the heat on my neck from the flames, the engine whining, and then the impact, the airbag slamming against my face and the water pouring in. Swallowing me. I remember watching the manuscript in the plastic bag, the much-awaited book, lift off the seat as the water rushed in. I could have grabbed it but I didn't. I just let it go. I didn't want to be a writer anymore and I didn't want anything to do with that or any other book. For so long I had believed in the divine power of words. But there was nothing divine in Jody's death or what her death did to the hospital.

As the water rushed in, pinning me against the seat, the thought running across my brain was not the next breath or swimming to the surface, but why?

That was nine years and 197 days ago.

People have long asked how could the death of an innocent young woman who was not my daughter or wife affect me so much? Did I have an "inappropriate relationship" with Jody? The question offends me and, no, I did not. I loved her but everybody loved her. Jody's death hurt me but it wasn't her dying that sent me through the concrete wall at a hundred and forty miles an hour.

The bus that hit Jody broke or shattered thirty-seven bones in her body. After all she had already suffered and survived, I simply could not—then or now—make sense of that. Jody died of internal injuries and the bleeding that resulted. All the king's horses and all the king's men could do nothing but stand around and watch. In shock and disbelief, I drove to the spot where she was hit, her blood still staining the street, and found myself screaming at the top of my lungs, "If this is how all our hopes and love and good intentions end, then why not put a bullet through each one of us and call it a day? Why put us here, give us each other, and fill us with dreams and gifts and expressions, only to spill them across the street like cheap paint!"

We buried Jody, her tender echo faded from the hospital halls, and I found myself in an angry place where joy is fleeting and suffering is constant. Where the power of words rests not in what they could do, but in what they couldn't. So I pushed my foot through the floorboard and took a meteor shot off the southern tip of the continent hoping to drown myself in gin and salt water, and bury me and my gift at the bottom of the channel. Three days later, I woke naked on the beach to a wrinkled old man in a white robe, smoke rings exiting his mouth, and a fishing pole in his hand.

Steady took me home, did his best to address the wound. But I never let him at it, so I've been hemorrhaging for a decade. Then a few weeks ago, for reasons maybe only Steady understands, he shoved the jagged piece that is you in the gaping hole that is me.

And it worked. I stopped bleeding. The evidence is in your hands.

There's one more thing: Door number three is not an exit. Not a way out. For you, it's a backstage dressing room where you can hear the performers on the stage and the audience response, but you're forever barred from joining the show. For me, a world filled with paper, but no ink. On this side of the door, we live alone with our memories, stripped of the expression of the gift but not the remembrance of it—or the need to use it. That remains and grows. Unsatisfied.

Katie, turn around, walk back through. Write your own story. Start with a clean page. One with no words. Where the ending, the next turn, next twist, next reveal, next conflict that demands a resolution, is unwritten. And where the resolution is unscripted. And when you get there, standing in the spotlight on a pedestal made for one, spill your bag of pieces on the stage and tell the world—tell them all the way back in the cheap seats—"This was once me . . . but it isn't anymore."

Chapter Thirty-seven

I hitchhiked home. Couple of guys in a thirty-year-old Ford pickup carried me to Everglades City. I wasn't very hungry, but I bought some groceries. Fifteen minutes after being home, I admitted that in all my time aboard this or any boat, I'd never felt more alone.

The argument in my head was two-sided: I should've done something, anything, to keep her from hurting herself. The flip side argued that, in reality, what could I do? Even if I hovered over her like a helicopter 24/7. If someone is bent on hurting herself, she'll find a way to do it. She was a grown woman; sooner or later, she was responsible for herself.

It didn't help much and I didn't believe it, either.

I spent the evening on the back of the boat, staring out across the Milky Way, watching shooting stars scratch the underside of heaven's floor. Mosquitoes were buzzing my head. I lit a citronella candle and when they finished laughing at it they kept buzzing my head. I was chewing on something Steady once told me: "By your words you'll be acquitted, and by your words you'll be condemned." When he said this, he was pointing his finger in my face.

Sitting on the back of that boat, I was wrestling with that. I thought a lot about Jody, Rod, and Monica, the kids on the floor gathered around me as I read, the shuffling feet, long faces, big round eyes, the scars, Band-Aids, IV lines, approving looks from doctors and nurses, my life before this one. There was a time when I would have done anything for those kids. Anything. When the reservoir of my hope was deeper than I ever imagined. Deep enough to live by. But, now? Some might say I'm a coward. Maybe that's true. Pain is a powerful deterrent. Especially pain of the heart. I know that. And I think Isabella Desouches knows that, too.

I sat there trying to name that thing that scared me. The fear I walked around with, or walked around with me. The fear that had me living all alone on a boat in the middle of nowhere where nobody could get to me and nobody could hurt me and nobody could make me cry. And yet, there were tears on my face. The image appeared: the hospital. The idea of setting foot in that hospital, sitting on the floor and reading a story to a bunch of misfits, scared me. I'd seen what it had done. Could do. Then I saw what it couldn't. And somewhere in there, I broke.

I cried loud and long. Ten years' worth of tears.

I woke as the sun cracked the tops of the mangroves. I'd slept in a chair so I was stiff. I brewed some coffee and sat with my legs in the water. Trout in the current called to me, my poles hung above me idly, but I didn't want to fish. I didn't want to do anything. I spent the day moping around. Feeling sorry for Katie. Feeling sorry for me.

At noon, I called Steady. He listened, and said little. The truth hurt him. And, in retrospect, his tone of voice told me he was disappointed. That we'd failed. That I'd failed. I told him I'd stay close to home in case, for some reason, she decided to find me. She might feel safe here. He hung up quietly and I didn't wander out of eyesight or earshot from my boat until the days ran into weeks.

But Katie never showed.

By April, I was knee-deep in a pity party so I drove out to the memorial. The place was packed. Three hundred boats dotted the waterline. People were swimming and partying everywhere. The swollen masses surprised me. I stopped and asked one man in a float tube with a beer in his hand, "What's all the commotion?"

He looked at me like I'd lost my mind. He proffered his beer at me. "Dude, it's Easter."

In my solitude, I'd lost track. "Oh yeah, sure. Right."

I circled the growing circus of anchored boats. Kids in floats, Jet Skis cutting the water, go-fast boats sitting restless, bikini-clad Coppertones from South Beach, beached whales from Long Beach, and the purely curious. The air smelled of coconut rum, cigarette smoke, suntan lotion, and pot. The number of white PVC crosses driven into the ocean floor numbered more than a hundred. All shapes and sizes. It looked like a game of pick-up sticks gone awry.

I shook my head and put the whole scene in my wake. Soon they really would have a reason to mourn. In the few times I'd talked with Steady, he had not heard from her. No email. No voice-mail. No "To whoever finds this letter" letter. We called her cell phone, the one from the safe-deposit box, but she never answered and neither did voicemail. My guess was that Katie had gone quietly. In her own way. Her own time. No witnesses. Regardless, I felt it was only a matter of time before someone found the body.

The pain in my chest was an ache without expression. I found it difficult to breathe.

I took to the backwater and got lost in old alligator and mangrove trails that no man had ventured into in a long time. Late afternoon I made my way home. The sun was setting.

Katie was ever on my mind. In truth, she was all I thought about. I wondered how she'd done it. And how was I going to live with myself when I found out. While I couldn't answer any of that, I knew I needed closure. Maybe Steady did, too. I'd stayed gone long enough.

Time to see the old man.

I bathed, rode to my slip at Chokoloskee, and drove to Miami, realizing my visit might well leave a bitter taste on his favorite day of the year. Other than his sunrise service, his eight p.m. mass would be the most attended. And a larger crowd meant it would be easier to get lost. I parked, pulled up my collar, and waded into the crowd looking like a guy who was punching his card on his once yearly mass attendance—the sound of my flip-flops drowned out by the nearly thousand people talking and echoing off the walls.

A thousand candles lit the interior. Lingering smell of incense. Hushed tones. Families hurrying to a pew. Rows squeezed tight. People kneeling, genuflecting, lips moving. Little girls in white and pink dresses. Boys in seersucker suits. Mothers fussing over their hair and tucking in their shirts. Fathers fussing over mothers fussing over kids who looked just fine.

Steady meandered near the front door, shaking hands, hugging babies, kissing children. Draped in purple, his smile wide. Face beaming. The gold stitching on his vestments reflected the candlelight. He liked to say that the church had bedazzled him.

I found a place in the back. The last row. On the end. A long way from the front and even farther from Steady's eighty-four-year-old eyes. I didn't want him to see me until after. Didn't want to ruin his service and seeing me alone, without Katie, would ruin his service.

The music started, as did the processional, and it's a good thing the fire marshal was not in attendance. Sardines had more room than us. I've often thought that Catholic services were good exercise and that Catholics were, or should be, in better shape than, say, Baptists or Methodists. The Catholics stand up, sit down, kneel, repeat. While most other denominations only stand up and sit. 'Course, the Anglicans and Episcopalians stand up, sit down, kneel, too, so I'm not sure what that says. Anyway, every time I attend one of Steady's services I am reminded of a term he once used with laughter: "aeroba-church."

Wasn't long and the entire congregation was

kneeling. I followed suit. Heads bowed. Mine, too. I fought the urge to leave. Drive to Katie's condo, see if she'd hung herself from the balcony, slit her wrist in the bathtub, or passed out in the foyer after eating a hundred or so pills. But something told me that was not the way she'd go out.

After the readings, Steady invited the kids up front. Sat among them. Explained why today was his favorite day of the year. Behind him, high on the wall over his head, the banner read: EGO SUM LUX MUNOIS. The kids listened, laughed. He had them eating out of his hands.

Following his mini-sermon, he returned to the altar, broke the body, and offered the blood with a smile, saying that it "speaks better things than that of Abel." Up front, the rows emptied as people made their way to the front, where Steady dipped a wafer in the wine and placed it on their tongue.

I sat and stared at the worn marble at my feet. A tear dripped off my nose and landed on the floor beneath me. Then another. Then another. The drops gathered in the vein of the marble.

Another was cascading down when a thumb appeared from over my shoulder and gently brushed my cheek.

She wore a scarf, sunglasses, no fingernail polish, faded jeans, flip-flops, white oxford, collar up, untucked. She placed her hand on mine and knelt. She was trembling. Her fingers wove between mine like vines.

Katie lowered her sunglasses and stared at me. She kissed my cheek, exhaled through a tear-stained smile. She pressed her hand flat across my heart. Tried to speak, could not, tried again, and still could not.

She leaned against me. Melting into me. Temple to temple. Worn marble floor staring back at us. Her tears mixed with mine. Up front, Steady showered us in Mass. His voice echoing. She scanned the horde around us, mustering her courage.

She took a deep breath, then brought her legs up beneath her, coiling, as if readying herself to stand. She pressed her lips to my ear. Her breath warm on my face. "You were wrong about one thing."

I looked at her.

"Words do bring people back to life." She held my face in her hands and kissed my lips. "Especially, yours."

Katie stood, walked around the back of the pew, and stopped in the center aisle. No script. No rehearsed lines. Katie Quinn was directing herself. Steady stood before her, forty or so rows forward. He saw her, squinted, then his shoulders rolled, he choked up, composed himself, and his smile spread. Maybe he let out a breath. Katie turned toward me, then gently untied the scarf around her face, pulled the sunglasses from her eyes, let them fall to the ground, and began the slow walk toward Steady.

A woman to her right screamed. Followed by another. And another. Whispers grew into loud conversation. People stood on the pews.

Katie approached Steady. Glassy eyes and a smile he couldn't erase. She stood before him, penitent. He dipped the wafer and placed it on her tongue. She bowed. He placed his hand on her head and his lips moved. Pandemonium might best describe the congregation at this moment.

I stood, slipped around the back, and pressed against the back door. Before I walked out, I turned. Steady was hugging Katie, who was crying, but his eyes were trained on me, and his smile was gone.

PART THREE

What began the change was the very writing itself . . . Memory once waked will play the tyrant . . . The change which the writing wrought in me was only a beginning—only to prepare me for the gods' surgery. They used my own pen to probe my wound.
—C. S. Lewis, *Till We Have Faces*

To die is nothing; but it is terrible not to live.
—Victor Hugo, *Les Misérables*

Chapter Thirty-eight

Katie returned through door number three. Once a one-way exit with "No Reentry" written above the frame, she tore the door off its hinges— proving the world wrong—once again. Her reemergence covered front pages all over the world. Head- lines such as THE MIAMI MIRACLE, EASTER SURPRISE, THE RESURRECTION OF KATIE QUINN, and LONG LIVE THE QUEEN! One French writer called it "The Summer of St. Katie."

Katie made the rounds, all the talk shows, news shows; Steady even appeared on a few. Questions abounded. Katie was appropriately vague. She took responsibility for all her own stuff. Had the scars to prove it, which she didn't bother to cover with clothing or makeup. The cameras zoomed in. She sat stoically. Unmoving. Unashamed. When they asked her why she'd come back, she said, "I met someone."

"Who?"

"Somebody who made me want to live again."

"How did he do that?"

She paused. Thoughtful. "He gave me a reason."

"And what reason was that?"

She stared into the camera. "Maybe someday he'll share that with you, too."

"What will you do now?"

A shrug. "Play somebody I've never played—whose script is unwritten."

The search for that someone was exhaustive; news agencies spared no expense, but they came nowhere close to me. She had kept her word. I was safe. Unbecoming Katie did not mean unbecoming me.

Katie visited the memorial in the gulf and thanked all the folks who had kept the vigil. One guy who had been drunk for the better part of the last two or three decades took full credit and shined for the cameras. Katie seemed more at peace, like the demon that tormented her had been cut loose. I know—I was watching.

I anchored *Gone Fiction*, loaded *Jody* with as much gear as I might need for a few months, even a year, and disappeared, moving farther through the islands. I traveled up the west coast, through the inland waters of Louisiana, over to Texas, and back down to the Keys—never spending more than one night in any one spot. About once a week, I'd find a hotel and hot meal. I'd fish some, record high and low tides, and stare off the stern. Months passed.

I was buying gas one morning in Key Largo when I picked up a *Wall Street Journal*. Katie had taken a lead role in a Broadway show that sold out within hours of the announcement. *USA*

Today said she'd signed contracts for a few movies. The highest-paid female in the business.

I put *Jody* in a slip, took a train to New York, rode the subway into the city, and stayed at a hotel on Fifth Avenue. Blue lights and neon. Seemed like everybody was drinking a martini but me. I bought a new suit, cut my hair, shaved, even wore black patent leather shoes. My feet didn't know what to do with themselves. The man tore my ticket, gave me my stub, and I sat on the front row of the balcony, staring down at the world Katie commanded. She was mesmerizing. Larger than life. Had us eating out of her hand. All the way back in the cheap seats.

I sat there shaking my head. Steady was right. She was the one. The standard by which others were judged.

At the end of the show, the audience stood for the better part of ten minutes clapping, whistling. She brought out the cast, introduced each one, and they all bowed and waved. People threw flowers. Some guy in the audience yelled, "Katie, will you marry me?"

She laughed. She was happy. Less guarded. She'd gained a few pounds.

I tucked the present under my arm and found an usher. An older gentleman, gray hair. I handed him three hundred-dollar bills and the present. I had hired a guy in Miami who works in rare books and asked him to find an older edition of

La Belle Au Bois Dormant. Something from another century with leather binding. He had. I figured she'd like that. I'd wrapped it in an Hermès scarf, then wrapped all this in brown paper and tied it with a bow. The usher looked up at me. I said, "Will you please take this to Miss Quinn? She keeps the gift. You keep the money."

He shrugged. "Sir, I can only put it with the others."

I nodded. "Fair enough," and handed him both the book and the money.

He smiled. "But I can put it on top of the pile."

I smiled. "I'd be grateful."

I turned and walked out into the street.

The train ride home was lonely, as was my life, now measured in rising and falling tides. Weeks passed. I kept to myself more. I thought a lot about my life and what it had become. And to be honest, it wasn't much of a life. Even I knew that.

The only person I saw was Steady. He'd drive out every Monday and Thursday, bring me some essentials, and we'd fish the last hour of the incoming and several hours of the outgoing tides.

The sun set. I read the water and followed the fish to a feeding frenzy on the northeast side of Pavilion Key—the same small island where Katie had spent the day quietly thinking before she asked me to walk her through door number three. Maybe, in a sense, I was trying to go back. Circle around.

I beached *Jody*, built a fire, and sautéed a few flounder fillets from the afternoon's catch. With the sun dropping below the horizon, I heard the faint whip and pop of a helicopter. It came in from the gulf side, circled the island, and landed on the far end, a couple hundred yards from me.

The pilot cut the engine and Katie stepped out. She smiled, waved, and started walking. A breeze washed through the trees, the waxy leaves smacking each other. Even the trees clapped at her entrance.

We met in the middle. She stood half smiling, hands behind her back, head tilted. I shook my head. "Figures that you'd find me."

She hugged me. "Thank you—for the book."

"You're welcome."

"You could have come backstage, you know. All you had to do was tell them—"

"I know."

She nodded, kissed my cheek, and brushed by me en route to the fire. The feel of her warmed me. She wiggled her toes in the sand. "What's for dinner?" She looked good. No. Scratch that. She looked fantastic. The scar on her neck had faded but she didn't try and hide what remained. The smell of her filled me. She knelt next to the fire, picked up my skillet, and began slowly eating my flounder. I sat, opposite her—painted in fire-light and bathed in her.

She held up a forkful of fish. "You hungry?" Her voice was strong. Resonating.

I shook my head.

She devoured it and spoke without looking. "Did you like my show?"

"Yes."

She forked the flounder around the skillet. "What'd you like about it?"

"I've never seen anything so wholly engrossing. You were phenomenal. I—"

She smiled. "Say something original."

"For three hours, you made me believe that the world onstage was real and the one I was sitting in wasn't."

"Funny." She pointed the fork at me. "I get the same feeling every time I read one of your five books—which I've read several times." She raised both eyebrows. "Which brings me to something I've been meaning to ask you." A pregnant pause. "Book number six—when can I get my hands on it?" She tapped my temple. "I know you've got it around here somewhere."

"Did my publisher send you down here?"

She laughed. It was easy. And she did not hold it back.

The helicopter blades had quit spinning. The pilot stood alongside smoking a cigarette. I said, "What are you doing here?"

"I had a night off. Came down to see Steady. He told me I might find you here."

"Figures."

"Was wondering if maybe I could convince you to come back with me." She stopped chewing and looked at me. "The show will be wrapping up in a few weeks and I'll have some time."

"Before?"

"Filming in Europe—with a good slice of time in northern France. Besides, the script needs some work and they're looking for writers."

I stared east. "I can almost taste those croissants." I studied her. "You look happy."

"You just ignored my comment about the needing writers part."

"Yep." I laughed. "It was purposeful."

"The world needs good writers, you know."

"And you ignored my part about being happy."

She nodded. "I am." An honest shrug. "Life's not perfect—but it is better. I am seldom happier than when I'm onstage."

"You deserve it." She waited. A measured pause. Silence in which she was comfortable and I was not. "Katie, I can't go back with you."

"Can't or won't?"

"Touché." I nodded. "Both."

Eyes on the water, she set down the skillet. "How's the fishing around here?"

A wide grin. "Fair." She stood, I handed her a rod and threaded on a four-inch Gulp! shrimp—

369

an artificial lure infused with the smell of shrimp—and she started throwing across current. She bumped the bait along the bottom. In an hour, she'd caught over thirty fish.

With the moon climbing, I fed the fire and we sat on the beach and pushed our toes through the sand. We talked about her life now—the show, the upcoming movies, the endorsements, the crazy pace that sought to squeeze the life out of her and the boundaries she'd set in place. She sounded good. Above and below the surface. She said, "Several publishers are asking me to write my story—the real thing."

I raised an eyebrow.

She continued, "They'll pay an unworldly amount for the whole thing—including the mystery guy who patched me back up." She chuckled. "They're dying to know about him."

"And?" I asked.

"It's not my story to write."

It wasn't until that moment that I knew how healthy she really was. How whole. Katie had made it. She'd unbecome herself.

Toward midnight, she stood. The pilot was reclining on the sand on the far end of the island. Every few seconds he'd draw on his cigarette, the tip glowing ruby red. She glanced at her watch. "Sure I can't convince you?" She waved her hand across the island and *Jody.* "Nobody 'round here will miss you."

"I'm sure."

She pulled on my shirt with both hands, leaned in, and pressed her forehead to my chest. Finally, she looked up. "Still hurts, doesn't it?"

I stared southwest. Across the gulf. Then down at her. "Every day."

She smiled. Eyes wet. A nod. "Me, too." She kissed my cheek, then the side of my lips, and began walking toward her helicopter. The pilot had climbed inside and begun his preflight. The blades had started spinning slowly. A few feet away, she stopped. Turned. And chose her words. "Sometimes, when I stand on that stage, I am reminded."

"Of?"

"That my gift isn't mine. And all of this—" She waved her hands across herself and her helicopter. "It isn't about me."

"What's it about?"

She smirked, almost spoke, held her words, and turned. Three minutes later, even the whip and pop had faded.

Weeks passed. All stories end.

It was Saturday morning. I was sitting with a cup of coffee on my lap, dodging mosquitoes, thinking about my life. Something I'd been given to lately. What had become of it. What kind of life it was. Resigned.

When I heard the small engine and saw the

small skiff approaching, I was surprised to see Steady sitting in the back with his hand on the tiller. Even more so since it was neither Monday nor Thursday. Seeing him had me a bit worried.

He cut the engine and I tied off the bowline. "You all right? Something wrong? Katie okay?"

He stepped out, straightened his robes, and stared at me a long time, finally touching his chin with his index finger. "I think you are my greatest failure."

Even through my sunglasses the sun's reflection off his robes was brilliant. "What?"

He straightened. "I'm sure of it."

"Is Katie okay?"

His finger shook when he pointed it at me. "A lifetime wearing this collar and I have had no effect on you."

"I'm alive, aren't I?"

He spat in the water. "I've seen bleach-white bones more alive than you."

"Nice to see you, too. Kind of grumpy, aren't we? Is this really what's got you out here this time of day?"

His eyes met mine. "It keeps me up nights."

I knew he was telling the truth. "Can't save everyone."

His answer was quick though not rehearsed. He was still pretty fired up. "I'm not trying to save everyone."

"I thought success and failure sort of went

with the collar. You know—win some, lose some."

He chose his words. Spittle in the corner of his mouth. "I suppose I should probably thank you."

"For?"

"Katie."

"I didn't give you Katie. Katie gave you Katie."

He shrugged. "Maybe." He pulled his pipe from inside his robe, packed and lit it, his cheeks pulling the air and drawing the flame. Smoke exited his mouth as he spoke. "There is still the matter of you."

I said nothing.

Another draw. "Get dressed. We're going for a ride."

"You don't want to fish?"

"I am fishing."

It was bait. I didn't bite. "Where're we going?"

He raised an eyebrow. "You grown particular?"

I showered, pulled on some jeans, a long-sleeved fishing shirt, rolled on some deodorant, and slid into my flip-flops. We putted back to Chokoloskee in his skiff, where the church van sat waiting. The tank indicator rested on full. It was never full.

An hour later, driving south on the Old Dixie Highway, he stopped at the toll plaza, paid the dollar fee, then drove up and over the Card Sound Bridge. It was my first time driving the entire span of the bridge. I'd been up it—just never down. I looked at the concrete patch in the railing. Dull, dirty, fading into the older stuff, but it was visible to the looking eye.

He drove another mile, pulled off on a single lane road. Card Sound sat north of us, the Atlantic to the east. Water on two sides. He wound his way through the trees to an asphalt parking lot. He shifted the stick into park and pulled the keys from the ignition. "Come."

I followed.

We walked through the soft sand to the water's edge and my memorial that had been built shortly after my death. A spiraling, black mass of pointed granite the size of a city bus standing on end—or bumper. Paper notes were stuffed into the cracks; memorabilia and plastic-covered books were stacked all around. Because of its general shape, and of what happened here, the locals call it Piet Hein's Spear. I suppose they think, in the end, that Piet Hein got the best of Pirate Pete. Maybe so. At any rate, I'm told it's a popular tourist attraction. My name appeared at the top followed by dates of birth and death and then the titles of each of my books.

Steady pointed. "Sit."

I did.

He stood in front of me. "Close your eyes a minute."

"What?"

"Close them."

"Why?"

"Because I said."

I did.

"They closed?"

"Yes."

"You sure?"

"Steady."

I heard a rustling of clothing, a grunt, and then Steady's open palm colliding with my face, slamming me against the granite. The taste of blood filled my mouth. My lip throbbed and instantly swelled.

His bottom lip shook and he stuck his finger in my face. Tears collected. "When are you going to stop feeling sorry for yourself?"

I spat—blood on granite. "Whatever happened to turning the other cheek?"

He struck me a second time.

I saw it coming so I dodged it. "I'm not feeling—"

"Don't lie to me."

"I'm not lying to you."

"Okay, then you're lying to you."

"Maybe"—my tone changed—"but I've never lied to you."

The thought of me was painful to him. I could see that. His face moved closer to mine. He was screaming now. "Then why do you stay here?"

And so was I. "Because I'm scared!"

"Of?"

I tapped my chest. "Pain."

"Then you're a coward."

I stood, my voice growing louder. "I don't want to be."

He backhanded me. My tooth cut his knuckle. He wrapped it in a handkerchief and spoke without looking. "You're not the only one in this world to have loved and lost."

I sat back down. "My head knows that—my heart does not."

He spoke through gritted teeth. "I'll leave you alone on one condition."

"Name it."

He reached inside his robe, grabbed a plastic bag, and handed it to me. "Read this to the kids in the Wyett Wing of River City Hospital."

My hands shaking, I opened the bag. Inside I found the dried but once-waterlogged pages of my sixth and last novel—the manuscript that had been on the seat next to me when I drove off the bridge. The pages were crinkled. Worn. Somebody had read it—several times. "You've had this all along?"

"Been waiting 'til you could read it again."

"How did you—?"

"You were clutching it when I first found you. It's how I knew who you were. You were unconscious, so I stowed it in the boat."

"You mean you stole it."

He nodded. "In a sense, yes."

Five hundred pages had never felt so heavy. "Steady, I can't—"

Steady straightened. He tapped the top page. "Seven pages. You read seven pages then you can leave and do whatever you wish. Drive off another bridge for all I care, but you owe me that much."

"Why seven?"

"Because—" He leaned in closer. His breath on my face. "If it hasn't hooked you by then, it never will."

Seven pages. The intersection of my deepest need and my greatest fear.

I nodded.

Chapter Thirty-nine

Steady drove six and a half hours north, stopping once for gas, once to let me change our flat tire, and three times to pee due to his swollen prostate. We spoke little. As we neared Jacksonville, I began to shake. I-95 was under construction, routing us around the western side of the city on I-295. We merged east onto I-10, drove over the Fuller Warren Bridge, and the Jacksonville skyline lit on our left.

The hospital sat before us on the south bank. Cranes spiked the air. The sign said something about a new auditorium. The size of the building suggested it was rather large. Steady rolled to a stop below the overpass and I opened the door and vomited on the concrete. When the light turned green, the car behind us honked and I vomited again, which seemed to silence the horn. Steady pulled up in front of the main entrance and said, "I'll be up in a few." Then, turning back, he tapped the side of his face and said, "Got some on your mouth."

I grabbed the manuscript, wiped my mouth on my sleeve, and stepped inside the hospital. The problem I encountered was that in the last decade, my stories had done well. Very well. And that meant a lot of money went to the hospital. The hospital, in turn, was grateful for that and not wanting to forget where it came from they expressed their gratitude by plastering my picture on almost every wall I walked by. I hid behind my Costas and made my way to the back stairwell, avoiding most of the cameras. I'd never felt more self-conscious in my life. I climbed two floors, exited onto a wide walkway, and turned left, taking me down a new hallway I'd never walked before. The walls were painted in scenes from my books. Each I knew well. The artist was someone named "John T." and he had done wonders with the pictures that had started in my head. Kids' rooms lined either side of the hallway. Nurses dressed in colorful garb walked from room to room.

The new wing ended and brought me to the

intersection with the older wing. White floor tiles met yellowed and old. A sign on the wall read PARDON OUR MESS. RENOVATION STARTING SOON. I slowed. The smell filled me. Sounds, too. Somewhere a child spoke—the echo wafted down the hall.

It had all started right here.

It was nearly eight p.m. when I walked into the empty room where I'd first played video games with Randy and read to Jody and the other island misfits. I sat, manuscript on my knee, and waited but no one appeared. No nurse. No kid. Nobody.

After ten minutes, an older kid, maybe ten or eleven, wandered in on his own two feet and disappeared into the library. He was skinny, curly red hair, and he took no notice of me. I gave him a few minutes, then followed him, where I was greeted by the smell of my books. He stood staring up at the far wall, his eyes focused on a row beyond his reach. He was moving the step-ladder into place when I idled up next to him. I said, "See anything you like?"

He nodded. Pointed.

I lifted the book off the shelf and handed it to him. I remember the first time I'd read it—where I was, and how, when I finished, I immediately turned back to page one and started over. "That's a good one."

He nodded, and tucked it under his arm. He eyed the shelves. A look of wonder on his face.

"Did you know that one man gave us all these books?"

"Yes."

He shook his head. "I bet you that guy knew lots of stories." A look of wonder and amazement. "Bet he had lots of friends." Then he turned and shuffled back down the hall.

I was scanning the shelves, saying hello to all my old friends, when Steady found me. He was using his cane more. His hair was slicked back and he'd splashed on aftershave. Two of my favorite smells—Vitalis and Old Spice. I glanced at the empty room and whispered, "Nobody here."

He nodded. "I know."

I was in the middle of saying, "Can we go now?" when it hit me. I'd been set up.

He sunk his arm into mine and pulled. "Come on."

We passed a trashcan and I turned, and dry heaved but no vomit came. I dry heaved again and Steady looked disapprovingly at me. "You 'bout done?"

A couple of nurses were staring—whispering back and forth. "I think so."

"Good, 'cause you can't be doing that once she gets you onstage."

"She?"

"Well, of course. Who else would introduce you?"

I steadied myself, both hands on the lid of the can. "If you weren't wearing that collar—"

"Come on, before I have to pee again." He shook his head. "Youth is wasted on the young."

Steady led me down a hallway and then a long ramp. People lined both sides, but none were staring at me. They were trying to get inside the twelve-hundred-seat Wyett Auditorium but couldn't. Standing room only. Several flat-screen TVs had been set up to show the stage. Several network cameras were transmitting. Katie had sold out another live show.

We stood in the back. Steady clutching me. Me clutching the plastic bag. The audience stood and whistled and clapped for several minutes when Katie walked out onto the stage. She stood at the microphone, smiling, waiting, comfortable.

When they quieted, she spoke. "Several months ago, I took a bit of a vacation. You may have heard—" More audience response. Extended applause. Whistling. "While there, I met someone, or—" She looked at Steady. "Was introduced to someone. A blind date of sorts. At first, he stopped me from harming myself. Literally, loosened the noose from my neck." A pause. The camera zoomed in on her neck. "Not one of my finer moments. As the days and weeks passed, he reached down into my heart and met me in places where I'd never let anyone meet me. Then, when I knelt before my young son's tombstone and hit my bottom, and I do mean my bottom, he did something no other person and certainly no other man had ever done. He returned to me"—she tapped her chest—"*la joie de vivre*." She paused. "He showed me that—" She stopped and her eyes found mine. And she quoted me verbatim. "'That love, the real kind, the kind only wished for in whispers and the kind our hearts are hardwired to want, is opening up your bag of you and risking the most painful statement ever uttered between the stretched-edges of the universe'"—she held out her hand to me—" 'This was once me.' I know him as 'Sunday' but you know him as someone else." She stepped aside and waited. Steady nudged me.

Shaking, I turned to him. "You did this on purpose."

A nod—a soldier's look in his eyes from fifty years ago. "Yes, I did."

I pressed my lips to his forehead. "I love you, old man."

He reached up, grabbed my arm, and whispered, "*Ego te absolvo, in nomine Patris, et filii et spiritus sancti.*" He brushed my forehead with his thumb and then I turned, beginning the long slow walk to the podium. Three rows from the stage, Rod and Monica stepped out into the aisle. He'd grayed. She'd put on a few pounds. Three children stood to their right. A boy and two girls. She stepped from her seat, her hands covered her mouth, and she shook her head, crying. After several seconds, she hugged me—clinging. He did, too. He put his hand on the boy's shoulder. "This is our son. This is our Peter."

The boy was probably seven. Maybe eight. Thick glasses. Good-looking kid. He extended his hand. "Hi, sir. Are you the writer?" He nudged his glasses up higher on his face. "We've read all your books."

I shook his hand. Monica held me for several seconds. Crying. Sobbing. I kissed her cheek and then knelt—speaking to the boy. Eye to eye. "I was once a writer." I glanced at the stage. "I think we're about to find out if I still am." He nodded.

The nurse who had handed me the birthday cake in the elevator leaned out from the aisle seat. Astonishment on her face. I grabbed her hand. "Your smile . . . warms me. It's a truly beautiful smile." When I turned Liza stood at my feet. Red hair short. Growing out. Julie Andrews as a child. No PICC line. No IV. Her color was good. I knelt on both knees. Eye to eye. She reached up, brushed my cheek with the back of her hand, then clutched the book I'd given her on Christmas Eve.

I climbed the steps.

Katie met me, locked her arm in mine, led me to the microphone, and whispered, *Mon cheri.* She placed the microphone in front of me then walked to the shadows and stood. With the spotlight on me, the audience began to make sense of my face, which appeared on all the screens. A few recognized me. Pin-drop quiet would be one description. The only sound was my short, shallow breathing echoing over the microphone. Up front, some one hundred kids sat woven together amid wheelchairs, crutches, IVs, thick glasses, casts, scars, and Band-Aids. I looked at them, then at the audience. I smoothed the top page, looking for an entrance. A place to start. I looked to Katie but she made no movement toward me. Steady stood beaming in the back. Sweat poured from every pore in my body.

I stood alone—need in one hand, fear in the other, hope just beyond my reach. "I—" It was a tough place. Maybe the toughest. "I—" No matter how I tried, the words wouldn't come.

Tongue-tied, I took the microphone off the stand, walked to the edge of the stage, stepped down onto the carpet, and sat down, cross-legged. I motioned to the kids and the nurses who assisted them. "Come on in. Closer. Gather 'round."

They scooted to the edge of their seats. The nurses offered a hand. Katie, too. A hundred kids engaged in a game of pick-up sticks. Logjam in front of the stage. I waited while they penguin-shuffled, crawled, or flopped down with me. It took several minutes. Many wore T-shirts depicting Pirate Pete or Piet Hein or *Long Winded* with her sails full of wind. A couple wore imitation brass monoscopes around their necks. Several were clutching older editions of my books. "It's always better if our knees are touching." They edged closer. The huge screen above my head showed me seated among a sea of broken and laughing children. I stared up at me and stared at myself staring at myself. A clear picture.

Seated among the misfits. My place in the world.

Many in the back of the crowd stood in order to see me. Cameramen from the networks filmed from the stage above my head and the row in front of me. Three rows back, my former publisher waved. My editor cried. I had some explaining to do.

Some of the kids hung back. Unsure. I motioned. "Come on. I'll wait, I don't bite."

They laughed. The pile grew.

I placed the manuscript on my lap. The once-waterlogged pages were wrinkled, yellowed, and oil from Steady's thumb had darkened the outer edges. I could smell the faint remnant of his pipe. I wondered how many nights he'd savored this. Jody's voice echoed from beyond the walls. Tears blurred my vision. I wiped my face on my sleeve, lifted my head, and said, "Hi, my name's . . . Peter Wyett—and I have missed you."

EPILOGUE

Katie said she wanted me to call her Katie, which I took as some relief. She'd had so many names that I was glad she settled on just one. As for her costumes and disguises, she set them aside, only unearthing them onstage, the other side of the camera, or the occasional trip to Paris. The absence of so many personas meant that Katie became Katie—comfortable in her own skin.

She calls me "P.W." in public and, occasionally—when no one is listening, *"Mon cheri."* I like the sound of either one, but the second does something on my insides that the first can't. For my part, I've taken to calling her "Bella" and she doesn't seem to mind. I don't think her father would, either.

Following our reemergence into public life, the publishing world went sort of crazy trying to get us to tell our story. Katie hammed it up and before too long they were all frothing at the mouth. Katie said she would only tell it if I told it. Sort of a two-for-one deal. I agreed. An auction ensued—five publishers competing—a contract followed. In short, we'll be making some more broad-scale additions at the hospital.

To get the story on paper, Katie postponed everything and the three of us spent a month on *Gone Fiction*. Steady took a leave of absence from the church and, in truth, was invaluable filling in the details that both of us had forgotten about our respective stories and how and where they intersected his. 'Course, we never let the writing interfere with catching a tarpon. It was a mending process for all of us.

Given that it was my first venture into non-fiction, I was a bit pensive and spent each night rewriting. Truth be told, it probably read a bit more like a novel than a typical memoir. Often, the sun found me just as the moon had left me. I wanted to deal carefully with what had been entrusted to me, because, to her credit, Katie opened up and revealed details I did not and could not have known.

With the writing finished, the publisher told us they'd love to put us on tour. She jumped at the opportunity, said yes, that she'd never been on a book tour and couldn't wait. Then she turned to me, thinking I would be equally excited. I said, "No, I'd rather not. Book tours really aren't my cup of tea."

She doesn't like being told no.

I told her to get used to it.

She pouted. Then she said, "Please."

So, I'm packing. So is Steady. Said he wouldn't miss this for the world. I, on the other hand, am selfish and I miss my hammock. Miss the quiet of the Glades. Miss the crimson sun off the tip of my toe. Miss the quiet rhythm of the tides. Miss the sound of my drag being peeled backward. Miss the kids at the hospital, where I'm now a regular. Katie picked up on my pity party and promised to get me back a day or so a week. She has a jet, so . . .

The tour starts at the hospital. Reading to the kids. We thought it fitting. Plus, they all wanted their picture with Katie. They like my stories but they love her.

This morning, Katie and I were guests on a live show. They sent a team to *Gone Fiction* to film us. Set us up on the deck. Sun coming up. Trout feeding in the current just off the bow. Smoke from Steady's pipe wafting over us. The anchor turned to Katie. "The book is entitled *Unbecoming Me.* Can you tell us about that?"

Katie never blinked. "Two reasons: When I was young, given my general physical appearance, I was told that I was unbecoming. Since then, I've tried to unbecome me. But doing so was like dying every day." She turned to me. "I went to bed dead. Woke up dead. Never knowing who I saw in the mirror. Ever fearful of resurrecting some-one I can't be." She shook her head and grabbed my hand. "Peter . . . changed that."

"How so?"

A confident smile. "He taught me how to live

without a script. A life where I get to write the words that become me."

The anchor turned to me, smiling. "It would appear that Piet Hein did not, in fact, get the better of Pirate Pete."

It was a good opening. I smiled. "The end of that story has yet to be written."

A nod. "A lot of readers will be glad to hear that. And none more giddy than my kids." He straightened, changing topics. "Nonfiction is a new venture for you."

"Yes."

"The book comes out tomorrow. As of this morning, preorders have placed it at number one. A lot of people are watching this broadcast right now, curious about you and this story. Wondering if you still have it. So, do you?"

Katie held my hand. Smiling. I said, "I don't know if I still have 'it,' meaning the gift of writing." I waved my hand across the camera. "You'll have to be the judge of that."

"What can you tell us about the story?"

I crossed my legs and said, "Allow an analogy. Imagine me carrying around a bag. Maybe like a big laundry bag that spans the length of my back—right shoulder to left cheek. Maybe it reminds you of pictures of Santa Claus that you saw as a kid only this isn't really a bag of gifts I'm all that excited about giving to somebody. In fact, I'd rather keep it hidden because inside the bag are a bunch of broken pieces—like a million—that once made up me. See, I was once one piece but then something happened and I broke, or shattered, and now I am many. Then, you and I meet and I realize that you're bleeding 'cause you've been broken, too, and all the king's horses and all the king's men could never put you back together again. And then I realize you're fading and in need of triage. You won't last the night. So, I give you the only thing I have—I hand you my bag and tell you that you can have any or all of those pieces to stuff in the wound. And what's more, they don't cost you anything. They're free. I paid for them in the breaking. And because you're desperate, and you've tried most everything else, you empty my bag across the floor, spilling them like splinters, and you rifle through each one, and somewhere in that furious discovery you find the one piece you've been missing. One piece out of a million. Or ten trillion. And when you insert that piece into the puzzle that had become you, it stops the hemorrhage, and for the first time in maybe your whole life, the wound starts to heal. And, when it does, you hand me your bag because I'm still bleeding.

"The book would be something like that."

"Can you read some of it to us?"

Katie nodded so I opened the book and read the first few lines.

" 'She knelt. Genuflected. He sat alongside the kneeler. Hands in his lap. She pushed the curtain open, to smell the Vitalis and Old Spice. She liked being this close to a man who did not feel compelled to touch her. To conquer her. She looked past him. Beyond the present. "Forgive me, Father, for I have sinned . . ." ' "

Afterword:
Doc Snake Oil

In 2000, I was hired to write a book. The assignment was to pen a biographical story about a fleet of hospital ships called Mercy Ships and the remarkable people that live and work on them. The process paired me with an early-sixties, salt-encrusted Kiwi named John Dyson who had traveled the world extensively as a writer for *Reader's Digest*—writing some two hundred stories over the span of his career. My assignment was to write the story; his was to look over my shoulder. Make sure I was on the right track. He was the mentor. I, the mentee.

So I flew to London, we met, had a delightful time. How do the Brits say it? *Lovely. Just lovely.* I learned he'd been a writer for a few decades, and had probably forgotten more about the craft and process of writing than I'd know in two lifetimes. For two days we met and he helped me outline the book I was to write. No real flags here. Just two writers talking. I liked him. Liked him, a lot. With the two of us "on the same page," I flew home and got to work.

Over the next four months, I spent a lot of time on planes. Africa. Central America. The UK. Several states. My research complete, I sat down and penned what I thought was a pretty good story. Eighty-plus-thousand words. When finished, I sat back and nodded. It was good. Even very good. Proud of myself, I let my mind wander and in my naive admiration I made a pretty good argument for how this story would soon climb the nonfiction side of the *New York Times* list, allowing me a platform for my soon-to-be-discovered fiction. This was my ticket. I was on my way. So I clicked Send and awaited John's positive praise.

It might be best at this point to simply let you read snippets of his response. An unadulterated view. To do this, I dug back through my inbox and unearthed a few of his editorial notes. They speak for themselves, so I'll let them.

Note: these are his words. Exactly. I've not altered a letter. Not one period. And yes, they still hurt and there's a reason why so many writers drink heavily.

This is a disaster.

Another ho-hum reversal of priorities at the bottom of the next page. Oh dear, what a bored writer!

Why the hell not?

The heart of the matter is the line-by-line quality of writing. You make strings of mistakes that do not appear in your notes, as I have pointed out often enough. It's not a question of voice but of accuracy and lack of snap. These problems are particularly frequent in the history section. I think you have found it difficult to stand back from the material and write with a sure and independent touch because you are polluted by it. This might be wholly understandable but it is also wearisome.

There's an awful lot of boring stuff in the history . . .

When it comes down to nitty gritty, I'm afraid you're not.

At the moment, in my opinion, it is confusing in many places, grossly overwritten in some places, and in other places underwritten.

I'm not proud of my initial internal reaction. I think it sounded something like, *Who does this clown think he is and who is he to tell me any of this about my writing?* I scratched my head. I'm positive that when we met in London I made it clear—maybe on more than one occasion—that I did have a BA in English, a Master's in journalism, and a PhD in communications. That should have sufficed.

More emails followed:

You're throwing this away. Very bland.

Rather a lot of awkward phrases and repetitions, many more than I have marked.

Bad start, as discussed.

This list goes on far too long. MEGO (my eyes glaze over).

Overwritten, too much introspection. Snap it.

If you can't do the cutting yourself you need to find a good friend to go through it with a ruthless blue pen.

Tell the story in a simple and elegant way and don't strive for effect. There's just one rule and you can say it in three words: story, story, story.

'Fraid this doesn't work. Overstated. Three/ four lines enough.

You have 27 sentences in this chapter starting with the word *As* and ten starting with *Following*. This is a passive way to present the story. In nearly every case these words are simply unnecessary.

I read the first ten pages or so in a state of ascending rage and disappointment because frankly it's a boring, tortuous, and badly written bag of bones.

Well, there are real problems with this chapter. It's too long. It hits all over the place, like carpet bombing. A lot of passages are not very well written, especially toward the end.

Bad sentence in every respect.

I'm missing emotion—

Let me say this powerfully. Do not overwrite. Overwriting is the last refuge of the writer who has nothing to say. Let the stories speak for themselves.

Wipe it off your disc.

I sunk lower in my chair. *Who is this guy!?* I felt undressed. Wounded. Laid bare. Downright mad. Somewhere in my office while throwing one of my tantrums, I might have given him the finger —several dozen times. And maybe said a few unkind words about his entire bloody lineage.

You might ask how and why I continued. Trust me, I did, too. First, I had signed a contract. But let's be real honest. Given the verbal hazing I was enduring, they could shove their contract. So, on to number two, which is much more honest— I desperately needed the money. What else was I going to do? I didn't have a backup. No plan B. But it's the third reason that might be the most important. Despite my sheepskin pedigrees, I had this sickly feeling that everything he said was right. No, I didn't like how he said it. Didn't like it at all. But once I separated the "how" from the "what," I began questioning, "Was he right?"

Something in me said yes. And although I told that voice to shut up on more than one occasion, it never did. Thus the lashing continued. So every morning I pulled myself off the floor and continued rewriting. And rewriting. And rewriting. In evidence of this, I rewrote the first chapter eighteen times. Yep. Eighteen. Baptism by fire.

About two months in, I made a snide comment over the phone. My bottom lip was sticking out far enough to trip over and I was swimming in self-pity. I said, "Well, hello John . . . it's just me and my warts."

He responded with curtness, "You know the old cure for warts?" I didn't respond. I was too tired for jousting. "Snake oil!" From then on, he signed his letters *Doc Snake Oil*.

I was ready to shoot him.

After three months, I'd reached my end. I could fall no lower. I called him on the phone.

My pride was gone. Self worth all but erased. My I-couldn't-care-less meter was pegged. I felt he had no clue about his total deconstruction of me and there wasn't much reason for small talk so I didn't. I said, "John, is anything I've written in the last three months any good?" My voice rose. "Any good at all?"

The pause told me my question had surprised him. Set him back. After a second he said, "Charles, bloody hell! We're not aiming for 'good.' "

That's when it hit me.

"Good" wasn't the goal. "Good" was never the goal.

Somewhere in the next week or two, his notes contained this phrase. "Getting there!" I think I screamed out loud.

Weeks later, this came through my email. "Love it!" Followed by, "Splendid stuff. I laughed out loud." So help me, at this, I pushed back from the desk, popped the tab on a cold beer, and propped up my feet.

Then this . . .

You are an excellent writer. You deserve to make a living at it and you are right to pursue it. I enjoyed parts of the book immensely and was totally absorbed by them . . . Substantial bits of the book are masterful . . .

It took nine months, but we finished that book, both satisfied with a well-told story. Despite the sweat, and the pain, and our best efforts to the contrary, it was never published. A tough pill to swallow, but that's fodder for another memory. Another day.

The point is not whether it was published. The point is what he and that process did in me. Until then I *had written,* but working with John, I *became a writer.*

Big difference.

Over the years, our correspondence morphed from teacher-student to the warm conversations between two invested friends. And, somewhere in there, maybe when my fiction sold and crossed the ocean and landed on the London newspaper beneath his nose, he quit critiquing altogether and became one of my biggest fans. (You can read his review of *Where the River Ends* on Amazon.com's UK website.) For reasons I do not understand, and to this day cannot make sense of, John Dyson had taken me from Good to Great. A beautiful transformation.

Just lovely.

We shared stories of our kids, wives, dogs, adventures, and pictures of all of the above. Much of his email he signed *Doc.* Even now as I read that, *Doc,* I don't remember the bitter taste of snake oil. I remember my friend, John.

John Dyson died in May 2012. Cancer. I wept

then. I'm crying now. In his last days, as he lay dying in hospice, his daughter told me she printed out a story I'd written and that despite the morphine, he read it. I like the thought of that. I'm sorry I wasn't there to hug his neck. To say all this.

I'm thirteen years into a writing career and you are holding my ninth book. If there's merit to my craft, John Dyson had a lot to do with it. He was quite possibly the finest writer I've ever known. And a dear friend. John once told me that my books had "impacted" him. Even greatly. That may be so, but if you look inside me, down where people touch me, you'll see his fingerprints. St. Bernard was right—we're all just dwarves perched atop the shoulders of giants. And I miss mine very much.

In one of his last emails to me, he penned these words. They were fitting then. They're fitting now. We were talking about the process of writing. We were talking about life.

White pages are not bad news. They're just part of the process. What's a sea voyage without long weary days spent crossing the blank bits of the map? It's how you get to the other side.

Reading Group Guide

Discussion Questions

1. Why do you think the title of the book is *Unwritten*? In what ways is that theme conveyed in the book?

2. Shortly after meeting Peter, Katie confesses to Steady, "I don't like the way I treat people." Why do you think she behaves the way she does? Is her behavior justified?

3. Why would Steady believe that Peter and Katie are more capable of helping each other than he is of helping either of them?

4. Do you think Peter did the right thing in helping Katie through door number three?

5. Were Katie's fans truly mourning her after her death? Is the act of mourning about the person lost, or the person who is mourning?

6. In what ways are Peter and Katie similar? How does it impact their relationship?

7. Why do you think Katie had so many disguises? Were they a help to her or a hindrance?

8. In what ways is Katie influenced by the opinion of society throughout her life? How has it shaped who she is?

9. Peter stops writing after he loses Jody, even though there are many children who love his stories. Why is that? Was it really about Jody?

10. Discuss the theme of forgiveness in the novel.

11. In what ways does Katie help Peter?

12. What do you think would have happened to Katie and Peter if Steady had not pushed them together? Could they have healed on their own?

An Interview with the Author

Are any of the characters in *Unwritten* inspired by real people?

No one single character in any of my stories is a representation of anyone that I know or have met, but most of my characters pull pieces from several people I either know, have met, have read about, or can dream up. I don't mean to make light of the process, but one of my favorite scenes in the movie *Toy Story 2* is when Mrs. Potato Head is getting Mr. Potato Head ready for his big journey—stuffing car keys, a golf ball, cheese puffs, and his "angry eyes" in his back. Every time I watch that scene I think to myself, "That's a lot like building a character." You think I'm kidding . . .

In what ways do you identify with Peter? How are you different?

One of the ideas behind this story, that forced it to the surface in me, is this idea of gifting, or calling. The idea that it's wrapped around our DNA, in each of us, and that no matter what, we can't shake it. Peter is gifted. Far more than I am. But something hurts him. Something dings him. And, in pain, he takes his gift and runs. Why? Because the expression of it has become too painful. Ask any honest, seasoned artist, and he or she will tell you that they've struggled with this at some point.

Not every reader, viewer, or consumer is going to "get" your art. Some will castigate, throw stones, spray paint on your water tower, and make statements about your heart when they have little to no idea what's actually in it. They will accuse you of ideas, thoughts, and intentions that are not yours, never have been, and never will be. But nonetheless, they say them. And that old adage about sticks and stones is a lie. Words hurt.

A lot. Because we're artists, and because we drink life through a fire hose, and because we offer our heart to others—our bag of broken pieces—we cannot help but be impacted by this. It's in our nature, our gifting, to feel. It's how and why we do what we do. It allows us—it allows me—to write what I do. And yes, sometimes it hurts . . . a lot. Peter is not me, but I can empathize with his life. With his response. Is it the right one? I haven't said that. I've just said I understand it. No matter how far Peter runs or how completely he isolates himself, he cannot kill or outrun his gift. It's Peter Pan's shadow. Never far behind.

At a recent speaking event, an audience member called out, "You write like a girl!" How is it that you are able to write novels that appeal so strongly to women? Is there something in your background that has influenced this aspect of your writing?

I grew up with three sisters, a mom, a female parakeet, and a female black lab. Maybe that had something to do with it.

It used to ding me when readers waved my books in my face and stated, "You write love stories." Made me feel like a windswept Fabio should be posing on my covers. I'd scratch my head and glance over my shoulder. "Why can't I write cool guy stuff like Vince Flynn, Clive

Cussler, Robert Ludlum, W.E.B Griffin, or Louis L'Amour? What's wrong with me?" But while I enjoy those stories and admire those writers, deep down I don't want to write like them. It took me a while to see that. To be okay with being me. I like what I write. That's why I write it. I used to joke that I write like me 'cause I can't write like them. I quipped, "If I could, I would." We both know that's not true. I'm writing the stories in me that I can't *not* write, regardless of how they come across.

When that lady stood up and screamed, "You write like a girl!" she was affirming that I write with emotion. That I don't bury it. That I say things that her heart and others' hearts need and want to hear. And yes, that goes for me, too. And I'm okay with that.

I wrote *Thunder and Rain* (in part) for this very reason—that us guys are good at living out of one side of our hearts but we stumble when it comes to living fully out of both sides. (This goes for me, too. Just 'cause I'm talking about the idea doesn't make me a pro.) We're good at storming the castle, at slaying the dragon, but we ain't too good at dinner table conversations in the weeks, months, and years ahead. "Good with sword and spear" does not necessarily equate to "Good at listening to wife" or "Good at engaging with kids." Maybe my stories are my attempt to awaken this part of my own heart.

John Eldredge is right—we are living out a love

story and yet we were born into a world at war. We are Londoners during the Blitzkrieg. I love the stories of the guys I've mentioned above, and if I was stuck in a bunker in London with the Germans raining bombs down on my head, I may very well read their stuff as an escape. We'd pass around their books and say how good they are and what we liked about them. But when I've turned the last page, and curfew has clicked off the power and I'm laying in the dark listening to the rumbling above me, I'm still wrestling with how to wake up tomorrow morning and put one foot in front of the other. Questions like: How do I fight for the heart of my wife? My kids? Friends? My own? What's it look like? How do I walk that out?

Yes, I hope readers like my stories. Yes, I hope they're entertained. Yes, I hope they pass them around and talk about them. But more than that, when the lights go out and they're facing a tough tomorrow, wondering how to climb out of bed and just stand upright in a world where the bombs are raining down, I hope that something about my story reaches down inside them where the world has dinged them, in the dark places they don't talk about, and whispers the words they alone need to hear.

Have you been to any of the places where *Unwritten* **is set?**

Yes, most (I think), if not all. Those I haven't been to, I made up. ;-) Rarely do I put a "place" in a story if I haven't been there. If I can't smell it, it's tough for me to write about it. I spent time in the Ten Thousand Islands, the Everglades, the Gulf, the Keys, Miami, New York, and France. My wife, Christy, loves it when I "research" settings and take her with me. After our trip to France, she thinks my next book needs to be set in Hawaii.

Where did you get the idea for the orchids Peter puts up in the trees?

We were driving out of Miami after a weekend there and drove by an orchid cart on the side of the road. Three for $20. Or four for $25. Something like that. Christy bought a few. While she was talking with the owner, my mind wandered to the Everglades and the Island. One thing led to another. How I got from that roadside cart to thirty feet up in a tree in the middle of the Everglades is a testimony to the wonder and majesty of story and one of my favorite things about what I get to do every day.

What is the most surprising question a reader has asked you? What was your response?

Not sure. There have been several. A few I can't repeat. But the thing that amazes me more and more is when people ask to take a picture with me. Seriously. And don't get me wrong, I don't mind. Take all you want. I'm happy to oblige and I'm happy you want to be seen with me. Please let me know if I've got something stuck in my teeth. I guess it's just strange. I can understand taking a picture with somebody famous, but I'm just Charles. I wear socks. I brush my teeth. I can be grumpy. I realize therein lies the difference. Your perspective of me versus my perspective of me. You see me as the guy behind the stories. I see me as husband and dad and son and dreamer.

Somewhere in this line of thought is the "thing," or one of the "things," that fed the writing of *Unwritten*. The idea that man is not made to be worshipped. To be praised. It's antithetical to our DNA. We're not made to receive it, but to reflect it. Want a good picture of this? Pour gasoline in a Styrofoam cup and you'll see what I mean. It eats you from the inside out, eventually spilling you across the sidewalk. And Katie, and Peter, and to a much less and smaller extent, Charles, can tell you a good bit about this.

The Author Answers the Discussion Questions

1. **Why do you think the title of the book is *Unwritten*? In what ways is that theme conveyed in the book?**

   Peter answers this far better than I in his letter to Katie on pages 292–3. I can't say it any better than that.

2. **Shortly after meeting Peter, Katie confesses to Steady, "I don't like the way I treat people." Why do you think she behaves the way she does? Is her behavior justified?**

   I think she's in pain. Justified? No, but that's not the point. She doesn't like it any more than we do. One of the things I love about both Steady and Peter is that they don't try to fix the symptom—the behavior. They're looking at the cause. The root. They realize that the water in Katie Quinn's glass is poioned and that occurred long before it entered the glass. So they follow the pipes, walk upstream, and pull the lid off the well where the spring is bubbling up. One of the two clicks on a flashlight and that's where they find the bodies. Deal with the bodies and the water downstream will take care of itself. I have found this to be true not only in the lives of the characters I create, but my own life and the lives of those I love.

3. **Why would Steady believe that Peter and Katie are more capable of helping each other than he is of helping either of them?**

Steady understands the nature of the pain Katie and Peter are living and knows that each can speak to the brokenness in the other. Did I "know" all this when I wrote this book? Did I outline all this in sequential multi-colored drafts pinned to the walls of my office and then work it into my story with a complete ontological and epistemological understanding of all the emotional complexities playing out between the pages? No. Not by a long shot. I wrote a love story about two messed-up people trying to walk down the painful road from broken to not broken, and now that you're asking me, I'm scratching my head and giving you my best guess. And that best guess is this story you hold. I'm attempting—after the fact—to dissect the whole and describe the intricacy of the pieces. Tough to do and I'm not very good at it. This is one of the beauties of Story—it answers questions that my intellect can't really wrap its hands around. And yet the answer satisfies and resonates as true.

Funny how that works. For more on this, see page 26. I spent four days writing those two paragraphs. Must be kinda important.

4. **Do you think Peter did the right thing in helping Katie through door number three?**

On this side of it, Peter would say no, but let's don't second guess what he didn't know at the time. He had to walk it out with her. Seemed like a good idea at the time. For the record, I agree with Peter so I'd have done the same. Also, you need to know that sometimes readers ask me questions that I can't begin to answer. I'm a writer. Not a psychiatrist with a couch. These pages are where I work out the stuff that's nagging me. Remember what I said above about "knowing" all this. Same truth applies here. Sometimes I'm discovering as much about my characters in the writing as you are in the reading. They make me laugh and cry, too. I find people are surprised at this. They ask, "You cried?" Like a baby. The human heart is pretty good at spotting counterfeits. If I'm not moved, then how will my story move you?

5. **Were Katie's fans truly mourning her after her death? Is the act of mourning about the person lost, or the person who is mourning?**

Not sure I'm qualified to answer this. Let

me try . . . In my experience, I've both mourned the person who's passed and I've mourned my interaction with them—or what they gave me. Just being honest. Last Saturday, I was at a race for my son. At the starting line, they played the National Anthem. I stood there listening while that perfect, angelic voice rose up out of those speakers. Halfway through, I found myself thinking, *Has this ever been performed any better?* As the recording finished, I realized how the absence of Whitney Houston still stings. How I miss her voice. I'm not sure I can describe what I miss about it other than I do. I miss what it does on my insides and the hope that she might be around to do it again. Is that selfish? Maybe, but we lost a great one in her and I'd be willing to bet I'm not alone in this. I just know that when that song finished, I missed something pure, good, and beautiful and the absence of it hurt. I imagine that those fans in the Gulf mourning the loss of Katie felt the same.

6. **In what ways are Peter and Katie similar? How does it impact their relationship?**

Both are uniquely gifted. Both drink life emotively. They "feel" deeply . . . intensely. It's how they're able to do what they do and resonate with so many. That trait amplifies both their joy and their pain. And . . . it's common among artists.

7. **Why do you think Katie had so many disguises? Were they a help to her or a hindrance?**

Anything that masks our true identity is probably a hindrance. Matter of fact, that might be a pretty good definition. Although in Katie's defense, she had lost all anonymity, so I think it's tough for anyone to understand that phenomenon who hasn't walked it. Myself included. Think about somebody like Will Smith, Tom Hanks, Oprah, or name your icon. Those people—and they're just normal people like you and me who eat, sleep, and laugh—can't go anywhere without folks like you and me hammering them 'cause we think we know them from their movies and because we love to touch our idols. In truth, we don't know squat. I'd be willing to bet most would pay—and probably do—a good bit to *not* be known. For anonymity and some sense of normalcy. I would. Kind of makes you wonder how many superstars are lonely. In Katie's case, there's a difference between masking her face and masking her heart. One is simply an outward reflection of an inward condition. It's the reason the scene at Steady's church on Easter Sunday is so powerful to me. Without giving away too much to those who haven't read it, let me say this—Katie can only do what she does there because she's already done that with the one on the inside.

8. **In what ways is Katie influenced by the opinion of society throughout her life? How has it shaped who she is?**

   Others' opinions of her hasn't shaped her nearly as much as her own. While others' are painful and sting, it's her own that hangs the rope around her neck.

9. **Peter stops writing after he loses Jody, even though there are many children who love his stories. Why is that? Was it really about Jody?**

   I'm not sure. I just know that when I closed my eyes and put myself in his shoes, the all-encompassing pain that had become his life was enough to put him in the front seat of that southbound Mercedes. And then keep him there. I know that.

10. **Discuss the theme of forgiveness in the novel.**

    Please see pages 7–391.

11. **In what ways does Katie help Peter?**

    I spent nearly a week writing the last page of this book. No kidding, five days focused on somewhere around four hundred words. I rewrote it twenty, thirty, forty times. It is, in my opinion, one of the most beautiful pictures I've ever scripted depicting the interaction between two people. And it's a pretty good answer to your question. Katie hands her bag of broken pieces to Peter and for the first time in a long time, the bleeding stops—and he starts to heal. As strange as it sounds, broken people are fixed by other broken people. It's God's economy. It's why soldiers who carried stretchers across the Bulge scribble beneath benches and become priests whose hands are stained.

12. **What do you think would have happened to Katie and Peter if Steady had not pushed them together? Could they have healed on their own?**

Don't know. I didn't write that story. In truth, I have no idea. "Healing" for you may look a bit different than "healing" for me, so I want to be careful I don't put it in a box of "it must look like this." I just know both Katie and Peter had Steady, or maybe Steady had them. Either way, I'm glad they did. Steady is one of my narrative treasures. I love him. If and when this thing is made into a movie, it will be fun to see who is tagged to play him. What a role. And no, I don't have anyone in mind. I don't see my characters that way, but it would be fun to play that mental game and see who we all came up with. Whoever he is, I hope he nails it and I'll be pulling for him.

Center Point Large Print
600 Brooks Road / PO Box 1
Thorndike ME 04986-0001 USA

(207) 568-3717

US & Canada:
1 800 929-9108
www.centerpointlargeprint.com